NO MORE TIME FOR SORROW

NO MORE TIME FOR SORROW

DR. ROBERT BEEMAN

AuthorHouse™
1663 Liberty Drive
Bloomington, IN 47403
www.authorhouse.com
Phone: 1-800-839-8640

This book is a work of fiction. People, places, events, and situations are the product of the author's imagination. Any resemblance to actual persons, living or dead, or historical events, is purely coincidental.

© 2010 Dr. Robert Beeman. All rights reserved.

No part of this book may be reproduced, stored in a retrieval system, or transmitted by any means without the written permission of the author.

First published by AuthorHouse 5/12/2010

ISBN: 978-1-4520-1621-4 (e)
ISBN: 978-1-4520-1622-1 (sc)
ISBN: 978-1-4520-1623-8 (hc)

Library of Congress Control Number: 2010905622

Printed in the United States of America
Bloomington, Indiana

This book is printed on acid-free paper.

Resemblance between any person living or dead and any of the characters in this novel would be strictly coincidental if they weren't so true to life. If you see yourself among my good guys, then you're obviously a real human being and a credit to the species. If you see yourself in any of my bad guys, then shame on you; you're sicker than me, and even in today's permissive world that's no small achievement.

And if you see yourself in my character Achmed Farouk, I know a psychiatrist who would treat you for nothing just for the case study.

"And bless our dear Troopers, the ones 'be done down,

Marchin' home to His 'Pipes on God's Mornin'!"

ACKNOWLEDGEMENTS

شكر وتقدير

I owe much of my plot to our current American government, who has provided all Americans the spectacle of a nation going about the world begging to be attacked. I never thought we would be so foolish or careless of our own safety, but we are. We offer to our enemies friendship seen as cowardice, negotiation seen as weakness, concessions seen as trash. We have handily surpassed the naïveté of the British seven decades ago who spent the run-up to World War II wishing and hoping and at the end *praying* that Adolf Hitler would honor his agreements. Today, we *pray* that the terrorists won't attack us again, and we support those prayers by offering them things they don't want and never asked for. Current American leaders have lowered the bar for commonsensical political acuity to new depths, right down through the floor, in fact. In so doing you have inspired me and galvanized me to write. Thank you.

To you specifically, Mr. President, I owe the vision of ideology trumping common sense. Hatreds of the centuries cannot be oiled away by bowing and shuffling and smarmy good will, yet you refuse to see it. Even when immutable conditions in the world have forced you away from the ultra-Left path you have tried to put us on, you refuse to acknowledge it. Those conditions have compelled you further into Afghanistan, further into Iraq, forced you to keep open our prison at Guantanamo, and stopped cold your program of freeing those murderers to continue their sordid acts. Events you cannot control by wishful thinking will soon force you to give over to our military the enemy combatants you insist on treating as rehabilitative criminals. Three major terrorist attacks inside our borders since 9/11 have killed innocent Americans but have failed to deflect you from your path of folly, not the least dangerous act of which has been to fasten upon the backs of our long-suffering defense community a chief security officer who refers to those attacks as "man-caused disasters." In order to test your post-American, Globalist view of the world, you have put our entire nation at risk. You thereby violate a sacred trust. The nuclear terrorists will hit us sometime during your incumbency because they perceive you to be weaker than anyone who could possibly replace you. Our enemies regard your term in office as their Moment in History. What frightens me most is your inability to admit your error even in the light of simple facts. After the coming nuclear assault, we will need a leader, a Father Abraham to show us the way toward our national destiny. Were you to add true humility to your intellect, you might amount to something then. But it's already too late to avert the next attack. You helped to bring it upon us. And for your ideological arrogance, we little people out here in the villages will pay a heavy price.

To terrorists everywhere who murder to make their political point, I owe the exciting and dramatic spectacle of a debauchery so evil that nothing I could write could ever succeed in describing it. I strove mightily to do it but in the end I feel my poor words have failed to convey the depth of your sin of killing in the Name of God. Nevertheless, I thank you for your consistency hating things you only dimly perceive, attempting to broker innocent lives for power, and your unremitting perversion of a God whose only wish is to be loved. Your horrors have given me a book. But more important, they have set the decent people of the world at your throats, which is right where they should be.

To the Lunatic Left whose diatribes against defense are as effective as your lunches against poverty, I owe your concentrated syrup of do-gooder control. Your relentless pursuit of that sociopathic sickness, socialism, and its requisite discard of human values, has given me a fat, slick, pulsing Target of Opportunity. Your theories of control by a power elite are already a continent-wide joke unequaled since the immortal question, "Doctor, what shall I do with these rectal thermometers?" You have done down good people into poverty and exploded our economy in debt. All of that can be put right. But your careless attitudes toward defense of our Homeland will visit upon America the whirlwind, and that cannot be excused. You are playing your silly power games with people's lives. Your desperate quest to become the power elite will harm many good Americans, and we do not deserve it.

But among those thorns, there blossoms forth here and there a rose. To my late wife, Lorraine I owe the vision and much of the substance of my book's heroine, whose first name is no coincidence. My darling, you were indeed my heroine all along. *Chief* Special Agent Lorraine Baskin is a true American Hero, as were you. You are she, my love, and I miss you greatly. This is your book as much as mine. You have set the Bar of Life at a mark toward which I can only struggle during what remains of my own.

I put into this story the disparate goodness of my friends, Howard's pragmatic patriotism, Terri's relentless support, the struggle and hard work of James and Diane, Dr. Bev's incisive deconstructions, Helen's invaluable insights, Larry's common sense, Doctor Joe's fatherly love, Desmond's lifelong attentions to the little ones of our planet, Meta's firm quiet patriotic resolve, the dear love of my three little puppies, Emma, Rachel, and Sarah, who will grow to womanhood while we are at war and will not see its end, and Carol's sweet inner little girl peering out curiously with perfect innocence at the tortured paths the woman who carries Little Beebee within her has determined to walk.

I put myself into the book in two minor places. See if you can find them by their single common thread. I would like to think I'm Cubbage. I'm not.

But you might be.

Dr. Robert Beeman, Bedford PA 11 September 2009

PREFACE

مقدمة

Some will consider this book insulting to the Religion of *Islam*. It is not intended to be. *Islam* is a decent, gentle faith, contemplative and lovely to behold whose sad lot it is to be hag-ridden and perverted by a vanishingly small minority, mocked and made ugly by self-styled "warriors" whose only real passion is for the money, the power, and the influence they hope their association with this well of decency and truth will bring to them. How can this be true?

> *Because no <u>decent</u> practitioner of Islam, no True Believer, would permit for an <u>instant</u> the murder and maiming of his own fellow Believers for any reason whatever.*

The *Qur'an* makes it quite clear: Those who kill Believers put themselves beyond God's Reach. This includes the demented murderer who explodes himself in a *mosque* or a marketplace and the *jihadist* who slaughters Believers of his own Faith. *Allah* is indeed Merciful, but He will assign to Eternal Damnation *any* premeditative murderer of the Faithful for gain. *Any*.

Unlike the Handwringers of Europe, whose rush to pander to a few religious malcontents gives new depth to "craven" and adds dimensions to "stupid," I pay no heed to religious zealots who collect insults to boost their own fortunes, who substitute the drama of false shame for actual contributions to the society they choose to live in. To the Muslim who feels insulted by my words, I suggest you look into your own heart to discover whether or not people are using your Faith to promote themselves. If you find it to be so, cast them forth from your tent. They pollute your Faith and they pollute you as well.

Suppose a group of people started murdering and destroying and then told everyone, *"The Pope told us to do it!"* How many nanoseconds do you think would pass before every Catholic in America – and no doubt throughout the world – was up on a table or a bench or in the streets with clenched fists shouting against that terrible perversion of his Faith?

Yet *jihadists* sanctify their atrocities by saying *Islam* tells them to do it. So to my fellow Americans who are also Muslims, I pose a simple question:

> *Where are your voices, my Muslim countrymen, shouting down this blasphemy against your Faith?*

Where is your *public* outrage against these murderers of innocents? Where is your *public* sorrow that your religion could be befouled to such un-Godly use? When I see that outrage, when I see that sorrow, I will take you seriously as Muslims, and as Americans. Until then, your silence convicts you. You are merely fellow travelers in *jihad*, supporters of murder and crime, and I trust you *not*.

And you *jihadists*. You murdering dogs. You exceed even the cruelty of the Nazi beasts. They practiced genocide in the name of politics. You do it *in the Name of God*… Rant and surge about; whip up your minions to a fever of destruction. Your coin being rage, your wages will be dust. Cease! Or be ground under.

Some will consider this book insulting to the political theory of Liberalism. It is not meant to be. I am liberal on many issues, but not national security. My book is entirely about the change in viewpoint toward this single issue brought about by a president casting us as weak and then throwing us on the defensive, and by his supporters who refuse to see simple truths.

Those of my readers who wish to keep us on this road should get used to dying. Try to become accustomed to humbling yourselves before our killers. I, on the other hand, wish to live. I wish America to prevail, so I hope the reader will pardon my one or two caustic comments about sweet people who hate our military yet scamper to duck behind them at the first sound of a cocking lever.

The Progressive movement peaked around a hundred years ago in a flurry of global finger wagging by America at the Bad Nations of Europe for squandering their birthright in a general war. Progressives view man as incapable of managing his own affairs without a power elite around that will show the underclass what to do. While never getting much play in America's capitalistic society, this idea of big government and quasi-socialistic governance forms the bedrock of American Liberal philosophy. In truth, American Liberals today should be called "liberal/progressives," since they have embraced their perceived role as America's power elite.

American liberal/progressives view the world as a wonderfully variegated pastiche of communities of peoples, gorgeously multi-racial, inexpressibly rich in diverse cultures, a pageant of wise and urgent souls in caftans and ferouks, robes and business suits plying their trades, spinning their tales, sipping their coffees, nuancing their relationships in a sweet dance of reason, moving here and there through an emotional landscape of light and hope, dispensing kindness to all, each earnestly seeking truth and happiness in a Global Village of peace. Ah, so beautiful…a lovely vision indeed. Until Reality rubs one's nose in the sad fact that some nations just want to have fun.

To those of us too insensitive to perceive how the Brotherhood of Man is ennobled by permitting psychotic dictators to convert their neighbors into pools of radioactive slag, these are merely rogue nations and need to be stopped. Cold. But in the Liberal world of situational ethics, where there is no moral compass of basic values against which to measure acts, holding a nation responsible for its actions is unacceptable because it creates *conflict* which frequently leads to *violence.* So when one of these *Significantly Unapproachable Nationalistic Risk Takers* or *Troublingly Violence Prone Self-Actualizing National Enclaves* begins to rattle the plutonium saber, the very most that will happen is they'll be asked politely to stop…and if they keep on, well…tut tut. If, despite urgent appeals to Rectitude, Decency and the Dignity of Man, one of these societies of *Disputatious Emergent Intimidators* should reach out and touch its neighbor with a kiloton or two, well, how could we deny their right to settle their differences by nuking each other back to the Stone Age as long as the debris field remains safely offshore?

Nobody would dispute the fact that Liberals and Progressives always know what's best for everyone else. The sad truth remains, however, that in their earnest attempt to be mommy and daddy to the world they can occasionally get a number of very good people killed. That's ok, of course, in the quest for the Greatest Good for the Greatest Number as long as it isn't the power elite doing the dying. Going about doing Good is a full-time job, and it's widely held among the Left that it should not be made more onerous by subjecting any of them to actual personal danger. Scrambling for cover might interrupt the flow of deep thinking, and of course nobody wants that. When you have an overwhelming duty to show the world how shallow is American culture and how destructive is American policy, most Liberals and Progressives agree that it's best to keep indiscriminate neutron flow to an absolute minimum, not to mention all those messy ruins. Care-givers have important initiatives to undertake on behalf of World Peace, and it's just a lot more difficult to get the point across, that America should trust her safety to sweet words and the United Nations, when your own skin is sloughing off.

So under this brand of tender, event-driven, Globalist analysis, American foreign policy has shifted from a strong counterforce against our sworn enemies to a series of sanctimonious wishes that these emerging nuclear nations should somehow...be good...and not...be bad. Everything will run along smoothly, the unspoken Liberal/Progressive subtext reads, as long as the inertial systems of these *Regrettably Argumentative Emerging Nations* are limited to deliver guidance at or below a launch parabola to the environs of Eastern Europe. Nobody seems to care until the mushroom clouds begin puffing out. For instance, rhetoric in the United Nations concerning Iran's incipient nuclear capability suggests that our finger wagging American do-gooders will be supported by Europe itself right up to an Iranian Ground Zero in the Vienna suburbs. Current intelligence credits the Iranian Air Force with an operational missile of 2300 miles range, 228 miles short of their launch facilities give or take, depending on whether you want to vaporize the Opera House. But never fear! The wonderful advances of the Iranian space program are already producing vehicles which, suitably tipped, could bring down the stern hand of a disapproving *Allah* all the way out to bad old Denmark who frivolously restricted Muslim immigration merely because they were taking over the government.

But what about those doughty *Sub-National Freedom Fighters* whom insensitive racist Americans insist on calling "terrorists?" What do American liberal/progressives have to say about these *Distressingly Argumentative Hostage Takers* who have no national borders and desire none, who slaughter Jews and Americans for *Allah* and occasionally just for fun?

Don't be angry!

Reach out to these *Bumptious Disempowered Islamic Strugglers* exercising their right to show their displeasure with us. Sit with them and help them realize that America was put into the world to fulfill their needs at the expense of her own. Embrace them with our love for their strong will. Reward them with our abiding respect for a world view that permits them to kill anyone they wish. Empower them with our sorrowful acceptance of their need to kill *us*. Share with them our pain for their somewhat dysfunctional yet dynamic and certainly understandable method of using American flesh to express their views. Join them in their condemnation of America's riches and of our selfish unwillingness to give it all away.

The thoughtful American will not journey very far down this road before beginning to suspect he's being made a patsy, a sacrificial symbol tailor-made to exalt the rest of the world at the expense of his own. To die to preserve one's homeland is a noble and honorable thing. To die to preserve a power elite who consider you their underclass is tragic.

Rogue nations with a nuclear punch might not be able to deliver their bombs here in the Homeland, *but they will shop their wares to anyone who can!* Terrorists will make their second great attack on the Homeland with nuclear weapons. The story tells who will do it, how it will be done, most likely where, and when.

This is a war story about what happens when mommy and daddy take over defense of the Homeland, about a country run by people in such denial that only a second mass death of innocent Americans could jog them out of their ideological stupor.

It's a story of courage and cowardice, the courage to stand head-up against power and the cowardice to sanction the murder of innocents for political gain.

It's a love story about men who love God so much that they're willing to sacrifice anyone but themselves, including their own Believers - about Americans who love power so much that they're willing to sacrifice their countrymen as long as their policies remain unquestioned - and about real Americans who love their country so much that they offer to sacrifice themselves in her defense.

It's a teaching story containing lessons about ideology trumping survival, political correctness trumping plain common sense, and agenda trumping truth, with a little character-building on the side.

But above all else, it's a story of Duty holding apart then welding together some very, very good people in the defense of America.

Some of the bad guys win; some of the good guys lose. Terrorists kill, bravery exalts, fuses ignite, and lovers find a way.

And it's a story about simple, average Americans watching their country's descent into danger and wondering why in the world common sense doesn't prevail - Americans kind of like you and me.

PROLOGUE

مقدمة

In order to be honest to my readers, I must try to paint an accurate, credible, fair image of how the liberal/progressive view of international relations compares to the real world. So let us call it *Cloud Cuckoo Land*.

While its loving, caring outlook and Tinker Bell Diplomacy may make the coffee cake go down more easily, sometimes the real world will no longer be denied. Occasionally, when drifting about, *Cloud Cuckoo Land* can become entangled in bothersome Reality, bumping gently into gritty facts that just won't be wished away. This happened a hundred years ago when, reeling under the devastation of their "victory" in World War I, The Allies decided that what they wanted was a little less of President Woodrow Wilson's high-flown principle, a little more *revanche*, and a whole lot more reparations. It happened again in the recent past when Iranians decided to demonstrate to President Carter that his pious platitudes were no substitute for a couple of dozen guys with Kalashnikovs who liked to beat up Americans because they were handy. And as our story opens it's getting ready to happen again.

Cloud Cuckoo Land has felt tremors against Reality in the recent past, but usually without measurable results. Embassy bombings were attributed to the youthful exuberance of frustrated folks expressing themselves in their own dear way. And even a twenty-four hundred square foot hole let into the side of a United States Navy destroyer by a half ton shaped charge compliments of *Struggling Islamic Disputationists* resulting in seventeen American deaths and thirty-nine casualties some of whom wished for death, was passed off as being our own fault. Ah, those zany *al Qaeda* guys – anything to make a point.

The most recent contact between *Cloud Cuckoo Land* and the real world occurred on 11 September 2001. The Twin Towers came down and jogged us out of our self-absorbed coma. We were convinced, for a while at least, that somebody out there really didn't like us very much. Three thousand American dead in our streets being difficult to overlook, we belatedly realized we were at war. For a while that snapped us out of it, and we got busy on defense. But after a time, constant vigilance came to be a lot of trouble, and besides, who were we to deny people the right to express themselves?

So we decided to call off the war and go home. To make our point, we elected leaders who declared the war finished, renamed the enemy soldiers "criminals," transferred them into our civil courts, and told the world that if they decided to hold a conflict, well, America was just not going to attend. But it turned out that it wasn't quite that easy. Terrorists rubbed their hands, straightened their *galabiyyas,* and pitched in to encourage the sick, disaffected people among us to start a great killing spree. As this is written, terrorist attacks in the Homeland are continuing and are likely to increase. Our Muslim "allies" abroad are hustling terrorists through training camps with only the thinnest lip service paid to cooperating with our military. Muslim opportunists who put that lovely faith to their own sordid uses are collecting fissionable material from North Korea and Iran fast as their trucks can scoot.

As our story opens, *Cloud Cuckoo Land* is on the verge of receiving a new kind of gentle nudge against the fleecy home of the Liberal/Progressives' beautiful vision of the world. This time the United States of America will be given an additional opportunity to atone for its sins by absorbing into its clay some tens of thousands more of its citizens than perished on 9/11, with another couple of hundred thousand so sick from hard radiation that they will wish fervently they had been in the former group now scattered here and there throughout the Homeland in lead-lined coffins. To wish this would happen in order to free us from the incubus of our current anti-American Globalist leaders – for it would surely destroy them and all their works – is too dastardly to contemplate. I hope my story isn't prophesy except of course for the lovers. They're good people. I drew them as the best America is able to produce. They should come out of this well and whole. But, then again, so should Alice.

ONE

دحاو

The plastic tape's sharp edges where it had been ripped from a roll chafed her legs where they were pulled together at the ankles and her wrists behind her back. She could feel a trickle of wetness and realized she had been fighting the bonds while unconscious. *How long was I out? No way to tell...who the hell ARE these people...no professionals would have taken me and my daughter in broad dayli...Alice!* The piece over her mouth had been carelessly, or perhaps purposely, swiped over one nostril and her muffled cry pushed it over the other nostril until she gasped for breath. God...*Alice!* The last thing Sheridan remembered was a hand coming from behind holding a cloth...then nothing. *Alice!* Her twelve-year-old daughter had been at the other end of the pool when whatever happened...happened. *Did they get her? Did she get away? Alice!...shit!...can't see anything... blindfold...God Almighty, somebody's going to* pay *for this...*

"Mommy?" A very small voice a few feet behind her brought Sheridan instantly full awake.

"Alice!" Sheridan screamed but the tape gagging her made it into a muffled groan.

"Mommy, where are we? Who are those men? Mommy! What's happening to us?" Alice's voice was beginning to rise but Sheridan could do nothing except listen in increasing pain to her daughter's increasing hysteria. Alice continued to call to her, voice rising, until finally she began to scream. A few seconds later a door opened and Sheridan heard several sharp cracks and a muffled thud. The screaming abruptly stopped.

Sheridan was frantic to get to Alice but her bonds held and the tape over her mouth prevented her from calling out. The thought came to her that this was a fiendishly subtle bit of torture, to permit her daughter's panic to reach her but prevent her from comforting her. Shortly she heard her daughter's muffled breathing so at least she was still alive. ...*still alive! My GOD! Eliot, help me, darling...ELIOT!*" As she slid back into a kind of nether world of semi-consciousness, Sheridan reached out mentally for the first time to her husband and was surprised she hadn't thought of him until now. She had always been self-reliant and her marriage to a man just like her, while a love match, had no component of dependency. Both Eliot and Sheridan had made their own professional marks, she in intelligence, he as an Army officer currently somewhere in Afghanistan with his squadron of pilotless drones. Their times together were brief and incandescent. The separations enforced by their work only seemed to increase the heat. Sheridan realized this was the first time she had ever needed his help. She longed for his strong arms, level gaze, and calm, wise counsel. It was that gaze that originally drew her to him, that first night when he met her eyes straight across the table, leaned forward, took her hand, and said quietly, "Talk to me." At that moment she felt a bond being struck that had since become unbreakable. When she had told him this long after, he replied with a loving eye that he had merely been trying to look down her dress. It was this attitude she relished – he was never serious about anything yet always serious about her. And of course about Alice. Sheridan recited the old love-phrase the two of them had used to quiet little Alice's fears of the dark beneath her bed "...*Child of learning, child of light...manatees and ladybugs, pups and armadillos*"...Sheridan choked a sob; *my God, my sweet little Beebee, what have I gotten you into?*

Sheridan's edge gave way and she felt her muscles relax as she drifted backward from the intolerable tension of her circumstances. Her mind drifted into old times with the three of them. Nine-year-old Alice had come home from school one day and told Sheridan and Eliot that one of her classmates was going to shoot up the school. Alice had told her teacher and the school principal but they didn't believe her. Sheridan passed it off as play talk but Eliot, although he was literally on the way out the door to his new Army deployment, had taken her on his lap and made her tell him all the details. He went to the web site Alice showed him, then was quickly on the phone. His people looked at the web site, contacted local police, and the boy was quietly arrested and placed in psychiatric evaluation. His parents were livid and not even the revelation of his web site, his cache of weapons, and his suicide note could quell their anger. They began agitating to discover who had defamed their innocent son, asserting to all who would listen that it was race hatred by whites that caused his incarceration in a hospital for the mentally insane. Since court records of Juvenile Court, as well as psychiatric records for all citizens, are sealed above subpoena, no facts were available to refute the parents' claims except Alice's earlier complaints to school officials. The parents of the sick child were black professionals from inside the Beltway. He worked for the Department of Urban Planning; she was an information specialist with a realty company. Alice's father, being military and by this time somewhere overseas, didn't really count. Her mother was…well, who knew what she did – some job somewhere that nobody really knew much about. Waitress maybe, prostitute. Nobody could really tell for sure. So the beat went on against Alice without letup. As a result, for Alice's part in saving the lives of numbers of her classmates and teachers, the following actions were taken:

--by the Commissioner of Police, Ann Arundel County, Virginia, [aired by Fox News but since the potential shooter was black, by no other network], Alice was presented a Resolution of Thanks signed by all three County Commissioners, her federal Congressman, and both Virginia federal Senators;

--by the 3550th Special Weapons Section, United States Army Intelligence Service, [again televised by Fox but nowhere else], Alice was commissioned Honorary Colonel, United States Army, commission backdated three days so that she would outrank her father who had just been promoted;

--and by the School Board of the Joshua T. Cuervo Middle School, [carried by all major networks along with file photographs of the potential shooter in a cute little soccer uniform] for "having recklessly endangered the self esteem of a fellow student and for engendering potential feelings of discrimination in a person of color…," Alice was expelled.

TWO

اثنان

"What the hell do you mean, she disappeared?'"

What with the FBI being forced to read *Miranda* Rights to captured enemy soldiers, with the House Speaker trying to get in front of her own stupidities by slamming his people, and with that idiot over in…Gordon Cubbage, Director, Central Intelligence Agency, was not having a good morning. And now this.

"Sorry, Jack, it's been a long week. Just tell me what happened."

Cubbage listened. He spoke again. He listened for a long time. True to his dictum never to let them see you stress, he kept his demeanor calm, his voice low and modulated, his language temperate, quite unaware that this was when his staff and everyone else who knew him would begin to shiver.

"OK, Jack, we'll get on it from here… …yes, she has one… …no, this is our first… …anything you can get on the perps will help of course, but if they're new at this shit we may have some trouble ID-ing them… …call you as soon as we have anything. Something new comes in, don't forget who loves you… …yeah, no channels. Send it right here."

Cubbage placed the phone carefully and gently down onto its cradle, insuring that it fit securely all the way into its little nook with the two tiny clicks that signaled full engagement of the metal clips that sent charging current from the base into the handset permitting call-forwarding, IPod access, internet services, and under certain conditions conversion of the unit into a charred, evil smelling lump. He performed this operation with great attention, not because it particularly required it — he could have tossed the handset into the cradle with as much result — but it was his habit when confronting situations like the one brewing at present to take special pains to avoid the appearance of frustration until it was time. The handset was secure.

It was time.

"Baaaasssss....kin!" His scream echoed through the three rooms of his office suite, out into the long hallway and down the stairwell at the far end. He was a half second too late. As the first syllable rang along the corridors a wood panel of his office wall pushed inward and Chief Special Agent Lorraine Baskin, Lt. Col, United States Army [ret.], BA, MA, Ph.D., LLD, C.P.M., OBE [pvtly cnfrrd], *Croix de Guerre* [pvtly cnfrrd], Order Of Lenin [pvtly cnfrrd], entered on long, shapely legs preceded by six full inches of bra-less horizontal cleavage surmounted by an aquiline nose framed by piercing green eyes that warned all but the most foolhardy against taking notice of any of it. She carried a dispatch case that never left her side and a nail file that frequently did.

"About time, Doll Face, - what kept you?" She had acquired her nickname the first time she had threatened Cubbage with a sexual discrimination lawsuit several years past and which had recurred approximately once a week since.

Chief Special Agent Baskin batted her eyelashes and looked demure, "Doin' my nails, chief...was this really, like, important or something?"

Cubbage was of the private opinion that of the eight thousand assets he had at his disposal, Lorraine Baskin was worth all the rest. He suspected she tapped his phone, proof of which would win for Cubbage a sizeable side bet from his Director of Internal Surveillance. For her part Baskin always accorded Cubbage her full attention, a privilege bestowed on the few men who had never begun a professional conversation by looking at her breasts. She had once accused Cubbage of ogling her from behind, to be met with a firm denial accompanied by the reasonable question, how could he see anything from that position? He had long ago filed this incident away in his mind under the General Heading *Days Of Torment I Have Known*, specific sub-reference, "*Quitteth whilst thee be ahead,*

Bigmouthed Asshole" because his next remark, that it would be like trying to determine the model of the aircraft by gazing up its afterburner, cost him a very expensive dinner at the *very* expensive Langley Headquarters VIP Dining Room. Having been requested by Cubbage to keep a low profile since the two of them worked closely and fraternization in the Agency was discouraged, Chief Special Agent Baskin arrived in an evening dress the cut of which created an instant sensation throughout the establishment. A marvel of seemingly strutless cantilevered support that refuted every known principle of civil engineering, it was the hit of the night and caused the Swedish ambassador to stand over her chair exchanging pleasantries for six full minutes.

Cubbage leaned back in his large chair and spoke quietly and deliberately. "Holloway just called. Walker and her daughter are down. On vacation in Morocco. Last contact yesterday, missed the morning check-in. Nothing at the hotel, no sightings, no perps, couple of scumbags hanging around but couldn't tie them in with anybody, otherwise nothing. Jack thinks she was grabbed but no hits on the MO so it might be a new bunch trying to make their bones."

Baskin was thoughtful. "Hard to tell with these scum; can't trust them to be professional and just grab her up and try to get a few bucks for her. Doesn't matter who they are…sooner or later one of them starts waving the *Qur'an* around and spouting Ancient Truths. They all start pumping themselves up, everything hits the fan and we've got body parts. The only defense we have is to get them back quick before the pixies get big heads about Serving *Allah* and start carving. Where are the fucking Commies when you really need them? At least they knew how to negotiate."

Cubbage sighed and rubbed his head with his palm. "Concur. So tell me what to do."

Baskin turned on her heel and spoke into the phone that had magically appeared in her hand, "IDENT? Charlie? GPS intercept Agent Walker, Sheridan, 3 meter fix. [Hand over mouthpiece, to Cubbage: "Working, Chief…"] then back to the phone. "Where?… …no… …yeah, if you get a sig/term, pass right it up to the top…… no… …yes…… HELL, no!…

...hmmmm... ...you wish!... ...HELL YES... ...OK, eight o'clock, don't be late......don't bother, I'll tell him; he's right here."

"She's in Damascus, chief, address on the way. No input from her since she started moving, so it looks like a snatch. Charlie figures they got both of them, mother and daughter. How old is she, fourteen? Twelve! Damn. She shouldn't be in on a thing like this. Taken in Marrakesh, eh? And Jack already has them in Damascus? Hmmm. Lots of quick transport showing here – fast movers. These aren't your usual towelheads grabbing up somebody to play with. If they can slide her across the Med that quick, we've got some real shit going on. Charlie says hello. Sig term direct to you if it happens."

Every CIA agent traveling outside the Homeland was being fitted with a surgically implanted GPS device monitored by local CIA station operatives whose signal fed back to a central database at Langley. This required each agent to check in daily so their trackers could know they were still their own master. As soon as a field agent missed a check, the Agency went on full alert. The unit was powered by heart motion. Signal Termination indicated death of the host.

Lorraine was thoughtful, "OK, so we know where she is and what happened to her. So you want me to tell you what to do? Ordinarily I'd say go get her no matter how we have to do it. But we both know that's out of the question now. DHS is running things and those people don't have a clue in the world how to run overseas ops. I can't think of one of them who had any military service, much less worked for the Agency. So that was then, this is now. Since the last election they've been hanging us out in the wind. So what do we do? Who the fuck knows? I don't."

Cubbage knew she was right. He'd incurred the wrath of several members of congress who dissed the CIA and expected him to sit and take it because he was an administration appointee. According to their political viewpoint, he owed The Party his job and his future. Cubbage hadn't quite seen it that way, so he stood up for his people when he had to and when there were hits to be taken he offered himself as the bull's-eye. Because of this attitude he came to be ignored by Congress and worshipped by his staff. He knew it had forestalled several high-ranking CIA resignations, but he also knew his days were numbered. Department of Homeland Security, for whom he and his FBI counterpart, Feeny, both worked these days, took a dim view of subordinates who refused to take hints how to behave, and *really* didn't like subordinates who roiled the calm waters with silly problems like kidnappings. But, Cubbage sighed to himself, he'd never been much of a hint taker where principle was involved. He noticed that Baskin was still speaking –

"...a lot more inside, and since the last election. So, since you ask me in my official capacity as your valued assistant, I now advise you to get on the phone to Human Resources, call in your Early Retirement Option. I'll run down to Arlington, hit one of the banks, and we'll fade away into the sunset."

"Cubbage almost smiled. "I've had worse offers from better, Doll Face, but for that to happen I'd need to see some really big tits..." He looked straight into her eyes and way back in the corner of her mind a tiny part of her wondered whether he actually knew she was female. She returned his gaze straight on making a supreme effort not to stick her tongue out at him.

"...but that wouldn't do Walker any good, would it?" he went on. "Rain check, Angel Eyes; offer noted and filed. Now what have you got for me that *will* work?"

"Send Reynolds, Byrne, and Getchell from Covert. Call in a marker on Hutchinson down at Andrews. Counting rollout, his BF-129s can have them in country in about six hours. Jack's CH-64 jumps them to the safe house; they reason with the pixies without worrying too much about staining the rug, bring out Walker and her daughter fast and easy. But get us in there and grab her back before they start fucking with her in the Name Of *Allah*. These little sweeties get to doing some tall thinking, petting their grievances and stickin' their hands down their pants, and all of a sudden – "

Cubbage nodded. " – Yeah...I know, and I've had a bad feeling about this one ever since I took Jack's call. No threats, no knife waving, no blubbering about *Islam*ic Law, no leaks to the murder-press...nothing. Nobody seems to *want* anything from us, and that scares the hell out of me. This may be another Daniel Pearl in the making." Cubbage referred to the kidnapped American journalist who was abducted by a group of *Discourse Challenged Hostage Takers*, tried in their kangaroo court, and ultimately publicly murdered. No rescue or exchange was possible because the sole purpose of the kidnapping was to obtain a Westerner whom they could torture and ritually execute. Cubbage shuddered inwardly as he remembered *al Jazeera's* gleeful broadcast of the *Distressingly Single-Minded Freedom Fighters* shouting *Islam*ic verses while one waved in an outstretched hand Daniel Pearl's severed head.

"But," he went on, "We don't have the decision anymore. Now that we're part of Homeland Security we have to…ah…consult with the Director before we put people in harm's way. Send your data to Counter, tell them what's up and that this might not be the day to take a long lunch. Get me Homeland Security, DHS Secretary, private line, priority scramble."

Baskin nodded and spoke into her phone.

Soon his red phone buzzed and Cubbage's voice became syrup: "Hi, Janine, Gordon Cubbage here. Got a minute? Good, let me put you on Speaker. Lorraine will be here shortly and on the call with me……yeah, that "Doll Face" [fierce whisper to Baskin, 'Damn you, who *else* knows about that?! – back across his desk a grin and shrug].

"Sure, no harm asking her sometime. She's, ah…spoken of you many times. I'm *sure* she'd *love* your side of the street" [from across his desk hands up and violent headshaking].

He went on, "No, no, she's a real asset here but of course nobody's irreplaceable and if you really need her…well, sure, absolutely, Janine, I'll make it a point to mention it to her. [upraised finger toward her side of the desk] "I'm sure she'll be in touch…. [head buried in hands across his desk].

Oh, ok, we're on Speaker now..." Cubbage was brisk. "For the record, present: Gordon Cubbage Director Central Intelligence Agency and Dr. Lorraine Baskin, Chief Agent, understanding to converse with Janine

Mastroantonio, Secretary Department of Homeland Security no others present this end…acknowledge?

"Yes, yes, Gordie, I'm here alone and will advise you of visitors. Now Gordie, we're being very formal today. What's this all about?"

"We've got a situation, Janine. One of my agents is on vacation with her 12 year old daughter and hasn't turned up for her 24-hour check-in. My station chief in Damascus believes both have been kidnapped and are still alive although he has no direct information on her daughter's health or whereabouts. He's following their progress from Marrakech where she was last seen."

"Does she have the GPS device?"

"Last month before she left."

"I always said GPS implanting was an excellent precaution," Janine went on. "I'm glad you saw fit to initiate it as my Committee authorized."

Major points for political correctness, Cubbage mused silently, but just shade wrong on timing. During her tenure as Chair of the House Covert Operations Subcommittee, former Congresswoman Janine Mastroantonio had continually blocked the CIA's request to implant these devices. It was explained to the Chairman that field agents had begged for this kind of support for years. Mastroantonio responded that no one was at risk at the moment, that CIA could not prove that lives would be saved if the Agency knew where a kidnapped agent was being held, and that the Agency might then be tempted toward some kind of heroic rescue that could endanger innocent locals. Worse, hamhanded rescue attempts might put the alleged kidnappers at risk without due process and possibly even violate their civil rights. The CIA's rejoinder, that these were enemy combatants, foreign nationals, and had no American civil rights, Mastroantonio dismissed as irrelevant. In any event, she had continued, her Committee could never be part of anything that might even potentially seem to lessen the self-esteem of a citizen even if they didn't hold actual American citizenship. To this line of reasoning the CIA could find no adequate response. When questioned more closely by fellow committee members about her opposition to these implants, Mastroantonio revealed that influential members of her Californian constituency had violently objected what they considered an extreme invasion of privacy, basing their conviction on a movie they had once seen in which citizens were controlled by their government through surgically implanted computer chips. Mastroantonio informed her committee that since her constituents *believed* this to be invasive and since what Americans *believed* to be true was more important than the truth itself, she would block any kind of request of this nature.

In American national politics, lights under bushels do not go unperceived. Janine's attitudes were duly noted by a new administration intent on moving America into world citizenship on an equal footing with all other countries irrespective of the American Constitution, which they felt should be subordinated to the UN Charter. She could help do this as DHS Secretary, they told her, by insuring all our Homeland Security forces treated all people in the world with the same rights as American citizens. Henceforth, "terrorists" would no longer be enemy combatants, but misguided and repressed individuals sometimes acting out their frustrations at being held down by American insensitivity to their special needs. As soon as Mastroantonio was tapped by the incoming President for her head job at DHS, the new Chair of her old congressional oversight committee, a 32-year, five-term Democrat, rushed through approval of the GPS tracker and urged Cubbage to expedite the implant process. Cubbage recalled all this in painful detail but reflected that it might not be just the right moment to remind her.

"Well, Janine, of course I remember your, ah…close association with the project. We just got it implemented about a month ago and Sheridan – my agent – is our first actual incident of an agent failing to report and being subsequently located using the implant.

"It certainly took you long enough to get it in place for all the grief you gave me," Janine responded tartly. "So, test working, is it? Have you got her back yet? She's probably in Cairo shopping or out at the Pyramids with her daughter and – "

"—Ah, no, Janine," Cubbage broke in, "I'm not calling you to report on the tracking project, although I know you're, ah…vitally interested in its success." [two middle fingers up and down, up and down, from across the desk]. "Walker's not shopping and probably not sightseeing. My station chief in that part of the world wouldn't make a mistake like that. We're reasonably certain she's been kidnapped and taken by force to Damascus. But none of the usual terrorist groups have claimed responsibility, nobody's MO fits, and we don't think they knew she was Agency when they took her."

"Gordie, I wish you wouldn't use the word 'terrorist' to describe people who might simply be misguided local patriots. We don't know for sure they have harmful intentions or that she isn't simply off with some of her tourist friends [head in hands across the desk] and besides, if she really was kidnapped we don't know what your agent might have done to provoke this."

Cubbage realized Janine was merely echoing the mantra of the new Administration, that the hatred and attacks were America's own fault, but Baskin's patience came to an end, "Nor do we know what excesses might have been committed among the locals by her twelve-year-old daughter." Cubbage made throat-cutting motions, but Janine appeared not to have noticed the sarcasm.

"That's irrelevant, Ms. Baskin. [a whispered *"Colonel Baskin, you cow!" and Cubbage put hands over ears]* She's – what's her name...Walker? Walker is an American citizen and accorded full protection of our embassy people. I'm confident that they can negotiate any situation that arises. So for the moment let's consider this a mysterious disappearance and go from there."

Taking a firm grip on the arms of his chair and on what was left of his temper, Cubbage spoke carefully in small words, "Janine, this is one of our top agents and one of my managers. She knows much about our operations that we might not want revealed in that part of the world. Anything we can do to protect that information we should do right away. That means getting Agent Walker and her daughter back, and if we move fast I think we can. We know where she is, and if we get in there immediately we have a pretty good chance of recovering her and her daughter both. Our problem is that the longer we delay the more danger she's in. These terror – ah, these...people might get tired of keeping Walker and her daughter and simply kill them but maintain the fiction that they are still alive. Or, if they discover she's Agency they might use tort...ah, extreme interrogation methods on her. So I need you to give me the go-ahead as quickly as you can. I repeat, Janine, if we don't get to them in the next day or two there's a good chance one or both of them will be killed. We *must* get in there *right now* and--"

"—Now of course I want you to get your agent back, Gordie," Janine interrupted, "But I can't just slam this thing into drive without some associative guidance. Every time you get to running one of your operations we end up offending some very important people in that part of the world, and in my position I can't just willy nilly risk creating more dissention and possibly getting some of these folks hurt. And of course there's the whole issue of the rights of the hostage takers under *Miranda*. Let's not forget the troubles we've had establishing their Constitutional framework for arrest and the flack we've gotten for reading *Miranda* rights to the people we've captured in Afghanistan. Suppose I let you go in on one of your operations, and some of the hostage takers become injured before they can be brought back here and put into our judicial system. What would we look like then but a bunch of thugs? Remember, Gordie, the doctrine of presumptive innocence is now going to be applied worldwide. Our president has seen to that! We'll just have to accommodate ourselves to some of the little rough spots along the way."

"At all costs we have to avoid giving more offense and making them feel, well...offended. It would ruin the delicate high level initiatives the President is currently involved in to bring America into true conformity with the real rest of the world. But I want you not to worry so I'll let you in on a little diplomacy that hasn't yet been made public. When the President was over there at the start of his term, he negotiated ironclad agreements with each of those countries that neither side would use those horrible torture methods anymore. We're going to be firm in keeping our side of the bargain so of course they will, too."

Cubbage tried one more time. "Janine, don't you have a pre-teen grandson? Suppose it were him and we knew where he was? What would you want us to do?"

"Gordie, that's not germane. My grandson would never be put into that kind of danger. Thank God my family is safe here at home. As our president has already said, Walker, like other soldiers, signed on for this kind of danger and should be prepared to accept the consequences.

Cubbage forced his voice to remain calm, "Then you're telling me folks like you are smart to keep their families safe, but Walker and people like her who put themselves in harm's way for the country…when they get hurt they…sort of…get what they asked for? Is that what you think?"

Janine didn't seem to hear him. "I think this can keep until we can prepare a reasoned and intelligent response that takes fully into account the rights and desires of every participant. But I need to talk to some people. Let me get right back to you…" and the line went dead.

Cubbage replaced the handset, this time with both hands, willing them not to shake. Everything today had a spin and at this exact moment he knew Director Mastroantonio was on the phone with Chief National Security Advisor Jeremiah Ayers checking political fallout. Until she got a political clearance his hands were tied. He wondered whether his own view -- that nothing was more important than the safety of an American soldier whether in or out of uniform -- was held by anybody but himself anymore.

"I do, Chief." Mildly surprised to find Baskin still there, Cubbage realized he had been thinking out loud. He sighed. He didn't like making excuses to a subordinate, but Baskin was his best. The woman had commanded a unit of M1A1 *Abrams* tanks in Iraq. Still carried scars from the war! So falling back on "organizational integrity" just wouldn't cut it, not with her. Nevertheless, reaching down into the deepest recesses of his loyalty to the chain of command, Cubbage tried to be fair.

"Janine's ok. Not a professional…and like most of the new ones never been military…you know…just doesn't get it…about America being in your gut…about being on the front lines. And she has to balance our interests against a lot of people breathing down her neck who *really* don't get it," a sidelong reference to the numerous advisors and bureaucrats brought in with the new administration who were actively hostile to the American military and took scant pains to conceal it.

"Chief, may I speak freely?"

"Absolutely not. You're a pretty face and a good pair of...legs, and I only keep you around here for the ornamental value. Your actual opinion is worthless to me."

Baskin smiled, "I'll take that as a 'yes'." Then she was serious, "Secretary of Homeland Security Janine Mastroantonio is a left-wing political hack shoved on top of DHS by the current occupant of the White House to keep us from pissing off the leftist lunatics that elected him. They hate us and they hate our soldiers. She's doing a balancing act all right, but it's a balance between keeping us on a short leash and yet not getting hit again here in the Homeland. That's the only thing that really scares these leftist idiots. They don't give a damn whether Americans get killed, but the President knows that after the last guy kept us safe for years, getting hit again here at home would destroy his presidency and take his party down with him. Not even his wackiest supporters could avoid the simple fact that his Shuffle and Bow Diplomacy got thousands more Americans killed in our streets. The President's not a bad guy and probably even likes being an American although it would be death for him to admit it. But he never served his country and he has to keep those lunatics happy who are ashamed of America and especially ashamed of our power in the world. They don't want our military to seem to succeed, but they know that if they get us hit again they'll be crucified."

Baskin shook her head, "So good old Janine was put in place to make sure CIA and FBI keeps the scumbags away from our soil. Her mandate from Mister Apology is to keep us hobbled as long as nobody hits us here in the Homeland. But if we do get hit, she's to make sure the military gets the blame and not him. I'm sorry, sir, I took rounds for this country and I don't have much humor for sidemouths like her or handwringers like him. She also has to tap-dance fast enough to keep our own Agency people from deserting in a big rush. Most of us are still here only because we're loyal to this country."

[And to you, Chief], Lorraine thought quietly to herself but did not say.

"If we start bailing it'll cause a lot of talk. If enough of us leave and then something happens...well, they're already feeling responsibility tickling their asses like a burner flame and they really don't like it when they can't just wish away trouble. They bank on our loyalty to this country and they use it to get what they want even while they're laughing at people called patriots. But if we get it here in the Homeland after they've pissed away our best people…they'll hang."

Cubbage noted that his colleague was beginning to redden from the recesses of her collar spreading up to her ears. Military through and through, Lorraine Baskin detested criticizing a superior, especially her Commander in Chief. She was right, but he knew it didn't matter. She, and he, and the rest would keep on doing the job they had in front of them and to hell with the politics because they *were* patriots and they *did* believe in all that stupid stuff about honor and duty. So Cubbage waited until she had run down, and then grinned, "Since everything in this office is recorded, when you slam me with your sexist lawsuit I'll be able to Dennenberg you right out of the Hemisphere." Herb Dennenberg had been an Assistant CIA Director who had made the mistake of arguing with newly appointed Director of Homeland Security Mastroantonio that his people should not be punished now for faithfully carrying out certain orders given them years ago. The Agency was able to save his pension but not his job.

Cubbage had tried to defend the indefensible, but Lorraine was too savvy to buy any of it. So he gave up and leaned forward in his chair. "When you were commanding that tank unit in the desert, if the President or any of his people had started talking about you guys lying to them, or had said they were going to investigate you for something you'd done in good faith years ago when things were hot, what would have been the very first thing to happen?"

Lorraine Baskin considered for a few moments, "Well, Chief, the very first thing would be about six hundred emails going out to about six hundred families telling them to start raising hell about it with their congressmen."

Cubbage nodded, "Precisely correct. Now when the CIA is accused – by the Speaker of the House of Representatives no less – of *lying to Congress*, and the Attorney General says he's going to start investigating things our people did in good faith under specific orders years ago, what's the first thing *our* people would do?"

Baskin was puzzled. "Well, Chief...nothing."

Cubbage's voice dropped with emotion, "Exactly right, Chief Special Agent Baskin. And why would that be?"

"Well, what *could* we do?" Lorraine replied, "Each of us has sworn not to take Company business public and if we do we can be prosecuted as a traitor or even a double agent!"

Cubbage was grim, "Right again. And this is precisely why CIA gets slammed every time the President has to demonstrate to his lunatic supporters his contempt for the American military. *He and his people hit us because we can't fight back!*"

Lorraine was surprised. "I never thought of it like that...a bunch of fucking street-corner bullies getting down on the little kids...shit...ok, I get it...damn! So CIA's the fall guy for the military because Congress can't touch our soldiers but they can fuck with us all they want? Thanks for sharing that. Makes me feel heaps better."

"Sorry, Angel Eyes, but you need to know where we stand. As a federal agency, we're the whipping boys because we have to keep our hands in our pockets. If the Speaker and her...associates...were to go after the military which is their actual target of choice, our soldiers' families would carve them new assholes and they'd do it on the Six O'clock News."

"I get the message, Chief. Well, now what?"

"So you and Holloway round up all the data you can on the target group. Try to find out what they want and whether they know who they have. I don't think they do. Walker wasn't on assignment. She had her daughter with her, for God's Sake! So we don't want to show too much interest and get them poking around but we've got to find out what's on the ground out there and who's pulling the levers. You know as well as I do that every minute we don't act might be the minute they decide

Walker and her daughter are too hot to keep alive. We've got to get in there quick but the new prez says I can't authorize anything unless Janine approves it. So…while the Secretary does her consulting…" Cubbage frowned down at his hands locked together on his desk. "…we wait. And hope to hell she won't be too long about it."

Lorraine Baskin frowned. "Are we going to leave Walker to State to bargain for like she says?"

"Lorraine!" Cubbage had never before used her first name; she was mildly surprised he even knew it. Her gaze went to his face and saw him smiling a smile aimed at the wall behind her that chilled her to her backbone.

"Do you remember the old saying from your service time, 'No Soldier Left Behind?' Nice motto. Well, we don't have any mottos around here to put up on the wall. Wouldn't even if we did. But understand, Chief Special Agent Baskin, *Walker's mine* and *none of my people get left behind either*. She and her daughter are coming home."

And as he said this Dr. Lorraine Baskin, published academic, combat tank commander, CIA spook, mother of three, looked deep into his eyes and felt a stirring that for these many years had lain dormant and forgotten.

THREE

ثالثة

The cracked, grime slathered windows of the cheerless room were dulled to exclude most of the light passing in and out. This was exactly what the owners had wanted for one had to be careful; painted-over panes might have indicated secrecy but who would notice one more dirt-obscured window in this section of town? It was easier to guard against stray noises. Tightly sealed against sound with rubber and insulation, the room was stiflingly hot. Pungent with sweat, it breathed the odors of decades wafting over each other blending into a faintly fecal stench rising from every square inch of surface in the waves of heat that never dissipated.

The group of men reclined silently around a central table, marinating in their own perspiration while their bodies tried vainly to rid themselves of their internal temperature through heavy desert robes worn not for comfort but for effect. Each simmered unmoving in the fetid air. Hard men all. Tempered by hard lives, hard choices, they had much in common. Each was devoutly religious. When he killed, he could always find a reason for it. He was a sensitive Arab man who found the deaths of children most distasteful, the deaths of women irrelevant, the deaths of his dull, loyal instruments of suicide exhilarating, his own death an Affront to God. But each was after all a mortal man, a hard man from hard packed sand inside of whom a small boy peered out trembling at the Endless Dark. Fear of death or dismemberment shrieked silently behind cold eyes.

Each man, on his personal journey to sit steaming in this room on this particular night had killed both children and women or had caused them to go to their deaths, sometimes willingly, to strike a blow for what he believed. Feeling himself destined to be of The Movers, not The Moved, he planned his blows through others. The small, the ignorant, the…expendable would do the dying, the exploding, the writhing in red billows. The little people, the Little Faithful, would gaze mournfully at shattered limbs, sometimes their own…and the man would nod and smile and genuflect before his God in their behalf all the while insuring he was seen by others of The Faithful since there was always a need for more…"ammunition" so to speak. To each man here this night in this furnace of a room, fully occupied in mastering or suppressing or simply hoping to conceal his fear, his own life mattered greatly because he and he alone was Larger than Life, More Faithful, More Effective in *jihad*, obviously more important to God than his fellows and thus worthier to go on. The other lives in the room mattered not at all to him except as they could be used to bring him closer to God. He would preserve his own life even at the expense of the rest because being more important than the rest, by surviving he was doing his God a great service and when he finally died God would give him treasures in reward. Each man would have killed every other man in the room just as willingly as each would have done away his own family and of the twenty-four present at the table this night, two already had.

So these hard men from hard lives who would kill without remorse the lowest and meanest of helpless human beings sat waiting without remorse barely containing their nervousness at what was to come. One tapped his fingers on the table over and over. One stared motionless at the door willing it to open. Achmed bin Farouk ground together two cartridges round and round, over and over each other slowly, hidden in clenched fingers wishing he could slide home the cocking lever of the Kalashnikov slung over his shoulder and when the door moved, spray it with welcome. He slid a calloused hand lovingly down his leg to the smooth steel of the barrel. The newer AKM version weighed a couple of kilograms less but it's stamped steel parts weren't nearly as sensuous as the machined forged steel receiver and the thick, substantial solid wood handgrip of his old AK that now fell smoothly to his secret touch. The solid wood of the butt stock was out of reach behind his armpit, but he savored the memory of its firm cushion against his shoulder and its urgent rapping when he converted Infidels to heaps of rags in deepening, spreading pools. Besides, if you crushed one of the newer model's plastic clips it stayed crushed, but his old metal clips could be worked out and eventually reused. He caressed the curves of the 30-round banana clip protruding ahead of the trigger guard. He'd done a lot of business with this old warrior. Carrying it caused some laughter but was not nearly as damning as almost being caught with the *Galil*, the Israeli AK47 knockoff, he took the night he found the Israeli Defense Forces trooper in a dark place failing to mind his own back. If they found him with an IDF weapon, he'd face certain execution for that little bit of business. But he was smart enough to fence it along with the trooper's pocket effects; the money from the trooper's wallet bought him dinner; nice looking wife; cute kids…fucking kikes. Not like killing Americans who these days didn't seem to care how many you killed as long as you kept on accepting their money. Truly puzzling, these whore sons of Satan… truly. They were easy to kill but hard to convince that you were serious about it. He had been watching *Al Jazeera* when it aired a tape of the new American leader going around the Middle East *apologizing* for being American! Who would have thought after the Great Lesson of 9/11, *The Great Holy Day*, that these people *still* wouldn't get it: we don't want them to apologize, *we want them to die!*

The man who would soon enter the room whom they were all waiting to receive held the key to the group's final triumph and therefore to Achmed's own personal triumph. He was powerful, this Visitor, in ways that Achmed would never be powerful. The Visitor had the force of intellect to command obedience, the charisma to make it palatable enough to shield him from the consequences of error, and thus enough power in prayer to be listened to by God. Nevertheless, being forced to ingest facile, unarguable logic and smooth, sympathetic manners merely because he needed The Visitor far more than he needed him made Achmed feel stupid and unworthy and Achmed hated the inference of impotency that lay behind it. He detested needing anyone and detested needing powerful allies almost as much as he hated Americans and Jews. His hand caressed the long, thick wood of the muzzle's heat shield nestled beneath his burnoose and this time, as it always did, its smooth warmth made him think of nipples distending from huge, swollen breasts heaving upward eagerly to his trembling lips, his rock-hard shaft parting slick lips sinking into writhing flesh thrusting upward to take him deeper and at the same time feverishly trying to eject him. But he continued driving down further and further into her heat knowing that she, like every woman, was created by God expressly to yield to a

Chosen Man's devout desires. But this one offered him an additional joy. The coupling was all the sweeter since he was acting as a Messenger of God executing on His behalf righteous *Sharia* law punishment for her shameless enticement of him.

He loved submitting to *Sharia* and submerging his manhood and his will in the calm, logical ocean of its higher intellect. *Sharia* – *"path to the watering hole."* Achmed, a *Sunni,* accepted *Sharia* as his code of life, a body of laws derived directly from The Prophet's way of living offering Muslims a moral code as does the Christian Bible. But unlike the Bible, whose words Christians believe are immutable and cannot be added to nor detracted from, *Sharia* embraces whatever consensus is built within each Muslim community, for would *Allah* permit an entire community to be in error on a basic Islamic principle? And which *hadith,* which "report" or "narrative" of the Prophet Muhammad, were actually true? Fortunately each Muslim *imam,* each spiritual leader, was on hand to interpret. Therefore *Sharia* could be changed to fit circumstances, while Christian and Hebrew morality must always hark back to Biblical teachings that never change. Achmed's *Shafi'i* school of *Sharia* was strict, but he bent willingly to its stern pronouncements. *Haram* offenses required punishments of a bygone day. Pregnancy unmarried was *prima face* proof of *Zina,* adultery bringing severe flogging and sometimes death by stones.

His life thus far was turmoil and struggle, and *Sharia* was his rock towering above the desert sands...yes! That was the image that defined his Faith, a rock amidst the shifting dunes of his life! He was of course subject to these punishments, too, but after all, he was a man, and men ruled. *Sharia* was always able to accommodate a man of pure faith, and sometimes such a man was put to use by The Law as a rod of punishment to Believers who strayed from the path.

Built on the consensus of the Muslim community interpreted by its teachers, *Sharia's* logic was both inexorable and inescapable. It's simple truths rang through his head like a bell, a deep sonorous toll of clear, clean thought that even an uneducated man could take into his heart: he had been aroused by this woman, brought to a fever pitch of desire, his own hands finally stealing beneath his robe stroking and caressing himself and hating himself for succumbing to her devilish ways, finally to feel his pulsing shaft swell up to burst forth spurting and pumping over his stomach.... yet how could this be? He was a faithful follower of the *Sharia* instructions and therefore presumably safe in the folds of its admonitions, secure in his humble acceptance of his role under its many Codes... So how could he have been debased in this way? How to explain it? *Sharia* logic supplied the clear, simple answer. He marveled that he hadn't seen it himself: He was a loyal and accepting disciple of *Sharia* and a Messenger of God. *Therefore*...his acute arousal could not have been his own failing but must have been the product of her enticements. *Therefore,* it must have been because her demonic ways were stronger than his Faith. *Therefore*...she debased herself and attempted to turn One of The Chosen from his Path to God... *Therefore* she must be punished. *Therefore*...*therefore*....*therefore*... His finger twitched lightly on his trigger and with an effort he willed his hands to stillness, but he had long since ceased trying to will away to stillness the vision of Shakala, his twin sister.

The door creaked and slowly opened ushering in a breeze just slightly cooler than the room. The figure framed in the doorway filled it with height to spare forcing him to bend his head, a gesture that in most other circumstances he rarely made. The light behind him shadowed his face and picked out the crag of chin and eyebrows. His burnoose flowed around him, then when inside and safe from other eyes landed on a chair, revealing the piping and accolades, braid and gleaming medals of a military uniform.

Rasoul gazed easily around the room, looking deeply and without the slightest hurry into each man's eyes in turn, seeming to weigh his soul and plumb the depths of his conviction. It was a technique the officer had learned years ago and worked every time to bring civilians to the same inner state of attention as raw recruits on a parade ground. Without betraying the slightest emotion, he sighed inwardly.

[*This rabble is what God gives me to do His work? Well, accompanied by the Hand of God, the righteous craftsman can fashion gold ornaments from the sand of the Great Sand Sea...very well then, so let us begin.*]

In this conference of the armored and yet conference of the naked, where no one need do anyone's bidding but where all knew that eventually a bidding would be asked and must be done, to speak first would name the servant and last the master. All of the men at the table wished to know who was master here and sat silently waiting for it to be confirmed. Rasoul lifted his gaze, walked erect to the foot of the table without seeking his path, and took the vacant cushion at the end of the table reserved for the most humble. It was always good, he reflected, to seem humble before humbling others, that at the proper moment they might see themselves fall all the further. Rasoul made his eyes look lower toward the center of the table and began to wait.

The scream cut the silence like a rocket grenade, rising high and warbling through the room, shrieking, trailing off into coughing, seeming laughter and sobs, then rising into the peaks and valleys and harmonics of the truly insane. The men looked at each other except for Rasoul whose gaze had never moved from the rough surface of the table. One of them slid a machine gun from beneath his robe, laid it gently on the table pointing away from the others, gathered up two of his companions with a nod and strode out of the room. After the passage of some time, one of the men remaining glared down the table at Rasoul, angry at being provoked into first speech. "We must do this business," he growled.

Rasoul said nothing, but smiled warmly around the room. More time passed. "We must do this business *now!*" The Speaker was gruff and becoming agitated.

Rasoul looked directly at him. It was time to show who was master and who servant. Where these men walked, an insult spoken could bring instant death even when the death would be counterproductive to the task at hand. So each man who walked in the way of *jihad* was careful to couch his true meanings in soft phrases each of which contained a subtext that would not fail to be fully understood, yet, since unspoken, unactionable. His voice came well modulated and softly as though accustomed to being sought to be heard, "You have powerful friends who recommend you to my attention. So I have come to you quickly to discover what you seek from me. Ask what you will and in their name I will give it."

[You have no influence with me, only through your friends. I am here on their sufferance and this had better be important. Be brief; I haven't got all night to waste on unimportant buffoons. If you get anything tonight it will come from me, and if I do anything for you it's because of them, not you.]

The group's Speaker was barely able to control his rage at this effrontery. "We are warriors in *jihad* against the Evil Ones who loll behind their oceans in the Great Satan. Since our last attack, eight years have passed. At first they became hard, but now soft like before. Now is the time to *strike!*" The Speaker pounded his fist down on the table. "We seek from you a weapon to deploy in their very homeland. We will provide the logistics, the operational command and control, weapons deployment and delivery." He paused. "And of course we will provide funding at whatever level you desire.

[So you are nothing more than a common merchant, foreign pig, Bring us dates and coffee.]

At this insult several of the men shifted in their seats. Rasoul smiled hugely.

"Not knowing your requirements, I have brought nothing with me, but considering the size of your group and your abilities, I could perhaps find several hundred launchers and enough RPGs to – "

"—Honored Guest," the Speaker sent the words through clenched teeth, "We are planning a major attack upon the United States of America within its borders. We will deliver and detonate a nuclear device somewhere in America. We wish to inflict maximum casualties especially among those harlots and young vermin whom America and her partners in evil consider 'innocents.' I refer to women and children. We wish to kill and maim as many of them as we can and thus demonstrate to the world that the power of Righteousness can reach out to anyone anywhere. We need no missiles nor other complicated delivery systems. We need access to an existing nuclear device that can be transported, maintained, deployed, and detonated by non-expert civilians, We further need training and operational maintenance documentation, and service and assembly special tools and spare parts as might be required."

"My people will smuggle the device into the United States. Our route will depend on the size of the device and whether or not it can be reduced to subassemblies to minimize the chance of detection. We will then use the excellent American shipping companies to transport pieces of the device or the entire object to the selected target. Since the Great Holy Day we have worked to acquire safe houses and other locations in which to service the device and perform final assembly. We intend to deploy it near a large center of population or an installation, and trigger it at the moment when it will gather to *Allah* the greatest number of these Infidel souls to serve Him as His slaves for Eternity. We have agents already embedded in the country, smuggling channels arranged, escape routes mapped, and liaison with other groups planned.

In addition to nuclear devices, we wish to deploy chemical explosives encased with radioactive material. In order to get that material into America, we have made an agreement with a South American drug cartel to use their smuggling agents. They will bring in the material to our people already in America. All we need is the nuclear waste to transport.

Each of us has sworn to accomplish this mission or die in the attempt. Each has fought in jihad for years against the western evil spreading over our lands. Each has killed with his bare hands the hated Jew, and done to death Jewish harlots and many of the lice they call children. In 1943, my own grandfather was *SS Obersturmfuhrer* in the Nazi's *SS Handschar* Division of Muslim recruits. The name is from our word for our curved Ottoman knife, *khanjar*, and I myself am proud to have served during its recreation in 1993 when we slaughtered Serbs and their Jew handlers in Bosnia.

If you wish to be a part of this glorious enterprise, we will welcome your assistance. But if not, you may go in peace with God and we will continue our search."

[*You've seen our faces and you know altogether too much about our plans. Consider carefully your chances of leaving this room alive.*]

Rasoul heard the threat beneath the words, squinted his eyes, and by a supreme effort of will refrained from laughing out loud. Soon now his hosts' external security would discover that he had been accompanied at a discrete distance by a combat team armed heavily enough to reduce the building to a smoking ruin. He was in no personal danger, but he had a job to do and it was time to get on with it. He had indeed come at the request of "friends" as he had said. They were several high-level officials in his home country who sent him to check on rumors of yet another bunch of crazies with a crackbrained scheme that never came off but which had to be looked over nonetheless. Rasoul was astounded to discover there actually was some substance to it and was impressed at the advanced stage of the group's planning and its thoroughness. Maybe he ought to take these reeking goat herders a little more seriously after all.

Rasoul made his face joyous. "Honored hosts, this is truly a welcome and glorious announcement! You will be revered in the halls of all True Believers. Prayers will be said for you in every Mosque in our land and especially amongst our Brethren in the United States. I applaud your diligence and foresight and I speak in the name of my friends as well. Please tell me more of your enterprise so that we may decide how we can best assist you."

[*OK, you're not much to look at but somebody here is obviously on the ball and Thinking Big, so for now you have my full attention. Convince me you have a ghost of a chance of actually pulling this off and you might get what you want.*]

The door opened and one of the group who had left to investigate the scream went to the Speaker's side and exchanged in a low voice. The Speaker motioned his comrade back out the door and turned back to Rasoul.

"Honored guest, a slight complication has arisen that might serve to delay our discussions. We have had entrusted to our care two Americans whom we are holding pending their Trial and Judgment. The sound you heard earlier was one of them being, ah, interrogated. We regret this inconvenience but we will not permit it to deflect us from the true path we have outlined to you tonight."

Rasoul was intrigued and careful. *This could complicate, maybe ruin, everything. What in the WORLD were these gobblers of fecal matter thinking, that they would allow themselves to drag in a side issue like this?]...* Rasoul smiled inwardly realizing that he had begun to identify himself with the project...*[got to be careful of that kind of slip or you'll occupy the same common grave as these jackals...ok, let's sort out this shit and get it behind us]*

"I praise your organization for its capability to operate on two levels simultaneously. Would you care to share with me the details of this... ah...auxiliary operation?"

[You assholes had better make this explanation fast and had better make it good or you won't be getting goatshit nukes from me and I'll pulverize you where you sit!]

The group's Speaker had just been informed by ear radio of the armored personnel carrier whose 106mm recoilless rifle was even now traversing to encompass his humble abode. Putting that together with the hesitation in Rasoul's last words, the Speaker went white. He willed his own voice not to shake. "Our greatest task is, of course, to kill Americans," he went on hurriedly. "However, we are stuck with these prisoners *[God grant he not discover we harvested them ourselves. Thrice DAMN those ignorant goat offal in our own ranks who forced this upon us! Allah curse them for getting us slaughtered before we can raise our fists against His enemies!]* "...and now with regret we must make the best of it. However, we will be overjoyed to relinquish control of these Infidels to you and to your massively more powerful and infinitely more effective techniques to squeeze from them the maximum benefit to Our God, if you would but instruct us..." *[So I'm going to stick them up your ass you big-city scumbag...now they're YOUR problem!]*

Once again Rasoul suppressed a smile...this was almost too easy. In order to keep these dung beetles focused on the Prize – and the prize they sought was truly considerable! – this side effort of theirs had to be eliminated immediately. How better than to let them give the Americans to him so he could get them out of the way?

"My honored host," Rasoul was as obsequious as a man could be who pointed 106 millimeters of shaped charge at his adversary's china closet, "You are most gracious and your generosity exceeds every expectation and even eclipses your former extravagant kindnesses shown to this stranger in your midst! Although it will pose enormous difficulties for me [*I'm pointing a 106mm shaped charge at your china closet; I suggest you get off your dead asses and follow my lead…*], "I will assume the burden of these two Americans if you will but assist me in their care." [*You owe me, son of a harlot, and I will not fail to collect be it even from your worthless skin.*] "Would you and your group care to dispose of this annoyance immediately so that we can turn back to the truly Godly matters you have in hand, and so that we may free your intellect and your attention to the wonderful tribute to* Allah *that you are now shaping?" [*Get this bullshit moving, Goatass; I didn't come here for pleasure but if there's fun to be had from Infidels, especially if they're the Great Satan's children I want in on it.*]

The group's Speaker ducked his head slightly and spoke into a throat mike that Rasoul hadn't noticed. [*I'd better stop selling these people short and start watching my own ass or they'll hang it on the wall!*]. In a moment he turned to Rasoul, "I am having the whores brought before you as we speak."

Rasoul nodded. [*"…brought before you"… nice touch. When we finally restore The Caliphate I can see there'll be no shortage of servile jackals to scurry about doing the bidding of the Chosen.*]

"Do you feel it might be more in keeping with the clandestine nature of our mission for me to view these Infidels without them seeing me?"

"Of course. Your pardon. One moment…."Rasoul waited, not quite tapping a finger on the table. The Speaker muttered into his throat mike.

"Honored Guest, if you would come with me…?"

FOUR

أربعة

Cubbage looked at Baskin and frowned, "Got a hunch we might need some out of town talent on this one." In the days since the news had come in about Sheridan Walker and her daughter Lorraine Baskin had determined that Sheridan's GPS signal had not moved from the industrial warehouse where it had come to rest after its flight down the length of the Mediterranean Sea. She had to assume Alice was there, too, since she hadn't surfaced anywhere else. The station chief in that part of the world assured Cubbage that his people were primed and ready and could retrieve Sheridan and Alice on instant notice with a minimum of collateral damage. Cubbage had passed this information along to DHS and received no response. Now he and his Chief Agent were at the end of their resources.

He took from a desk drawer a small handset, keyed in a string of numbers, listened. ..."And *Shalom* to you as well, and good morning; is Ari available?... ...yes... ...Gordon Cubbage... ...oh, OK, very well. May I ask when I could call back... ...thanks... ...my best to Ari and would you be certain to ask him to pass along my respects to Colonel Rutter? Thanks so much Please be sure to remember me to the colonel; that's Rutter, R-U-T-T-E-R......yes, and to you as well."

Cubbage rang off. "That was Aliza, Ari Dayan's assistant. Didn't you run into them when you were posted to the Beirut bureau?"

Lorraine nodded, "Sure, knew both of them pretty well, used to hang out with them once in a while, but we go back farther than that. Worked with Dayan when he was over with the Regiment setting up our tanks for the desert. IDF had a few tricks up their sleeve that helped us a lot. Never on ops with Aliza but I heard a lot of stories. He's good, but she's a piece of work. Wet work, that is. Recruited her out of one of those Soviet Afghan internment camps before they caught on she was a Jew. Taught her a lot of front-office tradecraft but she liked the back alleys; a real Mack The Knife although I hear she prefers a silenced Glock Seventeen or, when she's traveling light, just a garrote. The covert stuff threw them together a few times. Somewhere along the line a light bulb went off for both of them and they've been together ever since. Got The Fever when they were on some sort of op in the Negev out in the middle of nowhere. Pretty soon they discovered they both had the same strange notions about matrimony. So they dug a rabbi out of one of the nearby patrol brigades and got married on the spot. Hell of a place for a honeymoon. Spent their wedding night in a sand bunker under a rocket attack. Aliza told me later she fell in love with Ari chiefly because he was the only guy she'd ever met who always knew how to show a girl a good time."

"He still gets out of the office once in a while but she doesn't do much field work anymore; too well known. I guess I know Ari and Aliza as well as anybody who's not in Israeli intelligence. Where did she say Ari was when you called?"

"Apparently he went out for lunch. She said he was eating at the Y, replied Cubbage and to his surprise Lorraine dissolved in raucous laughter.

"what the hell -- ", Cubbage began --

"--Are you *sure* she said he was eating," choked Lorraine.

"Yeah, what about it?" Cubbage was getting annoyed.

"At the Y?" by now Lorraine could hardly speak.

Cubbage, even more annoyed, could only nod.

Getting control of herself, Lorraine grinned, "Never mind, you're too young to know, By the way, Chief, can I stay in the loop on this side of it, too? I have some drag in Jerusalem and maybe—".

"—Sure," Cubbage cut in, still annoyed but now curious. "That's why I wanted you in here when I called. I'll keep you up on things as this matures. Now what in the world were you laugh—?" But Lorraine was already halfway out of the room.

"By the way, Cubbage called after her, "tell Charlie thanks and not to leave any marks you couldn't explain away in a press conference."

The door closed gently behind her receding upraised finger.

FIVE

خمسة

Jeremiah Ayers, former Chair, Department of Political Correctness, University of Southern California at Berkeley, currently National Security Advisor to POTUS, smoothed back his bushy hair with both hands and allowed himself to sink further down into the deep folds of his leather desk chair. Slowly he opened his eyes and permitted his gaze to rest lovingly around his small but sumptuous domain just a short stride from the Oval Office, and reflected that life was almost good. Damned good, in fact, since POTUS tapped him out of the blue for this unbelievably important job. Strange that the acronym should convey more sheer power than the full title: POTUS…President …Of…The…United…States. Ayers mouthed the syllables silently, savoring their rich, heavy feel on his tongue. POTUS was what the uniforms called the prez and how the suits on duty marked him for protection. Ayers' contempt for all things martial had been a byword at the University and had gotten him significant preferment among academics whose chief badge of authority was undiluted anti-militarism and contemptuous amusement at American values. Yet in Jeremiah Ayers it masked an underlying question that seldom occurred to his colleagues privately and was of course never broached publicly:

> *Instead of making a career of being <u>against</u> things, what would it be like to stand up and declare oneself <u>for</u> something?*

He had frequently asked himself this question during his first years at UCLA, and then less and less as it became more and more apparent that the road to power in academia depended on preventing that particular question from ever being asked by anyone.

Dr. Robert Beeman

POTUS was the most powerful man in the world by simple virtue of the guns and missiles and stiff, saluting troops he commanded. Their presence, oh so discreet but never far away, imbued him with an aura like none other. This seemed paradoxical to Ayers since the incumbent won the presidency in no small measure because of his stand against all war and his implied dislike of our military forces who were still battling overseas. Now in office, he used that same military to raise his image of power. To Ayers' completely pragmatic mind this made perfect sense. When you need to impress the people for whom you are doing good because you know better than they do what Good is, who otherwise might not quite understand the favor you're doing for them, just shove in more guns and uniforms and they'll catch on. They'll either be cowed into agreement as in the European countries and the old Soviet Union where the masses who used to be subjects give the exact meaning to the word "proletariat," or they'll be convinced you know something they don't, as with the Independents in the United States who for two hundred years have yearned for the Man On Horseback.

This was a new thought to Ayers. He was almost shocked at his unconscious acceptance of a similarity between the scurrying, shoulder-glancing, favor-currying European masses and spine-straight Americans ruled by what Europe with a sneer calls the Cult of Individuality. Ayers realized that POTUS had identified this similarity early on and was exploiting it in exactly the same way proponents of European Statism manipulated their populations to produce Socialism without popular recourse. Ayers laughed out loud. So *that* was where POTUS was taking us -- toward socialism with a small 's' while the big 'S' waited in the wings for the proper moment! Ayers felt at once pleased to have reasoned out by himself what must be a deep state secret among the Democrat Left, and at the same time relieved that he would surface near the top rank of the Givers of Good. Not a good thing to be lower down in the Socialist pecking order, Ayers mused. Those down at the bottom who actually *practiced* "from each according to his skills; to each according to his needs," usually ended up spending their lives waiting in line for cabbages or toilet paper. No, clearly, the key to success under Socialism was to be one of the power elite who *determined* what everybody else "needs" and what everybody else "gives." not the guy who has to live with the determination. And at that very moment Ayers was near enough to the top that he'd be riding the crest of the wave, not tensing in the undertow beneath. If he didn't fuck it up.

Well, if POTUS needed uniforms here and there then he should have them. Hadn't been many uniforms around back at Berkeley before Ayers Answered His Country's Call – he liked to think of his appointment this way – almost like shouldering a rifle but of course he'd never allow himself to be linked to anything so politically incorrect as an actual gun. No, his patriotism – Ayers considered himself a patriot although he would certainly never use that silly word in public – was much better utilized in high-level decision-making than stomping around wearing one of those uniforms and gurgling the *National Anthem*.

Ayers had known POTUS was grateful to him for his hard work lining up California Convention delegates, but he knew it wasn't just that which merited his new sub-Cabinet yet Oval-Office-level reward. In truth, however, he had been vastly surprised to be named to his present post. He had always assumed the National Security Advisor job went to somebody, well, who actually knew something about national security. His only connection with that subject was a monograph he had delivered a few years ago to the Conference on Correctness In Academic Thought, <u>Globalizing America: Applying Political Correctness to National Security to Refocus Foreign Policy Towards America's Responsibility For Global Victimization</u>. In his paper Ayers argued that America's place in the world community of nations demanded that she admit her guilt for provoking other nations to hate her. He called on the US to repudiate narrow concepts of national defense and national self-interest and instead to base our entire foreign policy on discharging America's debt of guilt to the rest of the world. He went on to suggest that from that basic premise, turning over national security to the United Nations and collecting American wealth to pay into developing nations would naturally follow. He cited scholars who called for the first "post-American" US president, the first chief of state who would put his American citizenship second after his global responsibilities. He called for immediate repudiation of the Cult of Individuality, to be replaced with a new attitude of humility and service toward the rest of the world.

Most of the people in the ranks of American Liberal/progressives had no idea in the world what to do about anything diplomatic, they just knew what they hated – American unilateral power, Responsibility, the American military, and Individuality if it was somebody else's. So tackling these ideas head-on set Ayers apart in his world as a forward looking and courageous thinker. The buzz and acclaim ended up settling upon Ayers shoulders the mantle of National Security Expert. His thesis that correct "spin" – Ayers hated the word but sometimes nothing else would do – was just as important in international policymaking as in domestic issues, brought him instant international acclaim, a huge grant for further research from the United Nations Committee on International Relations, a request from the German Government to address the *Bundestag*, and in due course a call from the White House telling him that the new President felt his type of thinking was essential in moving American foreign policy toward a true partnership of nations and would he consider coming to Washington?

It didn't matter to Ayers that he had been more or less swept into office on the President's popularity and if that hadn't happened he'd still be a nobody out in the academic wilderness. He knew that otherwise he'd never have been able to make it past his Chairmanship at Berkeley. He had no skills, even in teaching. Deep down he knew he had never added a jot to the sum of human knowledge, and he also knew that on several occasions, by forcing thinking into lines more acceptable to the Limousine Left, he'd actually subtracted from it. He knew he had nothing to contribute to American culture except spinning the truth to push a Socialist-Globalist agenda. Jeremiah Ayers *wanted* to have convictions, but in the dim recesses of his very sharp mind he was afraid that if it weren't for clawing his way up the do-good-for-others ladder he might find himself without any at all. He had asked himself once whether he'd do the same thing for Conservatives if it meant high office, and he was immensely gratified to hear himself render to himself a resounding "NO!"....it never occurred to him that since Conservative philosophy didn't require spinning facts to force them down suspicious throats, or a sheep-like underclass for whom to Do Good, a society run under Conservative values would find him entirely useless. But this was the New Globalist Order for America and those who could think their way through to new solutions, kind of like parenting to the rest, would prosper. Or so POTUS had remarked privately to his close staff in a talk that was certainly NOT for publication.

So National Security Adviser Dr. Jeremiah Ayers swiveled in his chair and thought how much better it was to be shaping the thinking of millions of needy little people than slam dunking a bunch of ignorant students who figured they could just believe anything they wanted to, or occasionally cutting the legs off a colleague who dared voice his own views. Nevertheless, sometimes he got so caught up in the sheer magnificence of his sacrifice of a brilliant academic career for that of a humdrum civil servant that he forgot that to admit favoring one country over any other was unacceptable chauvinism and actually found himself *liking* being American. It was horribly bad form and he made sure he kept it to himself. Why, a few months ago when that Army recruiter somewhere out in Flyover Country was regrettably gunned down by that poor misguided American who had been brainwashed by those equally misguided middle-eastern religionists, the bonehead Cubbage over at CIA had actually suggested POTUS make a public statement of sorrow about it! Surely Cubbage knew that POTUS was in the middle of a delicate series of apologies being offered to some real heavyweights in the Middle East world to show them we're very sincere in wanting their friendship and wanting to discuss how we could make amends for...well, for being Americans. To support our military and thus be seen to side at this moment with one of our military against people with connections to powerful Muslims could ruin everything. One or two uniforms dead was really sad of course, and his heart certainly went out to their families, but that couldn't be allowed to interfere with this very important initiative. And that idiot Cubbage had been a POTUS appointee! Well, POTUS knew best of course. Until he could consolidate his hold over the American economy he still had to give some lip service to conservatives. Ayers assumed that appointing Cubbage to CIA was part of that. Maybe Cubbage was just too new at this. Maybe he'd come around in time. If not...well...they were developing their ways to seal off protest and stifle discontent, so Cubbage had better watch his ass.

An unsettling thought: maybe the danger of becoming politically incorrect went with the territory. That being so, Ayers had better take a lesson from Cubbage and be doubly careful of his own words. It was really hard to maintain one's politically correct viewpoint that America was the cause of most of the world's troubles when you had all these inconvenient and scarcely deniable facts flowing around Washington and bursting out everywhere for just anybody to hear long before they could be *shaped* into a politically correct form. Damn that stupid *Muslim* asshole anyway, gunning down an Army recruiter in plain sight! And that ignorant *jihad-crazy* officer shooting up those Army guys on that base down south. Bound to get the mudmind Conservatives all up in arms and bring even more fools out of the closet ranting and raving about keeping our solders safe. And for what!?

Couldn't these stupid gunmen see that we're moving to give the Religionists what they want? Just have to go slow with it that's all. Still some muttering, though. Make a mental note to put some spin on those two incidents. Interviews with the shooters' families, maybe; little bit of lip service to the Departed and ignore the wounded. This can be ridden out if you take the proper tone right from the start. Thank God POTUS grabbed the ball and ran with it, able to deflect most of the rage by talking about a *crime* instead of a terrorist act. *Religionists*. Good word POTUS came up with. Much better than *fighters* or *extremists* or that horrible word *terrorist*. Better than *militants* even, because it strips out the idea that anybody might be trying to take things into their own hands against a central authority. Lord knows there's enough of that silly notion of individual responsibility already floating around this country without doing anything to encourage it. Yes, *Religionist* gets rid of all the negative spin and conveys the image of a sort of earnest lapel-tapper.

Yep, this job had its pitfalls right enough. Out at Berkeley he didn't have to worry about keeping his compass pointed properly. All his colleagues hated being American and especially hated the fact that the US was powerful enough to call our own shots without consulting anyone else. Most of all, they hated the American military because it was our soldiers who made this terrible arrogance possible. What was that ignorant rant..."read and write?—thank a teacher...read and write *English?*—thank a soldier!" What crap. When we're done everybody will read and write and who cares what language? And they'll read and write what we tell them to. Simplifies everything.

And the students...well, a student never thinks past the next beer bust or bluebook or getting her rocks off...*his* or her rocks off...and anyway they were there to be molded into proper thinking and the less thinking they did for themselves the easier that would be. Once in a while one or two students would question this, but Ayers had managed to stamp out any really original thinking in his own department while he watched his university developed a very efficient method of correcting general thoughts. Instead of forming faculty committees in each discipline, groups which might develop ideas of their own, UCLA had gathered its mainstream thinking into a Department of Political Correctness wherein thinking on all subjects could be efficiently and effectively defined. But among academics – especially in the hard sciences where facts tended unfortunately to carry their own weight of truth – it was getting tough to find someone who combined the moral integrity to insist on a single standard flowing from the top, and the depth of sensitivity necessary to be able to beat each student into compliance.

But the University didn't get to its current level of prominence by failing to utilize talent when it appeared in its ranks. Being named Chair of the new Political Correctness Department was the capstone of Jeremiah Ayers' career. In so doing, his school had uncovered a natural. He very quickly brought students and faculty alike rigidly into line. Expulsion was a powerful persuader to a student just about ready to graduate and get on with their life. And the University had given him the power to expel any student who – how did the Manual put it? – "…threatened to undermine the constructive consensual value system derived by learned educators to ensure ecumenical harmony and universal self-esteem." Withholding or termination of tenure was equally effective in stifling individual thinking among faculty. His crowning achievement was creation of Consensus, a departmental newsletter that gave the politically correct version of virtually every new event or line of thought that might enter campus purview. The newsletter came to be used as a bellwether of proper attitudes and was greatly influential in campus decision making where the University officials had to thrash out their stand on controversial topics.

Yes, life had gone on from peak to peak in those days. Occasionally a little discord as when that lunatic shot up the student union and killed a few of them. Stopped dead – no pun intended thought Ayers, laughing – by another student's personal pistol before he could really get a body count going. Lots of unavoidable publicity but fortunately Ayers was able to hush up the part about the student taking initiative to protect the rest with his handgun, so the ironclad *mantra* that all guns were evil hadn't been compromised. Close one, though. The rumor of a student with a carry permit saving a bunch of lives even had the *SF Chronicle* sniffing around but the Brady anti gun people got to them in time and had the reporter pulled off the story.

His years at Berkeley had made Ayers an expert at turning inconvenient truths into acceptable realities, showing impressionable students how to climb upward past the limitations of a fixed and continually judgmental single morality derived from one's own moral compass, and tumble forth into the verdant savannahs and warm sunshine of universal acceptance where anyone's idea had merit and all opinions are equal. He recalled with a pleasurable wiggle that enfolded him deeper into the soft leather of his office chair the standing ovation he had received in a past Commencement address using that very phrase. Got him the Chair, it did. The task of discovering a universal morality was daunting, and measuring each situation against your own moral sense was a great deal of trouble. Usually you ended up having to deny yourself something and that wasn't much fun. He smiled to himself, and once again wondered why everybody couldn't see how easy it was to gain power simply by being willing to take from the shoulders of others the heavy burden of thinking for themselves. The key to success, Ayers had realized, was to surround oneself with people who never did much thinking, for they would be grateful when you gradually usurped the little they actually did. Most people yearned for a simpler way to live, and Ayers was there to provide it.

In Ayers' world no one was judged for their beliefs except of course those who needed to be judged, and he, like most of his colleagues and the bulk of his political friends, was willing to spare others that regrettable burden. Crime, for instance, was no longer considered "bad" *per se,* merely inevitable. Perpetrator and Victim were merely two actors in a dramatic situation in which each was a kind of victim but there was no right or wrong to it. The perp was a victim of his upbringing and the victim, well, she…*he* or she Ayers reminded himself, should have been more attentive to circumstances. After the drama of the Chase, the Capture, the Attorneys, the Trial, and the Sentencing, the perp would be tucked safely away to be rehabilitated by the general prison population, and the victim would receive as reward her…*his* or her…Fifteen Minutes Of Fame. In the unfortunate event that the victim became inconveniently dead in the process, well, there were always plenty of relatives to console and sometimes to compensate. The Great Wheel Of Approval would begin to turn through the delicately sympathetic frown of a News Anchor referring to the Poor Victim, past the earnest Feelings Of Pain of a talk show host and on through local B-roll interviews with Sorrowing Neighbors until the entire cast of characters had been equalized with any other cast of any other characters in any other made-for-viewing docudrama. It helped enormously that those people pretty much all looked alike...oops...*[now Jer, he chided himself, you'd better stay far away from that little indiscretion. The President...YOUR President...is one of 'those' people and he would be very unhappy if your prejudices started leaking out all over this lovely desk].*

No, racial slurs would never do. It was critical for the event itself and all its participants to be washed clean of color and individuality so it could take its rightful, inconsequential, place in Life's Rich Pageant as an inevitable though highly regrettable outcome of inevitable though highly regrettable events. Only in this manner could America be persuaded to tolerate the increasing killings and crimes that were always the end product of separating individuality from responsibility. People had to think that each crime was nothing more than a short drama being played out for their entertainment in which everybody was a sort of victim except of course for the Givers of Care who could never be victims. Nothing very bad ever happened. The victims, whose lives up to their Moment Of Fame became dissected and displayed in all their boring complexities by a somber anchorperson, were just folks getting along. Just bundles in the street getting basic union scale for a non-speaking part, local color entirely unconnected to solemn graveside ceremonies. Hey, did you ever see a victim there? Just a big box and a bunch of people with very bad taste in clothes, right?

Perps were sort of victims themselves in a way, being driven to act by a callous, uncaring, society created by the crass, uncaring Rich and ministered to by a woefully underfunded social support web ready to care and share for everyone as long as nobody tried to take their own safety into their own hands. Perps were more sought after than victims because, well, they just had more A-roll appeal. They were a hell of a lot more interesting because they *did* stuff instead of having stuff done to them. Interview a perp and you might get cussing or weird logic or maybe if you're really lucky even the n-word. The more bleep-outs, the pithier your piece and the closer you drift toward a Pulitzer. In and out of prison…knew about guns…maybe even used one!…shot his wife… raped a kid…maybe some kind of weird fetish or kinky psychodrama going on that might peek out if you twist them a little. Real free spirits these perps. Always give you good solid copy.

And perps had their compensations, too. They might do some time but it wasn't very bad in jail – better than most people lived, in fact. Warmth, food, entertainment, the occasional knifing…what's not to like? In Ayers' world there was no such thing as punishment. Instead, for having given the Truth Makers new opportunities to show how they were helping the unknowing multitudes, the perp got a real ego boost, showered with media attention, poking hush mikes and jostling cameramen during the Runup To Arrest, then carefully handled from car to room by attentive guards, listened to by important lawyers and powerful judges who cared for them and worried about their every need. A bunch of jurymen who hung on every sordid little scrap of detail about a life that nobody in the world ever gave a damn about before, or would thereafter. Each perp became the center of media and public attention, the worse the crime the more attention and care. Then afterwards, each perp was carefully placed into a chauffeured car and simply driven away, probably to McDonalds for lunch.

All this care and concern came at a price of course. In a universe where the amount of caring and sharing one exhibited counted more than the content of one's character, Individuality had no place. So individual thinking was discouraged. When, instead of letting the attacker work his will and then hoping to survive long enough to call the cops, someone rashly tried to protect themselves, the entire web buzzed and vibrated and everybody worked to cover it up. No victim was *ever* shown helping himself out of a jam. Nobody was *ever* shown foiling a robbery, saving a child, or dropping a serial shooter in his tracks with a legal handgun. To admit that this might actually work would give people Ideas. People shouldn't get their ideas from each other but only from what the Care Givers handed down to them. When individuals acted to protect and defend it diverted attention from the Care Givers themselves. That was tantamount to admitting that in the course of a tough day on the streets the Care Givers really didn't matter very much.

It was critical to keep assuring everyone that nobody was *really* safe unless Under Care. So in every crime there were shown to be two classes of people: The Sufferers – perp, victim, relatives on the one hand, and on the other, the care givers – The Stars. These were not necessarily the police, or at least the police never really pushed this image. Police went out into the streets, targets in blue, and tried to do a good job. No, it was the parasitic Care-ers About You And Me, the Professional Hand Wringers, the Limousine Liberals, the Social Activists…whatever you wanted to call them, who thumped the drum. Ayers knew this; he'd known it for a long time and it was ok with him. He didn't care about the sarcasm of the labels. This had set him on the road to a comfortable living and now – wonder of Wonders! – it had somehow propelled him into the White House Oval Office! Or at least down the hall from it.

Nothing was more threatening to that value system than the ugly emergence of individual thinking. When students…oops, *constituents*… for a moment Ayers had forgotten where he'd risen to, began thinking for themselves, why, you lost all control and no telling what would happen. People might even think you had made mistakes or were wrong sometimes, and they might not always keep firmly in mind that you were actually acting for their own good. Professor Ayers' job at Berkeley, and indeed the reason he had been recruited out of a comfortable obscurity to sit in this beautifully soft powered chair enclosed in a lovely office at the world's nexus of power, was to stop that kind of thinking cold in its tracks. Sure, he gave up a major academic career to serve his country, not to mention all those toothsome coeds envisioning their resumes trashed with a Did Not Graduate or, even worse…EXPELLED, and coming to him desperate for a pass…. His was a major sacrifice, to be sure, but as long as his President needed him Ayers could offer no less. And it was in order to do that job for The President Of The United States that he sat in this *very* comfortable chair behind this *exceedingly* technological desk in the center of this *impeccably* furnished office *in the White House no less!!!!*…the exclamation points rang through his head and made him almost dizzy with disbelief. And immense gratitude.

SIX

ستة

Rasoul wanted this attack. Wanted it with his soul. Wanted it for all the usual good reasons – to strike a blow, to make a statement, to send a warning, to kill profane, blaspheming Westerners, to harvest the souls of dead Infidels as slaves to serve *Allah*. But above, and behind, and before, and underneath all of those very excellent, highly honorable, and most devout desires lay another dream, one that had existed in Islam among the truly devout for decades. It existed only as a faint murmur, a fleeting unformed wish, always yearned for, always unvoiced, because this dream threatened the *jihadists'* very survival.

The nation-state is the strongest enclave a society can devise to protect its culture from outsiders. Therefore, it is truly ironic that the *jihadist,* whose avowed purpose is to protect his culture, can only find safety outside the nationhood model. Global terrorism has no government with which its enemies can treat, no territory to occupy, no citizenry to cow or to exalt, no allies to suborn, no agenda to negotiate and no promises to keep in order to forestall somebody else's dagger going in between the first and third rib. This is the *jihadist's* main strength. Any *nation* who practiced the terrorists' method of wholesale killing to make its political statement would be cindered by decent people and the ashes scattered to the winds.

Yet the *jihadist* can lurk in the shrubbery out of the searchlight's sweep and take aim at well illuminated targets without much fear of reprisal against anything held dear since nothing is held dear. Acceptance of subnational and extraterritorial status keeps these *Vociferous Islamic Strugglers* safe, or at least it did until The Great Holy Day. After 9/11, the United States' new policy of holding accountable host countries who harbored terrorist groups dramatically reduced the safety of havens like Afghanistan. It tended to discourage terrorist-wannabe nations like Libya who had already felt the stern hand of censure in the form of a visitation by American F-111 fighter-bombers from England and were not anxious to invite them back. As soon as became clear that nations would be added to America's List of Terrorist Organizations as well as groups, Libya renounced her support of international terrorism, disbanded enough training camps in the trackless wastes of her southern desert to give bare substance to the gesture, and enlisted on the Side Of Good.

Below the national level, a number of groups of *Emergent Indigenous Protesters* likewise hastened to mend their ways. The Irish Republican Army knew they could operate with impunity only as long as Britain lacked the money to take the field against them. Upon contemplating the billions of American dollars that would immediately deluge the English *Exchequer* the instant they were added to the American List of Terrorist Organizations, IRA disbanded its military section and nothing was heard of violence henceforth. So America's original policy of forceful response actually worked. Such a pity.

Global *Risk-Prone Communicators* – "terrorists" to folks less worried about offending than surviving the next marketplace bombing, seek virtue right enough, but their quest has nothing to do with religion. These run-of-the-mill Third World have-nots seek the interlocking virtues of Money, Power, and Influence. Their plan is to kill enough innocent people so that decent nations will give them what they want just to stop the slaughter. The Americans most familiar with this approach will be those who tell a woman to give in to a rapist because she shouldn't participate in the violence that would be created trying to fight him off, or those who tell a father not to keep a gun to defend his home because "there's too much violence already." Although these groups of *Activist Weapons Handlers* possess none of the worldly trappings of nationhood, and seek none, there is something they want, something which until recently had been so remote as to be on the moon, something that only a small number of actual nations have managed to achieve. Nobody in the global community of *Tumultuous Non-Ecumenical Instigators* talks about it; few think consciously about it; everyone yearns for it.

And what is this until-recently-unattainable Grail?

Each wants to be a card-carrying Member In Good Standing of The Nuclear Club.

Under certain controlled conditions, when bombarded by a neutron, an atom of uranium or plutonium can be made to release three additional neutrons and enough energy to carve out a harbor from an Alaskan wilderness or win the occasional war. The three neutrons thus freed are now available to strike other atoms nearby, thus freeing more and more and more and more…and all of this occurs near the speed of light. If you are able to keep this *chain reaction* from going wild, you can run a toaster or a medium-sized village. If, however, you let it go its carefree way undamped, it will give you a Cleansing Sun. Every cadre of global terrorism dreams of being able to back up their demands by exercising the nuclear option or the threat of it. Their logic is inescapable: if killing Infidels and exterminating Americans and Jews a boxcarload at a time with Improvised Explosive Devices is Godly, then vaporizing them by the hundreds of thousands with a nuke would be positively Beatific. So these *Emergent Embattled Radicals* do not crave nationhood or recognition or even acceptance, merely the weapon. Their target list is already fully populated. It is impossible to appeal to their better nature because they have no better nature. Convert or *die!* Bow down to *Sharia* or be ground underfoot. In *jihadist* eyes the Unconverted, the Infidel, the Unbeliever, is simply human garbage, his death eagerly sought as a Gift to the Almighty or merely to test the alignment of one's gun sights. There is no regret beyond a fleeting frown at the rising cost of ammunition.

The fools in the decadent, profane West who reach out to these men offering them what they do not want are to be tolerated for a time, perhaps even encouraged occasionally, and, when a nuclear device can be obtained, instantly obliterated. Herein lies the great danger of permitting nuclear weapons to these groups:

> *They have no incentive <u>not</u> to use them.*

Back during the Cold War, why didn't the Soviets give us a little lesson in humility by taking out Cleveland? Because we would have traded them Minsk, Pinks, Leningrad, most of Moscow, and Tsarskoe Selo not to mention a whole bunch of Second Strike bullseyes painted electronically here and there, not a few of which included the Politburo's comfy *dachas*. Both we and the commies realized that even though one of us smeared the other into luminescent glue, retribution would be inevitable and it would be equally horrible. This was because of the inescapable, irreducible Truism Of Nuclear Exchange: "You can kill a lot of cities, <u>but you can't get all the sites</u>! So, no "victors" here, only survivors. And not very many of those.

However, for *Action-Oriented Overcompensating Militants* who have no lands, no population, no *daschas*, the incentive is just the opposite:

> *"Use the damned thing before we're discovered and somebody takes it away!"*

These *Emphatically Overcompensating Rebels* care nothing for reprisals and even less for opprobrium. "*Allahu Akbar*! Push the button! Detonate!"

A great sadness has for years lain over these unfulfilled *Regrettably Dispossessed Extremists*. They lamented that nobody could lay hands on any of these marvelous nukes, and even if they did it would be impossible to deploy them. The only ones who possessed these treasures were actual nations who, after using them to strike a wondrous blow for the One True God, would quickly disappear in a cloud of radioactive vapor courtesy of the Great Satan whose blasphemous policy is to try to keep the incineration of its own citizens to a practical minimum. So extremists within the governments of the nuclear Haves of the Third World realized that a program of nuking Infidels or Americans or Jews, while certainly satisfying and most blessed, would result in the conversion of large areas of the Islamic heartland into radioactive glass. This, they realized, might not be a positive outcome.

So in their desire to smear the West into a thick high-energy paste, the nuclear nations among The Faithful languished, fearful of disappearing forever in their own swirl of accelerated particles. And they kept all those lovely little devices strictly to themselves under lock and key. At the same time the subnational groups around the world who, if they had bombs, were perfectly able to ship them, arm them, and light them off where they'd do the most good, languished because they couldn't lay hands on any.

> *Problem: How do you bring together the two indispensable groups, 1, owners of the weapons – who could not tolerate the result of deploying them, and 2, people sharing the same hatred of Western culture, who could?*

Rasoul was a trusted member of the first group and had now managed to forge an unbreakable tie with one of the second. In promising them the means to raise God's Righteous Fist and bring it smashing down upon the Profane, he was as good as his word. Better, in fact, for out of his nation's arsenal and from other nations in his area with whom he shared a cordial hatred of America, in addition to four hundred pounds of highly radioactive tailings in granular form, he supplied the group with several actual nuclear devices, all sub-Hiroshima grade, each easily disassembled into small innocuous subcomponents untraceable except by bulk-lot numbers back to the European firms who manufactured them. In addition, along with the hardware came simple, easy directions to rebuild them into weapon status.

His technicians showed the group how to arm the weapons and detonate them but cautioned that to try to detonate remotely would almost certainly fail. These weapons must be wielded by devout sacrificial heroes. They would need to be Americans so as not to cause talk in the small towns and out of the way places where these bombs would go. Fortunately, American mosques and You Tube could provide a ready supply of these wondrously committed Servants of *Allah* to act as transporters, assemblers, and ultimately fleshly triggers. The show trials of 9/11 conspirators, dubbed by one commentator "Justice By Ringling Brothers," were a huge impetus to recruitment of American Muslims within the US, especially after all charges against one defendant were ordered dropped from failure to Mirandize, resulting in a chief planner of The Great Holy Day being freed out the courtroom door. Recruitment among American Muslims skyrocketed. Instead of gratefully accepting anyone who showed interest, terrorist groups now had a waiting list and were able to screen applicants for aptitude and slot them into specific tasks. Human Resources Planning had finally come to the *jihad*.

The bombs themselves were much less trouble to custom tailor. Forget the thermonuclear behemoths tipping the Soviet SS55s and USAF *Minuteman* ICBMs of yesteryear. Those 150 megaton city-killers were the dinosauric outgrowth of an arms race between two superpowers with cities to spare and a *first-strike capability* to flaunt. Call it Western technological arrogance, cultural *hubris*, a misunderstanding of the concept of "progress," failure to Connect The Dots weapons-system-wise...call it what you like, the bald fact was that Western culture applied the twin myths of bigger-is-better and what-have-you-done-for-me-lately to nuclear weapons development and concluded that in the years since Fat Man and Little Boy tumbled into the crisp air over Japan to etch an indelible line across human history, "bigger" was "better." Mere kilotonnage became *passé*. The kick-ass hydrogen bomb people prevailed: an atom bomb was only good for setting off the Hydrogen Biggie. And in those easy times, the tiny grain of truth, that a low-yield weapon could become everyman's political statement, simply didn't matter much to Cold War Warriors whose currency was the Tupolev TU-160 and Boeing B-52.

Well, nowadays nobody needed those thermo-nuke monsters. Nobody wanted to kill cities out to thirty or forty miles of vaporized wasteland... well, maybe they *wanted to* but wise terrorist heads knew they didn't *need* to. All that was necessary was to throw a single nuke against the West...or the East if it came to that, for the Eastern Communist nations were no less blasphemous than the Satans of the Western Hemisphere and would surely reap their own special harvest when the time was ripe. But their time was not yet. In their deluded hope of using The Chosen as their instruments by supplying them with the implements of destruction, they contributed the very nuclear tools and technology that would eventually return to them as cleansing suns direct from the Hand of the One True God, vaporizing and immolating the slant-eyed yellow vermin who dared attempt to harness the True Faith.

Allah never employed a single jot more than He needed, and devout followers who understood Him better than their duller brethren realized that He was Directing them towards a basic weapon that could be assembled, armed, deployed, and detonated by the Hosts of The Faithful but without a lot of complicated engineering knowhow. Science was, after all, the corrupt tool of the Infidel West, so the less of it that could be employed by The Faithful in their destruction of the Infidels, the better.

In accepting this realization, the global terror elite achieved a breakthrough in strategic thinking that left the West quantum levels behind. Since the fall of the Soviet Union and its regression into a covey of client states, each of which was now a separate sovereign nation and thus henceforth diplomatically irrelevant, Western strategists had bent every effort to prevent old Soviet missile technology from "falling into the wrong hands," not realizing that the *last* thing *Unfortunately Disruptive Contenders* wanted was to be saddled with the care and feeding of an ancient, high-tech, maintenance-prone, cranky weapons system with a thermo-nuke on the top. Having been Members of the Nuclear Club so long – Charter Members in fact – the West could not envision someone who might not want to be elected President of the Club but wished merely to gain a ticket of admission.

Most of the nuclear weapons in Rasoul's home country were designed to tip his missiles or be air-launched, and were therefore not especially suitable for this particular use. Their circuitry ran in and around all the other missile circuitry. They were heavy in devices that generated telemetric crossput integrating with the highly sophisticated inertial guidance that would permit him to hit a parked car, say, in front of Calcutta's School of Tropical Medicine at the corner of Chittaranjan Avenue and Angarika Dharmapal Street where a student had her hood up with trouble getting the old bus started, or perhaps that delivery van that blew a tire just after turning off Braunhubert onto the one way at Ehamg Street in the center of Vienna and had to sit at the curb waiting for a repair truck. Lacking satellite-response guidance, Rasoul's weapons were necessarily old-fashioned, and current standards of 10-meter accuracy could only be achieved by ground-based radar or GPS repeaters located at the target site, for instance built into a delivery van or maybe inside the trunk of a medical student's old coupe. But even this was too much complication. For purposes of global terrorism, the weapon didn't need to be *delivered,* merely installed. His group would see to that. It didn't need *situation-specific detonation,* or *target-identification feedback* or any of those neat features that kept a nation's own missiles from homing on the Premier's back yard barbecue. No, all they needed was the clapper – the mechanism that drove together two mirror-polished concave blocks of uranium at just the right speed with just the right force and at just the right angle. And of course, the uranium itself.

Of all the nuclear weapons to have come and gone over the decades, the one closest to meeting the requirements of *Troubled Infelicitous Islamic Exploders* was actually the original device cobbled together by Manhattan Project scientists, petted, pampered, nicknamed *The Gadget*, and hoisted up into a hundred-foot tower on 12 July 1945 in hopes of demonstrating that the thing would actually work. The test in our desert that hot July morning was calculated to spare its designers – not to mention President Truman – the embarrassment of delivering to scenic downtown Hiroshima an extremely expensive dud, to the consternation of the City Fathers, the huge delight of Imperial Japanese Army Public Relations, and the joy of the Japanese scientific community who was just getting around to building one of these things anyway and could certainly use an almost-working sample.

At the moment of detonation of this first-ever nuclear weapon, existing state of the art of conventional bomb weaponry centered around several models. The General Purpose AN-M34 and the AN-66 were filled with a hair over 1000 lbs of TNT with an all-up weight of around a ton. The Light Case AN-M56 gave much better filling-to-weight ratio, weighing twice as much as the others but carrying a ton and a half of explosive. There were of course larger bombs – the Demolition T56M121 at 10,000 pounds all the way up to the T12 at 42,000, but these were special purpose devices for busting bunkers and sinking battleships. For strategic destruction of wide-flung targets like marshalling yards and factories, or for exhibiting dudgeon to the local citizenry, The AN-M43 or AN-M64 weighing about 500 pounds all up, half of which was TNT fill, were the weapons of choice. Whereas the 1000 pounders dug big holes, the smaller sizes caused an agreeable amount of wide-area damage and had the added virtue that many could be carried so as to spread the devastation around. They were all dropped free-falling, unguided, and produced craters fifteen to fifty feet across. They were simple to build, safe until dropped, reliable as cocoa, and the heavy bombers of the day could carry multiple units. The four heavy bombers in wide use during the war could carry twelve to sixteen of these [B-17, B-24], the British Lancaster twenty-eight, and the B-29 an impressive forty.

The Gadget, it was hoped, would replace the current crop of small bombs, large aircraft, many over target, limited destruction, and the heavy casualties attendant upon repeated multi-plane air strikes against a given site, the defenders of which knew you were coming back and were already considerably annoyed by your previous visits. About the destructive potential of this new weapon, the designers needn't have worried. Milliseconds after being triggered at the seriously inconvenient hour of 0529 on 16 July 1945, *The Gadget* vaporized the tower upon which it sat, produced a crater of molten glass fused from the desert sand *ten feet deep and a quarter mile in diameter,* and generated a shock wave spreading outward across the New Mexico desert felt a hundred miles distant. Of the actual power The Gadget unleashed that morning estimates vary, somewhere between fifteen and twenty kilotons, fifteen and twenty *thousand tons* of TNT explosive, or somewhere between thirty and forty *thousand* of those good old AN-66 thousand pounders. *The Gadget* was a test bed, not designed to kill anybody. Alongside it was developed the uranium bomb *Little Boy,* 9700 pounds, and Fat Man at 10,200, with a destructive potential that nobody could assure. That meant that for the equivalent weight of about five AN-66s, you got a debris field maybe two or three miles in diameter and a mushroom-shaped cloud that signaled to the world that you were now Somebody.

But returning to the chief concern – finding a bomb that *Indigenous Emerging Cultural Advocates* could employ to make their sociopolitical points to the decadent West – we must note that these first bombs were not at all suitable for *jihad* use. They were full-fledged aerial devices made to drop from 30,000 feet down to a couple of thousand before triggering by their internal barometric proximity fuses. Their thick shell was supposed to keep their components safe and not spread too much radiation around the hangar. They were big and clumsy – clearly not the weapon of choice to roll underneath Beaver Stadium just before the Pitt-Penn State Game. So during the first decades of the Nuclear Age, while *jihadists* dreamed their exquisite dreams of fulfilling Islamic Destiny in a mushroom cloud of Infidel souls, the race was on among profane Western nations for bigger, better, stronger, and higher-yield nuclear weaponry. Finally, when the West crossed the destruction threshold into *thermo*nuclear territory in which nation-killing could be measured in *millions* of tons of TNT instead of puny thousands, the simple, old kiloton-level atomic weapons and their klunky predawn technology were quietly shelved. Well…not quite, but we're getting ahead of things.

During the decade before the H-bomb, it's undeniable that by the limited standards of those days those first old sub-thermo bombs made a satisfyingly big thump. When triggered at 1900 feet over the city of Hiroshima, *Little Boy* vaporized everything within a 2-mile circle and destroyed 90% of the rest of the city. Three days later *Fat Man* detonated 1650 feet over Nagasaki vaporized a mile area, produced temperatures at Ground Zero to almost 10,000 degrees, and generated winds of 625 miles an hour. Now this level of destruction, while no longer front-rank in the Thermonuclear Standoff, would nevertheless do quite nicely for a group of *Regrettably Stress-Challenged, violence-Prone Risk Takers*. It was immediately evident to their planners that for serious work among the Infidels the uranium version was the style of choice. I had a simple triggering mechanism…you could almost make a blast by shooting a pellet at another down a gun barrel. You avoid the complicated implosion sequence required for a plutonium bomb. Much easier to transport without getting things out of alignment, and if you had to, it's actually possible to repair the thing in the field. Yes, some kind of *Little Boy* device was the best choice but without *Little Boy's* heavy protective casing and integrated construction. So *The Gadget* would be the model for assembly using a uranium core instead of the original plutonium.

In *Dangerously Rigid Perpetrators'* parlance, with respect to deploying this kind of weapon, two *delicacies* existed. The first involved the clapper, the 'gun' that slammed two pieces of fission-grade Uranium together to make a critical mass. No rocket science there. You could make it out of any mechanism that would furnish a specific speed and a specific impact force for a onetime event. But…! No tests, no trial runs, no tinkering… everything must work exactly right and work exactly right only once. The *delicacy* lay in making that 'once' be the very first time.

The second *delicacy* involved the uranium. The two pieces of metal had to be of a specific mass shaped very carefully to engage their entire surface area when slammed together. A chip, a crack, a malformed angle, and when clapped together they'd make a big mess alright but not a

Cleansing Sun. The Good News: these shapes were already formed and ready right from the arsenal and could easily be re-shaped to a smaller yield. More Good News: to construct the Ultimate Improvised Explosive Device Of All Time you need Enriched Uranium, Isotope ^{235}U.

There's a good deal of natural Uranium around, but ^{238}U must be processed to get 235. The International Atomic Energy Agency [IAEA] "attempts to monitor and control enriched uranium supplies and processes, in the Agency's words, "…to curb nuclear weapons proliferation." The quietly huge word in that sentence is "attempts…" IAEA goes on to say there are "about 2000 long tons of highly enriched uranium in the world." The quietly huge word in *that* sentence is "about…" The Agency does a pretty good job locating the stuff and monitoring it. But it can't find it all. Moreover, its works under the assumption nobody's making it and not telling. Ooohh…how naughty. Nobody would do that! Would they? Now that Iran and North Korea are processing the stuff – it's a simple operation involving centrifuges much like watching a DNA test tube being whirled on a crime show – the bottom, in one of Abraham Lincoln's less memorable metaphors, is now out of the tub. Fission grade Uranium will henceforth be available to anyone able to prove a legitimate use, such as building a bomb to support Muslim takeover of some country in Western Europe, or just vaporizing a bunch of Jews and Infidels before lunch.

The Bad News: these hunks of Uranium, once shaped, had to withstand transport, concealment, bumping, grinding around, and possibly even impact at the hands of careless baggage handlers or stevedores and still retain their critical shape. So as The Group's job began shaping up, safeguarding during shipment became their major concern. The mechanism could be disassembled into components shipped separately by common carrier. The issue then shifted to reassembly which could be handled in several ways. You could teach someone in each bomb team to do it. On-site assembly offered minimum movement of the final assembly and maximum security since parts would be innocent subcomponents longer, but implied different levels of expertise at each bomb site. Or, send one of their own around to assemble each one. A road show would insure the same expertise at each bomb site, but would require the first assemblies to sit in concealment fully assembled for a longer time and thereby become subject to discovery. No backup would be available in case the assembler got rapped with a speeding sentence or simply mugged. And the assembler expert would leave a trail traveling that might be picked up and followed, thereby seriously compromising the cell-approach in which each bomb unit acted alone. They needn't have worried. Rasoul's technicians had anticipated this problem and before delivering the clappers, had reworked their detonators so they could be broken down into sub-assemblies and reassembled to completely accurate tolerances by almost anyone familiar with basic hand tools.

The material from Iranian weapons-grade stockpiles was machined in the huge underground facility nestled inside the Naybandan Wildlife Refuge just south of Dagh-e'Ali Reza Kahn off Highway 91 a goodly number of trackless miles east of Nayband itself. The installation existed courtesy of UN nuclear inspectors who patiently negotiated with Iranian officials specifically tasked by the Government of Iran to keep the UN people talking until all the building was done. Everything important was far underground. To save excavation time the Iranians had roofed over an old quarry then began their work completely out of sight of Infidel satellites. To mask the project they even went to the extreme of passing trucks in only at night and smoothing the ruts of their passage with special sweepers an hour before dawn. The ancient rail line that had served the quarry was quietly refurbished, then buried here and there under a thin coating of desert sand. From the air or from orbit it appeared as though it was just another abandoned section of track slowly being reclaimed by desert dunes. Nothing showed above ground but a few lazy Arabs sprawling outside their colorful tents, and some small structures associated with the Refuge administration. Deep in the earth far below the old quarry floor Iranian scientists and technicians assembled their processing plant to make weapons grade plutonium for the *mullah's* rockets and a few pounds of fission-grade uranium on the side for a couple of their friends. The melon-sized spheres of pure enriched uranium were truncated into a complex three dimensional concave pyramid of certain dimensions then mirror polished with laser guided electronic scrapers that shaved the surface into conformance with its electron-microscope-determined shape molecule by molecule. Each uranium "pup" was beautiful to see and a quite a noteworthy artistic achievement as long as you kept out of your thoughts that this particular artwork's sole function was to cancel art, or perhaps Cancel Art, possibly forever. When the pups were finished their impact surfaces had been polished and burnished so that each molecule lay flat with every other, ready to accept the second pup's same surface in complete cohabitation.

Now all that was required was a device of some sort to drive the pups together at a certain speed and impact pressure. That was the easy part. The hard part was ensuring that the flat surfaces met each other on every square micro-millimeter of surface at the same instant. Now *that* would be an achievement! To do it, Rasoul's technicians went back in time. Buried in the Manhattan Project's construction files they found a schematic for Dr. Oppenheimer's original proposal: – "If you want to make noise, shoot a gun!" Shoot a Uranium bullet into a Uranium target." This method was rejected by wiser heads who thought it might not work being dropped 25,000 feet. But if all you wanted was a mushroom cloud somewhere noticeable, then it would work just fine.

For *jihadist* purposes the device had to be small and it's subassemblies had to look like anything but what they were. The smallest lump of ^{235}U that will give you critical mass is a sphere about 7 inches in diameter weighing about 100 pounds. America's old 1950s W33 nuclear artillery shell was about three feet long, eight inches around, and weighed just under 250 pounds. Inside each shell a small single gun fired a Uranium projectile into a larger mass of the same substance, making a critical mass when the two came together. This size device would be optimum for terrorist needs. And as far as Making A Statement goes, of the four variants produced of these shells, Model Y2 yielded a whopping 40 kilotons, twice the Hiroshima blast, although it may have been boosted with a deuterium-tritium gas. But forget all those refinements like wrapping the core in a neutron deflector and so on. As in purchasing a new car, don't worry about the accessories; just go with the stripper out in the back of the lot. Models Y1, Y3, and Y4 would each deliver a satisfactory hump at a 0.5 to 10 kiloton range. If all you want is a mushroom cloud, then this might be the only case in the pantheon of human evolution where size really doesn't matter.

So everything was coming together. Rogue nations supplied the material and hardware. *Jihadists* provided the deployment, and American Muslims stood ready to provide the "triggers." What's not to like? All that was left to do was get the parts into the American homeland, put the thing together, and suddenly every Muslim in the world gets the message that *Jihad* has taken the weapons of The Great Satan and turned them against the Devil himself right in his own parlor. Now it was time to select the souls who would be harvested by the Cleansing Suns to pass into *Allah*'s Eternal Service as slaves for the Chosen. Choosing targets was a candy-store operation but must be done wisely to avoid exposure. One team's capture would turn over the scorpion's nest and might jeopardize all the other bombs. Not even Americans as naive as the current government or in such deep denial as its supporters could ignore a nuclear device found within their country. No, targeting must be done carefully and with great patience, and as the *Qur'an* points out, patience is a major virtue.

SEVEN

سبعة

"Jeremiah? Hi, Janine Mastroantonio here."

"Hi, Janine, always glad to hear from you. How are you?"

"Jeremiah, we have a situation over here that I think you and the President ought to know about right away. Gordon Cubbage just told me one of his agents, a Sheridan Walker, and her teenage daughter were kidnapped yesterday. His people tracked them to Damascus where they're being held. He knows the location precisely and wants my permission to go in and get them. I told him to wait."

"Good work, Janine. You did good. We need to think this out. In the past, most of our foreign policy mistakes were made by people who went off half-cocked based on duty and patriotism and honor and all those other silly ideas. We don't have room for that kind of baggage anymore. Nowadays we make a judgment based on the global situation as it is at the moment, what we see in front of us on the ground and not on the stupid emotions that dragged us into all those wars in the past. We don't want anybody committing American power to support those outmoded ideas. POTUS...ah...The President...showed us how to do this during his glorious world tour right after he was elected. He promised to bring in Change, and this is part of it. Our new world is based on a reasoned assessment of each situation as we find it on the ground in front of us, kind of like the clear pragmatic thinking of the old Communist states."

"I wouldn't want to make that comparison in public," Ayers chuckled. "Too many Americans around who aren't sophisticated enough to understand where we're taking this country. So our Dr. Cubbage wants to ride in there like the Lone Ranger and untie the damsel from the railroad tracks, eh? So what are your thoughts?"

Janine was careful, "As DHS Secretary I have a responsibility to keep America safe. But on the other hand, I have a pressing responsibility to make sure our president's initiatives overseas are in no way compromised by anything I do here. A rescue mission to that part of the world right at the present moment might conflict with the president's attempts to win friends over there. Lord knows he's working hard at it!"

"Yes, Janine, I can assure you he will greatly appreciate your attitude when I inform him. His mission is to undo all the arrogant me-ism we've laid on the rest of the world in the past century. America needs to own up to its faults and this president is going to see to it that we air them to the entire world. If we give the slightest indication now that we disagree with anything these countries are doing, his overtures could be seriously compromised. We both appreciate your sensitivity in calling us…ah, calling me."

"Jeremiah, what do you want me to do? Cubbage is on me to approve a rescue. I've been stalling him off but he says the longer we wait the more chance she'll be murdered."

"Well, Janine…this, uh…Walker is a CIA agent, right? Hmmm…you know, these people sign up for that kind of danger and if she got herself into trouble, really, Janine, we shouldn't mix into their operations."

"Gordon says she was on vacation at the time. And Jeremiah, her twelve-year-old daughter was taken along with her – " Janine Mastroantonio's voice broke and for a moment she couldn't continue. "Jeremiah, *what are we going to do about the little girl?*"

"Now calm down, Janine. We're going to do everything in our power to get both of them back home safely. I want you to remember that… *everything in our power.* But sometimes we don't have the ability to do just whatever we'd like. Now here's what I want you to do. First of all, we'll keep this office and the White House out of it. Contact State, give them the full situation, and have them begin feelers to the Syrians but very gently. No need to complicate things by telling them she's CIA.

After all, she was on vacation with her daughter so in fact she's just a citizen. Nobody special, right? So just treat it that way, like we're not too concerned but maybe her daddy has some pull or something and he's raising hell with his Congressman…you know how to handle that. And we'll get things rolling."

"Cubbage insists that speed is important. He says they're liable to kill them if we don't hurry."

"Well, Janine, consider the source…she's Cubbage's employee and if she gets in trouble maybe some of the shit will splatter over onto him. I've always suspected these James Bond Types do a little too much drama anyway. They love the stage and the dark corners. If she was on vacation and not actually spying, why would anybody want to hurt her? I think we'll proceed with all dispatch but keep it below the radar for the moment."

"Very well, Jeremiah, you know about these things."

"Thanks for your confidence, Janine, and thanks for consulting me on this. We're both trying to protect the president's diplomacy here, and it just wouldn't do to have a lot of…situations…roiling up the waters. You've really done a service calling me. That's why the administration thinks so highly of you. So let's do some worst-case planning. What do you think is the worst possible outcome here?"

"Well, I guess the two of them murdered, eh?"

"No, Janine, that's not the worst that can happen; the very worst would be America finding out about the kidnapping. Americans would immediately see Walker and her daughter as underdogs, especially with a little girl involved. Then we'd be on the spike to get them back and the president might be forced to back off his "Softer America" program, especially if one of the countries he's talking to is involved. How could he keep on reassuring Americans that Muslims aren't terrorists when they have an American mother and daughter captive? He's gone to great lengths to switch us away from the old "war on terror" toward the much softer approach where each incident is a kind of "crime" that will fit right into our own judicial framework instead of calling out soldiers. He intends to shift control of terrorist response to politicians and away from the military. We in government are much better able to mold thoughts and ideas than simple soldiers. Now that we're in power, the way to stay here is to make sure Americans think what we want them to think and not be making up a lot of silly conclusions on their own. When soldiers run things they have a tendency to give out facts and events without the proper...orientation. So citizens are liable to believe anything. All too often it puts their government in a bad light. It's a matter of basic loyalties to keep that kind of dissent to a manageable minimum."

"Consider what would happen if Walker and her daughter were killed and it happened while the rest of America was watching! What a terrible blow to the president's credibility! You and I can't let that happen, Janine. If they're killed we have to make sure Americans understand the Bigger Picture, and if they won't, then we have to provide them with a believable scenario they can swallow. We'll work behind the scenes but if this goes public I want you to put some space between her and the Agency. Rogue her out if you have to. Let out that we're investigating a possible defection. If they kill her we'll just let the "investigation" die. The good media will run with a defection story then switch to a lot of wet-eyed commentary on the "man-caused disaster." Good phrase of yours, by the way. Sets just the right tone. The bad guys on conservative cable might bitch but they won't be able to prove a thing.

"I don't like it, Jeremiah. What if she's released?"

"Well, then, Janine, we just keep quiet and welcome her home. Give her a medal or something and make her a hero. Why don't you start planting questions about her loyalty in the next day or two. Nothing overt, be very subtle. You know the media guys who ought to be called. Just 'happen to mention; a few things – strictly off the record of course."

EIGHT

ثمانية

Sheridan and Alice lay bound and gagged on rough folding beds guarded by one of the group, a small man who carried an ancient machine gun and who hovered over Alice and never let his eyes stray far from her. The two women could not see past the glare of a high-wattage trouble lamp the Speaker had positioned next to the door shining inward. Rasoul thought for a moment, then switched off the light. He regarded them silently while Sheridan and Alice blinked away the glare. This was the first of their captors they'd seen without a mask and Sheridan studied his face. Despite her situation as a prisoner she had to admit he didn't run true to type with these other desert rats – well-formed, broad shoulders tapering to a slim waist, bulges barely hinted at muscular arms beneath his battledress. The uniform she couldn't place; Records would have a pic when she got back…if she got back…["*can't think about that now. First got to get Alice the hell out of here. Then we'll see about reaching out and touching these sick fucks whoever they are.*"

"I am Rashid," Rasoul began. "You have been…detained…by units of the Glorious *Jihad* for judgment by The Chosen Ones, stalwart fighters for God." [*stick that up your audio recorder, goat turds*"].

"You have been chosen to represent the sins of your nation before the worldwide *jihad*. Those *Muslims* unconverted to the Holy War will see your condemnation and will choose Life over living amidst their current pestilence." [*that should hold you scum for a few minutes while you look up that last word*].

He came close to Sheridan and knelt down as if to examine her bonds. He whispered, "I am not of these people -- he stopped when Sheridan, fluent in Arabic, shook her head to signify she didn't understand. He continued in English, "I am not with this group; I came here on other business and was handed this mess. They're recording audio in here but didn't have time to set up a video, so just let me talk to the mike. When I pull you out of this room it will be to another one that they haven't had time to wire so we can talk. Indicate you understand." Sheridan made a quick, small nod and Rasoul stood up.

To the Speaker who was standing outside the door: "Have you a place in this abode where I can be alone to think?" The Speaker showed Rasoul out and down the corridor to a small day room, one door, no windows, desk, chair, small sofa bed. The room adjoined the conference room with a door between and Rasoul knew that they would never dare to surveill him.

"This will do very well. Before you visit upon these sinners the Righteous Judgment of the Sons of *Allah*, I would request a moment to question the woman. She may have information I can use in my own line of work. I will use this room. Thank you for providing such excellent facilities."

The Speaker hesitated. He dearly wished to eavesdrop through his clandestine audio and video links but wasn't equipped in this office. Besides, he reflected, I don't need to know this pig's "other" business, just get the damned bomb and forget anything else. "I will have her brought here immediately, Honored Guest. You may have all the time you require and you will not be disturbed in your questioning."

Sheridan rolled over and felt the tape binding her hands behind her cut into her wrists again. She had been carried from the room alone to this place and dumped unceremoniously on the sofa with the comment in Arabic that the issuer was unaware she understood, "Well, Whore, you're going to serve the Masters now!" Her head ached and her shoulders pained her from the fall. She thought that if she could pull a piece of the tape into a cut, she might free herself, but it curled at the edge and resisted every effort to rip. [*Shit! What do I do now? ALICE!!!!..need to concentrate…ALICE!!!...got to get free and out of here…got to…ALICE!!!... DAMN IT stop that! She's where she is. Can't help her except by getting free…focus, damn you, lady, FOCUS!"*].

At that moment she felt a cool sensation on her forehead as the damp cloth was sponged over her head and face. Her eyes, tight shut in concentration on defeating her bonds, opened into quizzical eyes examining hers and a clean shaven face, dark with short cropped hair, inches from her own. His hand with the cloth stroked her face and neck with the only soothing relief she'd felt in days of bound torment. Involuntarily she smiled and in doing so remembered he was an enemy who was part of the gang who had her and her daughter here at their will. [*Alice!!!!...damn you, Sheridan, FOCUS!*] She went in and out of a kind of dream about her daughter being safe, being pillaged, being rescued, being back in the States...with an effort of will Sheridan pulled herself back from her abyss and regarded her captor who in a low tone had begun to speak.

Sheridan assumed she had been kidnapped because she'd been recognized, but she couldn't play that card...not yet, if ever. If they knew she was Agency they'd torture Alice in front of her. No agent, male or female, could withstand that kind of pressure, balancing information you have in your head against harm to your child and being forced to watch. She interrupted him and made her voice tremble with what she hoped sounded like panic. "Sir, I don't care what happens to me, but my daughter's twelve years old! She never did anything to you people. She's innocent, just a child. Do what you want to me, but let her go...please!

Rasoul went on in English in a low voice, "I regret you have been abducted, Madame; I assure you I had no hand in it. I am here on other business with these gentlemen. They exceeded their instructions and their authority in taking you and had I been here I never would have allowed it. I will have you and your daughter freed as soon as we conclude our discussions. I cannot free you at the moment, but later. I will have your daughter taken to another, safer, place." Now I am going to assault you. They will expect it."

Rasoul reached forward and pulled her shirt apart spilling her breasts out over the folds. He stood up and dragged her skirt down away from her hips and, taking a knife from the scabbard at his belt, sliced the tape binding her legs and arms. Knowing she was helpless anyway, Sheridan made no move to hinder but lay quietly waiting for what she knew was to come. Rasoul spread her feet apart and stepped out of his trousers revealing his swollen member stretching his undershorts into a banana shape gently pulsing outward until he drew his garment down and away and brought it nodding and beckoning between them. Crouching, he mounted her as he pushed her knees up and away, lifting her hips and causing his member to drag upwards between her buttocks. He was becoming urgent now with the feel of her cheeks involuntarily gripping his shaft. His member, as if with a life of its own, abandoned the search for her vagina and began probing for her anus. Her legs were high In the air so he reached wide behind him and spread her cheeks the better to find entry. When his tip went in a few millimeters and he felt her anal lips scrape against the side of his shaft. Their harsh rasp only heightened his frenzy. His rough, calloused hands squeezed her buttocks further open to accommodate his fully engorged and swollen member. Sheridan felt him thrust inside her and whimpered with the pain of jamming his large member into her anal cavity. She cried out as he thrust up into her heedless of her pain but only wishing to lubricate himself with her anal juices. As the lubrication took effect, he began sliding in and out, pumping his hips, jamming himself fully into her anal tract and back out again to thrust inward hard and fast until Sheridan gasped and groaned with each movement. This was not pleasurable for her but she endured knowing he was her only hope to survive this insanity, and survive she must for the sake of her daughter. Sheridan pushed down her own horror and disgust into a little box inside her labeled "Not Now…" and thought of Alice in the next room, bound and vulnerable, counting on her mother to do whatever was necessary, endure whatever what required, in order to save her. Finally the continual driving in and out began to take its toll and Sheridan felt herself drying out. Her anal walls were becoming stiff and frictioned.

Feeling a rasp against his shaft, Rasoul withdrew fully, and released Sheridan's cheeks. He moved further over her and with a whiff of feces unmistakable even in the noisome air of the room, brought his member up over her face. "Take me in," he whispered, "They're watching." Sheridan grasped his member and guided it to her mouth, the sharp, acrid taste as she sucked him almost making her swoon with the knowledge of its origin. She sucked and pulled holding his member in one hand drawing it into her mouth, tasting her own discharge, with each pull feeling his testicles gently bouncing against the curve of her wrist. Finally he withdrew from her mouth and slid backwards to a position over her, his member drawing a trace of saliva down between her breasts and over her stomach down between her legs to her vaginal cavity. As he probed with his tip between her lips, to her disgust Sheridan felt herself becoming wet and slippery with his insistent push. He never completed the movement into her, but backed himself out each time to continue to stroke and butt. It was the pulling back that was arousing her. Each time he'd push a few millimeters further in, then pull back out again scraping over her roof near her opening, then in just a bit more. With each withdrawal into the cooler air his shaft remained colder than her vaginal walls and when he re-entered her the temperature difference tingled her forcing her attention away from the sheltered place in her mind she was trying to crawl into and back to what was happening between her thighs. She tried to wall her conscious mind away from what was happening to her body, but thoughts of Alice had brought her to the ragged edge of panic and the soft, insistent strokes kept breaking through her concentration with their buttery smooth message of hope.

Rasoul paused, stroking his tip up and down between her lips and butting her clit and gently rolling over and around it. Sheridan felt heat begin to rise in her and tried to keep her hips from pushing outward to engulf him. She was having trouble staying still and finally when the heat became too unbearable, she gave in and in spite of herself felt herself begin rhythmically pushing her pelvis up against his tip to draw him deeper inside. She could feel his mouth searching her breasts and she felt her nipples rise up as his mouth felt for them and sucked them in one by one, abrading them lightly in and out with his teeth as his tongue slid over them and curled around each one in turn. Then he began rolling her nipple between his teeth moving his jaw side to side in a buzz saw effect. Each time his teeth slid back and forth sideways across her nipples a wave of electricity pierced down to her thighs and jerked them tighter around him. Suddenly he pushed himself up over her so that her knees pressed down beside her breasts as he drove deep straight down into her, forcing himself deeper and deeper, pulling back and then thrusting harder and faster. By this time she had given up holding back and was meeting his thrusts with her own gyrating hips, groaning and slamming herself at him in a frenzy of release, feeling herself begin to orgasm uncontrollably and continually as she rotated her hips to take him deeper. She felt him begin to swell and the swelling travel up his shaft. With one final lunge he buried himself deep inside her and she felt his tip, now bulbous, distended and slick with semen, begin to vibrate and gush his hot fluid into her, washing her like a fire hose. And as she retreated from her plateau of release, away in a tiny corner of her mind which stood by dispassionately observing all that was happening to her, Sheridan with immense disgust realized that the dirty little secret about rape was that…sometimes…it wasn't entirely rape at all…

NINE

تسعة

When Achmed met him at the door Rasoul was wiping his hands on a bit of cotton waste. Past him through the door Achmed could see the American whore, apparently unconscious, lying spread-eagled on the rude bed she'd been tossed on, displaying her open legs in a most inviting and disturbing manner. He had a sudden urge to push past The Visitor and gush his own bottled up semen into this Infidel slut. But while doing the whore would excite little comment, it would be a travesty of respect to abuse the image of the Honored Guest, obviously One of The Chosen, so soon after he had administered his own… instruction…to the Infidel. No, Achmed, thought to himself, he'd just have to…well…he'd just have to pray. But after so many years on his knees and forehead praying for forgiveness, it got to be a little old, especially when every minute of every day his loins never ceased crying to him for release. Correction and instruction of women was the responsibility of every *Sharia* Man whenever he found that regrettable burden necessary to shoulder, and Achmed had certainly done his duty that way. Too bad it had to turn out like it did for his sister Shakala, but of course the aftermath of her *Sharia* instruction and punishment was in God's Hands, praise His Name, and as long as he did his duty by *Sharia Law* he was absolved from the outcome.

Rasoul was relaxed. He turned to Achmed, "Honored Host, I thank you for your hospitality and for this opportunity. I have questioned the whore and received everything she possesses that might assist me in my own missions. If it please you, shall we return to our business at hand?"

Pleased and grateful that this august person would deign to notice him much less address him as speaking for the rest, Achmed drew himself up, "Honored Guest, we can reconvene at your complete convenience in the room adjoining this one. Shall we just go through this adjoining door?"

"You are most kind and efficient, Honored Host. Let us then move forward."

Swelling with pride at the high compliment from this obviously important and devout man, Achmed ushered Rasoul into the conference room, pausing to look back through the open door at Sheridan's still form, breasts swelling full and round up out of her open shirt, thick chestnut hair tumbled over her face hiding her expression. Achmed left the door ajar and took a seat across the table from the open doorway where he could fill his eyes with her. He decided that whatever instruction The Visitor had administered, this Godless American Infidel whore would require a great deal more of the same from him later on. And then there was her daughter. Nothing that little slut had that he couldn't enlarge. Achmed smiled to himself and he felt his shorts tighten. The rest of the group was filing back into the room. The Speaker began.

"Honored Guest, fellow Warriors of *Jihad*, we are here to discuss our planned attack on the Great Satan and to request from our Guest certain services." He turned to Rasoul. " We have outlined our plan to you and we trust it meets with your approval. Faith and courage we have in abundance. What we do not have are the tools to carry out our attack."

He took a deep breath.

"Therefore, with greatest humility and mindful of our solemn partnership with all Faithful everywhere to prosecute *jihad* against Infidels everywhere, and in view of your position in the high reaches of power and policy, we respectfully request that you assist us in our service to Our Lord by providing us with a nuclear device that we can deliver into the homeland of Satan and there detonate it to God's Eternal Glory."

When the Speaker had finished there was dead silence while they waited for Rasoul to respond. In the next room, Sheridan lay perfectly still and tried to shut out all noise but the conversation she could hear coming through the open door. Rasoul leaned back against his cushion at the low table and assumed the patriarch position. Once more he surveyed each of the men at the table, keeping his eyes straight ahead and moving his head to engage each one's gaze in turn, thus giving the unspoken impression of concentrating his whole attention on the man he was looking at and taking him and him alone into Rasoul's innermost confidence. As always with men in the ranks, it had a powerful effect. Returning his gaze to the center of the table, he spoke in a low, barely audible tone that required each man to lean forward to hear.

"Honored Hosts," Rasoul began, "We have been deflected from our duty by the presence of these Infidels among us. Let us return now to our reason for coming together and move forward in *jihad* that we may prove to be true Instruments of His Will."

Nods from around the table. Achmed settled into his cushion with one eye through the open door to Sheridan's still form in the next room. Rasoul went on.

"I have no doubt each of you is of The Faithful. I know you can be trusted to carry out Our Lord's Will against these Americans who are truly Children of Satan. Europeans and friends from South America and Asia and Africa send us money and recruits but only when we show them performance. They hide us and protect our followers but only the successful ones, the ones who show them killings. They look for bodies, for demonstrations, for political terror influencing governments to do our bidding. These people support us but they are not Believers. If we cannot provide these things, the money will cease to flow, the safe havens will be closed, the weapons and channels of communication will disappear. So we must make use of these fellow travelers until the day when we can spread our cloak over them and cause them to disappear."

"For this reason, this small group of yours does double service to Our Lord: your plan strikes a heavy blow at the American Satan and at the same time it will open the fountain of support once again. These people who furnish us money and logistics merely want to see Jews and Americans heaped up dead around the world. They don't really think we can destroy Israel, so they fund us merely for our willingness to kill and so they can participate in the sweet joy of killing Jews. But they are results-oriented. For years they have been asking us, 'Why have you not attacked since the Great Holy Day of 9/11?" All we can reply is that after the attack America suddenly became strong and resolute and until recently has kept us at bay. But now America has chosen a leader who is determined to return his nation to its habits of thought before 9/11. They are ceasing to war against us. They view our attacks as police crimes. This is wonderful news for us! It will make many problems of insertion and logistics connected with our next attack simply disappear. In addition, since we are now "criminals" instead of enemy soldiers, it holds forth the possibility – at least to the American fools – that we might rehabilitate and change our evil ways."

[*laughter*]

Rasoul nodded his encouragement. "Consider, my friends, an additional blessing. We will now be tried in American public courts that offer us a recruitment pulpit without parallel. Already the American President is moving to close the Cuban dungeon of detention and intends to move our captured fighters into the American prison system. Imagine! Our stalwart Faithful let loose amongst their most dangerous criminals! Imagine the thousands in their prisons who await instruction in jihad! What a wonderful opportunity for recruiting new Sons of *Islam* to our war, and what hardened fighters they will be. At a stroke *jihad* will leap their borders and erupt into the American heartland. These American criminals and gang members will never be truly of the Faithful of course. All they want in return for making our attacks are money and narcotics, and naturally we shall supply endless amounts of each. The Americans wish a 'redistribution of wealth?' We will help them!"

[*great laughter*]

"In addition to the money and the garbage drugs, they will receive mountains of weapons and a continual drumbeat of intelligence from our people within the American police forces, places to hide in our Mosques and limitless money to help these Americans evade the law when they strike a blow for us. It will not even be necessary for them to succeed in their planned crimes, for we shall underwrite them a thousand fold more money than they could ever steal."

Rasoul raised his hand palm out to the group. "And now you tell me you are partnering with the drug cartels in that part of the world who will convey nuclear material into the American homeland?" He closed his fist. "This is exciting news and fits exactly into our own plans. The cartels almost own the American prisons, on the inside at any rate. We can use their prisons to keep contacts alive between our fighters and the cartels with zero outside interference. And more good news. The new President has brought with him into power the silly people who used to be ignored by the previous leaders, who think they can negotiate with us." Rasoul suddenly pointed at the table with arm outstretched. "Tell me, my friends, what do you want of Americans?" Rasoul's listeners erupted in shouting slogans and growls of hatred, "Nothing! We want nothing! We want them to DIE!" Rasoul let them rail and finally when they began tapering off into muttered threats, he continued.

"Why is America only hastening her doom? Who knows? We had despaired of ever being able to strike another blow in their homeland. Under her former leaders America had become vigilant, strong, ready for battle. If we showed the slightest movement they were on us like a scorpion on a toad. But today…" Rasoul laughed. "TODAY! Today we see only weakness. Today…our Iranian brothers construct their final answer to the Jews and all America does is to whine. North Korea is preparing to take back its southern provinces and settle accounts with the verminous yellow scum to the east, and America groans to the United Nations. They almost weep with shame for not having presented more of their heads to our righteous swords. Soon even their president's head will roll from his shoulders, but that time is not yet. How Believers must have laughed behind his back when he bowed to us! Now surely we will PREVAIL!" Rasoul raised both his arms fists clenched and the men came out of their seats shouting and gesturing.

"And now, my Children In *Jihad*,"… Rasoul used a phrase of familiarization that brought his listeners forward in attentiveness, "Now we will discuss your plan of attack."

"My government is one of the world's nuclear nations, yet we cannot pursue Our Lord's Instructions in *jihad* as we might wish. If we did, we would suffer a worse fate than Iran, who has no enemies in her region except the Eternal Enemy, Israel, and yet who cannot smear those scum into the sand for fear of unleashing upon herself a nuclear reprisal. My own nation has enemies at its throat who are also nuclear powers. They would not hesitate to bury us if they thought we were involved in *jihad* and these enemies are outside our very gates. I am here with you because my superiors have charged me with developing subnational assets, groups that cannot be connected to us but with whom we can partner in a blow against the profane West. In this way we will survive in order to keep fighters like yourselves supplied on the front lines of our Holy War. From our vantage point the two most important aspects are secrecy and effectiveness. We must never be connected with you publicly, and we must be absolutely sure you are able to carry out your plans. We supported bin Laden until he was driven into hiding, and we quietly rejoiced at the part we played in the Great Holy Day of 9/11. You have asked me to provide you with a nuclear device and this is a request I am well able to honor. My nation has placed at my disposal nuclear devices in all kiloton ranges. Whether I will decide to do so or not will depend on the answers I receive to two questions: The first – how do you intend to deliver it? – you have already addressed with great ingenuity. Let us begin there. Why use the drug cartel mules to bring in piece parts? Why not simply ship in?"

The Speaker cleared his throat. "Honored Guest," since 9/11 the Americans have heightened surveillance of air and sea routes, so these are closed to our purposes. Even with their new leadership relaxing vigilance, their lower level people are still committed to protecting America. However, in their stupidity, they see their southern border as dangerous only from immigrants and drugs. Make yourself out to be a potential voter and you could smuggle in camels. In caravans! The new idiots who replaced the old ones are even stupider about the border. They cut back money for their local police and wring their hands about the "rights" of "undocumented immigrants" and so on. They make it <u>easier</u> for us to sneak in and to stay in. So far most of our operatives have simply walked into the United States across their southern river. A few of them were caught here and there and instead of being questioned they were simply sent back south…to try again until they succeeded! Our people are already in place, but for bringing in fissionable material we intend to use drug mules in the same way the cartel employs them. We will reduce the material to ingestible portions and send it north inside the mules just as heroin is shipped today. After their crossing they'll evacuate the material to cartel receivers and it will be delivered to our safe houses where it will be recombined."

Rasoul, impressed, nodded assent. "Have you considered that the life expectancy of these mules, once having ingested this substance, would be fairly short and not especially pleasant?"

The Speaker smiled, "Their lives are of no consequence to us, Honored Guest. They will never be of The Faithful and are therefore expendable. However, since these deaths and sicknesses might be noticed, we have taken pains to recruit actual handlers from the Mexican wilderness. In cases where we absolutely must handle material within the United States, we have used the casteless Asian riffraff and the homeless, who will work for liquor and never be missed. These people are despised by their own culture and their illnesses are considered chronic and unremarkable. In addition, we will schedule the aggregate loose bomb material that requires bulk handling for the very last, after everything else is completely prepared. Even if they are discovered there will be no time to react against us."

"Apparently the new American leadership has also made laws inviting these illegals to flock in. This is good for us because it helps us to hide, but it poses another problem. We're finding that the chief trouble we have is ducking their pathetic attempts to give us automatic citizenship! When captured, we are not interrogated, but offered a voting card! These new people in power see the stream of illegals as millions upon millions of potential voters, all of whom are guaranteed to their party. We have to be mobile and we have to have support if one of us becomes ill. So all we wanted was a driver's license and enough identification to use their emergency room services. Instead, we are almost begged to accept full citizen status. But we managed to get the licenses and med card anyway. These fools welcome us and press them upon us like ritual coffee. All they seemed to want is for us to register to vote…can you imagine? I don't understand these people. They're Americans but they hate their country. They hate their power. They hate being Americans. They hate their riches. They hate their fellow Americans. They seem to hate everybody except for us who are trying to kill them! And now this hatred has apparently become national policy…look at their Head of State going around the world telling everybody how sorry he is to be an

American. This new political change and the new President might be a Gift to us from God, but sometimes I wonder if it's worth the trouble. So, Honored Guest, we crafted a plan to bring in our device in pieces using cartel mules and border sliders. The drug people will want opium and we will ask it of you. Tons of it. Fortunately, drugs are easy to ship in. The border sliders will want support getting into the US. This we will do through the cartel, who will want additional drugs and money from you for that service. If you have quantities of the poppy we can do anything we wish in that region."

Rasoul smiled. "I guarantee that if we partner, you will have all the opium, uncut, or processed, that your contractors could desire, delivered in absolute safety to the destination of their choice. If a shipment is intercepted we will underwrite its replacement at no cost to them. Now, how will you assemble and deliver the device?"

The Speaker was on firm ground now. "When the parts are delivered by drug mules across the border area we will have them shipped to the locales we have chosen for the strikes. We will strike several places simultaneously and we will use their UPS and FEDEX and their excellent postal department to ship the parts from the border to our attack sites. They will then be assembled into the final devices in our safe houses. We already have recruited a number of Americans to act as triggers. These are devout Believers just like the Army officer who struck a great blow from within their own army post. The Americans would rather ignore these fellow citizens who have chosen the Correct Path than seem to be discriminating against them by making investigations. The officer – foolishly, it had appeared to us -- made his Faith well known among his unit and yet they ignored him. Amazing! But this will encourage the others and aid us, so no matter how bizarre, it is good."

Rasoul was thoughtful. "That would work for the bomb's subassemblies. My technicians can break it down into small piece parts for you. Nothing except the trigger would cause any concern if discovered, and even that would be recognizable only to a trained observer. If anyone is intercepted his cargo can be easily replaced out of our stocks." He was beginning to think this might actually work. He came to a decision.

"Good. I will arrange for the processed uranium to be delivered by ship to Mexico, then north across the border into America by train and private car. My country has resources in that part of the world, too. Long ago we set up delivery conduits just in case…"

Not wanting to go deeper into his country's clandestine intelligence operations, Rasoul changed the subject, "And how have you chosen your targets?"

"Honored Guest, our most cherished targets lie in Washington, D.C., but while their current leaders seem not to care about being struck again, they do indeed care about their own personal safety. So we judge Washington defenses to be unbreachable and even if it were possible, the effort would be too much for our group."

Rasoul nodded. "Yes, Honored Hosts, you are correct. These new American leaders are quite ready to expose their citizens but of course not themselves. Much of this attitude comes from what they call their Liberal Left, who refuse to believe we are at war and who shrink from defending themselves as long as none of them are harmed. But we need not strike at their leaders to make the blow felt throughout the world. In my own nation many true Fighters for *Allah* exist below the political power structure. We are fervent to continue *jihad* directly. It will be sufficient to our purpose merely to detonate somewhere inside the United States. May I request, Honored Hosts, that you consider deferring discussion of specific targets for your weapons until our next meeting?" [*YOUR* weapons…*that should slide your hands down into your pants, dungeaters.*]

At the phrase "your weapon" the group, as though prompted by Rasoul's unspoken thought, buzzed with muttered conversation; several of the members smiled and the Speaker nodded in happiness.

"Honored Guest, we take your meaning into our hearts and we welcome you and your nation to join us in striking a heavy blow against the Great Satan. We are glad to postpone target selection and will welcome your further advice. We will choose targets that not only show our power to snuff out Infidels wherever we wish, but which will, as you point out, yield a sweet, full harvest of souls to serve Our Lord and our illustrious

Soldiers of *Jihad* who have already joined Him. We are all fully aware that neither you nor your nation can be in any way complicit in our deed."

Rasoul sat back and let them talk about targeting. IT was obvious they knew very little about United States demographics or even simple geography. He was silently thankful that so many American Muslims were eager to join *jihad* against their own nation, for without them, no attack would be possible on American soil. Finally he sensed it was time to sum up.

"Honored Hosts," Rasoul was as deferential as was possible for one of the Chosen to be toward beasts of the field. The project would go forward under *his* direction. It was time to bring tonight's charade to a close, "You overwhelm me with your knowledge of America and her weak points. You have all made valuable suggestions and with your permission I will note these targets, particularly your suggestion a minute ago of Forest Lawn Cemetery, and forward them to our planners so that in future we may benefit from your astute knowledge of your craft. I have had some small experience in America – nothing like your reservoir of knowledge, I admit, but I have noticed that the target population you seek, women and children, tend to congregate around the places of entertainment such as sports stadiums and amusement parks. May we then defer actual selection until our next meeting?"

The Speaker, who knew as little about America as any of them, pounced gratefully, "Honored Guest, we are pleased to let our target selection be guided by your astute and worldly knowledge of America which we, I fear, cannot equal."

Rasoul smiled. "And now, Honored Hosts, with your kind permission I will regretfully take my leave of you. My people will be in touch with you soon to arrange for the nuclear devices and radioactive material. Until our next progress meeting, then, may God grant you His Peace and Infidels to serve you."

The group rose and bowed.

Through the open door Sheridan, who had been conscious although careful not to move and had heard every word, muttered to herself, "Holy SHIT!"

The Speaker escorted Rasoul through the door to the courtyard outside the building. Just in time remembered his captives.

"Honored Guest," we have not finished our transfer of those two Americans to your keeping."

Rasoul looked grave for a moment [*Shit! I forgot all about them*]. "Honored Host," now that I will be busy making arrangements for your...ah...deliveries, I will not be able to remove them from your charge."

The Speaker was puzzled. "Then what do you wish us to do with them?"

Rasoul considered the problem. Far too many people knew he'd been here and seen the prisoners, so if he was going to supply nukes to these monkey spawn he needed these worthless whores out of the way for good.

"Get rid of them but see that you do it quietly. Make sure the bodies are never discovered. They're nobody in particular and from the sound of things the Americans no longer much care about their citizens' welfare anyway. They certainly have not made any effort at all to look for these two. In the meantime, I will begin the task of procuring for you nuclear weapons. We will meet at a future date to discuss your plan and how I and my friends may support it. It will be my honor to host you and your exalted fighters in my humble abode in order to discuss your future plans and targeting." [*You're on my turf now, camel dick, and I'll be calling the shots from now on. See that you comply.*]

Rasoul spoke into his phone and stepped into his waiting car as a turreted armored car and two truckloads of soldiers moved out of the shadows from down the block and drove slowly past the courtyard. The Speaker stifled an involuntary shiver of relief and turned back into the room. The group, talking animatedly across the table, fell silent when the Speaker opened the door. He looked from face to face much as Rasoul had done, but this time there was hardness in his eyes.

"Which of you is responsible for the capture of those whores?" he asked in a quiet voice. They all started talking at once until the Speaker raised his hand. "We are brothers here in this room. We have a job of work to do and many plans to make. Each of us is sacred to our combined duty and cannot be spared. I desire two volunteers – you, and you. Discover who is responsible for this stupid kidnapping and make sure nothing like it ever troubles us again. You – he nodded toward Achmed, find a way to dispose of these liabilities. Be quick!"

"In the meantime, we will continue our planning, but this time…the Speaker paused, too filled with emotion to speak…THIS time – he raised his arms to the ceiling – when we attack we will caress the Infidels with the very Hand Of God!"

TEN

عِشْرَة

The huge storm cell sat like a giant pile of warm feces directly over the point where his road met the horizon. He was running fast, pushing his motorcycle hard trying to make his motel before it hit, rolling his throttle wide, pipes, normally loud, now blaring and reverberating out across the desert. His fairing gobbled up the right lane of this two-lane New Mexico secondary as lightning flashed out of the black underside of the cloud ahead. Beneath it he could make out a solid curtain of rain fuzzing distant objects near the ground. His wife had taught him rain didn't matter. "Watch out for the grease coming up in the first half hour, then ride like it isn't there." Hell of a rider; hell of a woman. Hundred thirty thousand miles on her own bikes all over the country when the cancer took her. Why she had chosen him he still hadn't a clue even today, but they had thirty great years together and that was good enough for him. No, the rain didn't bother him; he was well prepared for that. Lightning, now…that was something else.

He was too long out of his mirrors watching the storm cell and thinking about riding directly into the lightning, so the vehicle coming up behind him caught him by surprise. [*Holy shit, it's The Man! damn. I'm running over The Ton. Going right to jail. God Almighty…*] But instead of lights ten feet behind him and a light bar flashing red white and blue in his mirrors he saw the car swerve left at the last second to rocket around him, and then he was entirely occupied working to control the bucking motorcycle as the big sedan thundered past inches from him. Its wake rocked him towards the berm and he fought the bars back toward the center of the lane. He manhandled the big road bike back to vertical from the right hand lean shoved by the passing wind of the car and watched it recede into the distance in front of him. *Jesus!,* was all he could think, and speculated whether it was too late to convert the epithet into a prayer of thanks. Probably not, he mused, so he apologized.

Hector Escobar lifted his foot from the accelerator and the heavy luxury sedan immediately began to slow to take the relatively mild switchbacks on the way into the town. They were mild at any reasonable speed, but you didn't get anywhere at less than a hundred miles an hour. *Fucking gringo biker; should have shoved him into the weeds like the last one.* Hector liked cutting it close to motorcycles but only when there were no witnesses in case the bike got out of control. He remembered a couple of cars a half mile behind. They'd remember him and get the cops on him and fuck with him and...well...he had bigger things to do. *Well*, Hector consoled himself, *If I see him again I'll finish the job*...but then Hector reflected that Uncle Encino had given him strict orders about that. What Uncle *Mejillasdulces* Encino had called needless violence Hector viewed as simply getting his *machismo* out in the open once in a while. Reluctantly and with a feeling of sacrificing for the greater good, Hector dismissed the asshole biker from his thoughts. Fast driving gave him a feeling of power and importance almost the same as emptying himself into a woman. Hector reached beneath his belt and stroked himself in anticipation.

There would be a woman today, he reflected. His people didn't use men to mule drugs much anymore -- too much macho and bulling around, especially the low-class scum they had to employ. Got the cops all stirred up. Sometimes they were too high already to remember not to flush after they shit it out into the john. But a *mujer*, especially with a *mujerita* in tow with pigtails and dragging a Tickle Me Elmo doll...now those were perfect transporters. Bat their eyelashes and wiggle their tits a little and the *gringo* border guards look the other way; wave the doll around and the women guards get all shitty about the little girl...yes, women were best in this role and it was lucky for him they were. He liked women and the pleasure they could give him, old or young. There was always pleasure at one of these pickups. Sometimes they complained...stupid bitches, didn't they understand fucking him was part of the deal? What was it they didn't understand about being bought and paid for? Hector swerved the big car through the last of the S-turns dropping him down into the sleepy wide spot on US 60 that maps called Quemado. There it was on the left, The Largo Motel Rooms And Eats, fifteen rooms, no shade, no pool, Real fucking dump. Uncle *Llenavejiga* Encino should rot in hell for getting him into this bullshit.

But in the back of his mind Hector smirked. The minor favor gained from the transfer of semen from his late father to his *putita* mother which made Hector a relative to the mighty, would insure him a low level job at a certain wage for the rest of his life. But *madrechinga!* The favor he was now undertaking for Encino Escobar, *el presidente* of the *Pasorobles* cartel, not only would be enough to set up Hector for life, but would prove his manhood and his courage once and for all to those other *pendejos* looking for favors from his dear old uncle. Unconsciously Hector slid his hand down beneath his belt again and felt for his manhood... *Damn that mule pig laughing at his size!* Well, after feeling his knife she wouldn't be laughing at any other man and going off like that when he was doing the daughter; Shit, she brought the little cunt with her full of packets. *What does she think, the little fuck isn't going to pay me like everybody else?* With all that screaming he had had to use his knife on both. Couldn't have the little girl around to finger him. Uncle took care of it; the border cops didn't care - just one more greaser carving on his hump. But the little girl would have caused some talk if they'd found her. *Gringos* are real...funny...about kids turning up with knife holes. But since it was close to the border they were able to sneak her south and bury her so no more was heard about it. Uncle Encino was really mad and made Hector promise not to do that anymore and to be honest it wasn't all that satisfying anyway since Uncle *Chingador* Encino took the costs of disposing of the brat out of Hector's share of the drug money.

And what the hell was the old bastard thinking anyway, sending him way up here? The only thing that had made it work at all was being close to Mexico. Up here in *Gringo* Gulch a hundred miles from home he wouldn't have any of that good, solid backup. So he had to be very, very cool on certain things. Luckily this was Hector's last pickup. He had a trunk full of this new stuff with strict orders to deliver it to some kind of processing center in Shithole, Virginia. "New style drugs" and a "new style factory" Uncle Encino had called it. So Hector had to get this pig's shipment, drive out to some toilet in Alabama, trade his beautiful comfortable car for a fucking panel van with the rest of the shit packed in, and slam all the way across to Lynchburg in it. Well, at least he could fly home first class like a real *hombre* drinking wine and shooting up in the bathroom, maybe taking one of those airline *chicas* back into the lav like that flight to Phoenix and doing her standing up. Crazy bitch, came back to bring him a drink and when she bent down to serve him he slid his hand up between her legs and with the other took her free hand and pushed it into his crotch. She was real nervous about somebody seeing but started stroking him out right there in First Class. Back in the WC, could hardly get bent down low enough in the tiny compartment to get him in her mouth and almost bit him off when they hit an air pocket. Took it nice and deep though when he jerked her head up and shoved her foot up onto the toilet. Got some on her, but who the hell cared about that? *Old* Cara de Mierda *Encino had better make this one worthwhile,* Hector thought with annoyance. All this trouble was way over the top for a little dope. He'd better come through with the dollars he promised or there'd be more dead about him than his *pene muerto.*

The sign taped to the motel office window was so old and faded as to be hardly legible: "To our dear customers: please get your room at the cafe next door. We have closed this office temporarily." Hector cursed, "Shit! Now I've got to be seen by these *maricones*. He was grooming himself mentally for a senior management slot in the cartel and felt that he should be careful not to be recognized. After paying cash and getting his key, Hector walked outside and saw the yellow Ducati with bags and duffel pulled up in front of the restaurant. *Screw you, asshole, you got off lucky this time but don't let me catch you on the road tomorrow.* Hector moved his car around in front of a room three doors down from his pigsty room. Not quite the suite in the *Ciudad de Mexico* he was used to. *Well let's get on with it. Where are you, pig? Let's get this ON!* As though summoned, a nondescript car pulled in and parked a few spaces away from Hector's. A woman emerged and walked straight through Hector's half opened door and into the bathroom. *Not much to look at,* he mused...*take her up the culo, that way you don't have to look at her face.* Hector regarded the closed bathroom door. *Shit, no daughter this time.* Soon through the bathroom door he heard grunting and a sighing scream. He'd heard this before. When a mule evacuated the cargo – the condoms in which the heroin or other substance was secured – it always hurt traveling down the anus to be fished out of the toilet. Some of his colleagues like to watch that part but Hector was no pervert. Eventually the toilet flushed and she emerged with a number of packets encased in latex. Hector looked at the packets on the table. Close to a mil on the street, he guessed…well, he *would* have guessed except Uncle Encino had told him he was getting ten million American dollars per packet. Now *that* was real profit. So this must be some really cool shit *verdad?*

Usually his uncle was pretty indulgent about Hector skimming off a couple lines here and there as long as he wasn't selling it on his own but merely using it himself. But this time Encino was almost angry with him telling under no circumstances should he use this new stuff. In fact, the old turd made him promise on the bones of his whore mother not to do *any* of it. The men that came with Uncle Encino warned Hector not to handle it or get near it except with the gloves Encino had given him and while wearing that stupid plastic coat…what the fuck!… and then he was supposed to drive with it in one of the *lugares especiales* under the rear bumper, the "special place" furthest from the driver's seat. He made Hector promise, but what he didn't address was how the hell Hector was going to get out of this shithole town without a little chill to help him steer. The stuff didn't look like much, not silky and smooth and white like what he was used to, drifting up his nose or into his arm and carrying him away on its blossoms…this shit was pebbly and granular, kind of brown and gritty and to snort it you had to mash it up between two spoons like the really old time shit and even then you didn't get much of a rush. Must be real dynamite shit after it's processed to get that kind of wholesale money. At normal profit margins its street value would have to be over… Jeez! Well he'd have to figure out some way to keep a little out for himself. At that kind of money, a few packets put away and he could quit this bullshit forever.

"Fuck it, let's do some," Hector said to the woman in a tone that was not an invitation. The woman shrugged and they put lines out on the table and inhaled them. She threw her head back and pulled her long hair loose, shaking it down into thick walls past her sunken cheeks. Hector felt a tightening in his groin. This was the part of the delivery he liked. He always fucked the mule if she was a woman and he especially liked the ones that brought their daughters. They got double pay for both of them ingesting the heroin packets and evacuating them at their destination, and he got double attention from women who could not afford to say no. He'd always take the daughter first, the younger the better and the best times were when these *putas* would permit their preschoolers to make money right alongside side their mothers by feeding them packets of their own to carry inside.. Some of them screamed and begged but he broke them in anyway. After the daughter, then the mother while each watched just to make sure they went away knowing who's in charge. And if they brought their son he'd make the son suck him after he did the old lady so he could taste his mother on Hector's cock. This one knew what was coming and silently spread her thin legs. After Hector had finished with her she left clutching the wad of bills Hector threw at her on the bed.

Up the street on the left in front of the TEACC grocery, a sunburned woman, long thick hair pinned back and disheveled with the day's work, was rummaging through her cluttered truck. The motorcyclist had made it to his motel before the downpour. He basked in the approach of the storm that now held no malice for him and exhibited, he reflected, a certain robust natural beauty. He had come out of the little store with a candy bar and seeing her pushing and pulling things in her car, asked her whether she was having car trouble. "No," she smiled, "just looking for a buck. I'm a buck short paying for dog food; rescued fourteen dogs a while ago and...." The biker hauled out a fist full of quarters and put them in her hand. 'I'm on my way from Pennsylvania to California. Got an old girl at home. Here; feed your dogs and God bless you."

Next door and across from the motel at J&Y's Auto Service Complete Car Care and 24 Hour Fuel, a middle-aged lady was dressing down the J of the sign in a loud voice: "You've had my goddam car four months and I don't care if you can't get parts you get that sonofabitch fixed and you do it now, and another thing…" All J could do was smile weakly and nod because it was one of those vehicles that he just hadn't wanted to work on, so he shoved it back behind the grease rack and forgot about it. The biker, filling his tank, was glad he'd used a credit card to avoid interrupting the flow of harsh words and high language being carried out to the pumps that indicated each of the participants was having a rattling good time.

In the parking lot of the Largo Motel Café across the street, an elderly English pointer held stately court in the back of his masters' pickup while waiting for them to finish eating. He nodded and wiggled at each small attention from patrons passing by the truck. The biker, who had pulled in beside him, read a special welcome as he scratched up the old ears, but that was just the man missing his own fourteen-year-old special girl who every night had tucked in beside him on her warm furry back and had carried him after his wife passed. This dignified diplomat safe in his pickup bed never let any of the attention go to his wise, grizzled old head. When his masters emerged from the restaurant and smiled at a man obviously in love with another but showing it to their friend, the dog immediately left the biker's stroking hands to greet his own special loves.

But Hector didn't notice any of these things. He was having trouble finding a vein.

ELEVEN

أحد عشر

A quarter of the way around the earth and several worlds away from the posh, sumptuous offices of the Central Intelligence Agency, in a decidedly non-sumptuous and by no stretch of the imagination posh set of rooms in one of the shabby buildings of no particular distinction crouching around the perimeter of a squared *cul de sac* off Ge'ula Street in Tel Aviv's wharf district, the Political Action and Liaison Department of the Israeli Institute for Intelligence and Special Tasks conducted its business. It was known as "The Institute" within Israel and throughout the rest of the world by the Hebrew translation of that word, *Mossad*. The location had been chosen with care, a block and a half inland up a one way street from the Community Policing Center that sprawled across from the *Schlomo Lahat* Promenade bustling with businessmen and sightseers, Israel's answer to Atlantic City's Boardwalk but without the casinos, that shepherds tourists along the picturesque shore of the Mediterranean and into the many shops to be relieved of their vacation play money, then out into the happy throng of pickpockets tacitly permitted to operate along the quay since hardly anyone carried cash these days and the credit cards were all insured. They were pleased to be able to ply their exacting and delicate trade more or less under police scrutiny and caused no trouble.

The Institute's offices were far enough away from the police compound to shield certain visitors from casual observation which in some cases might get them casually dead, yet close enough to call up the sizeable mobile cadre of Israeli Defense Force soldiers stationed in the precinct's basement garage. The true genius of placement of the offices lay in the choice of Ga'ula Street itself, a regulated one-way to the left past the front of the offices on down the blocks to the police station with no intervening side streets or alleys. Anyone wishing to depart rapidly after doing a mischief would be forced either directly past the station house, or to buck the wrong way up Ge'ula Street's heavy vehicle and pedestrian traffic, thereby attracting instant attention. Buildings on either side of the Institute's modest holdings had been bought up quietly over the years by one firm or another who never seemed to have much business traffic but were exceedingly and unobtrusively well guarded.

One of the entirely unremarkable rooms in this entirely unremarkable building bore a small hand lettered wooden placard, itself entirely unre... well, you get the idea -- fixed on the door as if the room behind it had been a janitor's closet temporarily made over into an office:

A. Dayan

Special Services.

A closer look revealed it had never been a closet at all, but the home of the once prosperous firm of Bubic And Chandler whose faded gold-leaf letters were still barely visible on the door. Indeed, this was the feature of which the covert-portal designer from Israeli Intelligence's Engineering Section was most proud. The monumental difficulties in ageing gold leaf lettering to make it appear half a century old he would describe in great detail to colleagues, some of whom were hearing it for the ten or fifteenth time.

The rare visitor would be greeted inside by a small cubby filled with papers and books overflowing the shabby desk, by several ancient floor to ceiling bookcases and by a very polite, extraordinarily pretty, exceedingly curvaceous, and remarkably well armed receptionist. The retinal scan taken secretly at the entrance when the visitor signed the "guest book" would be transmitted upstairs and compared with whomever eventually opened the door. A mismatch triggered any of several unpleasant consequences, Usually, if no weapons were in evidence on the closed-circuit scanner, the caller was merely anesthetized from a ceiling vent and assisted to the basement Room of Welcome for a closer look. If vetted, he was supplied the antidote.

But upon a retinal match and confirmation by Marcela, one of the bookcases slid noiselessly aside to reveal a corridor which the visitor was silently invited to enter. At the end a door of rich inlaid wood opened into the office of Ari Dayan, Colonel, Israeli Defense Forces, seconded Israeli Counterintelligence, Chief, Clandestine Section, *Israel Medal of Valor, Israel Medal of Courage, Israel Medal of Distinguished Service* [three bars], *Medaille militaire, Israeli Defense Force Brigade Commander Citation* [*Tzalash Mefaked Hativa*]. At the sound of the telephone, Ari Dayan raised his head from where it had been buried between Aliza's thighs and looked at her inquiringly. She listened a moment, mouthed "Cubbage" to him over a covered mouthpiece, and continued to listen.

Dayan whispered, 'Wow, Gordon Cubbage! It's been years. Tell him I'm in the middle of something and I'll get right ba... --"

Aliza shook her head and held up her hand for silence, then whispered, "You are no longer in the 'middle of something', my love." She returned to the phone, spoke quietly, listened for a moment, then keyed off.

Ari had moved back up to his chair across from hers and regarded her silently until she finished. Seeing the look on her face, he was instantly serious. "What is happening, my darling," he asked with a frown that was also a smile. "It's not like you to be distracted during an important conference."

Aliza hesitated, also frowning, but hers had no hint of a smile and when she at last spoke her voice was very low. "He said The Name," she replied quietly with no visible emotion. "He needs something from you, Ari, something big. I want you to be careful of this one."

Ari came immediately to his feet and took the phone from Aliza's outstretched hand. "Thanks, my darling. I'll take it from here."

"Do you want me in?" she asked.

"Don't know," Ari was puzzled. "There are no open ops between us at the moment. Don't know what he could want. Besides, these aren't the Old Days. Whatever he's after, I can't see it being a killing matter so...," he smiled. "No dearest, I don't foresee us requiring your...ah...special talents this time." Then he grinned, "But stick around, Gorgeous; I'll find something for you to do."

Then Cubbage was on the other end of the line and Ari, ordinarily taciturn, was jovial in spite of himself, "I can't believe it's James Bond calling! How have you been you rich, feckless bastard? And how are all the other Profane Children of Satan? Tried to shop you to some Syrians a couple of months ago and they were interested in the agent I used to know, but now that you're always on The Hill and sucking up to those left-wing garbageheads I wouldn't get a shekel a pound for you. So what do you want from me, asylum?"

"Same old Ari," Cubbage chuckled, "Still trying to get by on your looks. We do go back a ways, don't we? You know, with your talent and ambition, if you'd worked real hard, by now you could have had your own used car lot."

Cubbage had been a budding field agent when Dayan came to the CIA for help in extracting from Paraguay *Herr Professor Doctor SS Obersturmfuhrer* Hans Joachim Rutter, German Army, retired, former Nazi Commandant of the Treblinka concentration camp and dabbler in National Socialist medical experiments which even in today's modern, permissive, outspoken society, do not bear mention . Rutter was the last of the Wiesenthal Nazis painstakingly tracked down by Simon and his group in their unquenchable thirst for justice. He was not only the last Nazi at liberty, but was considered by most to have been an amalgam of Mengele, Bormann, and Eichmann with hardly any of their social graces but all of their cumulative murderous intent. Wiesenthal finally ran him to earth in Paraguay, but laying hands on him was another matter entirely. Rutter's genius in choosing a hiding place lay in its openness and size. Everybody in Paraguay almost literally knew everybody else, and if they didn't, then Uncle Carlos or Aunt Esmeralda or Cousin Jorge did. So strangers stood out like an American flag at a Liberal rally. Moreover, the entire Paraguayan Jewish community consisted of less than six hundred souls nationwide, so Jews arriving or departing were easy to surveill. Most of the country was anti-Semitic to one degree or the other, so Rutter was hiding in a glass house with no doors where Israeli agents would stand out like nuggets in a sewer pipe.

Having found Rutter, in due course the Prime Minister of Israel consulted with the American ambassador. Madame Ambassador consulted with the President of the United States. The President consulted with his CIA director. And since the President at the time happened to be Jimmy Carter, whose enduring devotion to the rights of man stopped curiously short of helping Jews, the CIA Director was instructed to just let it slide. So the Buck Stopped There at the President's desk, and everything just sort of...faded away. But the CIA Director with whom the President had consulted possessed a grievous flaw of character, a grave stumbling block to advancement serious enough to make contemporaries wonder how he could have risen so high in government service. He was an honest, honorable man and he didn't like Nazis at all. So he talked it over with his senior managers and told them to see what they could do and try not to get him fired over the page phone.

The Israeli Prime Minister, seeing nothing was happening, turned to other avenues. The Israeli Defense Force had come to rely on a Captain Dayan whenever they needed work done that would be difficult to admit to later on, so Ari was handed the job of extracting the good Doctor Rutter from Paraguay to bring him safely to trial in Israel. It was critical, they told him, that Rutter be kept safe while in Israeli hands to avoid the accusation of assassinating him. Moreover, since the American President had shelved the matter, any help Ari could get in the Western Hemisphere would have to be completely outside channels. Any American intelligence people discovered to be helping him would be ruined.

Dayan returned to Jerusalem, took a long look at the situation in Paraguay, and picked up the phone.... The CIA being what it was in those days, senior management sought a low-level staffer to head the operation on the theory that if he managed to pull it off without getting himself killed that would be fine, but if something went public, they could hang him out in the breeze as a rogue agent and that would be equally fine. The name they came up with was Gordon Cubbage.

Not wishing to complicate his operational planning with a lot of needless details, and what with one thing and another, Cubbage's superiors never did get around to making him privy to the part of their strategic plan that had him twisting slowly in the wind, so Cubbage went forward overwhelmed with the honor and responsibility given to a junior agent like himself and swore a great private oath to carry it off no matter what. And as a matter of fact he actually did. Junior Foreign Service Officer Second Class Gordon Cubbage planned the operation, recruited a team, and arranged logistics, insertion, extraction, arms, ammunition, road maps, band-aids and toilet paper. CIA people heloed in one night, snatched Rutter as he ambled back from a campground coffee shop, and delivered him to a waiting Israeli intelligence unit for transport to Jerusalem. To Cubbage's surprise and the immense astonishment of his superiors the operation went off without a hitch, with the result that Cubbage received a fitness report that glowed with its own inner light and found himself bumped up to Assistant Station Chief in one of the worlds hot spots, Beirut. Rutter, confronted with mountains of evidence as well as a gallery of former inmates each of whom in his turn testified at length, was duly convicted and hanged.

During the decades that followed, the rise of Cubbage and Dayan in their respective organizations almost paralleled each other. But where Cubbage eventually moved into Army Air liaison and on to administration, Ari Dayan had stayed in Israeli Intelligence in the field,. He eventually rose to command the Mossad's equivalent of the British SOE Special Operations Executive, a picked body of exceedingly dangerous men and women who took any assignment too dirty or difficult for anyone else, including killing anybody their superiors told them to. When diplomacy failed and armed intervention was not an option, Ari's group was Israel's court of last resort. Dayan and Cubbage came together once or twice but never worked with each other again. Nevertheless, they shared an understanding between professionals of a debt unpaid and an unspoken agreement that the mention of Rutter's name would call in the marker. Since passing classified data such as the GPS intercept of Sheridan's location, even to a friendly power, was a capital offense, and since he knew both his people and Dayan's were probably listening, Cubbage chose his words carefully.

"I have a situation I'd like to get some...advice...on. Could we chat together for a few minutes sometime?"

"Of course, my friend," said Ari immediately, "Your place or mine?"

"Well, it's difficult to get away these days… damned Bridge Club counts on me, you know, and what with having the office redecorated and all --"

"--Never mind," Ari broke in, "Suppose I drop in sometime and we can share recipes."

"Great. Thanks. I'll be watching out the front window for you."

Cubbage had hardly hung up when Lorraine walked in. "So, Boss, I just dropped by to see if you needed anything. Cup of coffee? Massage…?"

Doing something about troubles always put Cubbage in a better humor. He narrowed his eyes at his agent, "You seem to have a wonderful facility for showing up just at the proper moment. Someday I'm going find that phone tap, Junior, and when I do you'll pay for that night at dinner."

"Promises, promises…The techno-asshole hasn't been squatted out yet who could find that…oops."

Cubbage laughed. "At least you have the delicacy to blush. Get your lovely motivations down to Internal Surveillance and tell Gandy how you did it so he couldn't find it. He's been looking for it for months so don't expect him to be cheery. If you make it back up here alive, I want you to stay on top of this abduction thing with Walker. Everything about this stinks to hell and I hate it when that happens. Anyway, I'm on to meet Dayan at the time and place of his choosing but locally and covertly. "

"So what now, Chief"

"Now we wait for Janine and whatever she decided for us to do. Anyway, we just wait."

"Well, Chief, you know that every minute we delay makes it that much more certain that Walker and her daughter won't be coming home."

Cubbage ran his hand from his forehead down over his face, pushed his cheeks into his fists, and, straightening up, sighed, "Thank you, Chief Special Agent Baskin, for sharing that with me. To tell you the truth it had completely slipped my mind. I see now what you get the Big Bucks for."

TWELVE

رشع انثا

The *Ritz Carlton Damascus* baked in the desert sun, its alabaster walls reflecting as much of the punishing desert heat as modern caloric engineering could exclude. Inside its overheated stucco exterior, cool, quiet rooms accommodated cool, quiet men with singular purposes. They were not always in concert with the wishes of the management but always with the benign concurrence of the Syrian government under whose benevolent and ever watchful eye all business was conducted. Every utterance was duly recorded by *Aluminium-Muchabarat* and reported, suitably analyzed, to the President of Syria. Syria had not been implicated directly in a terrorist act since 1986 and, in view of the new American attitude toward governments who dabbled in *jihad,* preferred to keep it that way. With some of the highest proven petroleum reserves in the world, she felt safe enough from anybody rolling tanks over the border bent on major souvenir hunting. Whomever would be rash enough to try that would instantly find ranged up against them every other oil consumer on the planet wanting to insure their own flow. But the Syrian government also knew that were they implicated in anything really dastardly, the Americans would come, and by the time they departed, all those lovely Rolls-Royces and *very* chic, *very* expensive water fountains would be just a memory. So the Syrians became the first Middle Eastern nation to adopt toward *jihadist* plotters an attitude of "pat– them– on– the– head– but– don't– lose– your– *keffiyeh*." The government turned a blind eye to the goings on at the *Ritz,* and gave tacit assistance right up to the point of actually doing something. The *jihadists* thought this was just fine because they needed a place to get in out of the sun and do their operational laydown, and besides, there would be plenty of time to settle accounts with backsliding Believers later on.

In one of those cool, quiet rooms held to a reasonable seventy-three degrees Fahrenheit by a seriously large and scrupulously silenced enclave of HVAC units on the roof, curtained, wainscoted, carpeted in toe-engulfing velour, a bevy of sweet servers made ready their delicacies, hair loosely tied back but always threatening to fall free and beckoning over their cheeks. Their uniforms were chaste but with a hint of wanton sexuality in the way the bodice rounded below the sharp inward curve of large, full breasts and flowed over wide, hospitable hips, subtly promising men of the desert untold earthly delights yet never so blatant as to cause even the tiniest frown from the most devout *imam*. The Management knew that men of the desert, being deprived of female companionship except for the occasional *Sharia*-ordained corrective activity, would arrive through their doors with imaginations aflame. Blatant sexuality could be kept to a minimum because almost anything would be enough to trigger pre-heated desires. Titillating the passions of men who must repress them in order to remain alive was always good for business.

Rasoul waited patiently for his guests to arrive. He had chosen the accommodations with care. Not ostentatious enough to overawe his guests, but sumptuous well beyond their custom. They would be suitably impressed without awe, respectful without anger, and ready to take his subtle direction without resentment. The project conceived by these storehouse scuttlers who had lately and quite unwittingly become his subordinates excited Rasoul and he was determined to make sure it succeeded. To do this he needed to imprint over the existing plan an internationalist's understanding of the geopolitics involved. *Allah* awaited a new blow at the Infidels and had appointed these tree frogs to administer it. But they were weak and divided, required a stiffening of real leadership, and Rasoul knew that to *Allah*'s great glory he was the man chosen by Him to do it.

The group filed in one by one trying hard not to gape at surroundings that they had only dreamed existed. Rasoul noted with a suppressed smile that the little man had brought his machine gun, artfully but none too successfully concealed beneath *jellaba* straight out of *Lawrence of Arabia*, bejeweled *akal* included. Rasoul sighed inwardly. Men like these were useful in doing God's work...essential actually. But would they ever realize that all the desert paraphernalia and wise oracular sayings in the world weren't worth a couple of sabot rounds from a

210mm tank cannon? Well, he guessed not, so he'd just have to play the game with these Sheikh-of-Araby wannabes and chalk up the wasted time to the cost of doing business. Rasoul came from an educated family – pediatrician father, scientist mother. He had absorbed enough pragmatism to understand that the *jihad* had nothing to do with God or *Islam*, but was entirely about money, power, and influence. Yet his Faith in *Allah* was rock solid; he believed in the teachings of *Islam* down deep into his soul and thanked *Allah* for putting the power to interpret his otherwise gentle Faith into the hands of *imam*s whose *fatwah* permitted him – urged him! – to kill in God's Name.

This was where *Islam* would triumph over Christianity, Rasoul believed. Christians had only their *Bible* to guide them through these modern days. The Christian preacher who strayed too far from its teachings could be branded heretic and in some extreme cases the Antichrist. *The Bible* was truly bedrock of their Faith, its ancient allegories and outdated metaphors warmed over and over in an attempt to apply them to modern history, but the bottom line was "love your neighbor," and this was the Christian's Achilles heel. Christians would tolerate enormous indignities before striking back, and would bend almost to the ground to accommodate other faiths. This was where The Righteous would strike at their Christian foes, for truly all Christians were enemies of the True Faith. Into this crack in their armor the Righteous would pour their acid, eating away Western civilization slowly, day by day, until *Sharia* prevailed over their blasphemous system of civil law. And now into this crack Believers would insert a little device invented by the Christians themselves that would tear a wide hole in their culture and even their religion. Nuking *anything* in the West would establish forever the ascendancy of *Islam* over their puny, powerless Christ. Simple, righteous fighters of *Islam* would appropriate a device that required the profane sons of Satan billions to develop, and turn it against them. Ah, what satisfaction! Every Believer in the world would begin to think seriously that *jihad* might indeed work! Every *Muslim* in the world would heed the call to *jihad*. He who was unable to fight would contribute – his money, his sons, his own life if needed. All this would flow from even the smallest nuclear event as long as it took place somewhere within the Great Satan's homeland.

Rasoul longed for the Caliphate's return while at the same time knowing in his mind that unless *Islam* could produce a miracle, it would never be. With all their accommodating, Western culture would never tolerate *Islam* past a certain level of sanctimonious acceptance. The best his people could do was to insinuate themselves into Western fabric and try to make what changes they could before Western countries finally became fed up.

But a nuclear attack against Satan Himself would be a true miracle!

Among *Intransigent Overcompensating Militants,* Rasoul was one of the elite, an educated, devout man who nevertheless eschewed the gentle teachings of *Islam* to grasp eagerly as a political weapon the mindless violence which *jihadists* tortured the *Qur'an's* decent, kindly phrases to permit them to unleash. And when, inevitably, Western backlash against the drumbeat of killing finally erupted against his people, Rasoul intended to be in position to direct and channel that anger back toward the west's own destruction. The current American government gave him enormous hope. The leaders of the United States went about the world assuring his fellow Muslims America was standing down from its defenses and indeed, Rasoul's own intelligence networks had confirmed a relaxing of vigilance to go along with the hatred of war and dislike of the military that were features of the new regime. Rasoul marveled that the new American president permitted members of his own party to attack his intelligence services while he himself showed open contempt for his soldiers by hesitating to support them.

It was wondrous how *Allah* brought forth strength upon strength from the most humble source. The plan hatched by these basket monkeys now entering the room, after polishing and adding the discipline of rank, offered a priceless opportunity at exactly the right time. The current American government was playing to Americans' fear of being disliked, their love of self, their hatred of war and their dislike of the military -- their own military included! Instead of raising a hand and declaiming "this far and no farther shall you go!", these new leaders bowed and scraped and apologized to their enemies around the world, and sneered at their own defenders at home.

No More Time For Sorrow

If this would go on long enough, Rasoul mused, by the time our next blow is delivered against them, Americans will have become accustomed to blaming themselves for being attacked and we will go completely free! Rasoul knew this was a farfetched idea, yet he observed that even now these new American leaders were actually releasing Blessed *jihad* fighters from their prisons back into the fray! He almost forgot where he was and chuckled. After he unleashed God's Cleansing Suns, Americans would redouble their efforts at "understanding" his people and "negotiating" with them. Rasoul and his fighters would redouble *their* attacks until the entire fabric of Western culture simply rotted away and fell to the ground. The other Western nations were irrelevant. But challenge these soft sheep who today ruled America, and you've won the battle! Look at Europe sucking and bowing for a generation as we fill up their countries with our Faithful and slowly but inevitably take over their administrations.

Reviving the *bhurka* had been, he reflected, a true inspiration. It never had anything to do with religion or Islam or being devout. Yet Westerners are falling all over themselves to provide for it! Look at the French pigs groveling to accept the *bhurka* and one American state is even going to permit a woman to have her identification picture taken in it! They think they're being kind to our women, but wherever we forced governments to permit it to be worn it symbolizes our power. And it cloaks our people against identification. The *bhurka* is also a symbol of our ability to turn the enemy's own strength against him. If we can force the Infidel to aid concealing us in his very midst, we have forced him to hold the dagger at his own throat *with his own hand!*

Rasoul shook his head a few millimeters. Of course, the people behind this new American leadership from down inside their own states and territories were far too naive to realize any of this. You could put all these thoughts into a book and, very simply and plainly; tell everybody exactly what was coming. And still these – what do they call themselves,...Progressives? – would be in such denial and such wishful thinking that they'd just dismiss it out of hand. He once again marveled in amazement at how people could go through an attack like the Great Holy day in New York and Washington, and *still* try to wish away the idea that they were at war. Oh well, he smiled to himself, even though we may never have the opportunity to convey our thanks to them before we make of them dust, these Liberals or Progressives or whatever they call themselves are our staunchest helpmeets.

And Rasoul's devout brethren needed all the help they could get. It was worrisome and difficult to spread *Islam* against the vibrant, world-wide culture of Western democracy. While grievously profane, it was also undeniably much more attractive than the austere, male-dominated *Sharia* covenants of the Middle East. Yet in addition to an ancient outmoded Bible from which the Christian Infidels could not depart, Rasoul's Gracious God had given his people a second invaluable weapon contained within the structure of *Islam* itself. While Christianity had to conform to its ancient traditions, an *imam* of the true Faith could issue a fatwa 'interpreting' *Islamic* scripture, sometimes completely reversing a commonly held *Islam*ic belief. If glib enough, logical enough, and *applicable enough to current events*, it could move his people in entirely new directions. From this shifting base *Muslim*s worldwide had made a career of being discriminated against. Their touchiness gained them some ground, but finally the Western cultures that controlled the world began to have enough of this and stopped worrying about insulting them. At this point the *imam*s took over and set Muslims on the road to *jihad*. *Allah*'s Chosen Ones owned everything anyway and besides, it was certainly better than grubbing out a living working for The Profane. When *Allah* sent His Prophet to his children to light their paths to Heaven, guiding them toward slaving in some desert sweathole was surely not what He had in mind. After all, wasn't the Prophet himself a successful businessman? It was far better to swoop about on horseback in long, flowing robes brandishing flintlocks – or their modern equivalent, the pickup truck, ski mask, and Uzi. Condemning the Profane and enforcing *Sharia* against the Devout, even if it meant cutting off the occasional hand or raping a woman once in a while to teach a lesson, was a lot more gratifying than running for City Council.

All this was good, clean fun of course, but it was a lifestyle that demanded numerous slaveys in the background to curry the horse, press the robes or change the oil in the 4x4, and pick up the body parts when required. So if all *Muslim*s were destined for greatness, it was essential to find someone else, not quite so great, whom they could persuade to peel the pomegranates and take out the garbage. Enter the Infidel, supplied by a Loving God to slave for his Righteous Followers. Didn't Merciful

Allah promise them slaves and virgins aplenty in *Heaven*? Well... shouldn't the go-getters among his children try to get a head start?

God takes care of slave management Up There, but down here slaves are deuced difficult to control, chiefly because in disappearing two centuries ago, slave economies failed to leave behind a lot of comprehensive operational literature. So wouldn't it be a good idea to start learning the technique now? Ruin enough slaves through mismanagement and sooner or later you start driving the price up. Of course nobody wants that, but all you can do is breed them and not even the wiliest *imam* making the closest reading of the *Qur'an* and applying the most torturous logic could justify slave breeding pens. So with a sigh you use Infidels as best you can and try to keep some of them around to work for you even in the face of having to tolerate pockets of Christianity here and there around the Caliphate. The Good News is that the Great Satan holds millions of robust candidates who don't believe you want to enslave them and who tend to regard international diplomacy as a walk through the rest of the world sprinkling Pixie Dust.

So as Rasoul's group of *Deeply Religious Homicidals* filed in and found seats in the overstuffed chairs placed around the room seemingly at random but each subtly aligned toward the small sofa upon which Rasoul took his ease, he reflected that of all the men in this room he was the only one who saw the *jihad* for what it really was: a way out of the desert. The question these freedom fighters never asked recruits but which always underlay their pitch, was simply, "would you rather be riding around in a pickup truck wearing a ski mask shooting your ak47 in the air, or squatting on sand dune waiting for your next meal to happen?"

Finally they were all seated with tea and fruit.

[*"Well, looks like everybody's here that's coming. Let's get this show on the road"*]

"Honored guests, I am overjoyed to at last be able to repay even a small portion of the kindness and hospitality you showed me at your own home. Please accept all that this humble and unworthy pigsty of a hotel can offer you in the way of comforts free with my enduring compliments. My brothers in *jihad*, I believe I can help you more than you have imagined. You will receive the nuclear devices you seek. And, I offer you my extensive knowledge of American culture and politics to assist in guiding you toward success. Would you desire me to continue?"

The men murmured among themselves for a moment. The Speaker finally nodded to the rest and addressed Rasoul, "Benefactor, we would be honored to include you in our planning. We have stout hearts for the fight but we freely acknowledge our limitations in knowing the broad strokes of strategy. Our chief lack is knowing what targets to attack and where. Please guide us."

"Very well, my brothers, let us begin. As you know, we have no interest in trying conclusions with the American military. They are too strong for us and will always win a standup fight. So we are left with three general types of targets. The first is what I call an *International Symbolic* target. On our Great Holy Day which the Infidels call 9/11 we struck two of these: the Twin Towers and their Pentagon building. Regrettably, since the Holy Day most of these targets inside the US have been hardened to untouchability. Even in the stand-down mode of the present government they remain too well guarded, chiefly because the members of that government frequent these places and do not wish harm to come to themselves. So I suggest we eliminate this kind of target from our planning. However, even if we do, we are still presented with two other target types that will be most fruitful."

[*some muttering and head nodding at hearing this*]

"*National Symbolic* targets are those that matter greatly to Americans but might not make a world-wide statement. These would include national monuments and treasured locales, places that Americans love which, if destroyed, would sink a dagger deep into their souls. For example, Hoover Dam, the Gettysburg military battlefield, Mile High Stadium, Cape Canaveral, or, any university would produce outrage and sense of futility and loss."

[*murmuring and smiles from the chairs surrounding the sofa*]

"And the third type is self explanatory: *Body Count,* a target whose destruction would produce tens of thousands of victims, chiefly women and children."

[agitated muttering throughout the group, some muffled laughter].

"Any theme park, any large sports event, any political rally would produce the desired effect. But political events are rigidly surveilled because government officials of the current American administration are inordinately afraid of what they call 'right-wing extremists,' who seem to be anyone who does not share their political agenda. Oddly enough they seem to fear *them* more than *us*, a choice I prefer but would not particularly endorse!"

[loud laughter among the group]

"American leaders fear harm to themselves, so each travels in an impenetrable cloud of security that descends upon each place they go. We are much more likely to be discovered by accident if we are near these places. So political events are not viable targets. I would not brand the president or his followers so cowardly as to suggest that they consciously offer us targets among their citizens in place of themselves, but the facts are hard to overlook. They have let their border defenses fall into disarray. They have attacked their own intelligence service that might otherwise easily thwart our current plans. They sneer at their own soldiers for fighting under their own orders. And at the same time they have heightened their personal security. So what are we to make of this? Simply that we must not attack where they are, but somewhere else in the heartland toward which their own fears for their safety have directed our hand. And if that serves to keep them safe until the Time of Reckoning, then so be it. Satan's leaders will feel our righteous wrath soon enough."

"This new government in America offers us a great opportunity. They have declared themselves weak and ready for another blow. By their unspoken approval of our brothers in Iran making nuclear weapons, they call to us to chastise them. The wondrous miracle of this new American attitude affects our planning in two important ways:

"First, we must make certain that none of these American officials would likely be present at our target. Their actions and attitudes in their own press have signaled to us that as long as they remain personally safe, we can do what we wish with the rest. They have begun to call our blows against them 'crimes' instead of the acts of war that they truly are. Since they view crime in their society as inevitable, we interpret this change to mean that the 'crimes' we commit distant from their centers of power will be tolerated. And since they also view crime in their society as rehabilitative, we conclude that they don't see our activities as anything more than an inevitable annoyance."

"Second, we must strike quickly while the current President still holds office. Even now the mass of the American citizenry is slowly beginning to realize into what extreme danger they are being led by this President's foolish diplomacy of apology and his reluctance to commit his forces against us. Their next change of government is certain to bring to power a much more suspiciously watchful and tough leader who will understand that we do not negotiate with Infidels, we kill them!"

[shouting from the group].

"A wonderful window of opportunity this new government offers us. Their ridiculous attempts at sweet reasonableness and scraping favor are great help to us everywhere we go in the world. So we don't want to see the American president or any of his regime harmed in the slightest bit!"

[much laughter]

"You may well laugh, my friends, but even as I speak, the new American president is beginning to undo all the progress the Whore of the West has made against us since our Great Holy Day. Behold! He speaks of inviting our friends in the Taliban to return to the Afghani government! He thinks this will endear him to Muslims everywhere…and he is right! We love him for it!"

[much laughter]

"So we are getting ready to leave our stinking cave-holes and villages in the mountains, and return to the comfortable quarters and global interconnections in our old camps. In return for this wonderful gift I ask us to offer a prayer of thanks:

> *"May Allah Bless and keep the United States President safe from all harm. As we, His servants, guard and protect him by deflecting our righteous blows elsewhere, so do we call upon the Living God to watch over him. He does God's Work!"*

Rasoul raised his arms to Heaven and the room became a bedlam of shouting.

One of the men spoke up. "But Benefactor, are we not to be able to strike a blow to equal the Great Holy Day. You say they are weaker, yet it seems they are denying us every prime target. Is this weakness?"

Rasoul was patient, particularly because the question was directed to him and not through the group's Speaker.

"My brother, their weakness lies not in their hardening some of their targets against us, but in their change in attitude towards us. For years after our attack America was vigilant. Their government reached out against us in Afghanistan where we were based, and drove us into the mountains where we cannot travel easily nor train our fighters. They harried us and worried us and kept us off balance, forcing small actions that do not gain the attention of financial backers and potential recruits. They made a flanking movement into Iraq. The pretext was flimsy, of course, but any pretext would have done. Although we have no borders to defend, we were forced to draw fighters from all parts of the world to oppose the new Iraqi democratic government. If it takes hold, our influence in that region will be finished. Their former leaders saw this and cunningly applied it. This is a chief reason we sit today in caves eating stale bread instead of jetting through the world tending to our business. That is one answer to your question."

"But the most far-reaching and important answer to your excellent question is something else entirely. We are reaching to pluck a much greater fruit than simply to make it easier for our fighters to regroup. The United States is the third largest country in population, fourth largest in land area. Every square kilometer of the United States is occupied by about 3.2 Americans. Of course, we want our strike to count by killing as many Infidels as we can with each bomb. But no matter where we strike, no matter how many we kill, no matter what destruction we achieve, *if we succeed in setting off a nuclear bomb in America we are suddenly as powerful as the Great Satan! Every Muslim in the world will see jihad as equal in power to America!* They will see that Islam can take the Devil's own tools and turn them against Satan himself! This will be a demonstration of God's Power that no one in the world could possibly misunderstand. And what would that mean to all Children of the True Faith everywhere in the world? *The Americans have lost stomach for the fight! We have beaten them!"*

[more shouting and fist waving].

"Of course you see what this also means!" Each member of the group nodded sagely, confirming Rasoul's opinion that they hadn't a clue.

"It means," he continued, "that with the money and recruits that will pour in to us after such a blow, we and our Al-Qaeda fighters will even sooner become ready for our next blow against the Infidel American pigs! Once we begin striking our continuous hammer blows, once we become a *nuclear power,* Muslims everywhere will join us!"

When the room calmed again, one of the men asked, "Are these Americans so arrogant that they invite us to attack them again?"

"No," replied Rasoul, "not arrogant, merely childish. Their leaders blind themselves to all reality in pursuit of their own agenda. They think they can talk away our righteous anger. This current crop of scum leading their country call themselves "Socialists" or "Liberals" or some such. Well, we can exterminate Infidels no matter what they style themselves. I'll happily kill 'democrats' or 'progressives' with equally pleasant feelings. No, my friend, these Americans are so stupid that they feel they can argue and talk and debate and slather us with their evil money and then we will abandon *jihad*. But all they do is make it easier for us to gather them to Heaven. I *spit* on their apologies and their insults!" Rasoul spat on the floor and the room erupted in shouts.

When they calmed down Rasoul went on, "They outflanked us by going into Iraq to cut our jugular, thereby almost negating our advantage of lack of infrastructure by forcing us to fight them openly. We must admit that they may still succeed, although I have high hopes that the new president's permission for Iran to develop nuclear bombs will end Iraq's flirtation with democracy, possibly in a large mushroom cloud. Soon after Iran offers to the Iraqi blasphemers the Cleansing Suns, we will return there and set them once again upon the True Path. After the Great Holy Day, Americans fashioned an impenetrable shield around their homeland and maintained it by declaring themselves to be at war with us. This attitude pervaded every activity and worked effectively to keep us away. But these new leaders are trying to restyle us to their citizens as poor, misguided people who can be won over by earnest talk [*laughter*]. Why, they have even stopped calling their actions a war, and now use some mealy phrase that says nothing. They have already hurt us grievously but they shrink from attacking us more fiercely for fear it would provoke us to reject their olive branch. We laugh at them of course, but we do not openly discourage their initiatives because the very attitudes that produce those initiatives make them weak and vulnerable and all the more ready to receive our righteous wrath."

A man was puzzled. "But Benefactor, I do not understand. Why would they consciously weaken themselves when we have sworn to exterminate them and have already dealt them heavy blows?"

"My brother, their country is run today by men and women who think they can simply wish away uncomfortable facts. These are rich fools who have been rich so long that they cannot conceive of anyone not obeying their will. Look at their top officials, never hungry, never hard pressed, never destitute, always softly cared for among their rich fool friends. And so I request humbly that you join me in a second Prayer of Thanks to the One True God for having brought about this change in America:

> *"Allah Be Praised to the height and breadth of His Heaven and throughout His earthly domain that he would send us adversaries so stupid and self-centered that they would open with their own hands the door to our renewed attack!"*

"Truly, I see the Hand of the One True God in their last change of government. He has removed the strong ones who almost conquered us and replaced them with these soft weaklings frightened of power and easily cowed. They think if they wish hard enough and speak softly we will suddenly throw down our arms, embrace them, and shower them with love. We will shower them right enough, but with the light of *Allah*'s Cleansing Sun." As he said these last words Rasoul raised his clenched fists as high as he could and the room erupted in shouting.

When calm was once again restored and the shouting had tapered off into muttering grunts, Rasoul continued.

"My brothers, now that we have eliminated attacks against world-symbolic targets and American politicians and their events, may I suggest we choose from among the national-symbolic and body count targets we have identified. if you would like to make the list I will be glad to support it."

The Speaker was positive and firm, "No benefactor, we wish you to select our targets and it is we who will support you."

Rasoul was grave. "My brothers, you offer me a heavy burden…" Then he smiled, "But on your behalf I will shoulder it. I can provide you with enough nuclear material and devices to attack multiple targets in the United States. I suggest we pick two national symbols and one place where we can kill and maim the maximum number of these Unbelievers. Let us consider first the national symbols. By destroying a seat of their damnable Christian learning, we will send the message that *Islam* will triumph over Christians no matter where they lurk in our Realm, that Christians' ideas of brotherhood and turning the other cheek will do them down to their deaths in the face of righteous *Islam*ic wrath, and that *Allah*, the One True God, holds sway over their puny Jehovah. I will leave with you a list of their universities that teach Christian principles. Any of them will do. In addition, we should attack a place that most Americans hold in high political and historical reverence, but which is not home to any of the senior government officials who guard their own persons with such loving care. This would rule out attacks in Washington or any American military base."

"As we move toward execution of our own Great Holy Day, we must be mindful to learn from history even if it was made by the Evil Ones of the Western democracies. I, too, would wish to strike down the American leaders. They are the most deceitful, the most profane, of all. But I have learned something from the history of Europe that leads me to be especially careful not to harm any of the current American leaders for fear of their replacement. I would recall to your minds the comment of their General Eisenhower during the 1945 War, when he vetoed a foolproof plan to assassinate the Nazi leader, Adolph Hitler, saying that it was best to leave him in place. At that stage in the war Hitler insisted on running his own armies and was making terrible blunders. Eisenhower felt no one could do a worse job and if the Allies killed him the Nazis might get somebody good. We will treat the current American leaders with the same care. They are trying to make America over into a European-style state with themselves in the saddle of power. Our attacks will be explained away somehow, probably through pious hopes at the UN, just as the Iranians' forthcoming nuclear attack on Europe will be explained away by European governments in some mealy fashion. I suggest we target an American national military monument or gathering place. I will send you a list that I feel would generate enormous anger and grief among Americans, yet which I know to be unguarded. We will show our disdain for American traditions and history and demonstrate that *Islam*ic furor spares no decadent symbol of Western shame anywhere in the world."

The group murmured and nodded among itself.

Rasoul noted the agreement with a nod. "And for our harvest of slaves to serve our God, we should present Him with a gift of suitable size to thank Him for His Love and Mercy in choosing us to do this task. I suggest that we target a place of amusement where Infidels go to whore and laugh and spend their time mocking true *Islam*ic law by their sinful recreations and entertainments, a place where we will harvest in one millisecond thousands upon thousands of American harlots and vermin, women and children who, if we do not end their sinfulness now, will continue to plague us and will grow up to fight against the true God. I will include in my list several places of sin and shame. Any of the choices on my list will do nicely, one from each category. Choose those that are most convenient to the preparations and locations you have already made."

As in any conference it was important to vary the input with time to assimilate new information. Rasoul adjourned them to the next room in which had been laid tables of juice, fruit, chocolates and other delicacies. Rasoul lingered in the conference room. He wanted them to be able to talk among themselves and to help each other understand the true immensity of their chosen project. As he reclined on his sofa the Speaker appeared in the archway and Rasoul beckoned him in. The Speaker was hesitant and seemed embarrassed.

"Benefactor, I do not wish to appear ignorant, but some of the things you said puzzled me. I did not wish to interrupt the sweet flow of your stimulating words. Perhaps I could ask now?"

"Of course, my brother. Please ask anything you wish. I know some of these things are beyond your experience and I am here to help you understand."

"Benefactor, nuclear weapons require many skilled technicians and soldiers. Faithful and resolute though we be, we are of the desert and not trained in these arts."

Rasoul placed a hand on the Speaker's shoulder. "Do not worry, my brother. The complexity of nuclear weapons is a myth. The small ones -- the old atomic weapons which are today only used to trigger hydrogen bombs, can be constructed with little trouble." Rasoul guided the Speaker over to an alcove of the room in which a thoughtful management had provided computer and copying services for the convenience of their business guests. He patted a Xerox DocuColor 260 standing along the wall.

"Would you like to own the original Operations Manual for *The Gadget,* the device exploded in New Mexico in July, 1945, by the Americans to prove their technology? Or the Deployment and Servicing Instructions for *Little Boy,* the twelve kiloton uranium weapon dropped on Hiroshima, or the DSI for *Fat Man,* the plutonium implosion bomb about the same size but twice as powerful dropped on Nagasaki? I can uplink to my staff and have these documents sent to this very machine. You will have them within the hour."

"Long ago my people anticipated a need for our *jihadists* to take into their hands God's Cleansing Suns, so we brought forth from the old archives of the West the technology used by their Manhattan Project a half century ago to build the first bombs. Foolish Westerners guarded their hydrogen bomb designs -- bombs that no one but superpowers could ever hope to build -- but failed to learn the lesson of the technological event cycle that the bombs were powering. The cycle was fueled by bigger-is-better. The first deployable nuke was about 11 kilotons. The plutonium implosion yielded about twice as much destruction for about the same size but still only an area weapon. Then the good Dr. Teller suggested using an atom bomb as a trigger to fuse hydrogen, and suddenly one bomb equaled one city."

"But the little ones left behind were cherished and sought by our righteous warriors. They are simple to make, easy to transport if you don't have to lift them to thirty thousand feet or throw them over a continent. We have tried our best to wage our holy war against the Great Satan. We have gathered up nuclear weapons technology made freely available to us by their historical services and public archives. Our great stumbling block was always how to obtain fission material to fill the bombs. Now we are being supplied by our comrades in *jihad* in Iran and by the dwarf monkeys in Korea. We went into the shadows and took America's declassified material on the old atomic bombs. All we need -- all we *ever* needed, was the enriched Uranium. And now that the Americans are permitting Iran to develop their weaponry, we will have an inexhaustible supply. I can name you at least three other nations who hate the United States and would eagerly supply the material except they fear retaliation. Iran is governed by Holy Men of our own Faith who fear no one. But they have no delivery system that will penetrate to the United States, and if they did, they would never be able to do enough damage to prevent instant retribution."

"There are three parts to a nuclear device suitable to our use. First, the fissionable material. The bomb The Great Satan used on Hiroshima, Japan, contained only 64 kilos of uranium and by using neutron deflectors we can reduce that weight to about 26 kilos, or 57 pounds, well within our ability to smuggle into the United States and conceal anywhere we wish. Second, the trigger, a simple mechanical device that we can either make here, disassemble for smuggling, and reassemble, or make on the spot if we absolutely had to. We've taken technology from the old nuclear-tipped artillery shells. When they were disassembled in 1992, we collected the disassembly procedures and reverse-engineered them. We have complete diagrams of both and could construct a nuclear 155mm artillery shell if we desired. We can also construct a bomb triggering mechanism about the same size, but vastly lighter since it doesn't have to be slammed out a rifled barrel and through the air. The third requirement is delivery. We need no missiles. You will be our missiles. You will process and transport the bomb material, making sure the uranium retains its configuration throughout transport and reassembly. This is the only real problem we face today. In prior years we hadn't a hope of getting near the United States undetected. "

"Today, however, with the relaxation of the southern border…well, as you have discovered in your own preparations, we now have avenues aplenty. Now that they are standing down from fighting our blessed brothers in Afghanistan, we will regain our old deployment and logistics bases in the desert. This time, of course, our locations will be as well hidden from satellite spying as are the current Iranian enrichment facilities in their own desert."

The Speaker laughed with Rasoul, then went on, "You used the phrase 'Cleansing Sun', and in the excitement of the moment I think it quite went over everyone's head."

Rasoul smiled and nodded approval. "My brother, you do not appear ignorant in my eyes. And you are right to ask any question that occurs to you. It is a nuclear weapon wielded by the servants of the One True God to further His Eternal Glory. The 'Cleansing Suns of *Allah*' are the sweet, mushroom shaped flowers that will blossom forth throughout His Kingdom here on earth wherever Infidels resist conversion to the true Faith. Wherever they contest the dominance of *Islam* as the world's one True Religion, there they will encounter the Cleansing Suns, quite literally the Hand of God that will enfold them in His loving merciful embrace and crush their disbelieving souls to dust."

THIRTEEN

رشع ةثالث

"Well, my friend, how can I help you?" As he waited on the stoop for Cubbage to unlock Helen's kitchen door, Ari Dayan shivered in his light overcoat. The cold snap had paralyzed York, Pennsylvania, with an icy rain, most of which seemed to be going down Ari's collar They were meeting at a safe house as far from Washington as Cubbage could manage. The home on Edgewood Road belonged to an old friend of Lorraine's. It was small and cozy and held the additional advantage of being highly defensible along all five threat axes.

"Have a drink, first. You'll need it," Cubbage offered as he and Ari went over the house room by room. As he checked for bugs, Ari admired the collection of pre-Columbian art stuffed into every corner, one or two pieces of which were truly magnificent. Helen had no connection to espionage so neither of them really expected to find anything covert, but they both operated on the theory that it was better to be safe than comatose.

"Hmmm…dangerous business, eh? Maybe I should have brought my wife along."

"Well," Cubbage said seriously, "I don't know…maybe…let me tell you what's going on and you can decide from there." Gordon gave Ari the full story – the kidnapping, the GPS implant trace, Sheridan and Alice's current location, and Mastroantonio's response forbidding him to go after the prisoners when he asked for permission to make a with-prejudice retrieval.

Ari heard him out without interrupting until Cubbage had finished, "OK, let me see if I understand the situation: your people are in trouble;

you know where they are; you're forbidden to pick them up; and you're running out of time before they get served up to *Allah*...so you want me to go in and get them, right? "

Thank God, at last a professional, Cubbage thought to himself. "Yep," he replied, "But it's got to be soon. I don't care if things get a little damp here and there but I want Sheridan and Alice out safely. How does your nuke branch put it: "If an operation is exposed, no matter whether objectives are achieved, it's automatically a failure?" Well, that doesn't matter to me anymore. If you get them back it will be all over the intelligence community like a rash so I've really got nothing to lose here. And if it gets out that I came to you for help when my boss told me to sit tight, and especially if they find out I passed the secret GPS intercept data to you to enable you to do it, I'll be tried for treason. I hate to put this on a personal level; it's not professional and I hate talking against my own country, but the squids running things over here these days just don't give a shit about anything except their own agenda. This bimbo Mastroantonio is willing to put a woman and a little girl at risk of death just to push the president's fucking socialist politics. Well, I'm not. So do this for me and I'll owe you as large as you felt you owed me. I called 'Rutter' with you because these are *my* people and I just don't have any more cards to play. I don't care what the Secretary wants. I don't give a shit about their goddam liberal 'hands across the sea' horseshit. These people running my show nowadays are garbage. They don't give a damn about their own; all they care about is power. And damn it, Ari, *I want my people back!*"

Ari Dayan looked at Gordon Cubbage a long time. Finally he said, "OK, I'll go get them for you, but there's liable to be some damage to the bad guys. My people aren't gentle and if I send my wife there's going to be red stuff all over the rug."

Cubbage nodded and Ari went on, "This I will do for you because of the Rutter operation, but I'll have to run this outside my own network and that means a lot more risk to me and my team. No backup if we get in over our heads. So someday I'm going to come back to you for something. It won't be anything you'll have a problem with but you'll have to trust me about that. I'll let you know what it is when the time comes. Deal?"

Cubbage sighed with relief, "Deal! Ask whatever you want. You know what's possible and what's not. Anything in my power to do that doesn't compromise my own mission...and you'll have it. But one thing, Ari, this is personal between the two of us. I'm ok with the favor but it's for you alone. Nobody else can ask it but you personally. I suggest you ask soon, because if you pull off this extraction it'll mean a big promotion for me, all the way up to Greeter at Wal-Mart." Ari chuckled and nodded assent. Cubbage went on, "Now how soon can you move on this?"

Ari smiled, "Well, my old friend, a short time ago my people got wind of a couple of Yanks being held by some of our local partners in *jihad*. Been nosing around for them for the past couple of weeks; found them yesterday, so I won't need your GPS data and you'll be spared pounding rocks at Leavengood."

"Leavenworth," Cubbage corrected faintly.

" My team's still in place from the Valparaiso job last month," Ari continued, "so they're just waiting for a phone call from me. "

Cubbage stared at him, then leaned back in his chair and shook with laughter, "Well! You conniving old son of a bitch! So you're ready to go, eh and all you needed was your Thirty Pieces of Silver!"

Ari winced and ducked his head.

Cubbage went on, "Well, you might well blush, my friend but I would have offered the favor anyway, so all your effort trying to trick this humble, gullible, naïve American went for nothing."

Ari was dialing his cell phone, "What would you have done if I'd said no?"

"Gone to the Russians and offered them New Jersey," Cubbage replied. "You know damn well that past you I've got nothing."

"Yes, I know. And as long as we're confiding State Secrets, I may as well tell you that I would have gone after your people even if you'd refused my deal. You Americans might well be...what did you say a minute ago?...gullible and naïve...? ['humble' my ass!]...but you're the kind of friends we Jews do <u>not</u> take for granted. Your people pulled our asses out of the fire in '72 and we stood by and watched The Cretin rocket our cities in '91 so you could keep your coalition together going after him. Could you have taken a few rockets into the middle of New York City and stood aside if we'd asked you to? There's a lot of – what's your phrase...blood under the bridge? – with our two countries?"

Cubbage chuckled, "'*Water* under the bridge', but close enough."

Ari paused and looked at Cubbage straight in the eyes. "We've been down different roads together, America and Israel. You had one or two interesting moments during the Cold War when you felt some heat between your legs, but with us that's a daily occurrence. We've had our backs to the wall every minute for each of the sixty-odd years we've been a nation. Every war we fight, and every day we live, we look over the border and know that if we fuck up, *on that very day* our families become the Front Line. You Americans have never felt that sting, but as you say, "that was then, this is now." Today with these scum attacking you, too, both of our countries have our families on the front line. With us it's "business as usual," but this is a new thing for you. Get used to it, my friend. We had to."

"When you kill a Jew to get his money, or you kill an American to get his goods, in our societies we call that 'murder' and we name it a very bad thing. And when you kill a Jew *just because he's a Jew*, or an American *just because he's an American*, we call that 'genocide,' and that's even worse. But when you practice genocide *in the Name of God*, that's called 'Evil' – Capital E – and it doesn't get any worse anywhere on this planet. Years ago the Nazis set a standard for evil that will live down through the coming generations. No one, particularly we Jews who survived, ever expected it could get any worse than that. But it has. As horrible as the Nazis were they never killed in God's Name. These terrorists do, and in so doing, they put themselves beyond the human pale and make of themselves animals to be persuaded if possible, to be hunted down if not. As long as terrorism remains global in nature, your people will be marked out for genocide just as we Jews have been for two thousand years. Whether you like it or not, my friend, we're all 'jews' now. So as one 'jew' to another, I'll get your people out for you if they're still alive. Now leave me alone and let me get to work."

FOURTEEN

أربعة عشرة

A section of the large room had been walled off with welding robes set on metal frames to provide a smaller enclosure. Several television cameras stood here and there not pointing at much of anything, just waiting, their thick cable trunks snaking out beneath the 'walls' of yellow plastic panels like prehensile tails. It was the best the television station manager could do on such short notice. Most of his film came from stringers or was streamed in from his own reporters on location. Hardly anything was ever shot in house. So a warehouse had to be cleared, a smaller enclosure erected within its cavernous depths, and all done in a big hurry. When the manager saw the size of the group's initial down payment check their urgency became his own. The renters not only paid handsomely but when the manager had brought them additional bills for cost overruns and for the special services they requested, they had paid the additional with many smiles. The producers were shooting a documentary about *Islam* to show *Islam*ic Faithful a representation of *Sharia* justice and the judgment and the resulting execution of an Infidel who dared profane it. They would use professional actors in each of the roles and would furnish their own studio props. Their objective was complete realism and as close to actual life and death as they could get. The filmmakers assured the station manager that his warehouse was the perfect location, and the faint echo produced by the high ceiling would not pose them a problem as long as he could provide several more of those excellent large plastic welding cloths to spread on the floor for sound deadening purposes and keep everything very hush-hush to avoid their competitors finding out how close they were to producing a finished product.

Large pedestal lights peered over the tops of the partitions and made shadowless the space within. An office folding leg conference table was centered over the plastic cloths on the floor and draped with another. Soon the station technicians began wandering in to begin warming up their cameras and microphones. An amazingly realistic plastic axe with a heavy two foot long painted blade and six-foot shaft stood in the corner of the room beside a small dais containing a podium. One of the camera operators focused manually and trained his camera on the axe head. He ducked into his lens hood and positioned his head in the rest that was already adjusted to the shape of his temples. He heard the sighing swish of the air exhausted from the section of hood over his eyes and felt the camera respond to the movements of his retinae as its computer acquired his retinal direction and focused itself on what the cameraman was looking at using the cameraman's own eyes. This was state of the art cinematography and the price paid by the station for this camera alone would have bought the technician a palace and servants for the rest of his life.

Once synchronized to his eyes, the camera would follow wherever his eyes moved and would maintain focus and clarity without adjustment. All he had to do was look at his subject and the camera would hold it in center frame and maintain the same focus as the operator. But this technique, like any that relied on a human/machine interface, had its down side. Making the operator a part of the camera so to speak tended to induce a feeling of intimate connection with the scene being viewed. The human operator became one with the action as though he was participating. He knew that this was because the complete synchronization between his eye movements and the movements of the camera lens gave such a strong impression of connection between them that the feeling of observing the scene vanished and the operator actually lived it. He thought this might be his most interesting shoot. Not that his own thirteen-year-old little darling would need the message being sent, but a mock execution like this would be good for backsliding Islamics to see; might keep them on the True Path. With this electronic connection to his own brain he'd be right up front with everybody. The first couple of times it was a little unnerving to feel the camera pointing its lens up and down seemingly on its own to follow its target and feeling as though he was actually performing in the scene being recorded. But by now the operator was accustomed to it and was exceedingly proud that he was trusted with the only cameral in their shop that could do this.

No More Time For Sorrow

At the appointed time the actors arrived, each in his costume of formal desert robes and a black ski mask hiding his features except one in a featureless sheet who seemed a little dazed, but the producers assured the manager that she was merely new to the screen and had taken a sedative for her role today. They reminded the manager how grateful they were for the enormous favors he had already done them and extreme trouble he taken to make everything perfect, particularly on such short notice, but would the manager object to assisting them just one final time by holding these payments to the Actors' Guild and forwarding them as soon as the shooting ended. The manager was glad to oblige and transferred the three inch roll of bills to an inner pocket.

Alice came to being walked by two men into a large building. She was still wobbly from the drugs injected into her. They strapped her to a table with some kind of yellow plastic cover on it and pulled off her mask so that her blonde hair streamed down over the end of the bench she was fastened to. Looking around, she noticed big cameras on rubber wheels with men ducked down behind them. One of her captors began to read from a paper. Alice understood not a word but it seemed to be have something to do with her. Finally, the man stopped and looked down at her expectantly. Alice had no idea what to do so she kept quiet. Then he went on,

"American whore, you have been given an opportunity to recant and to embrace the true Faith, but as a whore you have rejected the sweet comforts and earnest encouragement of the one true God, so since as a whore you have chosen to live, as a whore you shall be judged and as a whore you shall end your life."

He nodded away from her line of vision and she saw the little man who always carried a machine gun appear at the foot of her table, this time without it. Achmed moved into position between her legs and spread them apart. After his repeated sexual assaults of the past few days, sometimes holding the gun sometimes not, Alice hardly noticed him and tuned her mind away from what by this time she knew was going to happen. Achmed pulled out his member, now stiff, and, shoving Alice's legs aside, entered her. She whimpered at the pain of his entry but nobody seemed to notice. This was not unusual. The first time they had come for her three of them had taken their turns with her, lounging about laughing and joking amongst themselves. That first time it had hurt very badly; successive times it hurt less and each time she had withdrawn a little further into herself to be with her father and mother, and finally hardly noticed except when they slapped her around a bit to make her pay attention. This time Achmed was especially rough with her, driving into her repeatedly until she began to moan with the pain and muttering under his breath not loud enough for the mikes to pick up. The man at the podium read more from his paper, sometimes shouting and gesturing. The other men in the room were becoming more and more agitated, shifting one foot to the other, muttering to themselves, pointing to Achmed at the foot of the table and occasionally calling out, interrupting the man reading aloud who merely nodded and went on. They watched Achmed raping her at the end of the table and moved their eyes to the man standing next to the reader.

The cameras were shooting Alice's face and Achmed's repeated entries and withdrawals. One camera was on the Speaker and one followed the prop axe that one of the men had taken from the edge of the scene and now held with the fake blade resting on his foot, both hands on the shaft about two feet from the end. In her twelve short years Alice Walker hadn't learned much about the world. The biggest thing that had ever happened to her to date was when she'd tried to stop that little black kid shooting up her classmates; she had been taught by her school that maintaining political correctness with fellow educators was far more important than merely safeguarding the lives of the children in their charge. She had been taught by her peers that she was beautiful and would be sought for this quality alone, and she had been taught by her parents that these things were inconsequential, that beauty came from within, and that silly people who squandered their American birthright of stalwart individuality should be at best disregarded and when you couldn't disregard them, as when Alice's school turned on her, you simply laughed at them and moved on. But this situation beyond teaching her anything. What could she learn from it? That there were bad men in the world who hated little children? That there were even worse men in the world who would use little children? She already knew those things from the past days when men came to her to hurt her without reason.

Alice was on the point of crying out in fear and frustration when something suddenly calmed her, something her father had said right after the school incident, "Beebee, my little love, the bad people are not just the ones overseas who come here trying to kill us. You have already met some bad people in your own life very close to your own home. Your teachers who didn't stand up for you when you saved those kids' lives are bad people. Your school officials who hurt you and shamed you when you had saved their self-respect for the rest of their lives are just as bad as the people I fight against overseas. The people here at home who tell you not to be responsible for your actions are bad people, who tell you they know what's good for you better than you do...ignore them, my darling little lady. Hate every disgusting thing they stand for. I can't fight them with my ship or my guns; they're my countrymen. But you can fight them. Stand up straight and look them in the eye and say, "I am ME! You can never own me. You can NEVER take away my individuality. My individuality will *always* be more important than your collective. She hadn't been sure what that last part meant, but suddenly, tied to this table amidst these ogres, she finally understood. These men who were raping her and abusing her and now had brought her to this fearful place were the same as the school officials back home who tried to hurt her for daring to be an individual, for standing up for something she thought precious. Somehow in the midst of this horror, the thought calmed her. Her father had been right.

Alice looked up into the face of the man reading from a document in some language she didn't understand except that it seemed to be about her. Once he had stopped reading and looked down at her as though expecting her to reply to him. But she didn't know what to say so she kept quiet. After that he had gone on for quite a while. Then he was done, and said a few words to the man standing next to him who reached behind and brought up over his head a huge stick with something on the end. He stepped backward a pace away from the table. Alice saw what was in his hands and her breath left her as she understood what he was about to do. Into her mind unbidden came her father's code to banish fear, *"Child of learning, child of light...manatees and ladybugs, pups and armadillos...."* Alice whispered the phrase trying not to shake. The man raised his arms over his head. Alice, Child of Light, closed her eyes and began, "Our Father who art in Heaven, hallowed be thy Na--"

The first outsider to be brought to the realization that the plastic prop axe was neither a prop nor plastic was the cameraman whose retinal imaging camera had, by virtue of its seamless connection to his brain through his eyes, made him a participant in the unfolding scene. His heart and mind followed the axe blade upwards to the apex of its arc over its wielder's head, paused a moment for effect before the cameras, and rushed downward with it to its rendezvous with the throat of this "horrible danger to the Nation of Islam," this Infidel whore who so affronted *Allah* that He had Commanded she be put to death in this righteous way, this twelve year old vermin from the Great Satan. The blow took Alice in her throat and severed her head from her body. As had been noted numerous times by French during guillotining, at the blow the eyes snapped open and continued for a few moments to flutter as if trying to regain their sight. But this indignity was spared the group by a merciful *Allah* who permitted her head to roll beneath the table and out of sight.

The cameraman whose eyes and heart had followed the axe head downward into her neck was instantly violently sick into his lens hood. He then slumped away from his seat unconscious, his mouth open, eyes defocused, spittle dribbling down his chin. The second camera screening Alice's face followed her head drifting down to the plastic cover thoughtfully provided to avoid staining the warehouse floor beneath the table, her golden hair spreading and flowing in the lights coming into the camera lens. The cameraman who had been dollying this shot manually with his hand controls began to cry.

FIFTEEN

خمسة عشر

Sheridan awoke on the *nth* interminable day of captivity and immediately sensed a difference. She had been fed daily a thin soup spooned or poured into her mouth but remained blindfolded and bound on what seemed to be a folding bed. The occasional thumps and bangs in the room from time to time were her only communication outside her own mind for no one spoke a word to her. This time, however, she opened her eyes to a dim view of peeling stucco over rough board walls and realized the blindfold had been removed while she slept. She wiggled and stretched herself to turn away from the wall and toward the room. As her head came around she could dimly make out in the gloom a figure seated across the room and joyfully recognized her daughter's legs. Thank God they finally brought her back! Her mouth was still taped so mumbled and squeaked the bed trying to get Alice's attention but she was either asleep or unconscious. The thought of what they must have done to her made Sheridan sick with anger, and she vowed as soon as she got her daughter to safety she'd begin collecting payment from these animals. With that Sheridan lapsed back into sleep, her last thought being that when she awakened again she'd have little Beebee with her and would damn well work out a way to converse, then to escape.

When Sheridan again opened her eyes the room was flooded with light. Someone had reached in and switched on the overhead bulb. She eagerly looked for her daughter and could see her legs below the chair. Sheridan twisted her neck painfully back and forth against her bonds and finally felt them begin to loosen slightly. With a final wrench and a groan of pain she rolled to where she could see all of her daughter clearly.

Well, all but her head.

Dr. Robert Beeman

Her daughter's torso had been propped up on the chair slumped there as if asleep where Sheridan could not fail to see her. Sheridan gazed in horror and as she took in every small detail of what remained of Alice, she felt her mind begin to expand outward rushing away into the streets outside her prison where people even at this precise moment were passing and talking and if she were outside that wall there would still be Alice and sanity. She examined the notion that if she and Alice would be laughing about all this if only they were twenty feet to the left and she let go a little exploratory laugh just to try it on for size. But it wasn't just quite what she had in mind, so she felt her mind begin contracting back away from the world, down past Alice and into her head passing her eyeballs and her optic nerves and her sinuses bouncing against the back of her skull and back toward the inside of her face but not with quite enough power to escape outside again…then back down into a place into herself where no woman would ever willingly go, down, back, black, in, in, inside. And then Sheridan just stopped. She lay in the position she had squirmed to, eyes open, unblinking, drool seeping over her chin and never even noticed when the firing began.

SIXTEEN

ست عشرة

Pride of Sultistan, North Korean master, Liberian registry [they were finally learning that Korean-registered bottoms attracted instant surveillance], chugged on its last set of mainshaft bearings into Beirut Harbor past the lighthouse guarding what was left of the harbor mole and wheeled ponderously to starboard, pumps racing furiously to keep ahead of the leaks. In April, 1942, as one of the merchant ships built to replace those being sent to the bottom by Nazi u-boats, Henry J. Kaiser's Oregon Shipbuilding Yard had slammed her together in an impressive eighteen days, a feat that would not be bested until the *SS Joseph N. Teal*'s astonishing ten day build time later that fall. *SS Robert E. Peary's* had been assembled in five days but that was a race between shipyards and couldn't be maintained.

The spanking new C3 hull slid down the ways as the *SS David B. Yarrish*, and joined the British Merchant Fleet plying arms and food to England. For the most part her service life was uneventful, although on a crossing in 1943 the log reported that *Yarrish's* five inch deck armament had accounted for a German submarine. After coming about to investigate the fifty-two rounds of ammunition fired eagerly into the sea by the *Yarrish's* crew, the skipper of the convoy's escort, United States Navy aircraft carrier *USS Bogue*, reported that the surface debris encountered might have been from a sub, or, then again, might have been garbage dumped from the tanker ahead. After the war, The *Yarrish*, her deck gun prudently removed, had been passed around quite a bit across the oceans of the world and saw a lot of blue water under her bow. She displaced fourteen thousand tons and could load to almost six tonnes burden. Her twin diesels gave no trouble and sometimes the shaft bearings ran cool enough to yield almost fifteen knots. So even in the modern era of vast container ships piled to the sky with huge metal boxes, the old girl still had her special talents and special uses. One of those special talents was to slide her shallow 28 foot draft into ports where container ships couldn't venture. One of those special uses was to lift nonstandard cargo that wouldn't do well in a container that had to pass through the increasingly sophisticated electronic scanning and imaging machines that eagle-eyed Port-of-Entry customs agents employed to survey the millions of closed containers going by.

So *Pride of Sultistan*, nee' *David B. Yarrish*, slid her befouled hull creaking and groaning into the outermost reach of the Paris Street Docks, formerly home to cruise ships and chattering tourists but for the past generation a seamy, raffish collection of ancient sheds and rusting equipment. She came to rest at last, rocking at her berth in a slowly widening pool of diesel fuel, and waited for her five holds to receive into their into their fragrant, cavernous depths whatever lading needed her special skills. Crates of agricultural machinery were hoisted perilously up and over the hatch coaming to be lowered gently, slowly into the cavernous hold and dropped free-fall the last three feet by men who had no hint of the sea in their eyes and who harbored love only for the pleasures they could partake once past the twelve mile limit. Fortunately the contents of the crates were not particularly prone to impact damage unless impacted in just a certain way.

Sharp eyes on the mole observed *Yarrish's* arrival, eyes that took in the decrepitude of the hull and the filth of the upper works. They missed nothing, these expert eyes, and the ears accompanying them received with precision the faint clank each time the starboard shaft rotated past the flat spot on its once-polished surface. All these things were duly noted and in due course the captain received a visitor. The brokerage house consigning the cargo even now being loaded for Veracruz was concerned about the ship's powerplant. The captain jumped at their offer to repair it free of charge. Tax writeoff; wouldn't cost anyone anything!

6601 nautical miles and twenty-three days' steaming across the world to the west, each of the half million new cars that sail into the port of Veracruz every year slides through the A-Level Certified Customs House – one of three such in Mexico – whose personnel keep a wary official eye on the port traffic in general and imports in particular. Well, they don't *all* go through inspection. Most of them get a kick on the tire, a stamp on the paperwork, and are chained onto railcars for shipment up to the *Gringoricos* up North. Nevertheless, within the bounds set by their numbers and available time, sharp-eyed customs inspectors watch all, view all with a professional suspicion. Once in a while the inspectors would leave their coffee and bills of lading and beckon a skid or package or vehicle over to their warehouse for closer inspection. These random crates were taken apart down to the screws in the plywood floors and their contents minutely examined. The cars were started and actually driven. The theory was that random in-depth inspection once in a while discouraged more smuggling than cursory inspection of every load, since smugglers knew all the tricks of disguising packaging and falsifying documents, but had no defense against opening a carton and pulling their 'wares' out of a box marked Light Bulbs. But customs inspectors are not paid in the high brackets. Their days are hot and tedious, filled with minutiae about which nobody in the world gave a damn except to get their stuff cleared for transport inland. So after awhile even the best inspectors tended to become creatures of habit.

On this particular morning, none of them were especially happy to discover their kick-and-stamp routine broken by a stinking old tub wheezing into their pristine port tying up berthing that could have been assigned to spanking new container vessels that actually had some tonnes to show for their trip. Not only was *Sultistan* ugly and rusting, but its crew was fragrant in the tropical heat and looked as though they would do anything for money. The cargo consisted of large crates labeled "Agricultural Machinery," each of which, due to its size, would require special handling and really no end of trouble. The Lebanese crates carried impeccable paperwork, looked like they had been bounced around a few shipping docks and freighter holds, and in all respects just looked pretty normal. In other words, very suspicious.

So the Mexican Customs inspectors decided to give each crate The Treatment. When they were done prying and unscrewing and crowbaring and unwrapping, they were stunned at what they found. Agricultural machinery. Brand-new bright red and orange four-wheel-drive tractors with powerful diesel engines, glassed-in, air conditioned cabs, Category Two implement hitches and doubled high-traction agricultural tires hung four to each massive rear axle to breast the steepest, softest dune or guckiest swamp or most forbidding piece of Godforsaken hardscrabble real estate out near *Angel de la Guarda*. But The Treatment was The Treatment, so one by one each massive diesel engine was started up. Chuffing with great noise and satisfying vibration, the tractors were bumped around the dock to the delight of local children until the inspectors signaled their approval and each was shut down and parked. Each of the tractors sparkled in the hot Gulf morning. Each of them ran dutifully up and down past the garbage scows and container ships bobbing gently at their mooring bollards. The customs men gave each one a pretty good workout to prove its legitimacy and maybe just because it was fun to play around with them some, smoking and belching and rattling along, bringing a whiff of the countryside into an otherwise squared-off dockside day, although the kids soon tired of chasing them and wandered off to the *mercado* to steal lunch.

The company brokering the tractors was proud of its product and greatly pleased that they were able to sell the entire shipment to a farm equipment consortium in De Moines. But when the broker's agent at the dock started each of the tractors his experienced ears told him something was amiss. Unlike a twelve-cylinder diesel, whose two banks of six cylinders offered perfect primary and secondary balance and therefore hardly enough vibration to ripple your margarita, these V8 monsters, though powerful, rocked and stuttered and smoked far too much for brand-new engines. In the hands of professionals who knew what the powerful diesels were capable of, it was clear these particular engines not only vibrated hideously but would hardly pull more than their own weight. This would never do. There were four additional shipments of these excellent power units upstream in the pipeline consigned to this same buyer. If the first batch were problematic, the rest, although paid for, might be canceled thereby causing no end of paperwork and agony up and down the corporate ladder. That was the Bad News.

The Good News was that a Special Diagnostic Section had been set up with great foresight just across the border into the US by one of the buyer's vice presidents. Affable and knowledgeable, he had visited the buyers of the tractors in Des Moines, treating them to a flurry of dinners and credit purchases, trinkets for the wives and kiddies, making side jokes about the likelihood of reliability when you had machinery with Commie engines, Turkish running gear, assembled by Middle Eastern towel heads. He had come to the Des Moines dealer to make sure the initial shipment was absolutely perfect. After all, these units could be sold for a fraction of what was coming in from Japan and Korea, or China even! If the first ones worked, then the door was open to both firms to make handsome money.

Our goal, said the VP of the brokers, is to work out a way you can buy succeeding shipments and drop-ship them right from the dock to your customers. This first shipment is a test. If we can perfect this process right at the first, we will be able to make large savings in rail charges, a good portion of which we will be able to pass along to you. So we are setting up a special facility in Phoenix to service the units before they reach you if they need it. Don't worry, he went on, we'll pay for everything, special handling, quick service, top priorities on the rail bills. We're also sending a team of mechanics to the port at Veracruz to inspect the tractors right off the boat. Of course, in the unlikely event anything needs adjusted, we'll rebate to you a substantial late-shipment penalty for every day we have to have them in our shop. He mentioned a sum. The purchasing agent gulped and began smiling hugely. All we need from you, the purchaser, is to plan for a possible diversion of part of the shipment to our facility after it clears US Customs at the Texas border. The purchasing agent for the Des Moines dealership felt that wouldn't pose any problem at all.

Back in Veracruz, the brokers' agents worked feverishly with port customs inspectors to hasten the clearance of the tractors off the docks. It was necessary to pay to certain officials certain sums for certain special licenses, but the broker paid willingly because, he told port officials, he was being reimbursed every dime by the *gringos estupidos* who had more money than brains. In a day or two – an astonishingly short time for chattel clearance in Veracruz – the tractors were poked, prodded, stamped, signed for, and released by regretful port inspectorate whose every move for the past two days concerning the tractors had generated fulsome gratitude and showers of pesos. All that was necessary, the brokers' agents told port officials, was a small section of their warehousing for a pre-delivery inspection after clearing customs. We will, of course, pay any fees associated with leasing the space. In cash. In advance.

Well! – the port inspectors thought, what wasn't to like about that? They hastened to line off an ample section of their dockside warehouse. The brokers of the tractors immediately paid over a year's rent in advance, then walled in the entire area and began stocking with tools and parts, explaining that the locks on the doors and the armed guards were there to protect certain proprietary electronics that the buyer would be taking this opportunity to install. Even more good news! The mechanics who in due course arrived from *el norte* turned out to be a supervisor and a shop foreman who intended to hire local workers to do the actual wrenching. More local jobs! Excellent!

The tractors were towed into the buyer's section of the huge warehouse and arrayed in diagnostic stalls. Sometimes the rough ride was not always due to the newness and aggressiveness of the tire treads, but perhaps to be charged to certain material that had become lodged inside the tires where there was supposed to be air. The foreman instructed that each of the eight huge tires on each unit be deflated and removed from its rim to insure that no rust had crept into the welded surfaces. It was likely, he said, that material had collected there during assembly. Regrettably, the foreman's prediction was accurate and debris were discovered inside the tires. The mechanics shook their heads sadly at this serious assembly line flaw, scraped out the material and set it aside as instructed for a special collector of industrial garbage to remove. The foreman was very specific about making sure every gram of the debris was saved. He told the mechanics it was acidic and might stain the floor and advised using gloves when handling it.

The certain material was collected by an exceedingly courteous man of garbage who, being a waste-handling professional, was very careful not to touch any of it. He was much more careful, in fact, than the mechanics had been, three of whom were already showing signs of nausea. When the mechanics left for the day, the material was tucked safely and unobtrusively into fertilizer bags and loaded into a large truck whose payload had been considerably reduced by thick panels of lead shielding. Diagnostic instruments revealed that the engines of the tractors were only running on five of their available eight cylinders. Ordinarily the firm's extremely thorough mechanics would go the extra mile to insure proper tuning. But there were no facilities here to do a proper teardown and inspection, so the discrepancy was noted and the broker's agent duly informed.

When the tires were thoroughly cleaned and remounted, the tractors were chained down onto flatcars to be coupled to a double engine and pulled, along with a hundred other flats and covered car sheds, through one of the Port Exits, out to Puebla then north through Ciudad Victoria and Monterrey. The man of garbage paused for a moment on his way out of town to watch the flat cars bearing the tractors ease through the huge arch of the radiation detector on the Port's outer perimeter. He nodded with respect at the engineering achievement that the giant detector represented. It was sensitive enough to pick up one of the old radium dial watches and, in fact, had been tested using just such an artifact from a local museum. Of course, it wouldn't penetrate lead shielding, but then, he reflected, nothing was foolproof. He slid back behind the wheel and pointed his ancient sedan north on Boulevard Fidel Velasquez Sanchez to pick up *Estado Camino 180D* toward Ursula Galvan, then to the pike over to Jalapa and on north. As the tractors passed under the detector, its sensitive needle barely blipped up over background, but not enough to attract the attention of the operator who had finished texting his girlfriend and eating watermelon and was just getting ready to return his attention to the radiation counter he monitored.

The crates that had permitted the tractors to be stacked in the freighter's hold had been discarded in order to make it easier for United States Customs to inspect them. Since everything was open and visible, the inspection was cursory, consisting of simply walking down the line of flat cars comparing the number of tractors and their VINS to the manifest. Making things easy for US inspectors was top priority with the broker firm. This attitude was duly noted by American customs officials. They tried to cooperate where they could. Just after being passed through American Customs at the Mexican border, and just before the rail cars left the Customs shed to begin their journey north to their purchaser, the broker's VP worriedly notified the purchaser that problems had been discovered in the powerplants of a number of the tractors. To be safe, the entire shipment should be diverted to the broker's shops in Phoenix for inspection and repair. Since the flaws had been discovered three days ago, the VP was backdating his promised performance penalty payments to the purchaser to that date, and would be sending an initial amount of three times the daily sum agreed upon by electronic transfer, with each day's additional delay paid daily at the same rate. Des Moines called its rail connection and arranged for the tractors to be diverted to Phoenix.

In Phoenix, under the expert eyes of the shop foreman, local mechanics recruited by word of mouth from among the illegal immigrant community carefully disassembled each engine. A Diesel compresses its fuel-air mix to about 23:1, over twice that of the standard Otto-cycle engine found in most cars. The heat of compression is what causes the fuel to ignite instead of a spark plug. Simplify, simplify... Unlike the complicated fuel metering and bug-prone ignitions of Otto-cycle engines, give a Diesel engine fuel delivery and compression and there's not much to keep it from running. The mechanics were competent men and couldn't understand why all of the engines would run poorly without big jagged holes in their cylinder blocks, for that was just about all that would make an eight cylinder Diesel run on only five. They wondered as they chatted among themselves how each tractor could exhibit the same symptoms. The engines were *Yaroslavl* models from the excellent firm *Novye 12 Tsilindpovye Dvigateli Yaroslavskogo Motopnogo Zavoda*. How could these very good engines *all* have the same problem? We must look carefully into the places of pain that might obtain within these makers of power that we may observe obstructions that might enter with accident the bore of each cylinder and clean it of any obstructions that might have accidentally entered the cylinder bores and would thereby reduce power.

The mechanics found the three inoperable cylinders to be filled with packages most carefully wrapped and secured against vibration, items packed in thick lead coverings. These, they were told, were milling slugs that would occasionally be left in place at the factory for some engineering reason. Just remove them. – carefully! – and set them back and a factory rep would be by to collect them. Frequently the rep came early while they were still working and watched them remove each milling slug. These weren't particularly good times for the mechanics, for if they even appeared to be ready to drop one the rep went seriously crazy and berated them in a harsh and unseemly manner. The rep had the mechanics carry each of the packaged milling slugs to his van and carefully nest it with the others he had collected from the other tractors.

The milling slugs were picked up in due course by the not-so-courteous factory rep and transported across town to a similar warehouse where they were repackaged as wholesale assembly parts, then FedEXed to several destinations here and there around the country. Several of the smaller units went north to become components of exceedingly reasonably priced switchgear destined for an electrical equipment wholesaler in Montreal, there to be repackaged for retail distribution throughout Canada and the States.

SEVENTEEN

سبعة عشر

Monsieur le docteur Henri Traître ambled up the steps of 8709 Boul, Saint-Laurent in Montreal's industrial district, through the spacious reception area of *Elektrogrosshändlern GMBH* and with a wave to the receptionist, on into the carpeted recesses of the Sales Department. The amount of business he permitted these salesmen to write, selling him wholesale laptop components and industrial switchgear, had long ago entitled him to free access and a cheery nod from each cubicle. He returned the greetings as he passed through the warehouse door at the far end of the room, giving the room a wave as he went through. His own little desk, provided by the management to each of their very, very special six-figure retailers, was tucked into a corner of the cavernous distribution area. As he reached it the phone rang. He had timed it perfectly. The voice sounded male and nervous, "Your shipment of electrical components, 121 packages, has arrived in our warehouse and is ready for pickup. You may inspect the items at your convenience, Aisle 19, Bay 410C."

"Aisle 19, Bay 410C," repeated Traître and as he added thank-you the line went dead. He walked back past dim side aisles to number 19, then left to Bay 4. There was no 410C; the last three digits referred to labels on certain crates marked so as to invite his particular attention. There were twelve, on the outside indistinguishable from the dozens of other crates in this particular shipment except for the '10C' burned into a wooden slat on each side with a pencil beam. They had been marked by burning to avoid lost labels, water damaged ink, and a host of other accidents that might have moved one of the packages into Lost And Found. And that would never do.

Henri keyed a number on his cell phone and in a few minutes a fork lift rumbled down the center aisle. the driver and his safety walker loaded the 10C crates onto the fork's pallet and went off with them, leaving the genuine 121 packages in the bay. The 10Cs were grounded by the forklift in a remote corner and covered with sheeting. In due course over the next several weeks, the demand for these components increased, so Monsieur le docteur found it necessary to ship a portion of his stock out to several of his stores. The entire order had been prepaid along with a healthy penalty escrow held by the wholesaler, the disposition of the interest on which was neither here nor there. Since Traître used his own drivers and thus saved the warehouse owner even more money, he was encouraged to manage the shipping himself, which he was all too ready to do in order to accommodate such an understanding supplier. To each shipment as it was palletized and packed was added a 10C crate. Then they were sent out to the truck dock or the company's siding and dispatched overland or by train to their destinations, always in the United States.

EIGHTEEN

ثمانية عشر

Years ago Aliza Dayan had taken Ari's name gladly, proud of him and proud he would choose her, knowing he returned pride in her skills and her beauty. They had never been lovers before they were married in the desert. The heat each of them felt between their legs sustaining them as they crouched in a bunker on their wedding night under a vicious rocket and artillery bombardment delivered by people who challenged Ari and Aliza and all other Jews' right to exist. That heat had finally won out over their instinct for self protection and, moaning and crying they took each other over and over again as the explosions overhead deafened them and rained sand and dust down from the ceiling on their forms locked together in an embrace of unconquerable equals. Neither the emotions unleashed by that embrace nor the equality had never diminished. They loved and made love today just as they had done that first night when the bed jumped at intervals from concussion and Ari had afterwards had tried to make her believe it was his prowess instead. She had laughed at that but privately reflected that there had been similarities not to be overlooked.

Now her night vision glasses probed the rundown building across the deserted Damascus street trying to detect movement around the outside or on the rooftops above which would signal the presence of guards. She was not expecting any. Her outside team had discovered six guards on the roofs and five more on the ground up and down the block and in a few minutes there was no more movement. One of the ground figures might have been an innocent passerby but the team gave him the benefit of the doubt and dispatched him anyway along with the rest, each man's last impression being a rough hand over his mouth from behind and the low wheeze of air escaping from a deftly sliced throat. Aliza motioned to the men beside her, and clicked her cell phone twice. Bent figures ran across the dark street, paused at the door and the boarded window for a moment, held their pose rigidly still for the two minutes required to flood the room with fumes. Then an oblong of light flashed as the door burst open.

They entered what looked like a conference room which at the moment was filled by the fumes of the aerosol anesthetic pumped through the window. Several forms lay about, some weakly trying to rise but most of them inert. The team split up and raced through the building, each one moving along his own pre-assigned line etched on the map he had committed to memory days before. There were no surprises. Each team member knew every nail in this structure, every closet. They weren't sure in which room Sheridan and Alice were being held, or whether there might be more than just the two prisoners, so they were careful to use gas first in each room before shooting down the surprised occupants.

"What's for this lot?" Aliza's team leader motioned to the men gassed and retching lying here and there in the conference room.

Aliza was brief, "Keep an eye on them until we get the prisoners away. We might need to ask them some questions. Then kill them. I don't want witnesses."

The man smiled. His mother and two sisters had been kidnapped and "judged" by a similar band several years ago. They had not survived. He had been looking for the kidnappers ever since without any real hope of finding them. This bunch would do in their place… "It may take a while, Major…"

Aliza nodded and waved him away. She had been in the command center when they brought in what was left of his mother and sisters. She didn't care what he did to these animals as long as it stayed within mission timelines. Something had caught her attention and she sifted down through a pile of papers on the floor beside an overturned table to retrieve what looked like a picture. It was a print of an old photograph of several men in fedoras and baggy coats, a couple in uniform, standing next to a large object, a bomb it seemed to be. But something about it raised her hackles. It was no ordinary bomb. This was something more.

The caption in Arabic made no sense. *"Fat Man"* There was no fat man in the picture. She shuffled through more papers, then gasped, read part of one, and started stuffing as many as she could into her blouse.

"Found em." David's head and shoulders appeared around the door frame. "You're not going to like this…."

"Bring them out right now," Aliza ordered.

"Woman's coming out walking; no other prisoners. Kid's dead. They had their fun with her. I'll get somebody to bring her."

Aliza's phone vibrated silently against her leg. "Ephraim here; truck's been spotted – fire fight – Jaim's down but he's aboard – got to move *now!*" Get your team to the egress point – two minutes!"

"Shit!" Aliza called over her shoulder, "David! Are you sure the kid's dead?"

"Uh…yeah, Aliza, no question about it. She's dead alright."

"OK, forget the body; just bring the woman. Got to egress right now! Get the team out to the truck. When you come through here grab these guys lying around and throw them in, too. We've got to take them with us." Aliza heard their truck growl up to the door and counted the team as they ran past her out from the inner rooms, dividing up two by two to drag the unconscious men. The last two slowly half-carried Sheridan between them. Aliza took one last look around, filled one hand with as much of the scattered paper as she could hold, thumbed a thermal grenade, tossed it through the door into the recesses of the building, and vaulted into the truck as it pulled out into the street.

A long time later Sheridan awoke in a different room, clean, airy, in a bed with sheets and covers, a plasma stalk and instruments beside the bed. A man bent over her from whom she initially shrank until she realized he had kindest eyes she'd ever seen. Sheridan hadn't spoken since the rescue. Most of the time she was far away down inside herself not particularly caring what happened outside her safe place. She had taken Alice with her on a little vacation and thereby murdered her daughter in the most foul way. She summoned up her last strength and whispered, "Alice…" A huge hand descended gently over her mouth, "No…no…no…no…" a voice said softly. And as her mind confronted her last view of her daughter and began the long slide back down into the protective place inside her where it was safe, Sheridan Walker knew with her final coherent thought, that the hope she'd been clinging to – that the vision of her little Beebee's broken, bloody, headless corpse was a nightmare from which she would soon awaken – was gone.

NINETEEN

تسعة عشر

"Gordon!" Janine Mastroantonio's voice was sharp. "You have disobeyed my direct order and possibly for the last time! I don't know why you would do such a thing or think you could do it without me finding out. Your pigheadedness and unwillingness to work on our team has jeopardized some very delicate matters and I for one am going to see to it that you never have the opportunity to damage this administration again!"

When Janine Mastroantonio got angry her voice became shrill and went up several registers. If she was really incensed, she ranted. Her ire had been visited upon Cubbage before, most recently when the Speaker of the House of Representatives had tried to cover a bad political call by accusing the CIA of lying, and appealed to Janine, Cubbage's boss, for help in damage control. Cubbage, at that time a recent Presidential appointee as CIA Director, had been told to go along with the charade and offer his apology for his agency's alleged bad behavior. Instead, he memo-ed his entire staff that the Agency had never lied to its civilian bosses and he knew that on his watch it never would. The political fallout to the Speaker of the House was immediate and severe. The liberal mainstream media ignored the whole thing of course, but her attempt to use one of America's protective services to cover her backside caused her to be pilloried in the conservative press, whose following among Americans was extensive. These commentators had little humor for politicians who had never served in the military yet who tried to dirty the hands that kept America safe. The story was picked up by internet bloggers, most of whom had definite views on how the American guard was to be respected. In their assessment of the Speaker they were not kind. "Ignorant, arrogant anti-American pig" was one of the milder observations, which descended the scale from that point down into the biologically improbable. In due course, Janine Mastroantonio received from the Speaker of the House one of those phone calls whose tone and substance could be summed up in her opening salutation, "You toothless old idiot..." The Speaker then moved on to dwell in considerable detail upon Janine's disloyalty to her own party, her inability to control her subordinates, and her insensitivity to the Really Big Issues. The call had caused Janine much anguish and the memory was still green.

"Gordon, once again you have done serious harm to our country by your misplaced loyalties. You have lied to me and flouted my authority, not to mention disrespecting our wonderful president and his exciting visions. I'm speaking for a number of people who simply can't understand how you can constantly fail to see the Big Picture and – ."

"—Well, well, hello, Janine, how nice to hear from you!" Cubbage broke in brightly, "Having a productive afternoon?" Cubbage held the phone away from his ear. Janine went on for some time. When she finally wound down and paused for breath, Cubbage was seriously attentive, "Now Janine, it would be greatly helpful to me to know just a few little details about the subject under discussion. For instance – and in no particular order, of course – ah...why did you call?"

"You know very well why I called! Don't pretend ignorance. You spooks have much better sources than I do all over the goddam world! A few hours ago a representative of the Turkish Government summoned Ambassador Somers to a hospital in Ankara, and what do you think he found when he got there? Your goddam agent Walker lying in the IC unit with tubes coming out of her! Seems she was brought in by three or four people the night before, no notice, no paperwork. They *forced* the ER to admit her. No ID, no discussion, nothing. They made the ER people examine her and stabilize her, then they ran out! They drew a gun on a doctor! A *gun*, Gordon! On a *doctor!* The ER called the Hospital president, he called The Ministry of Foreign Affairs and they put him with somebody named David O'Glue or something.

Cubbage was impressed in spite of himself, "Janine, perhaps you mean Ahmet Davutoglu; the Foreign Minister? A fairly big cannon to be getting up in the middle of the night."

"Yes, yes, of course; well, this Achmed [*"Achmet," Cubbage corrected silently*] called Ambassador Somers at four o'clock in the morning and got *him* out of bed! Can you imagine the fallout I'll be getting from State for this?" According to Somers' people he kept using the term "Cumurbaskie – something."

"*Cumhurbaskanligi?*" Cubbage asked, surprised, making a manful effort not to laugh. "It means 'Presidential.' Holy shit! Sounds like this kicked over a pretty sizeable anthill." At this point Cubbage discovered he was dancing around his office and almost dropped the phone. He kept his voice steady "Uh, are you absolutely sure she's Agent Walker?"

"Of course I'm sure...! [the "you fool!" was left unspoken but Cubbage heard it clearly]. *They left a note in her pocket!*"

"What's up, Chief?" Lorraine was in the doorway with a coffee cup. Cubbage made shushing gestures and beckoned Lorraine in to sit. When she was close enough Cubbage mouthed silently "Walker is OK."

"What in the *world...?*" Lorraine broke the silence laughing and crying at the same time and could hardly speak. Cubbage just grinned from ear to ear. Lorraine Baskin's smile lit up the room. They high-fived and came to a stop silently face to face just grinning at each other. Faint sounds came from the phone dangling in Cubbage's hand. Janine had obviously not finished with him. Lorraine could hear her unmistakable nasal voice inflecting up and down with an occasional phrase she could almost make out in words. After a minute or two during which neither Lorraine nor Gordon moved a muscle nor took their eyes from each other, the silence was broken by a burst of garble from the phone. He glanced absently down at it as though it was the first time he'd noticed it was there, then back up at Lorraine. Holding her gaze with his, Cubbage slowly rotated the phone shut.

After a moment or two he spoke, "Well, Chief Special Agent Baskin, sounds like Walker's coming home! Ari got her out alright, Janine's blaming it on us, which is ok. I don't want that conduit blown open and neither does he. Left her in a hospital in Ankara to keep his people out of the picture. Not giving us a heads-up is his way of telling us he doesn't think we're secure here." Suddenly Cubbage shook with laughter, "God, Lorraine, it caused a stink over there!"

He dialed a number. "Sid, are you up on the Walker retrieval? Good... ...yeah, some good Samaritans apparently found her... ...ok, ok, no Samaritans, but we've got to leave it at that for now. I'll give you the lowdown later. Just heard from DHS she's ok but in Intensive Care so as soon as she's well we've got to get her home. Give me what you've got [Cubbage listened, made notes] ...who?... ...State? Absolutely NOT! Keep them as far away from her as you can. Let me know how soon she'll be ready to move. Listen, Sid, Somers is in the middle of this and ...yeah, *that* Somers...one of those lunatics the president – well, never mind that, just stay on top of this personally in case Somers starts flexing his diplomatic muscle. Apparently he hasn't had much sleep [*silent laughter from Lorraine*] He's liable to start pushing cookies and end up giving her away to the Russkies or something. ...ok, Sid, she's in good hands as long as you're on it. Keep me informed."

Cubbage keyed off and turned to Lorraine, "Walker's in the Hastanesi Hospital in Ankara. His phone rang again and Cubbage opened and listened.

"Ari, hi, how are you; it's been a long time."

"Gordon, my friend, I am well. Aliza sends her love. She wants me to ask you if you got our Christmas package. It's so difficult to send items through the mails these days. We took great trouble wrapping and delivering it to make sure it got to you ok."

"Yep, we got tracking numbers and my kids are really looking forward to it. FedEx says it's still at their distribution center over near you but I'm going to go get it as soon as it's ready."

Ari was brief, "Gordon, is this line secure?"

"We're bouncing this signal around to each of the twenty-three COMSAT satellites and with every third bounce it passes it through the Encryption Room of the *USS Stennis*. We're as secure as it gets on this planet, Ari. What's up?"

"When Aliza went in to bring your agent out, she interrupted some kind of conference among the kidnappers. One of the documents she retrieved was a picture she didn't understand. We've just identified it as a photo of a Dr. J. Robert Oppenheimer and a device we have further identified as one of your original atomic bombs detonated over Japan in 1945. The photograph is captioned in Arabic 'Fat Man,' There are no obese men in the picture. Could that be referring to the device itself?"

"I don't know, Ari. Squirt it to me and I'll have it checked. Why does this concern you?"

"Because of the other items she found. When she saw this picture she scooped up as much material as she could carry, but they were in something of a hurry and could only take out a few sheets. They seem to be part of a transcription of an earlier meeting. In it we discovered the following phrase:

...and in view of your position in the high reaches of power and policy, we respectfully request that you assist us in our service to Our Lord by providing us with a nuclear device that we can deliver into the homeland of Satan and there detonate it to God's Eternal Glory"

"Our linguists interpret this to mean the group was discussing deploying and detonating a nuclear device somewhere in the United States. My people assess this threat as credible and immediate, and I pass it on to you in that spirit. *Mossad* takes this seriously. If this document had referred to Israel instead of their slang for the United States, we would be on full alert. I urge you as a fellow professional and as a friend of Israel to take this threat completely at face value. Something is brewing. I do not know what it is and at this point my sources are dry. I might have more for you in a week or so; we will see. In the meantime, Gordon, you need to know that the lady in question wasn't the only retrieval during that operation. When Aliza saw that the documents she had stumbled across seemed to involve nuclear weapons, she ordered her team to bring out everybody left alive in the conference room. We assume these people had a hand in kidnapping your agent and I thought you might wish to chat with them. There are six and they're at the hospital, too."

"Thanks, Ari," Cubbage forced his voice to calmness. "I don't think it means much. These crazies are always shooting off about something like that. They all have a plan to knock over the Statue of Liberty or nuke Cleveland. You get used to it over here. But I'll follow up on it if you think there's something in it and you and I will talk again."

"What's up?" Lorraine asked, when Ari had keyed off.

"Aliza ran the Walker job for Ari. When she was inside she uncovered a plot to nuke us here in the States. I tried to damp him down a little because we need a lot more facts and I don't want him telling his people we think it's a credible threat until we can prove it is. However, Ari thinks it's genuine and if he thinks so, so do I. We haven't picked up even a whisper of this, so if Ari's right, who knows how far along it is? They might be ready to light it off right now!"

"Wait a minute, Boss, how can those sand fleas drop a nuke on us? They can barely pull the pins on their own grenades. When I was in the Sandbox driving armor they ran like piss down the side of a wall, and those were their professional troops! These people are just wannabes."

"Two problems with that, Lorraine."

[*There's that first name again,* Lorraine mused to herself *He's <u>got</u> to stop doing that!*]

"First of all, it doesn't take a missile tech or a hot shot jet jockey to deliver a nuke if all you're going to do is sit on top of it and put two wires together. Second, the damned things are so easy to build you and I and Home Depot could probably put one together this afternoon if we had the fission material. This is a threat, all right, very real."

Lorraine was puzzled. "But then, why are countries like Iran taking so long to get one?"

"Because they not only want the bombs, they also want a way to keep them in inventory and some way to deliver them outside the country. For that you have to develop processes, systems, hardware, missiles. Our Home Depot model wouldn't last on the shelf but it would be perfect for detonating 'as is, where is.' And that, Chief Special Agent Baskin, is exactly what I've feared for years – that these crazies would finally figure out that all the stuff surrounding nuclear weapons, the missiles, the troops, the lab coats, the clipboards, the silos...all that stuff is just eye candy. If all you want to do is join the Nuclear Club, you don't need that shit. Just build one, park it somewhere, light it up and let the mushroom clouds commence!"

"Okay, I get it. So we're looking at a poor-man's nuke triggered by crazies that could be anywhere in the US. So let's get on it. What are your orders, Sir?"

"Well, I'm going to get those monkeys back here and squeeze them dry. They obviously know something about this. Maybe they'll lead us to the real perps. Maybe by getting them we've stopped the plot. But I don't think so. Nobody has that much coincidental luck. Whatever happens, I can tell you one thing: we're way past flapping doilies in some Embassy. It's Fuck You Time and there's going to be a Fuck-or and a Fuck-ee. I'm going to try to pencil us in as the former."

Cubbage dialed. "Herb, call Sid and...oh, you've got it...OK...that's right, O-Z-E-L-G-U-V-E-N-H-A-S-T-A-N-E-S-I...yeah, on *Simsek* east side of the *Almanya* Basin a block over from *Guvenilk*. Listen Herb, this is important. The people that brought Agent Sheridan Walker in last night... ...Yeah, yeah, the "Good Samaritans," well, they brought in six other people along with her. We can't wait for her to get out of IC. Go get her right now and when you do, take out anybody that went in there with her... ...No, no, I don't mean kill them! Jesus! Sorry, I want you to *bring them out* along with her."

"Now Herb, this has got to be kept in-house; I repeat *in-house*... ...yeah, this is for us and has to stay that way for awhile... ...no, keep State out of this; I don't trust them. Also I want your DHS liaison out of the loop. They're the ones who held us back from going out and getting Walker when she was first grabbed. Might be some fallout from this [Cubbage realized what he had just said, closed his eyes briefly and shook his head], but I'll back you regardless.... ...right, Herb, there's more to this than I'm telling you. Just found out myself. Can't talk about it now but I'll brief you when I can... ...Yes... ...yes, get em all together and ship em here but I want maximum security all the way home. Two troop per body, weapons hot, repeat, *hot!*. Get em out to the Air Force's Air Support Element in Balgat. Be gentle with them if you can; don't know their condition and I need to have a talk with them. I'll have transport waiting at the field. Get on this right away; we need to move fast... ...no, I'm not expecting interdiction from those assholes...it's our own people, I'm afraid of our own people on this one and...other stuff... ...yep... ...right, *those* people. I can't take the chance they'll start waffling around about some political bullshit. We've got to get these people interrogated and fast. Try not to shoot any of our allies if you can help it, but keep those weapons <u>hot!</u> Tell your team not to assume they're safe until they feel the wheels go up... ...Good. GO!"

Cubbage turned to Lorraine, "Get Hutchinson at Andrews. Offer him anything – you – me – anything. I want a Cee One Four One with operating room, full med/surg team, and weapons squad on the way to Ankara Air Station as fast as he can get their little pink toes moving. Tell him I got no paper for him but I'll owe him for this Big Time No Shit: *Bravo Tango November Sierra* -- put it just that way. I don't care what he wants in return; give it to him and take it out of my next paycheck. Just get that piece of junk off the unstick end of One Niner with those sawbones aboard A-S-A-P."

"On it, Chief. He's a smokin' hot dude so I'll offer him me, but I'm billing you for overtime and cosmetics." Lorraine disappeared through the door, dialing. In a moment her head came back around the door jamb. "Say, Boss...how did they get the message to our people at State that Walker was American and ours?"

Cubbage wasn't paying attention. "Hmmm...takes a lot to explain... methods of intelligence tradecraft...Ari's team is very, very good... storehouse of old tricks..."

Lorraine cocked her head to one side and furrowed her brow, "Hmmph. Well, I guess it worked ok, but why didn't they just stick a note in her pocket?"

The door closed and Cubbage sat back from his desk in thought: get Lorraine on that picture coming from Ari and the copies of all the documents he retrieved from Sheridan's captors...get to Janine right away and tell her about this, then suggest she interrogate the captives coming back with Sheridan. Tell her to get them down to Gitmo where they can be properly interrogated. Get to Feeny at FBI on targets and ask him to work on possible ingress into the Homeland for the bomb parts especially the fissionable material.

Cubbage sighed and thumbed his intercom, "Please get me Janine Mastroantonio; urgent. Track her down." As he waited for his call to be made, Cubbage reviewed his actions one by one. Had he left anything out? Usually his split-second decisionmaking was pretty complete, but this time something nagged at him, wouldn't let him alone. He sat back in his chair and closed his eyes, willing whatever it was in his subconscious mind to come to the surface. Finally it swam up close enough that he could make it out clearly and he felt ashamed for being so consumed with gladness at finding his agent safe, and anxiety being so far behind the plot, that it took all this time to think of it. Janine had said Sheridan was safe. *Where was Alice?*

TWENTY

عشرون

They were all back at the sumptuous Damascus hotel, but this time in a much smaller room and minus the comely servers who were doubtless busy with other devout Muslim businessmen whose devotion could sometimes be dimmed just sufficiently to enable an occasional private indulgence. This was the final session before committing to an attack date, a last meeting to sum up preparations and insure everything had meshed. Rasoul watched as the group arrived in twos and threes.

[*Hmmm...I sense nervousness. Let's start by putting everyone at his ease.*]

Rasoul's voice, until now brimming with cheery good fellowship as he had greeted the members of the group, dropped almost to a whisper, "And now, friends, my brother fighters for *Allah*, my fellow conspirators in the most gigantically beautiful action that is certain to call down upon each of you God's especial favor, may I ask you, humbly, how it was that one of the stinking American whores, charged to your care, *ended up on the international network news?*"

The Arab TV satellite news channel *al Jazeera* usually had large news to report and seldom aired the drearily boring little morality plays that arrived in a continual stream from various groups who believed that since Arabs actually had an outlet, its first priority should be to trumpet the group's individual version of *Islam* to the world. Staffed as it was by experienced international media professionals, the Station usually pigeonholed these amateur efforts and forgot about them. The most junior staffer was always detailed to review everything that came in, and inevitably resented the job as beneath his abilities. The current incumbent slid the latest disk into his viewer and sat back ready once again to fight sleep. This time, however, toward the end, he sat up straight, ran the visual back a few seconds, and watched again. Now *this* was talent. How in the world had these people made this so...so *real*? He summoned his boss, who after a while summoned *his*. This was real theatre and would definitely make it into the next day's airing, but first they needed to find the producers to insure attribution and full credit. Search turned up nothing until one exceedingly intuitive staffer thought to check hospitals for possible injuries during the 'take.' He discovered that a cameraman from a local production house had been brought in almost unconscious. When revived, he had attacked his attendants and had to be restrained. He was diagnosed as having suffered very recently some kind of severe mental trauma, but doctors could get nothing from him about it except the word "splash," which he muttered over and over without apparent meaning. The *al Jazeera* staffer called up the sequence, reviewed it carefully, then informed his bosses that it couldn't possibly have been faked, but was indeed real footage of a real execution. Their reaction was, well, finally something better than these horrible plastic knives and fake blood! The tape was aired that night, picked up by Reuter's, and sent around the world.

At Rasoul's almost whispered question, a cold wind seemed to sweep through the room. Several of the seated men involuntarily shivered. The men in the room had rejoiced at the vision of Alice meeting her just rewards before the entire world. No one but the Speaker realized that this might derail the entire project. He had gathered his team together and told them that the airing of Alice's execution could change everything. His men vowed amongst each other to continue no matter what the cost. Each had joined this cadre to strike a gloriously heavy blow against the great Satan, not to be done casually to death like a careless prostitute then carved piece by piece into a disposal unit out of an upscale Damascus motel room. This "public" place was no place of safety. None of the men present had the least doubt that there waited outside for each of them three or four assassins – close at hand, instantly available - probably soldiers from the look of their host's uniform. Anything that might be done could easily be concealed from everyone in the hotel or on the street. They knew there might be a reckoning for their loss of the woman, that it might be viewed as incompetence, that the project might abort with the Benefactor withdrawing his nuclear weapons, that a sacrificial life might be demanded of them. Maybe of all of them.

Assuming that this question from Rasoul would be forthcoming, the Speaker had prepared himself.

"Honored Host and our Benefactor in this righteous cause," he began nervously, "When we were callously and murderously attacked by Jewish pigs—" Rasoul allowed the suggestion of a furrow to crease his forehead, looked down at his left hand where it lay over his right on his lap palm down and raised it an inch. The Speaker stopped in mid-word.

"Thank you, Honored Guest, I am aware of the circumstances of that treacherous attack." Rasoul looked up directly into the eyes of the Speaker…"But the publicity. Had we not agreed that in view of the importance of your mission they would be disposed of secretly?"

The Speaker wasn't certain whether it was fear or anger that was making his voice shake. "Honored Host, several of our group who are indispensable to the conduct of this operation are also considerably more righteously fundamental than others of us. These members saw the young whore as a symbol that might unite many *Muslim*s behind us…" Seeing that this was about as thin an excuse as would be possible to construct, and not wanting to put off the inevitable, the Speaker simply stopped and waited.

I assume the woman died in the attack? Therefore nothing could be discovered of our plans?" Rasoul asked quietly.

"Of course not Honored Host, our plans are known in total only to the men in this room. Others who must act for us outside this group know only their own tasks and not how they mesh into the whole. We have applied Communist cell theory strictly and rigorously in our planning and organizing and even our recruitment. And yes, the older whore perished in the burning building which consumed both their bodies."

Rasoul nodded in agreement. He was fully engaged with them now, but he had wanted to use the regrettable publicity surrounding the execution to cement his position as leader. It had worked beautifully. They were close to a perfect plan and on the evidence they were able to carry it out. The more he listened to these people, the more he *wanted* this for himself. He made his voice brisk.

"You have done well my brothers. And what good would your organizational plans be without a solid test of their security? In the weeks since we've met I have satisfied myself that nothing has leaked outside our circle. I presume this is your finding as well?"

The Speaker almost wept with relief. "Oh yes, Benefactor, "Nothing has come to us from our agents or recruits. Our plans are well along in production, so we have people in the field here and in America. We would know instantly of the slightest impediment placed in our path anywhere in the world. But this has not happened and we take from this negative occurrence our conviction that the...incident...with the whores remains unconnected to our main objective."

Rasoul smiled, "Then I conclude that these members of your group took the long view of history and acted so as to gather together in righteous wrath many of our fellow Faithful who have not yet committed to *jihad*. I applaud their zeal and their love of our God. I do not think they have materially harmed our cause or our current project. On the contrary, I believe they have offered a distraction that will tend to shift focus away from us should anything be revealed. Now would you review for me the status of preparations?"

"Certainly, Benefactor." The Speaker referred to his notes.

"As you know, we divided this enterprise into several Phases:"

"Phase One: <u>Insert logistical personnel, recruit local operatives and establish places of safe assembly in the US.</u> This has been going on since the Great Holy Day in 2001. We now have all our people in place and ready, not only for this attack, but for many to come. We had originally thought that recruiting local Americans would be difficult, but our Mosques have provided a broad highway to us for the many American Believers who embrace *jihad*. We have been immensely assisted by the current people in power who hate things American, which has been encouraged by the current government's policy of treating our attacks as crimes instead of acts of war, and our warriors as criminals instead of enemy soldiers. That policy has reassured our American recruits that they can help us without being viewed as traitors, only as common criminals who, in American society, are regarded more or less as celebrities."

"Our chief problem was to avoid compromising these recruited American operatives when inserting controllers and technicians from our part of the world. It was important to use our own Middle Eastern people to govern logistics and assemble the bombs. They are far more trustworthy and dependable than even the most devout American recruit. At the same time our people cannot move freely in their society. For that, native Americans are essential. Yet if the Americans were seen to associate with our people, it might cause talk. So we have been careful to keep our leaders in the background. This serves a dual purpose. Our American operatives receive the idea that they are controlling their own destiny atoning for American's sins, so they work doubly hard. And, if capture seems likely, we can throw these American pigs to the police."

"Phase Two: <u>Choose targets and sequester fission materials in the United States</u>. We have transported and distributed to our safe locations in the US multiple disassembled warheads and quantities of loose radioactive material to encase chemical explosives. The routing and transport is already well known to you so unless you have specific questions, I will move past that to target selection, except to say that in bringing the fission plugs into the United States through Veracruz and across the Texas border, we were required to spend large sums so as to appear to be merely drug smugglers. Without burdening you with meaningless details, we brought everything into the hemisphere by a non-container ship to avoid the sophisticated monitoring surveillance that container ships must undergo. Then, when the cargo had been cleared in Mexico, we split the cargo between the fission elements for the bombs, and the aggregate for the chemical bomb casings, gave the aggregate loose radioactive material to our cartel contacts to smuggle in, and sent the fission plugs north into the United States. By using two different routes, we ensured that if one shipment were compromised the other would be completely safe. Once across the border into America, our people extracted the fission plugs from their carriers and distributed them to our bomb assemblers. In processing these fission materials, we used illegal Mexicans as much as possible. Since they must stay concealed from American authorities, it aided concealing our own project as well. We even trans-shipped some of the material from out of the US, into Canada, and later back into America to further confuse the route. All this has incurred great cost, but we feel it is worth the expenditure if we can conceal our stockpiles in the United States itself."

Rasoul waived his hand airily to signify the irrelevance of any sum thus spent. "Money is the least of our concerns. Our poppy fields yield enough to pay any conceivable price. In fact, it's even more pleasurable to use that particular money, since most of it comes roundabout from rich American degenerates desperate for the drugs. In the matter of logistics, you have done brilliantly, my brothers. I am gratified at your skills and attention to details."

The Speaker continued, "In the matter of targeting, Benefactor, we have taken your advice. We have chose one target from each of your categories, one American historical place, one seat of Christian higher learning, and one mass event. You have already received the specific list and our rationales for each– ."

"—Excuse me, Brother," Rasoul interrupted, "but I wish to congratulate you on your selections. The targets you have chosen will strike fear into every American's heart and will destroy hundreds of thousands of them. You have done exceedingly well."

The Speaker came as close as he ever did to grinning and the rest of the group rustled and shuffled in their seats in prideful display. "Thank you, Benefactor," the Speaker continued, "We are greatly pleased at your concurrence."

"Now to Phase Four, <u>Assemble and Deploy</u>: If we wished only to make individual, uncoordinated attacks we could skip this step and go straight to detonation. But as soon as one bomb detonates it will cause an enormous police and military reaction, so we intend to synchronize the blasts. Each of the bombs is housed inside a service-type vehicle that can move almost anywhere unchallenged. The device can be assembled slowly and carefully inside the vehicle and left there as long as required without disturbance. Then at the proper time it may be transported to the blast site at the last minute without any handling of the device itself. This minimizes discovery and permits us to move a device to a safer location if one of the others is discovered prematurely. We developed this idea from the blast at Oklahoma City which, though, not nuclear, was very cleverly planned. The bomber was truly one of us in spirit."

"Phase Five: <u>Synchronize and detonate</u>. Each of our American recruits will drive his vehicle to its appointed place and will trigger the bomb himself at the proper moment. Each vehicle has been chosen so as not to stand out at the location, but blend in with other industrial items – a tour bus, for one example. Each recruit has sworn not to leave the bomb, but to go with it when it explodes. This is critical, for it will leave no witnesses, and it is important to conceal from the Americans how many of their citizens are already involved with us. We want them chasing off after Middle Easterners instead of looking around at each other. This will be a vital asset in future attacks. For, Benefactor, we are planning for the years ahead here as well as our initial strikes. We may be able to strike now and still retain devices and assemblies inside the United States to make future attacks."

"As to our status…" the Speaker couldn't help pausing a second for effect, then said simply, "We are ready. Our bombs are built; our delivery systems are concealed close to the target sites and ready to be driven there; and our recruits are fully trained and willing. You have our proposed date and time of the attack already, so all we need is your signal to go."

Rasoul was pleased. "My brothers, you have done splendidly. I cannot think of a thing you have overlooked. I bless your operation and bid you strike!"

"Allahu Akbar!"

TWENTY-ONE

واحد وعشرين

"Well, Gordon, I'm glad you were able to call back. It's a very busy time for me these days what with the president's upcoming trip to Syria. I'm working with State on the details and they just don't understand *anything*. How can the president show humility at being an American. And make these countries see that we're just thankful they're willing to be our friends in the first place when every little gesture of courtesy gets blown up by the right-wing extremists as some kind of "bow" or something? Honestly, Gordon, I'm beginning to think these tea-party people are worse than our enemies overseas, not to mention...."

Cubbage waited quietly until as she ran on, reflecting that the realities of American politics occasionally eluded her...in fact, almost always eluded her. But that wasn't his problem. He shook his head. He had been prepared to apologize for cutting her off the phone yesterday, but either Janine hadn't noticed or had forgotten about it. Finally he found an opening,

"Janine, I confirmed the identity of the woman in Ankara you called me about yesterday – it's Walker all right. I'm bringing her back to *Walter Reed* for observation. There were some other persons with her. Never know what problems Americans might be causing other people overseas, so in order to insure that we're not blamed for putting anyone in jeopardy, I've asked Turkish officials to, ah, release them to our care."

A lie was always more credible with a little truth in it, Gordon mused, and there was little enough in that one. The extraction mission had gone well. Dressed as Emergency Medical Technicians and a physician, Herb and his team had simply walked in the door of Guven Hastanesi

Hospital checked charts for location, and gurneyed Sheridan and the six heavily sedated kidnappers into waiting ambulances in the pre-dawn darkness. They had timed themselves to arrive just as the bleary night shift workers were concentrating on leaving and before the day managers had arrived. Amid the amiable confusion of shift change, nobody seemed to notice them.

The three mile ride to the Air Force's Balgat facility had been uneventful. The ambulances had driven up the loading ramp and directly into the C-141's cargo bay. Sheridan and the kidnappers had been removed and carefully strapped down with medical people clustering around. The instant the last ambulance cleared the ramp it began to lift back into place and the plane started to taxi. In a few moments the motion stopped and a rocking vibration signaled that the pilot was running up his engines at the end of the tiny runway. It was then that things started to unravel.

Lights were observed at the base of the control tower. A car came racing across the apron and turned onto the far end of the runway toward the big transport just as the ponderous aircraft waddled onto the runway centerline and slowly began rolling. The *Starlifter's* pilot, being a guest in that country and not wishing to give a bad impression, waved cheerily out the cockpit window as he gunned his sixty-foot-wide, quarter-million-pound aircraft toward the oncoming car. The impromptu game of "Chicken" ended abruptly just as his wheels came off the concrete when the car swerved at full speed out of the aircraft's path and skidded across the grass, coming to rest windshield deep in an open trench filled with what was later identified as municipal sewage. Days later, when the after-action report reached him, Cubbage was greatly pleased to discover there had been no casualties or serious injuries to the occupants who turned out to be Turkish police. His only comment when authorizing compensation to the Turkish government was to note in passing that the huge charges for extensive cleaning and disinfecting might have been considerably reduced had the windows been rolled up.

"Well, Gordon, what are you going to do with them?"

"They're on their way to Walter Reed, Janine, grounding at Andrews this afternoon. But that's not why I called. I have received information from some of our overseas contacts that a group is planning a new attack against us here at home. My sources tell me this time they're going to attempt to detonate a nuclear weapon and it's possible they might actually have gotten hold of one. We don't know how they're planning to get it into the country or how far along they already are, or what they're planning to hit. We might not want to go public right away to avoid driving them into deep cover, but I suggest you put the entire Homeland Security apparatus on full emergency alert."

Janine was silent for a full minute. "Who told you this?"

"If you don't mind I'd rather not reveal that. These people came to me in good faith and they would be at serious risk of death if it came out."

"Well…do you think it's possi…my GOD, Gordon, do you think it's POSSIBLE?"

Cubbage hesitated a moment, then said in a very quiet voice, "Yes, Janine, I do. Technically speaking it's easy. Simplest if they bring the parts in piece by piece and build it here then set it off with a suicide trigger. Politically speaking, we're much less prepared today than we were even last year. People high in our Congress dislike our military power and insult our military people when they come to testify. Some of them say right out that we have no business defending ourselves, that all these attacks are somehow *our* fault. But that's not the major issue. Our immediate problem is that this new administration – I include the President here – has made us look soft and yielding and defenseless to the whole world. So our enemies think they'll have their best shot at us while he's in office. Why wouldn't these animals take another swing at us? *We've been begging for it.*""

"I've told you this for months. Feeny's told you this for months. Told you and Ayers over at the White House and the rest. Our military doesn't say much about it because it's not their place to comment on politics. It's their job to shut up and do their job. But it's *my* place because I'm here on a political appointment, just as you are. Besides, by now the military's gotten the feeling nobody listens to them anyway. Look at McSorely in Afghanistan. Put there by the president himself. Asks to be reinforced and three months go by before a decision! Nobody listens. Nobody seems to care. "Do I think it's possible? *Janine, I think it's inevitable!*"

Cubbage decided to level with her. "But we have a chance of a possible outside confirmation. The men coming back with Walker belong to the group that kidnapped her. I believe they're part of the same group that wants to explode the bomb. They'll be coming into Andrews on the same aircraft. I suggest trans-shipping them to Guantanamo right away. I urgently request that you start a full program of interrogation on these men aimed specifically at finding out what they know about a nuclear plot. We need to know how many bombs, what type, how they'll be triggered, and what targets."

"All right, Gordon, let me get to work."

"Thanks, Janine. I'll let you know as soon as I get anything more."

"One more thing, Gordon. That horrible execution of that poor little girl that was just on all the news, did that have anything to do with this bomb plot?"

Cubbage was silent for a moment. "Well, Janine, I don't think the murder had anything to do with it directly. But these men I'm bringing back with Walker are involved in both. They either performed the execution or ordered it done. These are bad men, Janine, very bad men."

"But how do you know they did that terrible thing?"

Cubbage had a hard time even talking about it. "I just received a copy of the tape, Janine. From our development of the details on it, it's clear that the victim was Agent Walker's twelve-year-old daughter, Alice."

TWENTY-TWO

اثنان وعشرون

Sheridan Walker moved the chain adjuster nut two of its six flats to the right, causing the chain to tighten slightly between its sprockets. She then sidled across behind the lift to equalized the other swingarm's adjuster nut the same two flats to the right, pulled the rear wheel of the big road Ducati rearward to bring the adjuster stops in contact with the swingarm ends and spun the axle nut finger tight, then finished with a 30mm wrench.

"There!" she exclaimed proudly. "Chain's back at 29mm stretch. Now, darling, do yours."

Eliot Walker took the wrenches from her grimy hand and set about adjusting the chain on his own Ducati. "What was that torque value for the axle nut?" he asked.

"Railroad Torque," Sheridan laughed, "Tight as you can get it, then half a turn."

For years Sheridan had ridden cruisers, great ponderous, seven-hundred-pound behemoths, bars pulled back, feet out in front – or as her husband, Eliot, described it, riding a birthing table -- until finally he had persuaded her onto his old Ducati ST4. Seating herself in the saddle, she had complained bitterly of the forward leaning position and the rearward pegs that forced a small amount of her weight down onto her wrists on the bars. He paid no attention when she told him she could never ride this way, that it would ruin her shoulder muscles, and ok, she'd take it out but she'd be right back.

Six and a half hours later as Eliot was in his study putting the finishing touches on a report, he heard the boom-boom-boom-boom of his idle at the garage door below the log addition. When he got to the basement with the customary glass of Chardonnay in each hand, Sheridan had dismounted and was wiping down the fairing with Pledge.

"I'd ask you how it went," Eliot remarked, "but I'm not sure you could talk through that grin."

Sheridan came to him, took her glass, and embraced him, nuzzling his chest, murmuring, "You bastard! Why didn't you TELL me?"

Eliot cupped her chin and raised her eyes to his, "Well, my little rabbit, I did…but you don't learn from men until you try it out yourself. And now you know. That big hog you ride is for profiling. A Ducati is for your soul."

From that time on the two of them had ridden together, he on his old ST4 and she on a 1000GT. From having been a motorcycle operator she grew into a superb rider, fast without recklessness, decisive without aggression. Their work took them far across the world from each other. But whenever they were able to come together there was the bond of the miles they had shared and the thin, sweet song of the breeze ruffling through their hair as they stood of an early morning contemplating the sun coming up and lighting the chrome bars of their mounts. They rode a staggered close-trail formation, both in the same lane one three feet behind and slightly to the side of the leader. Occasionally they would come up on a gaggle of giant chugging chromed two-wheel behemoths, their riders and passengers plugged into country rock on their MP3, passengers sipping sodas and mired in their Blue Tooth receivers. Then Eliot and Sheridan would roll up to 90 and flash past in perfect formation. Once past, they'd glide back over in front of the group as though roped together, shrink and vanish into the distance.

But all that was different now. Whatever had happened to her overseas, the Sheridan who had returned to him was just a shell. The woman who inhabited her body was dug in far down below the surface with no path upwards and nothing to light that path if it could even be found. Her inner light of human emotion had been crushed down inside her. Indeed she had willed her own intelligence to follow as she dived deep into her sanctuary that was also her prison. The vision of her daughter was unacceptable. So Sheridan refused to accept anything else. She had been brought safely home by hard, tough soldiers accustomed to offering their views down the narrow end of an automatic rifle but who for Sheridan had only the gentlest hands and the kindest eyes, seasoned, unemotional professionals who after taking a good look at her and hearing from others about Alice, talked quietly among themselves of revenge. Meanwhile, mistrustful of the daylight that might bring her daughter back to her as she now was, and dreading the night whose cloak refused to shield her from the image of what had been in the chair, Sheridan crouched in the dark space below her skin and waited for better times.

Rushed home on compassionate leave, Eliot Walker vowed he would find her again wherever she hid inside herself. He set about his journey toward his wife with simple things, easy steps, familiar smells. Her daughters Reagan and Patton took turns watching and guarding. Each of them held her when she rocked back and forth keening a high thin, rhythmless song of unspeakable sadness when the image that had been burned behind her eyes came out and disintegrated the vision of her sweet little Beebee as she had been before. When the execution splashed all over the world's news media, the entire family made sure Sheridan never saw it.

Slowly, very slowly, the changes came. She began taking her own nourishment, sipping coffee with both hands around the cup, Eliot kneeling next to her helping her tip. She came to be able to choose shirts and shoes, sometimes matching, sometimes not. She sat on her bike with Eliot holding her in the seat, leaning her forward and carefully moving her hands onto the grips. And as the weeks passed she discovered to her astonishment that she was able to be alone for minutes at a time.

The Sheridan of the past had always made it a firm rule of her life to watch at least three hours of television a year. But now Eliot encouraged her to view as much as she could to immerse her deeper in things of the world, safe images to add to the familiar articles in her safe haven. They sat together most nights watching the comedy of MSNBC Nightly News, then turning for truth to Fox. One evening they broke in as the Fox anchor was threading one story into another. "...over what has become known as the Naweoba Massacre. Afghan military sources today confirmed one hundred twenty-seven dead and eleven hundred fourteen wounded in what is seen as the worst military setback this year for insurgent forces in the northern provinces. General McSorely credited a joint effort between Afghan and Pakistani military for the victory. And in a related story the White House today met with members of the Pakistani military on the progress of clearing the Uzhd Ghwazhai region along the Pakistan Afghan border. National Security Advisor Jeremiah Ayers is shown here in talks with the Pakistani delegation made up of senior Pakistan army and air force officers" – pictures on the log walls of the Walker's spacious addition vibrated and almost jumped off the wall with the concussions. The air filled with smoke and flame and deafening roar as the rounds from Sheridan's Beretta hammered the television screen into a jagged ruin.

"Don't know what it was, Doctor, something she was watching. Wasn't paying much attention. Something on the news."

The Walter Reed Trauma Wing physician stroked his chin pensively and gazed at the ruined screen, the holes in the wall behind it, and at Eliot. Eliot went on, "We're watching TV and all of a sudden out of the blue she pulls her service piece out of the magazine stand and unloads it into the screen. I'm sure that was the target. The metro cops thought it was me, but she's a crack shot and if she'd been shooting at me you'd be talking to a body bag."

Sheridan had relapsed back into her catatonic state and, sedated, was rushed back to the hospital. The doctor made up his mind. "Colonel, I don't think this is for me. We're doing our best for your wife medically. I'm going to hand the rest of it off to her own people. Something's going on here that we aren't seeing. Can you work with them directly or do you need orders from my folks up the line?"

"No problem, doctor. I'll call her boss and get this moving. I don't know what the hell is going on here either, but I'm sure this has something to do with what happened to her in Syria. She was doing fine and then all of a sudden she's back to Square One. If we could have retrieved Alice after...after what happened to her, well, maybe that would have helped. I don't know. Nothing we can do about that now."

Sheridan lay drugged and almost conscious, instruments and IV tree surrounding her bed. Once in a while a friendly face came into focus then went away. None of it mattered much to her. During the weeks since her rescue, she had begun slowly to regain her presence. The horrific visions of her last view of Alice were mercifully beginning to fade. She had seen dimly a stairway from her place of safety deep within herself upwards toward the light of the world. One part of her knew the stairway wasn't real yet she clung to the vision of it for it helped focus her mind on the slow progress toward regaining who she had been. She wished to run up those stairs and tumble out into the verdant fields of sanity. But steps faltered and lagged like an anxiety dream, trying to escape the bear chasing her but running in molasses. Nevertheless, through all the past weeks she had climbed painfully step by step until she could see clearly the welcome door on the landing above. Then suddenly something had tripped her and she had been flung back down to the base, slammed into the ground of her hideaway with her breath knocked out. The terrible thought came to her that although this had happened to her once, this time there would be no climbing out. She lay there inside her own mind knowing she had failed and would be doomed to inhabit this dark place for the rest of her life. She wailed a torment, cried out for her husband, begged for death, but nothing came to her except silence and the pressure of a hard lump that pained her back where it lay unnoticed partly protruding from under her while she cried. She could feel it poking her like a rake handle lying in the grass. As her sobs began to taper off into snuffles of self-pity, it occurred to Sheridan that there had been nothing here the last time she had been flung into this loathsome pit – yes. Now she saw it for what it was, not a safe haven but a prison, a Well of the Damned where, if she permitted herself to remain, it would be at peril of her very existence.

"I don't know, Colonel. She's one of our top agents but she was on vacation when this happened. I assure you she was not acting for the Agency. If she had been, I'd get you cleared for it and put you in the picture. You'd need to know what she was doing in order to help her. But there just wasn't anything, nothing at all...." Cubbage had given orders that any transmittals about Sheridan would come to him. The psychiatrist who contacted CIA had been routed direct to the Director's office and Cubbage had summoned Eliot. Every intuitive sense Gordon Cubbage had developed during his decades in intelligence screamed at him that he needed to find out what happened to Sheridan and do it fast. Eliot Walker was Cubbage's first step.

Eliot tried to keep the panic out of his voice. "So if she wasn't acting for you people, then whatever triggered this episode occurred during her captivity. And shooting up the TV came from something she had just remembered. So what the hell am I going to do for her? You've got to help me, sir. I know she's one of your people, but this is my wife we're talking about. She's all the way back to where she was when you first brought her back from Ankara. Jesus! What am I going to do?"

"Look, Colonel, I want you to stay on this for me. There's something going on here way past Sheridan's abduction and – I'm sorry to say this to you, sir – way past your daughter's death. I don't know what it is but my gut tells me something's brewing…something very bad…and Sheridan is the key to it. I have information that you're not cleared for that I need to talk to Sheridan about. I want her back whole again just as you do, but I need to know exactly what happened to her because I'm beginning to think this may be a national security issue. I know you're due to be redeployed off compassionate leave back to Afghanistan. I want you here with her. I'm asking you as an officer of our government to delay your duty overseas. We need to get to the bottom of this and we need to do it ASAP."

But this time, instead of getting lost inside herself, Sheridan realized she was not alone. There was a Thing there with her that had somehow come to her as she neared the top of her symbolic virtual stairway. It had accompanied her in her tumble back down into her prison. She lay where she had stopped falling, idly speculating on what it might be, feeling over her memories except for that one door that must never be opened. No, it didn't come from there, but near there, maybe from further down the same dark passageway that held the door.

The broadcast media was making an all-out effort to support the President in his "Softer America" Middle East policy. Part of it involved downplaying the execution of an American pre-teen by terrorists, trivializing the story as hearsay even though the film of Alice's murder was everywhere. Part of it involved giving full play to friendly contacts between nations of that region and the US. So MSNBC and others sent their best reporters and their most agile cameramen to record the Pakistani visit. TV experts lit the conference room to provide a soft, friendly setting while at the same time permitting maximum, good-photo-op exposure of the confreres. Sheridan cast her mind back over the events leading up to her relapse. She saw once again the conference room and each delegate seated around a long table. As her mind took her memory down the row of seats, she realized what the Thing was that had slammed through her brain like a locomotive and now lay beneath her in her dark solitude quietly waiting to be brought into the light. It was this Thing that forced Sheridan to realize she must climb that staircase once more no matter how long it took. Her duty demanded she bring this Thing up into the world. And maybe, in so doing, she'd bring herself back along with it. In the Oval Office conference room, lit and photographed by experts, carefully staged by White House diplomatic professionals, and reported by nurturing media anchors, the senior Pakistani military leader, a four star general, seated in the place of honor just to the right of Presidential National Security Advisor Dr. Jeremiah Ayers, was Rasoul.

TWENTY-THREE

ثالثة وعشرون

"I greatly appreciate each of you being able to attend today on such short notice and I'm sure you're wondering why I asked you here." Jeremiah Ayers was at his steel-hand-velvet-glove best this morning. He ignored the fact that that anybody in their right mind, receiving a "request" to attend a National Security meeting held down the hall from the Oval Office would probably get there the previous night and camp on the stairs. And he glossed over the fact that, being government employees, each of the attendees had to come Or Else! It was his gentle way of reminding them all that while they didn't exactly report to him, nonetheless he held them by the balls or their female genitalian equivalent.

Ayers had set up this meeting in a panic after a call from POTUS in Damascus late the previous day. Ayers hated being summoned on the squawker; it was invariably bad news and invariably required him to bust his lovely white ass to get something done *yesterday!* He should have been flattered. The president had called from the middle of serious and intensely publicized talks with the Syrian government. His visit to Syria was the centerpiece of the president's attempt to craft a new American image in the Middle East. "Softer America" he called it. He intended to renounce America's former evil ways under previous administrations, especially the last one whose incumbent generated lasting hatred among everyone whose opinions really counted by acting unilaterally to defend America after the 9/11 attack instead of seeking help and concurrence from the United Nations like any civilized folk would do. America, the president felt, should take its place as a humble and unexceptional member of the community of nations in Spaceship Earth's Global Village. His nation would be best off spending its time and its treasure serving others while being directed in those services by his care givers only this time on a global scale. The president realized that most Americans wanted America's interests tended to first, so he set his first job to replace that regrettably short-sighted viewpoint with a full understanding by his countrymen of how bad America really was. He planned to do this by encouraging open discussion of America's faults with anyone who would come to the table. He sought continual negotiation of all differences between America and any other culture that wished to raise its voice in protest at American perfidy, and he was ready to enhance and uplift those cultures even at the expense of America's own. America thereby fitted herself seamlessly into the global network and at the same time expiated her past sins. A neat bit of multi-tasking, POTUS chuckled to himself.

Apparently it was working. He had been invited for talks by the Syrians largely on the strength of his having marginalized the American observance of 9/11. During his first year in office he had been able to smooth it away from the theme of "Patriot Rage and Resolve" desired by ignorant Americans who did not yet realize that 9/11 was part of America's necessary punishment and substitute the trivializing idea of "Multicultural Remembrance And Service." The Prime Minister of Israel commented dryly that giving up one's moral position in return for conversation seemed not to be a very good bargain, but he was just a Jew and what did he know? His view was lost in the shouting of presidential supporters who took time out from their adulatory praise of POTUS to accuse Israel of fomenting violence among the obviously discriminated and blatantly exploited Palestinians, so the Jews' comments on this unrelated matter somehow didn't count.

Besides, pundits among his supporters noted that no objections were raised by other Middle Eastern countries, so obviously the initiative was paying off. Removing the idea of having been shamelessly attacked, and substituting a formless observance that was almost a celebration of 9/11 certainly appealed to the Syrians, and avoided the president having to acknowledge that ninety per cent of the 9/11 attackers were Syrian nationals. Yes, the president ruminated, ratcheting down the patriotism surrounding 9/11 certainly paid direct dividends to his foreign policy achievements and made a big impression at home, although occasionally some of his base went overboard. A plan by a left-wing political action group, the *Santa Monica Progressive Tide,* to stage an event on 9/11 commemorating the attack as "Multi-Culturalism In Action: An Indigenous, Disempowered People Reaching Out Into The World Toward Self-Awareness" was, at the request of the Administration, quietly shelved. He had had to call the promoters himself, but he was able to stop an event that of course had merit but would have brought millions to Washington in protest.

Where the Syrians were concerned, the president knew all he had to do was keep talking and holding out friendship to these people and soon they would respond to his obvious good intentions. Jimmy Carter had put this theory to the test a generation ago and had his rear end, and his second term, handed smoking to him by Iranian extremists. But in spite of this object lesson, POTUS knew that kindness and sympathy would prevail over hatred and even over *jihad.* To make that happen, he needed his countrymen to forget that 9/11 was an unprovoked attack by a terrorist army at war with America, and accept it as a criminal tragedy perpetrated by unfortunate have-nots who really aren't so bad once you get to know them. History must be rewritten to eliminate the rage and horror associated by Americans with 9/11. Well, he had no less an expert than Jeremiah Ayers to accomplish this for him. Considering the job Ayres had done out at Berkeley getting everyone on board believing just what they should in order for things to go smoothly during the campaign, this thing with the Syrians should go very well.

Of course Jerry had his work cut out for him. Instead of realizing that we had brought 9/11 upon ourselves, a number of misguided Americans still resented the attack. But Ayers was well on the way to substituting the idea that these *jihadists* were stalwart freedom fighters, loyal citizens of their own land attempting any way they could to counter a huge country's bad intentions, and that America should see this and give them whatever they wished of us in recompense for our past mistakes. If we did this, POTUS felt, they'd eventually see our new, more congenial face and agree to refrain from attacking us anymore. POTUS was certain, and Ayers agreed, that the people who attacked us and who ranted at us from their caves and secret enclaves would join in the brotherhood of man once they realized they were seriously and earnestly being invited.

So far everything was going beautifully. POTUS had made it a point to bow low to the Syrians and assembled ambassadors in front of news cameras. The photo op was designed for the Middle Eastern media to show to locals that the great American president came to them hat in hand. He wasn't spouting American interests but seeking accord. Double shot, he thought, because it also pacified his ultra-left supporters at home who wanted America to be seen to beg. These people had gotten him elected and he owed them big time. Actually, *triple* shot, he smiled to himself, because he actually believed in this line of diplomacy and was determined to carry it forward despite the reactionary right at home and the subtle yet clearly articulated disapproval of his military leaders.

The military…? Well, he ran the military, didn't he? When he was finished modulating their voice and reining them in, they'd spend a lot less time going around his administration and saying all sorts of things to Congress. It couldn't fail to relax the tensions in the world that the very existence of a huge American military structure created. Then it would be time to see about shifting the American legal structure just slightly into compliance under the UN Charter, with the long-term goal of placing *all* US forces under UN Security Council control just as Europe had. Bringing the US Constitution into line with the Charter would take a little longer but would become inevitable once US forces were divested into the UN. Europeans had the right idea: let a supra-national body be responsible for the safety of all nations so that each nation has no responsibility to its own citizens. After all, what real difference was there between America and Zimbabwe?

Yet POTUS knew he still needed to find a way to slip this across without a lot of dissent. Lord! If my real plans came out it would cause a civil war! I need a military NAFTA, the inspiration of a previous administration but regrettably applying only to trade on this continent. I need something like the recent health care reform bill that would entrench the people of my party – and by extension myself – as the final arbiters of each individual American life. Life itself was after all simply one's health, and what greater step could he take toward his vision of a true European-style socialist State than to control each American's health, thereby telling each of them who can live and who cannot and reminding them every day of their lives of the power held over them by the government. The twin hammers of withholding health care and twelve million new alien voters would secure his party's power for a generation. And after that time passed, there would be only one face on America...theirs. But better not even think about that now; the conservative Right was still too strong even in his own party for that bit of business. Later, after his policies had been endorsed by a second-term election, *then* he'd see about setting America into its natural place in the world as just another pleasant nation among many. They called him "the first post-American President,' did they? Well, they had no idea...no idea at all!

Then, during a break midway through the morning conference, a minor official on the Syrian President's staff took POTUS aside into one of the cool, dark rooms adjacent to the cameras and handshaking and in a quiet voice laid a bombshell on him that threatened the immediate destruction of his legacy, his administration, his party, and all his careful plans, "Our intelligence services have received information of a plot to detonate a nuclear weapon somewhere in the United States. We believe it will occur within a matter of days. We pass on this information to you in the spirit of our new accords of friendship and trust."

In an instant the Syrian was gone down the hall and POTUS was left standing in a cool dark room earnestly desiring to vomit. If the people whom he courted, the people who, he assured America, would respond with friendship to his new diplomacy of apology, succeeded in something on this scale, his entire foreign policy and most of his domestic policies would lie in ruins. He had built his presidency on an open-handed approach to these people underpinned with an acceptance of American guilt for their miseries. An attack now would mean they repudiated his overtures.

Worse, at this very moment his supporters were going about in America trumpeting our guilt at being wealthy and saying we had to be more like the other nations of the world in accepting government intervention in each life. He based most of his moves toward the true distribution of wealth desired by his party largely on eventual American acceptance of this wealth guilt and the submergence of individuality beneath a blanket of statist control, just as his party for generations had built its power on white guilt and the benevolent control of blacks...for their own good of course. In order to plant that guilt firmly in American culture, his party had forced American blacks to adopt a subculture of victimology.

The subtext was starkly simple: if a black succeeded in America it was not because he was *equal* to whites, but because he was leveraged and assisted and nurtured and encouraged and given special treatment *by the liberals and leftists who just happened to be white.* If a white man succeeded it was somehow because of his white skin; if a black man succeeded it was *in spite of* his black skin. White bigotry never diminished and could be identified *by skin color.* Blacks were *never* bigoted and could never be racist. In the liberal/progressive governing model, black Americans formed a single-issue underclass perpetually emerging toward, but never quite achieving, full equality. This dynamic could never be permitted to resolve itself, since liberal/progressives needed a grateful underclass to set themselves apart. If a majority of black Americans actually achieved a measure of equality, they would no longer look to the liberal/progressive power structure to sustain them. And, if not respected as Care Givers, people might start asking what it was that liberal/progressives actually contributed to society at large, and all those comfy social billets and all that friendly air time would vanish.

Now, his party was taking the broad step of shifting victim status to all Americans but this time *the party* would clearly emerge as the savior. Soon the "cult of individuality" – that wonderful European term carrying within it the glimmer of envy, would be dead, and Americans would have to look to their government for everything. A terrorist attack now – an attack by *Struggling Islamic Separatists*, he reminded himself – especially using the nuclear weapons he had tacitly approved of other nations possessing, would galvanize Independents, right-wing Democrats, and Conservatives alike behind the false gods of Patriotism and Duty. There were still many Americans who liked being American. This would change slowly but if challenged now would resurge and choke off any possibility of a Socialist America in his lifetime.

In order to meet the threat of nuclear attack just handed to him a minute ago, calling upon his military or police services was out of the question. The very existence of the plan would be almost as damaging as getting nuked. There was one ace in the hole, though, somebody who could be relied upon to spin the situation to his advantage no matter what happened.

The red phone on Ayers' desk buzzed.

"Jerry, how are you?"

Ayers was startled but forced his voice to calmness, "Mr. President, what an unexpected pleasure. How can I help you, sir?"

"Jerry, we have a problem."

["<u>We</u> *have a problem. Holy shit.*"]

"I was just informed by a member of the Syrian government that they have picked up a plot to detonate nuclear weapons within the continental United States. Do you have any intel on this?"

Jeremiah hoped the relief didn't sound in his voice. "Yes, Mr. President, my office has been in touch with CIA Director Cubbage through Janine Mastroantonio about it. When we rescued the CIA agent who allowed herself to be captured, she attempted to cover herself by claiming a plot of some kind. DHS thoroughly interrogated the captives from that rescue and came up with nothing."

"Are you sure, Jerry? If we're hit again it will destroy my "Softer America" diplomatic initiatives and make it very difficult for us to continue drawing in our old enemies as new friends. I've built my entire foreign policy on the idea we can convert these people to friendship if we just admit America's past mistakes. If we're attacked in the middle of these negotiations, and if the people I'm talking with are suspected to have a hand in it…well, you get the point."

"Absolutely, Sir. And I would guess that it would make the rest of your domestic policies fairly untenable as well. We can't permit that to happen. We must move in the direction you have cast for us. This could be the end of all of that. We subjected those captured terr… those captured fighters to our entire repertoire of legal and permissible interrogation techniques and not a single word came out of any of them about any plot. I can send you synopses of the interrogation transcripts, or the raw tapes if you wish."

"That won't be necessary. But I want you to stay on top of this personally, Jerry, and take the point on it. If I use NSA or CIA or

Defense this will leak to the world, the Conservatives will jump on it, and the outcry will be almost as bad as the attack itself. In order to accomplish anything *I must preserve the <u>appearance</u> of friendship between both sides no matter what the reality.*"

"Yes, Sir; I'll stay on it myself."

"If anything surfaces I'm to be informed immediately. And Jerry, just so we understand each other, we can't have any more attacks in the Homeland. Both of us will rise or fall on that one thing alone."

"Yes, Sir, I understand."

POTUS disconnected. Jeremiah Ayers took a moment or two of Personal Time to let his hands stop shaking. My GOD! Was there actually something to this bullshit that stupid cunt was peddling? And what the hell could *he* do about it? He could spin facts to make a giraffe out of a garbage can, but this was something else. Jesus! The President had just told him both their asses would be hanging out and it was up to Jeremiah Kerfucking Ayers to stop it! Well, the important thing was to keep everything quiet, and to do that he needed more information on this fucking shit and he needed it right now!

From deep in his solacing leather chair behind his huge desk completely bare except for a red telephone, National Security Advisor Jeremiah Ayers surveyed The House: Gordon Cubbage, conservative asshole who got his appointment God only knew how…Janine Mastroantonio, a no-talent sacrificial bimbo put in at DHS to keep the screw down on Security and make sure if anything happened the blame stayed in her house…The Walker woman who started all this shit getting grabbed like that and her stupid dau…well, don't speak ill of the departed…so let's get this shit moving.

"I greatly appreciate each of you being able to attend today on such short notice and I'm sure you're wondering why I asked you here."

Janine Mastroantonio was brisk, "Well, Jeremiah, we're certainly honored you've asked us here and we're ready to help with whatever it is you feel we can contribute. "

Gordon Cubbage was not in the mood for schmoozing and decided to get this over with. "Actually, Dr. Ayers, seeing the personnel here I would guess it's about the forthcoming attack. May I ask what's being done with my people's assessment? Are you following this up through our other networks?"

Ayers had to get the meeting back under control. "Director," I've asked you here today to discuss the atta…your report." I asked Janine and your agent to attend so we can prosper by a completely full and frank flow of information among us and decide how to address it. "'

Cubbage wasn't giving up so easily. "Well, from the short notice, I would infer that you're pretty worried about it. I am, too. In fact, before I came over I back-checked my entire file on this situation and re-analyzed all the facts just to make sure I hadn't missed anything. Dr. Ayers, there will be an attack by" – Cubbage searched for an acceptable phrase and tried manfully not to sound contemptuous – "*Self-Terminating Energy Distribution Experts* somewhere in this country in a matter of weeks, possibly days. We don't know the date, but we do know that the group is planning to detonate at least one nuclear or sub-nuclear radioactive weapon in the Homeland. We know their targeting parameters and we're guessing that some American historic place will be hit along with a social event. Our sources…my sources…have placed the attack within the next week or month at the most. My own analysts place the casualties at between ten and seventy thousand killed outright with an additional minimum of two hundred thousand deaths or serious illnesses from contamination. Now, sir, *what are you going to do with this information?*"

Ayers had finally regained a measure of his composure from POTUS' phone call and was now ready.

"Janine, what do your people say?"

"Well Jeremiah" -- the first naming was deliberate -- we simply haven't received anything even close to this information from our prisoners. Remember, these were the same people that had kidna…ah…detained Agent Walker and her daughter and were the men Agent Walker said she overheard plotting. We've interrogated them twice -- the last time at

Director Cubbage's specific request -- and each time they insisted there's no plot at all."

Cubbage shook his head. "Madame Secretary, how did you question these people?"

Janine was firm. "We followed the President's outline for acceptable interrogation techniques to the letter. Before we questioned them each man was read his Miranda rights and each man had his ACLU attorney present the entire time. We put all the questions to them that you sent over. Of course, no questions were asked that might threaten to violate the prisoner's Civil Rights – "

"—Madame Secretary," Cubbage interrupted, "May I point out for the record that these men have no 'Miranda rights?' They have no civil rights at all for the simple reason *they are not American citizens*." Cubbage's voice dropped low into the danger zone, "And do you mean to say that these ACLU lawyers *prevented* you from asking questions you needed to ask in order to stop a nuclear attack on the United States?"

"Well, Gordie, the way you put it sounds like we don't care! We do! But that's the way we do business these days, and I for one applaud it. These man-caused disasters must be addressed without hatreds and emotions getting in the way. It's much fairer to everyone and we Americans are supposed to be fair…to everyone. There's no evidence of an attack except what your agent says and she was under drugs and…ah…other influences at the time."

Cubbage strove to keep his voice from shaking, "But there *is* other evidence! I reported *Mossad*'s assessment to you as soon as it came in! They outline an attack with enough similar features to Agent Walker's report that it can't possibly be coincidence. And they have nothing at all to gain by deceiving us."

Ayers smiled the smile of One Who Was Privy, "Well, Director, they just might. The president is right now engaged in some very delicate talks with Israel's enemies and *Mossad* might just be interested in derailing them. Besides, *Mossad* uses discredited and forbidden extreme interrogation techniques. Their torture subjects are liable to say anything just to get them to stop."

Cubbage looked at Ayers a long time with such intensity that nobody else spoke. "Dr. Ayers, you've never actually done any interrogating, have you? You've never actually *been* interrogated. You've never actually *witnessed* what happens to subjects, to their minds. Have you? He went on without waiting for a reply. "You people *hope* that you'll get information your way. You *wish* to get it without what you call torture. But I say to you, sir, that right at this very minute you have no idea what's going to happen *because you haven't asked*! If we have even a hint of an attack we need to squeeze these prisoners as hard as we can to determine the exact targets and specific dates. Then, if it's immanent, inform the country of the impending attack and hope we can discourage these people from actually doing it by the sheer publicity. I don't think that will work at this late date but it's our only option. If we can't get any more intel out of our captives, announce it anyway and put everybody on full alert. If they do try to detonate any of their weapons, we might get the chance to save some lives and maybe even prevent the bomb going off. There's also a slim chance we might be able to get hold of one or two of them, or maybe some citizen will see something that will lead us to them."

Ayers wanted to show his superiority, "Director Cubbage, don't you think my people throughout our defense system are fully aware of the possibilities? We've listened to the generals and the admirals and you guys and frankly most of us have a real problem envisioning these simple desert people launching something as complex as a nuclear device – "

"—Dr. Ayers," Cubbage interrupted, "How can I make this clear to you? *There's nothing complex about a nuclear bomb!"* What most people know about nukes comes from watching Manhattan Project documentaries on the History Channel. Sure, it was tough back then for those guys to go from theory to fact. It took a lot of lab coats and blackboards and crossed fingers…but *once the bomb was proven to work it was nothing more than a few pieces of dime store hardware!"* The so-called complexity comes from the requirement to throw one of the damned things over the North Pole and hit a thirty-mile-wide city you don't happen to own. For that you need inertial guidance, vibration damping, automatic triggering, manual just-in-case circuitry, telemetric guidance monitoring, and enough rocket fuel to get it past the border. And if you're going to keep it around for decades 'just in case,' you'll need cryogenic storage, telemetric monitoring, and anti-radiation procedures to keep your people safe. All this shit is hideously complex. *But it has nothing to do with the bomb itself!"*

"An atomic device is two pieces of fissionable material shaped a certain way shoved together at a certain speed. That's it! That's all there is! You need the material, a ram, and a case to keep the rain out. It's nice to have some way to cart it around to where you want it to go off, but if you build it in place you don't even need that. That's *all* that stands between us and a quarter mile crater somewhere. If all you want to do is light off the sonofabitch somewhere inside a zone three thousand miles wide, why just load it into a vehicle, run it into a parking lot, and push a button. If you've got somebody stupid enough to sit on top of it, then you don't even need the button."

"Dr. Ayers, *we are at war with these people.* These prisoners are not *Action Oriented Zealots* or *Disputatious Islamic Life Takers.* They're not part of some "Planned Nuclear Event Encounter Group." These are *enemy soldiers* bent on our destruction. If they can get hold of nuclear weapons they will surely use them. Nothing we can do will stop them except to capture them or kill them. I think these prisoners who came back with Sheridan Walker know what the plan is, the type of target, and approximately when they intend to strike. They have information we need and if you don't go after it vigorously, whatever they do will be on your head. *Can you bear that burden, Sir?"*

The room was silent. Cubbage was finished, in more ways than one, he realized. Ayers rose half out of his chair and when he spoke his voice was shrill almost to a scream, "Director, we are not going to torture anybody! I don't care about the potential for lives saved. We are going to do what we know is best for this country *no matter how many get killed* and we will not be diverted by a bunch of hard-line rightwing scare talk! So if Janine says she couldn't find a plot, *then there is no plot!"*

With visible effort Ayers lowered his voice to a conversational tone. "But OK, suppose you're right. Let's suppose there really is a plot.

Let's worst-case this scenario for a moment and see what we can do about it. Suppose these freedom fighters actually do what you say and explode those bombs. The situation isn't all bad, and it certainly isn't irretrievable. We're in the best possible place to minimize the damage this would do. I think we can weather this if we act quickly after it happens, but we all have to act together and speak as one voice. First of all, we'll leak the fact that our intelligence services had known of the plot and didn't inform us in time. They're already under the gun for lying to the Speaker, or at least that's the conventional wisdom. Gordon, you'll have to handle that for us with your people. We're going to need a couple of prominent sacrifices. Since you're on our team it won't be you, of course, and in view of your sacrifice already" – Ayers nodded toward Sheridan – "you'll also be exempt." How about that assistant of yours…Baskin? We'll let it out that she knew about the attack and… well, you can handle the scenario. Do anything you like and we'll back you." Ayers smiled at Cubbage, who had already passed well beyond any further speech.

Ayers went on, "Then, we're going to have to throw a small issue overboard to preserve the larger ones, so I'll go on record that we got nothing out of our prisoners and maybe we should review our anti-torture policies. Hmmm…since we're going to have to back off of that we'd better not use the word 'torture'…"anti-extreme-interrogation practices"…that will work. We'll re-open Gitmo and give these prisoners back to the Army to guard. And maybe…just maybe…when things die down in a year or two we can start the anti-torture campaign again. Yes, that will send an excellent message to the rest of the world: 'Americans suffer just like other nations, and we're always ready to endure hardship for the sake of world peace…yes, I'll backfile that one for later." Ayers made notes on his Blackberry.

"Now, Janine," he continued, "The president has decided there's no more 'war on terror,' just misguided people with an unfortunate habit of communicating through violence. So we can't call this an "attack." It will be a "tragedy" like the thing down south where those soldiers were shot by that major. What was your phrase, "man-caused disasters?" I like it! We'll handle it as a kind of natural disaster like Hurricane *Katrina*. That way we can respond through our civilian police instead of the military. We'll emphasize our lessons-learned techniques from *Katrina*.

Let's all remember that the chief lesson we learned from that disaster was the need for speed, security, and control of the news to avoid panic. During the *Katrina* aftermath we were way too slow in getting there and security was far too loose. And we let just any reporters in there to poke around, so when the police took safety measures like confiscating guns, for example, there was an instant hue and cry. As a result, Americans saw the government as not being able to take care of our minority citizens. Fortunately this perception became fastened onto the previous administration. But this time with the foreknowledge that Director Cubbage has provided, we can deflect it from ourselves entirely. There was also a very bad precedent set where individuals took up arms to protect their own homes from looting. We have to make sure this never happens again. We don't want Americans thinking like individuals, that they can protect themselves. They should look to the state for their protection. If we're ever going to move toward the European model we've got to take every opportunity that presents itself to drive home that basic dependency. We can't have just anyone taking care of himself; sets a bad example by implying that the individual American is more important than his government and we all know that's not true."

"This time, though, we have some advance word so we can take care of a lot of these problems on the front end. Janine, I'll need you to mobilize your DHS people but very subtly so we can get to the bomb sites as quick as we can after the attack and show America that while our intelligence services may have failed us, the administration was as ready as it could ever be. I'm afraid we may have to hang a few more of our covert intelligence people out in the wind, but they're the only ones we have available who can't fight back through their families and Congress. On the security question, I'll need the FBI on station at each site as quick as they can get there. I don't want a single survivor taking his safety into his own hands like in New Orleans. This sets a very bad example for the rest of the country. As I said, we don't want Americans looking to themselves for their personal safety instead of the government. I also don't want a lot of lawsuits later on against our police. So the FBI is to be instructed to…ah…neutralize any situations where firearms are in evidence. There shouldn't be witnesses, either. Regrettably, this may cost additional lives, but it's for the greater good."

"Something very important, however, to stress to your FBI Director... have him tell his people be sure not to shoot any minorities. Whites with guns are no problem to explain away. They're right-wing extremists, or private militia, or something like that. But our minorities have to keep on viewing themselves as victims and beholden to us, and if they get it into their heads that they're subject to the same sanctions as whites, or they start thinking they can get a gun and protect themselves, then they're liable to get...well...uppity."

"So, people, if we hit the ground running right after this happens we'll be able to minimize the bad feelings about being attacked, and we'll keep everything secure without a lot of *ex post facto* unpleasantness. For my part, I'll make sure the correct media people get to the bomb sites right afterward so they can film your people delivering aid. And I'll do what I can to keep them off the FBI's back while they're furnishing protection and taking care of any right-wing gunmen. The conservative media will raise hell, of course, but if everyone plays their part nothing will show above ground and they won't be able to do anything more than cry about it. Besides, this will comprise a full-blown National Emergency and that will provide me a couple of ways to neutralize them that we don't need to go into now."

Gordon Cubbage had been given a chair that was just too low, that placed his chin about level with Ayers' desk. It was a common tactic of executives who had self-esteem issues and was designed to make him feel small in the presence of greatness. It hadn't worked. Slowly he gathered himself and stood, never taking his eyes off Ayers. He began in a voice so low that the others had to strain to hear it, and even Jeremiah Ayers leaned forward out of the safety of his chair.

"Dr. Ayers," Cubbage was calm, "I think I'm beginning to understand what's happening here and I want to thank you for clearing my mind on a number of issues. As you know, I was appointed by the President just as you were, but what you may not know is that I took the job because I like being an American and I want to pay back a little for the great things America has done for me. That would include trying to save American lives where I can. That opportunity doesn't come along very often. Mostly it's just slog along day by day doing little things here and there to try to keep us a little safer. So far my job has been pretty unremarkable, but once in a while something comes along where I can make a huge difference. I look carefully for those times and when I find one I treasure it and try to do the best I can."

"But you and Janine here see yourselves differently. You don't really like being Americans. You're here to boost the president no matter what, and you'll sacrifice *anything* and *anyone* to make him succeed. You and Janine got together and held me back from going in after Walker and her daughter when we had a good chance to save both of them. You shoved it off on State so the president wouldn't have to deal with it with the Syrians."

Cubbage willed his voice not to shake, "A while ago I got a heads-up from somebody in the press corps that some of their investigative stringers were going around trying to find out about a CIA 'defection.' They'd been cued that one of my people had gone over, *a female agent in the Med*. Of course nothing like that was in the works anywhere, and we first thought it was some kind of counter-intel plant from overseas trying to discredit us. But strangely, each time we back-traced the rumor, the source kept coming out Department of Homeland Security. I see it now. You set up Walker as a turncoat to cover your own asses for not going after her. And when the Alice tapes hit the media you knew your little game was up. How do you explain a rogue agent's daughter being murdered by the very people she was supposedly defecting to? Now you're talking about the needless sacrifice of tens of thousands of innocent American lives as though it were just political damage control. You don't really give a da –"

"ENOUGH!"

Unnoticed by the others, Sheridan Walker had risen from her chair and now stood with feet wide apart, arms straight down at her sides. Her exclamation silenced Cubbage in mid word. All heads turned toward her. Slowly she took in each one of them with a steely gaze. There was no hint of anger in her face, only resolve. Her voice was low-pitched and carried as much emotion as any sound could. Her gaze stopped at Ayers, who slid back reflexively into his chair.

"You weasel," Sheridan said tonelessly. "You faithless, murdering weasel. You and this whore -- she nodded toward Janine -- killed my daughter? For *politics?* You…beasts…my GOD…you…you…scoundrels! You preach and preach what's good for us but it's just not quite the same that's good for you, is it? And you, Madame Secretary, don't you have a thirteen year old boy? Would you throw him away for your goddam Socialist bullshit?"

She turned back to Ayers, who by this time was deep into his chair. "And you, sir, you vile…you offer us reins and bondage. Your fat lips suck up the cream and then you expect us to thank you for leaving the skim? Greatest good for the greatest number, eh? Sure. As long as *you* decide what's good for the rest of us, and it doesn't apply to you. As long as *you* have the levers in your own hands. Look at that sorry bimbo running Congress, hates the military, sells out my fellow agents because she hasn't got the balls to pick on a uniformed soldier. She knows if she tried to fuck with the visible military she'd be shit right out of that place on her wash and wear hair. I don't give a damn whether you people suck each other off dissing America. But you're going to get some people killed who really don't deserve it. In fact, you already did, didn't you? You deserve it but you'll never put yourselves in harm's way. That's for the little people like me and the rest of us who love America and end up doing most of the dying for her. We don't begrudge dying for our country but we sure as *hell* begrudge dying for the likes of *you!*"

"You never make anything; you never do anything; you scurry around pulling things down and think you're as good as the rest of us. Well, you little weasel, the only reason you and your liberal asshole friends can live and suck and scurry is because we keep you safe to do it. Get your asses out on the front line for a while and feel the wind whistle between your legs. You and your kind are the sorriest excuses for decent humans I can think of. And you threw my little girl to those murderers just to hide your dirty plans? You smirk around thinking that using people makes you powerful but this time, you little fuck, you've used just the very wrong people in just the very wrong way. Your master is over there tinkling tea cups and setting us up to get nuked with the people who killed my little girl, and the best you can do is cover up so they'll still shake hands with him?":

"Have you no shame, sir? Have you no decency?"

Sheridan leveled her gaze around the room, "For God's Sake, we're talking about a nuclear attack on our country! We have no more time for apologies and ass kissing, shuffling around the world head down begging favor from these jackals. We're going to be attacked, you fools! You're sorry to be Americans? *Don't you realize we have no more time for sorrow?"*

Sheridan gaze stopped moving she looked Janine up and down where she sat. "And you." Sheridan's voice went very low, "You…murdering…bitch…killing my daughter for your stinking politics…well, I thank you for the gift you gave me, showing me how low a human being can sink. And now I'm going to give you a gift in return. Here is my gift to you for the foul murder of a little twelve-year-old girl"…

Sheridan's voice faltered and then she seemed to draw something from inside, and her voice became firm again. "Every night for the remainder of your sorry life until the moment you go down to your grave, just before you go to sleep you will be accompanied by my daughter, Alice Walker. She will sit at your bedside where you can look at her. But of course she won't be able to look back at you."

Sheridan smiled with her teeth, "Shall I tell you why?"

"And every morning of your sorry life until the moment you choke and spit and roll over to die, just before you open your eyes, you'll have just the tiniest little hope that maybe this time my daughter, twelve-year-old Alice Walker, *won't* be sitting by your bedside as she sat in a chair next to mine when I was bound and gagged in that room. But of course when I opened my eyes and saw her sitting there I realized immediately that *she* didn't need to be bound or gagged like me."

Sheridan's voice went to a whisper, *"Shall I tell you <u>why</u>?"*

"You stupid woman, you and your kind will murder us all just for your own power. You have to call the shots. You threw Alice away as casually as you breathe, just as you endanger all the other decent, kindly Americans and their children with your stupid apologizing and your ignorant global-village bullshit. You dirty woman, you're dirt, and your kind are dirt, and someday we'll be rid of you. All you want is to tell us what's best. All you want is our liberty and our souls."

"Well, Madame Secretary Mastroantonio, you murdering ignorant liberal slut, I have no soul for you today, my dear, only the gift of my sweet little Beebee, child of learning, child of light –" Sheridan faltered and then summoned all the courage she had left. "'Manatees and ladybugs, pups and armadillos.' She'll be yours now, Janine, yours until you flicker and go dim. And believe me, Madame Secretary, I wish you a long, long life and many, many hours in which to enjoy my daughter's constant company."

TWENTY-FOUR

أربع وعشرين

Some say Bobby Lee was sick that day, others that he was too much caught up in feudal Matters of Honor not to throw it all on the pile occasionally. But never mind about that. The simple fact was he got himself sucked into a killing ground, not by anything Buford or Hancock did or Meade did, but by his own troops leading him away from what had been a very, very good plan. It was Lee's objective to get across the Susquehanna River well up into Pennsylvania near Harrisburg. Then who knew where he might strike next? Once across that broad, army-sheltering, army-destroying river taking sustenance from the endless bacon and full barns of the North, the Rebs could hit anywhere they liked. Philadelphia? New York? Boston? Washington, D.C.? Sure, why not Washington? Lots of troops down there but all the Confederates had to do was *feint* towards D.C. and the whoopla would begin!

The Butternuts came swinging down out of the mountains where they were safe sweating their packs and rifles and heavy cannons up along the Allegheny spine toward Harrisburg. Looking for trouble they were. For shoes? Maybe. They needed the shoes, but they didn't need the trouble. Lee had just over 75,000 troops, hardly a single one of whom anybody would call raw. This was a different kind of army from the forced drafts of scared, unwilling ranks whipped into battle by European princelings and strutting tinpot dictators. Lee's soldiers were their own men and were there because they themselves permitted it. This army was blooded and tough and not accustomed to moving an inch out of its path for any fool Bluebeaks. Everywhere they'd been they fought the Yankees to a standstill and once in a while made them run like chickens. A bunch of them hadn't cottoned to invading the North but wanted to stay in Virginia defending their homes until it was pointed out that it might be better to fight over the enemy's ground instead of through your own front yard. This made a certain amount of sense, so after considering the matter they allowed as how they'd just come along.

Shoulda…coulda…woulda….

General Lee *shoulda* stayed on the Harrisburg Road; Ewell's Corp was already in Carlisle and if the damned Yankees burned the bridges – and they did! -- well…didn't matter.

Coulda got across anyway because the river was low enough and Ewell was strong enough on the ground to guard the ford on either side while the rest of Lee's army splashed helplessly through the reeds.

Woulda been licked back in '62 at Antietam Creek if Union general McClellan had force-marched his two unused Corps down to the river crossings after the battle and pitched into Lee's exhausted and mauled infantry as they floundered back across. But he didn't, thus prompting Lincoln to write to General McClellan asking him, if he wasn't using the army right at the moment, could Lincoln borrow it for awhile?

And if Lee had refused action at Gettysburg, continued north, and shoved his bad boys over the Susquehanna and onto the broad, fertile, rolling hills and farmlands of eastern Pennsylvania, he *woulda* scared shitless an already panicky North, by this time half insane with fear at where he might go and what he might do. Might even have panicked them right into a change in government. And speaking of *panic,* thirty miles or so down the Susquehanna south of Harrisburg, Wrightsville on the east bank opposite all the excitement, *coulda* taken up a few yards of its prized bridge and denied Lee a crossing until federal troops could get there. But in their fear and desperation, the City Fathers burned it all, every stick, not to be rebuilt for seventy years. Huge stakes. North knew it. South knew it. Everybody knew it. Today, though, it seemed as if, among those who had the most to gain – the most to lose! – nobody much cared.

And so they came ambling down the Cashtown Road in the morning fog just beginning to burn off into a hell of a scorcher. Marching Order: ragged; Discipline: nonexistent; Eyes: side to side; Menace: absolute.

Grousing, about the heat, about their fool officers, too much dust and no damned coffee…same as soldiers everywhere when they think they just might be walking into sudden death and with a word or two and a quick joke try to keep it out of sight for just a bit longer. Could have been Hannibal's Legions stumbling and sliding down icy Alpine passes toward arrogant Rome, or the 7th Army shivering through a grey January dawn south of Remagen Bridge, or maybe the Tenth Mountain sweating along a trackless track through Middle Eastern sand, or a bunch of farmers and hunters more tough than careful peering out over mud walls too low, too far apart, not enough weight around the perimeter to stop a goat much less the four thousand regular soldiers encamped around a little church out in the middle of nothing called the Alamo. Didn't matter; they were all the same, tough, irreverent men, laughing at themselves, laughing at each other but with no nonsense about the killing. Men who couldn't use the word "courage" without blushing a little in order make it quite clear they weren't applying it to themselves, eating dust and chewing tobacco, spitting, passing the plug back and forth, trudging down just one more dirt road to nowhere with no particular courage except perhaps the highest courage and from no particular duty except perhaps the most profound duty, putting themselves where their better sense told them they had no business being while something they couldn't quite put their finger on told them that somehow they had no business being anywhere else.

General Buford saw them coming. Just a Union general of volunteers whose brigadier stars would disappear as soon as the war ended and bump him back to major in the Regular Army. But he hadn't gotten that brevet for sitting on a log drinking coffee, and now he did everything right. Deployed his cavalry regiment dismounted, short range carbines loaded, every fourth man back to hold the horses so he was already 25% thinner on the line but nothing to be done about that. When you fire dismounted you might actually hit something once in a while. Today accuracy might be essential. Besides, Doctrine said when attacked by infantry, cavalry will take cover and present a smaller target and if they're too strong in front of you, hope to hell some of your people are coming up behind. Great doctrine; looks real good in the manual. Like to have a minute with the guy who wrote it up…gets a good man killed once in a while.

Same old stuff...same as always when men go to war for what's inside. Buford's line of damned Yankees hunkered down behind whatever they could manage to throw up in front of them, regarding with a certain interest the endless grey columns coming toward them against the black backdrop of Blue Mountain through a shimmering midsummer morning.

> *"What the deuce are we going to do now?" [didn't use the F-word as much in those days]... "My God! Look what that asshole got us into!"..."Think he sent back to Corps for more men?"..."Better get that pigsticker on there – might have a use for it by and by."..."Jesus! Look at those bastards come!"*

So brevet General of Volunteers John Buford, a pretty fair soldier for being only thirty-seven, sprawled his men across the road and tucked them in behind the fencerows wherever he could to slow the enemy down. After awhile General Reynolds rode up with the Union Army's 1st Division, 1st Corps, lean, rangy men as good at soldiering as any on the continent which meant better than any in the world. Their nickname, from Pope's disaster at 2nd Manassas, which, they took pains to point out, was none of their doing, said it all: *"The Iron Brigade."* A not inconsiderable opinion existed, shared to a man by the Brigade itself, that they were the toughest sonsabitches on the planet. Nobody to fuck with, but today just not quite enough mass to do the trick against the miles of flashing, burnished steel flowing down out of the hills.

> *"Get your ass down to Meade and tell him to get his up here right away with everything he's got! I can slow em but I can't stop em and we have to hold that hill behind us where the graveyard is. Now get <u>going</u>!"*

Then they all sat and waited to see what would happen next.

Longstreet's Invincibles – that's how these reb soldiers considered themselves and actually not without pretty good reason – ran up against annoying fire and deployed into line of battle without anyone much ordering it, without their officers doing much more than making sure their lines were reasonably straight and nobody's flank was hanging out.

Somebody sent back to General Longstreet about it and he said go ahead. So they fanned out and started feeling for Buford's flanks which weren't all that far apart to begin with and weren't all that much trouble to get around.

Then the lines erupted in clouds of black powder smoke and the slap of ¾ inch bullets meeting flesh. The Bluebellies held on where they could. Took a lot of casualties especially down in some old railroad cut where Reb cannon found them and fired down the length of their line and they couldn't do anything about it except die in their tracks. Couldn't spread out far enough to keep their flanks solid and still mass their fire. Slowly forced backwards calling to their buddies, trying to form a line where they could find some cover, retreating in groups and bunching together for mutual support, some of them keeping their ears out for orders from their officers, others just shooting when they could and running when they had to, back through the fencerows, over lawns past farmhouses where frantic women gathered babes and sometimes fell down on them to begin the eternity of their own endless sleep, giving up their children to whatever might befall, drifting upward to The Lord, unwillingly willing their love ones to the tender mercies of decent soldiers and the impartiality of grapeshot.

Turning, looking back, firing and stumbling backward in the face of the deluge of grey coming out of the mountain. Drifting closer to their comrades for protection, funneled onto the only good roads, the market roads leading through Gettysburg itself. Too thin on the ground to stop Heth's grey sledgehammer driving them and killing them whether they stood or shooting them as they ran away. But not...quite...driving through them, always forcing them back, back, back toward the hill, bunching them in among themselves. Back they came through the streets and alleys and around the town, crouching, firing, loading and reloading, running like hell when they had to, keeping an eye on their comrades not to leave them hanging out but always moving south out of town, always further up the hill toward the graveyard.

> "Head for the goddam hill! Everybody up on the hill! Did you find Meade? Where is he?"

> "Two Corps coming up the Taneytown Road as fast as they can march. Says to keep those bastards off the ridge until he can get here. Hancock coming up ahead, Sir"
> "Very well. Get out to the west and keep em out of those fields. They can't get east of us; ground's too broken. I'm staying here across this road. Can't move fast unless they have it. Now move it!"

Longstreet sent back to Lee telling him something was brewing around Gettysburg and should he push more men in? Lee hadn't planned a battle until he was across the river; didn't need one here. The main Union Army of the Potomac was too far south. Couldn't get up north in time to prevent Lee from crossing. And when he did cross, what would happen next would be anybody's guess. But whatever happened, General Robert E. Lee would be the one driving it. Yes, Bobby Lee had it all right there in his fingers, but he didn't know it. His cavalry was off on an adventure and he was blind. Fuck it, said Lee, let's fight. And Longstreet sent word down the line to the rest of his troops: follow my boys down into that town and chew up what you find....

TWENTY-FIVE

خمسة وعشرين

Day Zero of the Cleansing Suns

اليوم صفر) في التطهير سنز

The fuel oil truck delivered its cargo to the pipes beneath the Administrative Center at Gettysburg Military Battlefield Park, although the driver had trouble with the truck's pump after offloading about fifty gallons. She apologized to the supervisor who had let her through the gate of the Park's maintenance facility and radioed to Dispatch to send another truck right away. Then, having no way to complete her deliveries that morning, she decided to return by way of the monument boulevard on the crest of Cemetery Ridge. It always gave her peace of mind to visit this most hallowed place in American Civil War history. As she moved the big fuel rig slowly and carefully between parked cars and laughing children, she once again marveled that so large a country with so diverse a culture could somehow find a common bond in this single place. But she thought she knew what was going on in their minds, maybe even better than they knew it themselves. The struggle that had taken place here a century and a half ago helped renew her own personal bond with her nation, and somewhere inside each of these visitors she suspected something similar was occurring.

The Park Service ranger escorting a group of Brownie Scouts through the cannon park just behind the High Water Mark smiled to see the fuel truck pull up at the crest of the ridge beside the Copse of Trees. He was standing at the small scrolled marker where Confederate General Lewis

Armistead had been shot down as he led what was left of his brigade through a breach in the Union lines and up the gentle hill past what was to become known as the Bloody Angle. The ranger was giving his Short Talk to the little girls whose attention span was seldom long at the best of times, and on this lovely, soft morning was almost non-existent. His remarks centered around courage and duty and how neither the North nor the South had a lock on either one. Noticing the truck, the ranger mused happily on the thought of a simple American taking a moment out of her busy work day delivering heating oil in order to commune with the sweeping fields and granite relics of one of his nation's most sacred places. His words caused the Brownie troop leader to reflect on talks she and her husband had over the past decade lying in each others' arms about pretty much the same things, agreeing with each other that while Americans didn't have a lock on that stuff either, they were glad to be Americans anyway. She couldn't believe her luck having Hal, nor his having her if it came to that; they were so alike.

The fuel truck eased into the pullout opposite the smoothbore cannons sited to face toward the phantom Confederate regiments eternally converging on the Copse of Trees, The driver took pains to get her vehicle as far off the road as she could so the continuous line of cars could edge past. Even at this early hour the park was filling up. She sat in the cab a few feet from the statue of Union General Alexander Webb, Medal of Honor at Gettysburg for grabbing up a rifle from a downed trooper and leading his men into the thick death at the Angle. Survived that and other battles and lived on to 1911 – how, nobody could guess, for in every fight he was always at the front of it. The driver carefully pulled the lever that set her hydraulic parking brake so that the truck couldn't drift into another vehicle as she sat, and thought to herself how good it was to be an American and to know these things about America. Her country was flawed, possibly irreconcilably so. But part of her job as an American was to do her small bit to move her nation into the correct path. She reflected upon her additional great fortune at being chosen a servant of God. All these years she had thought she was fulfilling his duty to her Lord, but then her *imam* brought to her mosque in Phoenix a visitor from across the sea, a most holy man who showed her and the rest of her class striving toward *Miraj* how the very soles of their feet were polluted by contact with the dust of a land not controlled by *Šarī* at *Allāh'*. He revealed the *Šarī a*, the path to end the rule of civil law in America and cause to blossom forth in its place *Sharia*.

But these were but idle exercises in logic until the great Enlightenment burst upon the class. The visitor pointed out how American leaders themselves were welcoming *Sharia*. By procrastinating and delaying America's fight against the Faithful, did they not show their contempt for their own American military currently murdering Believers overseas? Did they not tacitly approve of the Blessed Warrior, the American army officer in Texas who slew his comrades in the name of *Allah*? By endless talk and protestations of friendship even in the face of ugly provocation, did they not take pains to ease the path of Iran, a Muslim nation, in its attempt to develop God's Cleansing Suns to be used against Jews and Infidel Christians? In their silly show trials, have they not tried to provide to the Warriors from the 9/11 Great Holy Day a wonderful, irreplaceable forum to permit them to assure the world of the long reach and immeasurable power of *Islam* to crush Unbelievers? Then the visitor asked her and the rest of her class,

> *"If your leaders act so forcefully to bring Sharia to America, shouldn't you, as devout American Muslims, act as forcefully to welcome it?"*

This was a thunder blow to her complacency, the driver reflected. It had never been suggested to her that America *wanted* Islamic governance, but after considering these broad steps that her current government had taken to hasten it, which were now perfectly plain to her once the visitor had explained them, how could American Muslims stand by without taking up the cause? Surely the signal being given to us from Washington was unmistakable. It must be answered.

The ranger had just finished showing the little girls where a young man two years out of West Point lost – to the 130 guns of the Confederate's two hour barrage – all but one cannon of the six in his charge. When ordered to retreat out of harm's way replied, "No, I stay right here and fight it out or die in the attempt." The young artilleryman, already wounded and ramming canister into the last cannon in his tiny command, firing it like a huge shotgun point blank at the Confederates coming over the fence in front of him, died in his tracks when a ¾ inch rifle ball entered his mouth and confirmed his choice. The ranger told the Brownies that Lt. Alonzo Cushing, commander of the immortal Cushing's Battery, was no more hero than any one of them could be if they put their minds to it, and perhaps they wouldn't even have to die to prove it. He said it didn't matter they were girls, they were just as much American as Cushing as long as they had love of America in their hearts. What mattered was what they had for America in here, and he tapped his own uniform blouse gently, third button down. He was remarking to the Brownie Scout leader how this was the only park he had ever worked where Americans came back time and again, not for the history particularly, but just to walk around on what they considered their own hallowed ground, when the fuel truck driver, basking in her good fortune at being given a key role in God's Judgment against America, The Great Satan, pressed her button and the Day of the Cleansing Suns began.

At the Moment of Cleansing, the healing, cleansing light blossomed from the rear bay of the fuel truck heating the surroundings to about seven thousand degrees Fahrenheit, vaporizing its contents, the cab, the driver in mid self-congratulatory thought, then expanded outward in a globe of healing at $1.86 \times 10E6$ miles per second. But since this wasn't an air burst like Hiroshima, the beautiful symmetry of the nuclear globe was transected and inhibited by two unfortunate obstructions. On its way down below where the tires of the truck, the asphalt of the road, the marble of the statues, the Codori Farm, and the flesh of the Brownies had been, it encountered The Ground, which caused an immediate Celestial confrontation in which The Ground said 'no' and the Cleansing Sun said 'yes.' The result was that a simple ridge and monuments and cemetery and twenty-two thousand six hundred forty-seven people became in approximately three and one-half seconds a quarter-mile crater ten feet deep.

That was the easy part – force-in...dirt-out. Simple math; simple physics; easy to envision; nothing much to tell. More complex and difficult was that which followed. The second obstruction was The Air. Like the ground, The Air said 'no' and the Cleansing Sun said 'yes.' The result was an atmospherically propagated shock wave that moved outward from Ground Zero, then rushed back on itself, smearing and mixing everything in a mile circumference into a tangle of rubble

No More Time For Sorrow

bound together by rebar and the sobs of the survivors. ...Well, not quite everything. On its way down Baltimore Street toward the center of town it swept over a shallow declivity and in blowing out the insides and crushing the three-story brick house at 334 Baltimore Street, it spared the smaller, much older home at 332, not even breaking the china on the sideboard in the small, cozy dining room. A few nanoseconds later the Moose Lodge on the south side of Route 30 half a block from the square, along with its thirteen occupants and in the street outside three members of the Crips street gang who were taking aim out of their SUV at two Bloods dealing in their territory, was compressed into a compact mass approximately eighteen meters square which was then passed at roughly eight times the speed of sound through the foyer of the Kunstler Art Gallery across the street, taking with it four cars, two other pedestrians, the manager of the gallery, and eleven patrons who had come in early to see the Kunstler's Civil War document collection. At the same instant give or take a femtosecond or two, the Cleansing Sun reached the square and snapped off at its base the flagpole, the only remaining artifact from the Adams County Courthouse built in 1804 but spared this present indignity by burning to the ground in 1859, and sent it at just over one mile per second through the plate glass window of the Centuries On The Square restaurant in a corner of the Gettysburg Hotel, decapitating a diner and the concierge, then moving through the kitchen and out into the rear alley where the rest of the hotel was deposited upon it in flaming rubble. On the far opposite corner, the venerable Adams Bank building came apart into the square but somehow its clock standing sedately out in front on its own pedestal was untouched except for hands permanently etched and frozen at 9:16 a.m. It was only the heat, the solar-level, building-incinerating, lung-searing heat that found no opposition. On the contrary, the atmosphere welcomed the heat and improved it by retaining some of it as the shock wave past, to burst cars into flame and make of anyone who tried to run away a sort of candle, considerably greasier than the standard item used for lighting, and significantly noisier.

The Cleansing Sun healed the land and taught Infidels the error of their blasphemous ways out to a radius of about three miles give or take. Its efficiency related directly to line of sight and where hills or really large buildings like a hospital impeded its progress, the Cleansing Sun...well... cleansed. Gettysburg Hospital on Gettys Street about a half mile from the blast center was slammed into a flaming wreck. Its Wellness Center a few miles to the east was more fortunate. By the time the Sun reached V-Twin Drive it had been required to pass through many structures and instruct many Infidels, so the shock wave was somewhat diminished. The building remained intact while being lifted up, turned around ninety degrees, and deposited back where it had sat, Of course, no one survived inside. Outside in the spacious parking lot where the Adams County Renaissance Fair was in progress, fairgoers and presenters alike were swept up and pushed onto the building's foundation just in time for the building itself to greet them returning to earth.

Aside from the pleasant images attending the violent destruction of so many Western harlots and their verminous spawn each of whom had profaned *Islam* with their very existence, the true beauty of the Cleansing Sun lay in its efficiency. Every *Self-Destructive Islamic Life Taker* who served *Allah* by exploding themselves among the Un-Righteous, and each of their handlers, men to whom *Allah* had whispered they would serve Him better in a supervisory capacity, knew that car bombs and suicide belts worked pretty well in small areas, but the body count was woefully small. Injured and dead usually numbered only in the dozens. And most regrettably, the injured were not infrequently True Believers themselves who with exceedingly bad luck, just happened by at the moment of a Demonstration of God's Power. Sometimes it became frustrating that so many True Believers had to be dispatched to Heaven in order to take out one or two worthless Western Infidels. The Cleansing Sun, however, not only exterminated thousands of Infidels at an instant, but its blast of hard gamma radiation conveyed a lasting lesson to surviving Unbelievers, that they were better off dead than to reject the True God. Fortunately, though, most of the Cleansing Sun's casualties were either vaporized outright or burned alive into unrecognizable husks, so it was very difficult to pick out True Believers after the fact. This spared other devout Muslims from being troubled by the thought of *jihadists* murdering their own.

TWENTY-SIX

ستة وعشرون

Sheridan Walker lay across the Lancaster Best Western's king sized bed listening idly to the shower hissing and splashing against the tub curtain as Eliot shaved. Her exit from the hospital had been slow, prolonged by tests and consultations. Earnest men and women sought to contact the kernel of her remaining sanity that had been dragged into reality by an innocuous bit of liberal TV's Administration-puffing and punctuated by her thunderous reaction to it. The bulletin issued to Sheridan from her subconscious had used up a full clip of expensive ammunition and sent Eliot's invalid mother into a state resembling anaphylactic shock.

They brought Sheridan around carefully, but the most serious danger – that she would descend her stairway back into herself and this time never reappear, was gone. The shells from her service Beretta had ripped through the television set and into the wall behind, traveling through the pantry past an ancient Labrador who barely stirred in his slumbers, and on into the garage where they left a number of neat holes in Eliot's old Jaguar. When the car was eventually sent in for body work and paint, he instructed the body shop to seal off each one down inside the panel where it couldn't be seen, and then paint over them unfilled.

As the reports died away they masked Sheridan's urgent footsteps up her virtual stairway and her slamming the door closed forever that led back into that pit. The first outward confirmation of Sheridan's return to life was her insistence on seeing Cubbage to whom Sheridan was now able to give every detail of her capture and imprisonment. Then Eliot took her away to begin his own brand of therapy, a month-long bike trip down through Skyline Drive and back up the small coastal roads through the Carolinas winding past the inlets of the Chesapeake Bay. They sipped wine, cleaned drive chains, made love, and stood quietly beside a pasture in their boots and perspiration, glorying in having a horizon always just out of reach. Somewhere in the miles Sheridan came fully back to herself. Exactly *when* it happened she could never afterwards say, but she knew that the first face she saw was Eliot's. And of course that was what he had intended all along.

They wound their way up through the fields and back roads, blasted up Interstate 81 in close trail, two matching bikes seemingly locked together as they blew past. Today they were meeting their daughters, Reagan and Patton, granddaughter Sophia, and Reagan's six- and seven-year-old monsters Jackson and Beauregard. Sophia was a cute four year old, still taken up with her pandas and ribbons, but in Eliot's assessment, the Twins would end up either the first men to be elevated simultaneously to the Joint Chiefs of Staff or else hailed into court for attempting to restart the Civil War. Either way they promised unending agonies to their parents and to their grandparents, unremitting joy. The Old Folks, as Eliot and Sheridan were known in the family, could stoke their grandkids' independence, encourage their protests, subsidize their individualities, and then at the end of the day throw a leg over their motorcycles and depart, leaving the two little tragedies to their despairing parents, which is all the revenge on their children that good parents can ever hope to get. When managed properly, it's enough.

Eliot emerged from the tiny bathroom in a towel which Sheridan reached for as soon as he came near the bed, and pulled him down beside her. He slid his hand below her breasts to stroke her bulging belly.

"What a bonus," Eliot said as he moved his hand over her.

Sheridan laughed quietly, "You need some new material; you said that the last two times." She put her hands over his and became serious. "Darling, I need to talk to you about something. It's been bothering me and I need us to work this out."

Eliot moved his eyes to take her gaze and she knew that now she had his full, serious attention.

"I have to know…whether…my baby – our baby – is…really…is actually…." Sheridan stopped, not knowing how to say what she had made up her mind to force herself to say. She took a mental deep breath and started again, "Eliot, I want this baby. I want it to be ours. I just don't know. I just don't know if...if...if it's yours." It was out. Sheridan felt great relief and in a corner of her mind a huge gladness that she didn't have to carry this burden alone any longer. Eliot said nothing, knowing there was more.

"I was raped by that animal when I was kidnapped," Sheridan went on almost inaudibly. "I'm afraid my baby isn't..." The rest came in a rush. "I'm afraid it might be his child. When we get back I'm going over to Bethesda and get a DNA trace to make sure whose it is." Then she sank back to her pillow and stared at the ceiling. She kept her face expressionless, but Eliot could see the fear in her eyes.

He began quietly, "Babe, I understand about the rape. We've already been through that. You did what you thought you had to do to save Alice. You couldn't have helped yourself anyway even if you'd been there alone. We've always taught our daughters to fight off an assault, but in your case how would you fight with a house full of men ready to hold you down or maybe just shoot you? We have to bring ourselves to peace about Alice. In time we will. I knew there was more to come out of you about that. I knew there were things in there – he tapped Sheridan gently on the forehead – that needed to see the light of day but only in your own good time. This is one of them. We're going to have a conversation about this right now and get it out of the way for good. Now I want you to listen to me and listen very carefully. Here is my view and this will never change. You can do whatever you want to about the DNA survey, *but don't tell me the results!* This baby is from inside you; therefore, he's *my* son. Period. End of conversation on that topic. I don't care about the rape in that way; I don't care about the DNA. Since he's yours, he's mine and he always will be. Eliot smiled. "Is there anything about that I can clarify for you?"

Sheridan rolled herself over toward Eliot and took him in her arms. She found herself unable to speak, so she merely buried her head in his shoulder and tried to keep her wracking sobs of relief from punishing his deltoids. Eliot stroked her hair and gentled her, "Ok, Babe, let it out."

Eliot held her a long time trying not to move. Finally, Sheridan's muffled crying subsided to sniffing and then to silence. She nestled herself tighter into Eliot's embrace and sighed. She had put one more thing behind her that needed to be out and gone from the both of them. He shifted her head so he could see her face, and said quietly, "Babe, I didn't mean we couldn't talk about this later if you need to. I wanted you to know that there are three of us now and that's my take on it. So let's get the bikes ready, and we'll roll on over and meet the girls. This is going to be ok for us. We're going to do all right with it. Everything's going to be ok for us now that you're back home and back to yourself. And hey! I've got a *son* coming!"

Patton Walker had arisen early and made sure the desk at the Travel Lodge knew she was meeting her mother and father later that day. Reagan had already left with the boys. They'd never been to Gettysburg and her sister wanted to begin at the Visitor's Center. Patton and Sophia strolled down Steinwehr Boulevard toward the square, passing the shops and restaurants, idling along taking in the lovely smell of a country morning and looking for just the right place for a mother and her four-year-old to breakfast. Sophia chattered along at her side eager to see the monuments and to meet Grandma and Grandpa later for lunch. Sheridan and Eliot were on their way over from Lancaster and everybody was meeting at McClellan's Tavern on Gettysburg's square. Patton reflected with a smile that while the generals who fought it out a few yards away rated monuments and books, Union General George Brinton McClellan, who had squandered at least three priceless opportunities to end the Civil War in its first months, got a bar named after him. How fitting, she thought. She fumbled in her purse for the money to secure a Confederate kepi for little Sofia a few steps below the place in the cemetery where long ago a man had come from Washington to give a speech about it. The speech had gone over about as well as could be expected considering that the audience was accustomed to perorations of hours' length like the one orator Edward Everett had ended a few minutes earlier:

> "...*bid farewell to the dust of these martyr-heroes...and down to the latest period of recorded time...*"
> "*... in the glorious annals of our common country...*"
> "*...no brighter page than that which relates the Battles of Gettysburg.*"

The crowd clapped and stomped and though many of them were too far away to get any of the words in that unamplified day, most of them generally felt they'd heard something pretty big.

[Whew. Got our money's worth out of that guy for sure! Two full hours! That's something alright, lots of big words, great images, well put together. Loved it! Real entertainment.]

The man who stood up to give the next speech was tall and gangly. Some likened his features to a baboon. Well, his short two-minute speech would have to do because, being who he was, he had the right to short-change his audiences if he wanted to.

[Some speech! Couple of minutes long was all, hard to hear, and he sure was right that the world would little note nor long remember what he said here.... What was that about "...all men...created equal?" "That from these honored dead we take increase devotion...something...something..." last full measure of devotion?" "...a new birth of freedom...government of the people, by the people, for th...what? ...Can't HEAR.]

The man who delivered that faintly heard speech was worried. The fall of Vicksburg earlier that summer had split the South away from her western reaches. Almost at the same moment, on the very same weekend in fact, the United States Government in its victory at Gettysburg had made the inescapable point that if there was fighting to be done it would be done on Confederate soil. Nevertheless to many the War seemed to be dragging on inconclusively and without an end.

This man was different than the top-hatted, frock-coated Presidents before him. They had been ponderous of dignity where he was heedless enough of dignity to ride a horse to the cemetery where his legs dangled down past the stirrups. They were turgid of phrase where he was sparse and homespun, never using a long word where a short one would do. Many of them had been handsome. He was ugly, some said, but they had to admit that his simplicity and good humor tended to offset some of it. He was uncultured in the ways of the Venerable East, a brash, uncouth Westerner from a frontier that not too many generations later would be merely a whistle stop on the way to the real frontier over the Rockies.

Dr. Robert Beeman

[And anyway, why can't we have handsome statesmen like England and France? Why can't we have polished men of letters who can write a real speech sprinkled with Latin and Greek metaphors and complicated sentences that require real intelligence to unravel? We don't need short words that just anybody could slam together. We want somebody who can get up there and really zing one out, somebody who can give us stuff that would impress a man instead of just mumbling up a couple of sentences that aren't going to thrill anybody. And boy...embarrassing! No applause, or really not very much. Stone silence just about. Well, If he runs for another term next year maybe he'll do better....]

No, all in all not much of a "presence." Not much of an effort. Except that, curiously, within just a few years of its first reading on that chilly November afternoon, the two hundred sixty-nine words of that disappointingly plebeian, woefully short, indifferently received little speech ended up translated into every known human tongue. And for some reason — maybe from the force of its sheer humility and simplicity or then again maybe not — those ten depressingly ordinary sentences somehow continued to beckon the hearts and minds of men throughout the world from that first moment of utterance unto the present generation.

But that was long ago. At The Moment of Cleansing, in sending forth God's Fingers to grasp up the souls of the Infidels who stood against His Chosen, the Cleansing Sun paid the place where the man had read his speech no special attention. The marble marking his location dissolved among the dust of corpses planted there long ago and all were lifted by the Cleansing Sun and bathed in thundering streams of God's Radiance. Standing a little way away from the place of the speech, Patton and Sophia were instantly vaporized...well, not instantly. "Instantly" is reserved for God, not the relatively puny ebb and flow of neutrons bumping against each other, speeding here and there, missing and colliding and occasionally taking out a city. Semantics notwithstanding, they both disappeared in a blinding flash of light, the same light which approximately one times ten to the minus six seconds later illuminated Reagan, just emerging from the Visitor Center bathroom on the other side of the Park. Reagan and her two little boys happened to be sheltered inside an earthquake-proof ferroconcrete structure that lay behind the low end of Cemetery Ridge and out of the direct blast cone, so they were not vaporized but merely swept upward and crushed into a gelatinous mass between two of the sturdy beams of the ceiling.

A short interval after the Moment of Cleansing, Sheridan and Eliot had just taken the southbound exit ramp and were passing under the concrete overpass that carried US30 over US 15. The Cleansing Sun required one forty-seven-thousandth of a second to arrive to meet them where their motorcycles were just coming out of the sharp lean angle required for the right-hand ramp into the southbound lane. The hill intervening caused the shock wave and winds to veer upwards, interdicting the path of God's Cleansing Spirit along the ground and creating a vortex that lifted the massive concrete overpass in its entirety off its thick piers, crushing it down across the four-lane highway below.

Truly, the Cleansing Sun was God's Own Breath sucking the life out of these Unbelievers, leveling and smoothing their vile handiwork back down into God's own Firmament. And of course, as was true of all *Allah*'s Handiwork, the greatest Blessing of all was its eternal replicability. From this glorious day forward the Suns would blaze forth God's Anger against the American Satan as long as True Believers could be called to their Sacred Duty and the uranium held out.

And the souls. What of the souls? What of that indestructible part of a human being which some human beings, upon arriving at the end of their life and seeing what their fate will be for Eternity, might wish were somewhat less imperishable? Ah, the souls...they were taken instantly – this time in the exact meaning of the word – up to Heaven. Being Infidel souls from the Great Satan and thus inaccessible to God's Mercy, they were bound and yoked into service to the One True God for the pleasure of his Chosen People. Patton and Reagan, not being virgins at the time of their Ascension, were of course ineligible to serve God's Chosen as personal concubines. However, God never wastes anything so all was not lost. Places were found for them in the deep mines and other artifices of punishment by which *Allah* shows his favoritism toward His own Believers by grinding in Death the souls of those who refused His tender mercies in life.

Moreover, as thousands of degrees Celsius melted their bodies from around their encased souls, Patton and Reagan and their children, were given the opportunity to serve yet an additional joyous purpose. They had been released from their blasphemous existence by a nuclear holocaust engendered by energetic and unremittingly faithful warriors of *Islam*. Thus it was given by *Allah* to the regretfully departed warriors of this particular step on the road of *jihad* to witness Patton and Reagan's journey to Heaven as they were drawn helplessly and hopelessly to their doom along with the upward swarming -- or outward depending on one's vantage point – of the masses of other less identifiable yet equally culpable souls of Infidel American Sons and Daughters of Satan whom this Man-Caused Disaster had claimed.

The faithful, stalwart Warriors of God lounged upon their clouds or whatever one lounges upon in those regions of Heaven, nearby tables piled high with meats and drinks and other savouries. They were served by nubile young virgins one of whom was occasionally plucked from her rounds to enjoy one of the Chosen's personal attentions, afterwards, being no longer virginal, to be cast away into the maelstrom of damned souls languishing past. The Chosen lolled and laughed and beckoned, jollying along what was left of Patton and Reagan and the rest of the souls on their journey to Judgment and Eternal Damnation. The wonderful thing about being God's Warriors was that you didn't have to participate in a particular attack in order to enjoy its aftermath. Merely die in *jihad* and you'd be taken directly to Heaven. After a suitable orientation browsing amongst the food and virgins, slaking appetites acquired during your long years of deprivation and suffering on Earth, you could drop in on any operation you liked and savor the souls being dragged in for their punishment. Thus it was that many other warriors who had been dispatched during their own righteous fights or disassembled by their own suicide belts, joined the nuclear attack team on their clouds to enjoy the progression of Infidels moaning past. There were suicide bombers from Iraq who brought multitudes of Offending Infidels, and the wonderfully creative fighters from Afghanistan who, even though they lacked volume, shielded themselves behind women and children and thus always managed to bring at least one other soul with them into Heaven for *Allah*'s Comfort. Some of these were devout Muslims but God in His Mercy toward his fighters regarded that as an inevitable, though regrettable, consequence of the Infidels forcing them to do it in the first place.

TWENTY-SEVEN

سبعة وعشرين

Gordon Cubbage opened his eyes and tried to breathe normally. He felt as though he had never done anything like this before, although of course he had. His hands were filled with her thick, silky hair; his arms cradled her head. Where a minute ago he had gushed like a fire hose deep inside her, his tip nudging her cervix spraying and splashing everywhere through her virginally tight vagina, now he felt himself draining a solid stream into her like a full flowing kitchen tap rolling his fluid into her filling her up. She had moaned to him when her legs went over his shoulders, and gasped as he drove down hard through her, muttering "deep…so deep"…forgetting to breathe so he had to stop for a few seconds to let her catch her breath. He had brought Lorraine to orgasm several times, the last one continuous in a long drawn out cry that was both a plea and a release. But then their eyes locked together and made a connection between them that rendered their physical connection almost moot. He knew this was the end of him that evening. He could ignore the insistent urging of her vaginal walls pressing his shaft as it slid past, the curves of her great breasts in his hands and mouth, and her insistent moans of pleasure at his touch. Up to now he could put these things out of his mind and continue hard and dry for her pleasure. But when he looked into the endless years beckoning to him from within her bright green eyes commanding him to attend her and somehow at the same time entreating him to cherish and protect her, he felt himself losing control. She slid her hands up behind his head and bent him down for a long, lingering kiss. He could feel her ring muscles contract around his shaft as her lips sucked his tongue into her mouth. Then he pulled slowly away and with her legs pointing to the ceiling and her thighs straight upward he began to drive into her at first slowly and then faster and faster and harder and harder until he knew she could feel the swelling start at the base of his shaft, moving upward along his length, bulging her vaginal walls as it passed until his tip became slick and bulbous and he couldn't contain it anymore. Their eyes still drinking in the other, he jammed himself as deep into her as he could. She heaved her hips upward and cried out with the rush of fluid as he began to throb and spurt into her. He felt her nails go into his back, dragging out and down to his buttocks, on the way becoming slippery with his blood, clawing and sliding her legs up and down his hips, jamming her feet onto the bed and arching her back into him, locking her legs around his buttocks and squeezing him harder into her, groaning with her need to take him deeper when there was no deeper while their eyes gazed calmly into each other seeing nothing but the rest of their lives. Finally as his flow diminished he felt himself going softer and softer, and withdrew the last inch or two, rolling carefully over to lie beside her. She lifted his head and pillowed it between her firm, massive breasts and they breathed together for a time.

"I've never felt anything like that before," Lorraine whispered.

Sensing her vulnerability at this tender moment, Gordon marshaled his full male sensitivity and spoke from his heart.

"Virgin, eh?" he whispered.

Lorraine looked down at the back of his head buried between her breasts. The corners of her mouth twitched upward and her dimples went deep, "Yep, you were the first. The twins were a miracle – Immaculate Conception. When they came along nobody was more astounded than me unless it was Ernie. Tried to get some Sainthood stuff going with The Church, but you know how fussy they are...'So, Dr. Baskin, your birth was *sans coitus*, eh?. How nice...and twins! *So which one's The Messiah?* Shall I ask the Monsignor to flip a coin?'...and so on; lots of silly details. We just settled for *Ripley's* and let it go at that. So watch your ass with me Bucko; I'm *very* well connected Upstairs. "

"Every night I pray to The Pope asking him forgiveness for my sins," Gordon gravely intoned, "and I in turn forgive The Pope for the Spanish Inquisition."

"Holy shit! You're going to get me Purgatory for sure talking like that! How did I ever let you get to this point with me?"

"I don't know," replied Cubbage thoughtfully. "Might have been the begging…or was it maybe tying you up and putting a knife to your throat?"

"Was that you? Damn, I've got to get better control of my task scheduler!" Lorraine slid her hand to his neck and caressed his cheek. "Darling, you wouldn't have needed the knife." She drew him to her for a kiss, then murmured softly. "The restraints and anesthetic would have been enough."

"I'll remember that when the cheerleaders come over."

"No more cheerleaders, darling. From now on you don't date anyone you have to drop off at their college dorm. You're going to be mine and I take a dim view of my having to help your little "friends" with their term papers. Besides, that hideous old pickup of yours can hardly make it here from the airfield much less a bring up bunch of your…ah…nieces. Love your little airplane, though. What a sweetie! Could you teach me to fly her…you're a pilot, aren't you?"

"Well there are opinions about that," Cubbage replied, "But…sure, I can teach you. First thing you need to learn is when the instructor snaps his fingers the student unbuttons her shirt, lies back on the seat, spreads her legs…."

Gordon's thoughts drifted back over the events of the past day. After the meeting with Ayers in the Oval Office, CIA Director Cubbage had returned to his own office at Langley to discover a locked door and a letter handed to him by his receptionist. She had been crying and was still on the verge of tears. Reading the letter, Gordon discovered that during his drive out the George Washington Parkway he had been fired, probably right around the time he passed Chain Bridge Road. Considering what he had said to National Security Adviser Ayers, it had been done with almost exactly the amount of ceremony he might have expected.

His first thought upon reading his letter of termination was that he was being set up to take the fall for whatever might happen with this bomb plot. It was just like Jeremiah Ayers to cover both his ass cheeks at once, and a disgraced CIA Director who dropped the ball warning America was a very good political card to have in one's hand just in case. Well, Cubbage was not disposed to worry about things he couldn't affect, so he put it in the back of his mind with an admonition to himself to get out of the path of the steamroller asap. His second thought was for his Commercial Driver's License. Worked for him before getting him back into a paycheck. Of course, the pay of a tractor trailer driver wouldn't be quite what he had been making as a senior government official, but most of the disparity in income could be offset by not having to be pleasant to Janine Mastroantonio anymore. Maybe Schneider was hiring. Good outfit. Fully satellite dispatched and controlled. Violate federal time regs and telemetry shuts off your truck engine right in the middle of the Long Island Expressway. Loved it. Encourages the driver to plan ahead. He had hoped to see Lorraine one more time. There were one or two things he wanted to mention to her now that…but…oh well…

Just then she appeared in the office door and it occurred to Cubbage to wonder how a woman could appear in no makeup, greasy coveralls, hair back, smudges on her face, and still remind a man of the *Mona Lisa*. He showed her the letter. They left without a word and drove to the little airport at College Park, Maryland where at ruinous expense Gordon kept his 1946 Ercoupe, the single engine, eighty-five horsepower, two-place, open cockpit love of his life. Half a century after its manufacture Cubbage's 415C was not only old but slow – well, of course you could get almost a hundred miles an hour out of her if you put the nose down a little, firewalled the throttle, and blew real hard against the windscreen. Climb speed was about like going up a stepladder. Not much to look at, not much performance, cranky and high-maintenance, in other words, the perfect aircraft for any man in no great hurry yet partial to seeing over the next hill. With this dainty sweet little lady he had fallen in love at first sight, pretty much like he'd done with… Cubbage glanced over his shoulder at Lorraine buckling herself into the passenger's seat harness and smiled a vast inside smile.

Well, maybe there'd be time to discuss that later but right then Gordon's attention was on rollout. He finished his preflight noting that all three fuel tanks were full, climbed in, primed twice pushing the brass primer lever slowly in and out. Master on, mags on, throttle 1/8, carb heat off, clear the area, pull the starter lever until the engine rotated reluctantly, finally coughing into life and settling down grumpily into a lumpy idle as it began to warm. Radio checks, altimeter set, taxi out, mag and carb heat run-up to 1700 rpm, check the mag drop on each unit, one last look up the approach path for casual visitors.

"College Park Traffic, November One Three Niner Seven Juliet centerline departure Runway Two Seven departing runway heading." Throttle to the wall; the engine blares and the cowl shakes as your little ship starts reluctantly down the runway. A little back pressure to settle her weight on the mains and cock the wing against the coming lift, airspeed indicator out of the corner of your eye, at 45 the nose comes up, feel her wag her wings slightly as she shoulders her weight in lift and gets ready to shrug off the ground, then a sideways wiggle and the smooth rush of sweet ascent. Left hand on the wheel, right hand on the throttle…and suddenly the light caress of soft fingers over your right wrist – the other love of your life assuring you that she feels that same gentle tug against her heart that had always pulled you skyward.

Cubbage leveled off at 1000 feet, giving himself a 500 foot leeway under the first control bucket extending from 1500 to 10,000 feet AGL to slide beneath radar controlling Dulles and Reagan International. He wished to avoid meeting one or two of the Air Defense Zone's interceptors piloted by very competent, quite humorless F16 fighter pilots, weapons: hot, trigger fingers: itchy, no compunction about shooting him down if he wandered into forbidden airspace. When he passed Gaithersburg Airport on his left he tuned in Martinsburg VOR and flew the beam up the river for a while just to enjoy the scenery and to keep well clear of the infamous P40 Prohibited Area. The Presidential retreat at Camp David was definitely not a place to fly near, much less over. So Gordon and Lorraine stooged slowly up the north bank of the Potomac counting speedboat wakes and generally just reveling in being alive. At Martinsburg, when his VOR needle started the donkey dick dance that signaled he was directly over the VOR transmitter, Gordon swung right onto the 330 AWAY radial towards Bedford. He climbed to 4000 feet to avoid Hancock's traffic and noted as he passed over the field that there were at least three aircraft in the pattern. Lots of business, he mused. Now he was bumping in the updrafts from the Allegheny foothills below. He started looking for the tiny hamlet of Clearville, a sprinkle of two dozen houses tucked into the folds of treed foothills set amid miles of forbidding mountain fastness, but a sure beacon that he was on course. There it was just off to his left. He was right on the money for Bedford.

Key in Bedford AWOS…"Winds, 310 at 4; altimeter…."

"Bedford traffic, November One Three Niner Seven Juliet five miles south east inbound straight in approach to Three Two."

One more ridge and he could see the field. Five thousand feet of paved runway and his hangar off to the left. It was getting on toward dusk so he triggered his mike seven times and the field lights blossomed like a well lit door to home.

"Bedford traffic, November One Three Niner Seven Juliet three miles inbound straight in for Three Two. I have zero traffic in the pattern."

Turn to final, line up with the runway centerline. Carb heat ON; throttle 1400 RPM, airspeed about 70 mph, pick your spot just after the Numbers, runway getting larger, the part going away from you is ahead of your touchdown, the runway stationary spot is where you're going to do whatever it is you're going to do, fence coming up, throttle back to 1200, airspeed 60…hold it…wait for it…let her just nod up a bit…NOW, enough back pressure to start a sink, LEAVE THE POWER IN…feel her settle… CHIRP/CHIRP – there go the mains…power OFF drop the nose wheel, and you're not flying anymore, but driving. In this two-control ship it's all the steering you've got. Coast her down to the first available taxiway; waddle off the Active and Call Clear; "Bedford traffic, November One Three Niner Seven Juliet clear the Active, cheated Death again. Have a nice day!"

Carb heat OFF, Strobe OFF…*[Passenger Status…hmmm…still conscious…not too green…nice tits…]* "Darling, would you mind unlocking the man door and putting the hangar door up? Just push the UP button you'll find inside. When you exit the aircraft, go aft over the trailing edge and walk all the way around to avoid the propeller."

Gordon and Lorraine had dug his ancient Ford 4x4 out of the recesses of the hangar, pushed *Elinor* into the empty space, and had driven up to his cabin in the Allegheny hills. No phone service, no computer; no television, nothing but serene hardwood forest, a well stocked pantry, and bears. The only vestige of the world was the faint, slow whup whup of the giant wind turbine over the next ridge. They had spent the evening in a rush of words of love and endearment that had waited three years to tumble out of both of them. From the first moment they met and all during their association as non-uniformed soldiers in America's defense network, each had strained toward the other, knowing they'd found their life partner but forcing themselves to their duty instead of yielding to their desire. On this night the dam had burst releasing a torrent of passion and indulgence.

Gordon came back out of his memories and sighed, "No more cheerleaders, eh…well…I guess there are always sacrifices….But don't count my truck out just yet. It started once or twice last year…ok, two years ago…a little tuneup it'll run just fine. I'll get on it tomorrow. Maybe the next day. So, Angel, you probably think I brought you up here just to get in your pants, but there actually was a good reason."

Lorraine's voice was sugar, "Are you suggesting sir, that getting in my pants *wasn't* a good reason?"

"Ah…no, no…of course not, my darling. Ah…what I meant to say was…um…ah…something else entirely. I'll get back to you as soon as I, ah…think of…whatever it might have been."

"But in the meantime," Cubbage went quickly on, "I'm going to need your help with something and neither of us will have time for anybody else's homework. We're going to write a book about the nuke plot Sheridan uncovered and the likelihood of its actually being carried out. Thus far I've been out flanked, out maneuvered, out gunned, and chucked out on my ear by our own people. The bad guys have had it all their way. I had complete notes, audios, and transcriptions of all the conversations we've had with Ayers and Janine and all the rest, including a remote video I streamed back to Langley of that last meeting where Sheridan tore them a new asshole. Trouble is, I was locked out of my office before I could get the disks so we're going to have an uphill job reconstructing everything. And when we get it published we're going to have to find a desert island to live on so they won't be able to get at us."

Lorraine slid his hand between her legs and rubbed his fingers into the soaked flesh of her hips and thighs. "My darling Director…oops, darling *former* Director Granite Stud Muffin, take a moment and catalogue for me my assets as you have been able to identify them to date."

"Well, my love, let's see," Cubbage flexed his fingers and stroked her lips until she whimpered, "Immense, globular, succulent breasts, narrow waste, loving lips and flashing tongue, thighs that melt in my hands, long, thick, silky hair, lovely Roman nose set between exquisite green eyes…hmmmmm…fine ass, good tits…yep, I guess that's about it. Did I miss something?"

Lorraine chuckled and squeezed him hard enough to produce a yelp. "Well, my long, thick, juicy male chauvinist piggy-wiggy, you missed just one tiny attribute of mine that I think ought to be brought to your attention. Of course I'm all those things and far more than a man of your disgusting animal urges would ever notice, but also a conniving, sneaking, duplicitous, lying, vengeful bitch. And when somebody fucks with my man I turn into the Slut Of The World. But the talent I want to bring to your attention is another you haven't seen before: I burgle. Did you seriously think I was going to permit the man I love, the man who will follow me the rest of his life while I'm following him for the rest of mine, to stroll into Ayers' abattoir without somebody at his back?"

"Sweetie, when Ayers rounded you guys up that morning, I saw the writing on the wall. So while you were over at the White House sucking up to Ayers & Company I hung around Langley. I know you, darling, and I know those creeps. They were sure to try to fuck with you and I know you too well to think you'd do anything but tell them the truth. Truth isn't any good when dealing with this president or his people. They don't give a rat's ass for substance, only form. Your tolerance for suffering fools gladly is fairly small in the best of times and I figured you'd be coming back with a big bulge out your ass. So while you were over there picking your nose, I was picking the lock on your office door. Didn't know what you might want from there so I just copied everything. It's all under the bed. Didn't have time to review it but there seems to be enough stuff in there on Ayers and the president and his lunatic Socialist friends to flush 'em *all* down the crapper. Darling, *nobody will ever fuck with us again in this world or The Next.*"

Gordon grinned. "Well I'll be dipped in shit! That's my little girl all right. That means we can write this book from facts, not conjecture. And if those animals actually get any of those bombs to work, our book will be a nuclear detonation right under the president's chair. If we can show that we *told him* a hit was coming *before* they struck, it will destroy him and the rest of those lunatics he brought in with him."

"On that score, you need to understand something, darling. This book is a last resort for me. If I thought there was *any* other way to warn the country I'd do it in a heartbeat. But nobody who can act is going to listen. And the ones who are listening have no power to act. I'm just out of options. It's a good thing they fired me and did it in writing. Releases me from any organizational confidentiality except for the Official Secrets Act, and none of this stuff has anything to do with that. It's not an American state secret nor an ongoing covert op – God Knows I tried to make it one! I pleaded with them to take this seriously and at least stake out the places we thought might be hit. But Ayers and Janine have to cover it up so the prez can keep on glad-handing the Syrians. Hate the thought of Americans dying just to get a point across to that pinhead in the White House, but I did my duty and got shoved out the door for it, so I guess my hands are clean enough. Hope that plot fails on its own because we sure aren't doing dogshit to stop it. I could go public, but the firing takes care of that. They'd put out the word that I was just trying to smear the administration in return, and trying to get in front of dereliction charges. Then the bad guys would know how much we know. I can't let that happen."

Cubbage sighed and took her face gently between his calloused hands, "OK, Doll Face, we'll get on back to civilization tomorrow and start work on the book first thing. You need to know, my sweet lady love, that I won't be able to do this unless I have your full attention….your <u>full</u> attention."

Lorraine looked seriously back at him. Her face went severe, "My own true love, I want you for my life, but I want you to promise me something. You've plagued me with that nickname 'Doll Face' for years. You forced it on me and sniggered at my embarrassment looking the way I do and having to fight off every damned loose dick in town. And yet you never once, not *one single time* in all the years we worked together, so much as *glanced* at me any other way than business. Not *one single time*, did you ever ogle my tits or my ass or my waist or acknowledge anything *feminine* about me. You were always the soul of propriety and the absolute essence of honor...you prick with ears!. Can you understand how I *hated* you for that? You never came on to me, you shithead, not even when you let it slip that you loved big breasts and a small waist and long, thick hair. Do you understand how that made me so fucking frustrated and angry...Jesus!.I considered beating you to death with a length of pipe except it might have influenced my pension. I even bought a piece at Lowe's; it's in my car. Any time you don't believe me I'll give you the fucking keys! You damned... decent...sensitive...honest...b-b-b-businesslike...w-woman-promoting... *fucking honorable*...c-c-cleavage-ignoring...b-b-bastard...you shitheel, ignorant, h-hateful son of a b-b-b-....son-of-a buh...son of a bub!"

Lorraine collapsed against Gordon's chest, tears streaming from her eyes, shoulders heaving trying to contain her sobs. Cubbage pulled her close into his arms and gently slid his hands beneath her hair tumbling over her face, feeling it caress his wrists as he slid it back away from her cheeks and tilted her gaze upward so she could look deep into his eyes, "Son of a *bitch*," he said quietly.

Lorraine put her lips up to his, gently gnawed on his and sucked his tongue deep into her mouth until the two of them began to lose track of time. After a while she pulled back a little way, fixed him with a gaze that Cubbage reflected would dissolve almost any man or for that matter any reasonably thick piece of depleted Uranium armor plate into a kind of mush. She said softly, "And now that you've finally gotten off your *dead a*...ah, now that we're finally together, my love, I want you to promise me..." She held her deep frown for a full twenty seconds more, then lit up the room with a smile so tender that Gordon Cubbage felt the back of his head bristle with electricity, "...you'll *always* use it, that I'll be your Doll Face, your Angel Eyes, your Sweet Lips...and all those other horrible sexist names for as long as I'm yours, which if you know what's good for you, Bucko, will be a fairly good quantity of time."

He reached for her shoulder and slowly and carefully urged her over on top of him. She straddled and centered him between her lips. He pushed carefully up inside her and when he had moved fully in he met her gaze with his own smile.

"My love, he said softly, "do you remember what Sheridan Walker told Ayers yesterday, that we have no more time for sorrow? Let's use that for the name of our book, 'We Have No More Time For Sorrow.'"

"No More Time For Sorrow..." breathed Lorraine softly and was quiet for a time. Then she shook her head as though to clear it, "I've been thinking a lot about Alice Walker. We could have saved her if we'd been allowed to go in when you said. There's something I've wanted to tell you about. Didn't matter much in the great scheme of things, but I just never knew where to start. Not until now. Remember the video of the execution? Well, I took that tape down to the lab when it came in and ran it a bunch of times. No intel in it, but if you enhance it then run it forward on Slow Retrieve you notice that as Alice watched the axe come down to her neck, her face went calm and she was saying something right at the end. We'll never know what those last words were, but whatever they were, Alice Walker met her death with a level of bravery that these cardboard cutouts running this country would never understand. They don't believe in God; they don't believe in America... well, Alice did. Twelve-year-old Alice. God Almighty, Gordon, do we have to learn our lessons from the butchering of a twelve year old girl?"

Lorraine moved on top of him and looked toward the master bedroom's tiny window under the broad eaves of the old stone house. A faint lightening of the dark forest promised soon the sun would be coming up. She snuggled back into Gordon's embrace, him deep inside her yet completely immobile waiting for her thoughts. Lorraine felt the weight of her years and responsibilities slowly dissolve into certainties. She would walk with this man wherever he would go, and she would, in her turn, lead him wherever she needed to be. They would put their own puny bodies and meager strengths between their country and this evil that had come upon it. She didn't know how, but together they'd find a way.

"Yes," Lorraine said softly, "Just what we want to say; America has to start saying to the bad guys what Alice's mother said to our own bad guys, Enough!" She slid her hand down Cubbage's cheek. "'No More Time For Sorrow'...you know, darling, I think maybe Alice would have liked that."

EPILOGUE

خاتمة

Day Two of the Cleansing Suns

اليوم الثاني من التطهير صنز

The sun spread its first light across the dark deeps of the hardwood forest surrounding the lodge, graciously lightening the treetops against the ridge before dancing down into the rolls of fog caressing the creek bank, dispersing its billows into trembling wisps. Each blade of well-mown grass on the long lawns contributed its own tiny black sliver to the immense shadow now sliding backwards away from the brightness of morning and the two figures on the deck.

"Never in the world did I dream I'd be sitting here nekkid as a jaybird with you and all those lovely breasts," Cubbage remarked. "I've greeted the dawn many times in this old hot tub, but I've never felt a warmer nor brighter sun than the smile in your eyes when you look at me. These last couple of days with you have rebalanced my world. I need nothing outside it anymore. I never came on to you when we worked together. Loved you from the moment I saw you but didn't know what to do and sure didn't know how to say it. Well, now I can. I love you, my darling, my sweet lady, Love of My Life. 'Come with me and be my love, and we will all the pleasures prove.' Marry me, Special Agent Baskin. Bring with you into my life your sorrows and your joys, your fears and speculations. Come lie with me and drift to sleep to awaken each morning in loving arms."

Lorraine shifted herself up a little out of the hot tub's bubbling water, setting her shoulders back to give him a better view of her magnificent breasts. She fixed upon Cubbage a gaze overflowing with love. "Chief Special Agent Baskin," she murmured softly.

Gordon raised his wine glass toward his companion, "You're my Love and my Lady, Colonel Darlin', but always the first toast will be to the United States of America, God Bless my dear country."

Lorraine met his glass with hers and recited, *"And bless our dear troopers, the ones 'be done down…"*

"…Marching home to His 'Pipes on God's Mornin'." Cubbage finished the old tanker's lament and they drank deep to their loves, to their sorrows, to Duty, and to each other.

"Haven't heard that in a quite few years," Cubbage smiled. "What brought it to mind?"

Lorraine smiled back and shrugged. "Today we're fighting shadows. The people running things tie our hands. I get pretty frustrated. I guess I was thinking about a time when we were encouraged to win, and we knew if we had won or lost."

Cubbage nodded and she went on, "Back in the Sandbox I was rotated in to take over a tank unit whose commander had been killed in a firefight. They'd raised a whole lot of hell with the bad guys but got chewed up pretty bad. The medals came down on this crew like a shower. Commander got a posthumous Congressional and when they pinned them on the rest of them had to walk lopsided with the weight. Caught up with them at the refit laager and introduced myself, "I'm Lieutenant Baskin replacing Lieutenant Kitta."

"The gunner stopped what he was doing, looked me up and down real slow, and said, "Well, I guess I'll just call you 'Tits'," and went back to cleaning the breach of his 62mm on the forward glacis. Now you know, if you come right down to it, I suspect most officers would probably prefer 'Lieutenant' to 'Tits'. But these guys were very, very good so I decided to let it slide. Had to say *something*, though, something that would show just the right combination of respect for his achievements balanced with my command authority, so I turned to my new loader, who had heard what the gunner said to me and seemed to be trying to crawl up into the turbine's exhaust port, and I asked him, "Sergeant, am I permitted to shoot this man?"

"Jake considered my request for a minute. 'Nah,' he said finally, 'Don't do that. He's not much to look at but he can single-round that 62 and take the eye out of a social worker at three hundred yards. Besides, you don't want the paperwork. Big pain in the ass, the paperwork." That was just about the time I realized I wasn't assessing my new command, *they* were interviewing *me!*"

"A few weeks later we were out on the sand reconning a fuel dump. Big sandstorm came up, knocked out our comm; lost touch with the other units. No radio, no GPS, no nothin'. Storm passed after awhile and we found ourselves pretty much alone if you don't count the sand fleas or the Iraqi armored brigade coming down the road. Usual mix: ex-Soviet T55s, T62s, a T72 here and there but no missile launchers so we could take em all right. Trouble was there were so many. We could do 'em one at a time, one round each, but we'd never be able to fire fast enough. For that you need more assets, also to spread the incoming around a little. Taking all the rounds at once from thirty or forty tanks can spill coffee and sometimes interfere with concentration. So here we are, Gunny, Jake, The Wombat and Little Me, down behind a dune wondering whether it was too late to transfer into Accounting, and guess who everybody's lookin at...."

Cubbage was fascinated. "So what did you do?"

"Well, what would *you* have done?"

Cubbage hesitated, frowned. "Well...I don't know. Spent most of my time during the war up on top yankin' and bankin', and anyway when it comes to getting out in front of a 210mm High Explosive Anti Tank round I had always seen myself in more of an administrative role... but...well...let's look at the situation. Since you couldn't report in, your Mission Priority after finishing your recon became getting back to base to make your report in person. The Iraqis were between you and your objective. One tank couldn't survive a standup against a whole brigade. You had no backup, no firepower, no way to whistle up some air…I don't know, Lieutenant Tits. So what *did* you do?"

"The Wombat was on the periscope," Lorraine replied, "and when I asked him what he saw he just said, 'target-rich environment', so I knew we were in deep shit. We were safe enough for the moment. They couldn't see us and it looked like they'd drive right past. But if they saw us first we'd be creamed. And we were out there to find that dump and, like you said, we had no way to report it except to get ourselves back home. So it was with deepest regret that I realized we had to get back onto that road and to do it we had to take charge of this situation and make something happen before we were discovered. Got me to thinking about something I learned at The Point. Our history prof was big on a Civil War guy named Joshua Chamberlain. Commanded the left end of Hancock's line on Cemetery Ridge at Gettysburg. Colonel Chamberlain knew he had to hold that position or the whole Union line would have caved in. Rebs kept charging up the hill and almost broke through. One more charge would have done it for sure. He saved the Union Army that day and after the battle somebody asked him, 'Colonel, what was going through your mind at the time?'"

"'Well,' said the Colonel, 'It was turning out to be a pretty long afternoon. Longstreet's boys kept coming at us up the hill and after awhile about half my men were shot down. The rest were almost out of ammunition. My sergeant came back from headquarters with no reinforcements to be had. I could see the Rebels massing at the foot of the hill for another charge. So only one thing occurred to me to do: I had my men fix bayonets and we charged down the hill.'"

Lorraine's gaze went out to the ridge behind the cabin, She cocked her head and smiled a smile that her eyes didn't share. "'*Only one thing occurred to me to do….*' Didn't occur to the good colonel to retreat; didn't occur to him to surrender. *Only one thing occurred to him to do.* He saw the enemy in front of him and let em have it all. He went down that hill knowing it was all he had left to give, and he gave it freely. So I said to my own men, 'We're going to get out of this, but we need to be bigger than we are. What have you got for me?'

"Well, the Wombat rigged the smoke grenade launchers to detonate all over us right after launch to give us some local cover. Jake loaded HEAT rounds and set up the flechette and cannister in case we ran into some troop trucks, and Gunny…her eyes shone at the memory…well, *Gunny, he* reached around back of the ready ammo case and dragged out a set of *bagpipes!* So we dogged down, strapped in, lit the turbine, cranked on the air conditioner, and up we went over the dune, smoke billowing out everywhere, the Wombat slewing us around always heading for the last sand geyser figuring they'd adjust range and miss us with the next shot, me running the gun slamming HEAT rounds into the Iraqi tanks as fast as Jake could load me, and Gunny on the loud-hailer belting out *Alamein Dead*."

Lorraine took a sip of wine, relaxed her head backward onto the tub rim, and chuckled, "They ran like rabbits. Jake counted forty-two of them. My first four rounds brewed up three T55s and knocked a tread off a 62. I was traversing around shooting at whatever came up on the screen and suddenly we noticed every blessed one of them turning hull-down away from us rolling off over the dunes except for two hot dogs who tried traversing their turrets while turning and shot each other. Jake just rammed HEAT and I went from one to another boring them new assholes right through their engine bays until they disappeared into the desert. I think I maybe got five or six that way."

"So down the road we went and after a couple of miles we ran right into their main fuel station. Big dump, bowsers standing around, fuel lines all over the place. Really liked all the screaming and running away when they realized who we were. Didn't want to seem impolite, so we paused to pay our respects. Put some flechette rounds into a couple of bowsers to get them leaking out but it didn't get interesting until Jake rammed me a HEAT for the last one. Whew. What a sight. Must have lit off the underground storage tanks. Wonderful explosion; shit flying everywhere, rocked us on our damned treads! Huge plume…really made our day. We were having lots of fun so we stuck around and shot up the buildings, but you know how it is. Sooner or later you have to get back to work. It was getting pretty late so we figured we ought to be getting home."

Cubbage was concerned, "Champagne running low?"

"Worse," Lorraine sipped, "Almost out of caviar. Besides might have got back late for Happy Hour and Gunny did love his tot. When we were dismounting back at base, Gunny spat one up onto the gun tube, looked out past the turret, and said to me, 'Appears to me you got balls as big as your tits, Lieutenant.' He walked off and, you know, it was always "Lieutenant" after that."

Cubbage let go a long laugh, "Yeah, we heard about 'The Charge Of The Light Brigade.' Damn! So that was you, eh? My compliments! Something you might not be aware of, but one of my A10s was out looking for trouble that day and spotted the plume off that dump you rousted. Humped on over to see if he could get in on the fun and on the way counted fifteen wrecked tanks and a whole bunch of other tanks and troops kind of milling around. He went hot and was setting up a gunnery pass when he noticed all the hatches were coming open and guys were bailing out and running. He was ready to strafe 'em but when he got close he saw they all had their arms up in the air. So he radioed Ground Engagement Dispatch for instructions. I was in the GED that day when the call came in...

"Dispatch, Three Niner Sierra Whiskey Tango, squawking four niner three zero, This is an Alpha One Zero with a hot load; have an Iraqi armored column in sight and they seem to want to surrender. About two zero zero enemy on the ground with their hands up. Do I light 'em up?"

[*long pause*]

"Negative, Whiskey Tango, take the surrender and herd them bearing two zero five degrees. We'll send trucks to pick them up and transporters for the vehicles."

[*even longer pause*]

"You want me to take *what?*"

"They're obviously trying to surrender to you. T-a-k-e t-h-e s-u-r-r-e-n-d-e-r and herd em East"

"Hurt em?"

[Dumbass!]

"Negative negative, Whiskey Tango. *Herd* them. Hotel Echo Romeo Delta. Weapons cold; I say again, weapons *cold*."

"Whisky Tango, roger the weapons cold; roger the Hotel Echo Romeo Delta. Trouble is, I clean forgot to load any cattle prods into my weapons bay, so I'm EVER so eager to hear any little suggestions you might have on how the *fuck* I'm gonna *herd* em."

Cubbage laughed and shook his head. " Well, between the two of them they eventually figured it out. By flying over them on the bearing of march and putting in a few rounds ahead of stragglers in a marked, yet friendly, manner, the pilot managed to encourage them toward the trucks that were coming out until the helos got there and he could bingo for fuel. The working over you gave them was a real attitude adjuster. It's the only time I ever hear of ground troops and armor surrendered directly to a US Army aircraft."

Cubbage took a long pull and leaned forward to refill his glass, "So you made your nut with the crew, eh? How long was it before they invited you to the NCO Club?"

Lorraine laughed, "About two weeks later. They said they had strict rules about officers not being allowed in the Club, so they gave me a bag to put over my head to avoid recognition."

Cubbage smiled. "I fell in love with you a long time ago," *Chief* Special Agent Baskin, "but you worked for me and I couldn't see how to get around that. You're good…damned good. Best I ever saw. Suppose I had come after you. One of us would have had to quit, and I couldn't be a party to that. Each of us were serving our country and we needed keep that before anything else. How did Bogey put it: 'The problems of two little people don't amount to a hill of beans in this crazy world?' Well, you had my heart, Colonel Darlin', but Honor required me to keep my distance."

Lorraine swam over to him, snuggled close, and breathed deeply. "Now there you go, my love, using those big words on me again. You know you can get anything you want with those big words."

Cubbage chuckled. "Those old words...Honor...Duty...Integrity...Faith... they don't get much play these days with this new bunch. Well, they can go to Hell. I run deep with that stuff"...Cubbage grinned..."and so do you, Doll Face. That was some little stand-up you pulled out there in the Sandbox. Saved your crew, kicked some ass, got home to tell about it...and then – you shitfaced bimbo! – there's the little matter of quoting Joshua Chamberlain to me like I had no idea who he might be! Chamberlain was a professor of comparative literature and religion in a little one-horse college up in Maine. When the Civil War broke out, he asked his Board of Regents for a leave in order to enlist, they said no, highly inappropriate. So he asked for leave to study comparative literature and religion in England and they said, sure, go ahead. Rode over to Bangor and enlisted. Figured he'd probably be in trouble with his bosses when they found out, but it turned out when he got home after the War they never said anything more about it. The Congressional Medal of Honor he got for that little bit of business in Pennsylvania might have had something to do with that. Darling, you can judge a man's character by three things: First: what he's willing to put aside in order to do his Duty; second, the condition of shine on his boots... and I've forgotten the third thing."

Lorraine was silent for a while, then murmured, "What a lovely place," She looked out over the deck rail at The Girls grazing unconcernedly up the slope toward the house, their fawns playing tag in the brush. "Do you hunt them?"

"Used to," Cubbage replied, "Well, truth to tell I used to take my gun for a walk in the woods once a year. Always went out before first light Opening Day, carefully climbed up into my tree stand, the one over there behind that big clump. Very important to sneak up into it so they don't hear you and wander off in some other direction. Deer are attuned to their feelings about the woods, and if they sense something's different they'll change their grazing pattern. So I'd hunt for a while and when I woke up, I'd go back in for a coffee and that was it for the year. Nobody hunts them now so they're pretty tame; come right up to a car but not if you're outside. Wow, look at 'em run! The only thing that spooks 'em like that are dogs, or somebody walking around, or helicopter rotors."

Baskin and Cubbage looked at each other. "Helicopter rotors?"

As the sleek Army helo grounded lightly in the front yard, Cubbage made a mental note to have a word or two with the pilot for taking an inordinately long time circling the hot tub with his high vision glasses trained on the occupants.

'Verifying his location,' no doubt. Oh well...hot shot kids, Cubbage sighed to himself, wrapped a towel around his waist and went to meet his visitor. The Marine pilot seemed entirely spit shined from head to toe and almost gleamed in the early morning sun behind him. He strode up to Cubbage, snapped to attention, and delivered a salute so crisp that the wind seemed to whistle from the passage of his arm to his forehead.

"Director Cubbage –" he began, but Cubbage put up his hand, "Captain, before you proceed I should tell you that I am no longer in policy. I am currently not employed by the federal government in any capacity. I am a private citizen with zero security clearance. By the way, how did you find me?"

The officer didn't seem to care. "Sir, I have no instructions on that. I was ordered to fly here, locate you, and offer you this" -- the marine held out a cell phone -- "and to request that you key in your SSN, then listen. As far as finding you, sir, well, when I was given this assignment, nobody knew where you had gone. I happened to know you kept a ship at the Park, so I accessed your flight plan, flew up your line of bearing, pulled a little tap dance with your airport manager and got your address. Had to circle for awhile in order to make sure I was landing in the right cornfield." Reflecting on what he had seen looking down into the hot tub, the captain grinned.

Cubbage did not. He looked at the cell phone in the soldier's outstretched hand. "And suppose I refuse, Captain? What are your orders then?"

"In that case, sir, my orders are to return at once to my ship and vector back to Andrews."

Instantly Cubbage took the phone, punched the keypad and put it to his ear.

A few buzzes and clicks as relays opened and closed and systems shook hands, but from the absence of dialing tones and the very correct officer at his side, Cubbage suspected this was probably not Publisher's Clearing House. Then a familiar voice:

"Gordon, is that you?"

"Yes, Mr. President. How are you, sir?"

The President came right to the point. "Gordon, in view of what happened in the last few days, I want you to take over DHS immediately. Now here's what I need first – "

"—Just a moment, Sir, if you don't mind. Guck!" The act of interrupting the President of the United States had caused Cubbage to bite his tongue severely and it was a few moments before he could make any sound other than a kind of gurgling bleat. The President waited for Cubbage to resume.

"Mr. President," Cubbage said thickly, "I thinth you ougth to know that yethterday I wath dithcharged from my position at CIA, and frankly after what happened at the National Security meeting I'm just as glad to be out of there. I don't want to be around when these bombs get fired off. I told them it's going to happen soon but nobody would listen. After what Ayers said about damage control, I'm sure Janine will be much better able to handle--"

"—Gordon!" The President interrupted then hesitated. "How much do you know about the events of the past four days?"

Gordon reflected, "Why actually nothing, sir. Lorra…ah, Agent Bas… ah…Chief Special Agent Baskin and I have been up here at the lodge… ah…conferring since my termination. Figuring out what we're going to do with the rest of our lives. I'm sorry Sir, but, we have no phone nor TV, nor computers here, and..."

The President was grim, "Very well; let me bring you up to date. Day before yesterday between 0916 and 1719 hours three nuclear devices were detonated in the Homeland just as you had forecast. Disneyworld and the battlefield park at Gettysburg were almost completely destroyed, and a good deal of Liberty University in Lynchburg. The loss of life is staggering, almost all civilians. We're still assessing damage but I can tell you that we lost nearly a hundred thousand Americans killed outright and God Knows how many more from radiation exposure. We won't know the true toll for years because some of the radiation sickness… will…require…". For a moment the President seemed unable to go on, then regained his composure.

"We don't know how they did it or how they got the bombs into the country, but we're expecting more attacks any moment. FEMA's on the scene but there's not much they can do. The few police not caught in the blasts are going crazy with the refugees and looters, and..." the President's controlled his voice with an effort, "Gordon, *if they can do it there they can do it anywhere! No American is safe!*"

Cubbage broke in. It was easier this time.

"Mr. President, before we go any further, I think you and I need to talk a bit and you need to know where I now stand. It might make a difference to you later on. When I was commissioned an officer in our armed forces, I took an Oath to "preserve protect and defend the Constitution of the United States against all enemies foreign and domestic" I'm no longer a serving officer, but there is only *one way* that I can be released from that Oath. Since I'm still alive, I am still bound. So when you came to me to run the CIA I was of course at your service and I did the best job I could. But right at this particular moment I'm an American civilian. I don't answer to you. I don't answer to anyone. And I certainly don't answer to your ignorant lunatic flunkies. Your people have finally convinced me that as far as my oath to protect and defend our Constitution is concerned, *you and your socialist friends are the domestic enemy!*"

"There's a saying, 'annoy a Conservative by lying to him; annoy a Liberal by telling him the truth.' Jeremiah Ayers in your name had me fired by your appointee Janine Mastroantonio simply because I told the truth to liberal assholes who couldn't stomach it. Now, Mr. President, here's what you need to understand: going back in history, John Ehrlichmann and Bob Haldeman didn't do all those bad things because Richard Nixon told them to, but because they thought Nixon was the kind of guy who would appreciate it. *And he was*. Ayers and Mastroantonio didn't try to cover up that bomb plot because you told them to, but because. *And you are*".

"You wished away the War on Terror by changing the name to Overseas Contingency Operations. You 'opened a 'dialogue' with Iran and let them stall you until they got their nuclear weapons. What are you going to do when they unveil their nuclear missile and tell Europe to begin taking Muslims into their governments *or else!? What are you going to do if you find out they supplied the bombs that just hit us?* You let the Taliban back into the Afghan government and sort of trusted them not to be bad. And just how long do you think it will take for that murderous bunch to seize power and restore the Al-Qaeda training camps?"

"Your policies got us branded weak; your people got us hit, with their heads firmly up their asses, deaf to inconvenient truths that challenged their ideological agendas – *your* agenda, Mr. President. And all this became possible because you went bowing around the world to our sworn enemies apologizing for being an American, telling them we're weak and irresolute and wanted to 'negotiate.' You bloody fool! These people don't want to *negotiate;* they want to kill! So why is anybody surprised when they *do* it?"

Cubbage went on. "I thought we had more time. My sources described the plot but it sounded as though they were still putting it together. I hoped capturing those guys that kidnapped my agent and killed her daughter might have derailed it or at least set it back in schedule. They might have had information for us, *but you didn't even try to get it from them!* But the worst harm you did to our country was encourage those lunatic supporters of yours who think they can wave their magic wands and 'teach the world to sing' or some such bullshit. The world is what it is. We need to protect ourselves. You should have clamped on those pixies and you never did. Now you're reaping what you sowed, and you want me to sign up to it? "

"Sir, I take no pleasure in saying these things to you. I love my country and I revere the Office of President. I know you carry a far heavier burden than I do. And I sympathize with your present predicament. But please hear me, Mr. President: I stayed at CIA long after I came to believe you were nothing but an empty-headed agenda merchant like your idiot do-gooder friends. But I stayed at my post anyway and did my duty and got shitcanned for it. Now I'm your Priority One Target to blame for all this. So if you're looking for somebody to help Jeremiah Ayers and Janine Mastroantonio, you can take your goddam damage control and sho—"

"—Gordon! Listen to me!" The President was back in compelling voice. Cubbage shut up.

"I have reviewed the tape of the Ayers meeting. I repudiate everything that Jeremiah Ayers said. I'm not interested in "damage control," but in retribution for this dastardly act. Americans who looked to me for their safety now lie in the dust. I was wrong. Being myself part Muslim, - look at my middle name! – I thought if I forced America to reach out to these people and make a bridge with them that they would respond and thereby overarch the killing and the *jihad* mentality. I was wrong. I see now that we are indeed at war and these murderers will understand nothing but force. If you will accept the post of Secretary DHS, my first order to you will be to give your CIA a single mission: discover who planned this act, then communicate that data to the Joint Chiefs and help them plan appropriate action. I personally suspect the Syrians. I think they informed me of the plot late enough so we could not foil it but in order to get in front of accusations. Gordon, if we discover they are complicit, I will go into Syria, depose the regime, and establish a democracy as my predecessor did in Iraq. You should also know that Jeremiah Ayers is no longer with me and at approximately noon yesterday Janine Mastroantonio died by her own hand."

Cubbage was silent for a moment., "You're really serious about this Sir?"

"Gordon, I want you for DHS because I need somebody to go after these vermin and lay them by the heels!" Cubbage had never heard the President use such language. "You are right in saying I have surrounded myself with lunatics. They were instrumental in getting me this office but I see now that their world view is wrong and I have carried them far too long. I never realized how close to the edge we were skating. I wanted peace and I wanted disarmament on my own terms and a settlement with our enemies in a spirit of reconciliation. I never thought they'd be so…two-faced, such lying…sneaking…." The President's voice gave out and he paused. "Now I see. I never realized that what I said overseas would come back to us here in the Homeland. I wanted America to take a respected place in the world…I wanted that so much. And now I have nothing to show for it but mounds of corpses…" The President stopped, unable to go on speaking.

Cubbage waited for the President to continue, then after a few moments said quietly, "Mr. President, you have taken us down a very dangerous road overseas. We tried to warn you that these people don't respond to anything rational, only force. Like the Palestinians feel about the Israelis, these terrorists don't recognize our right to exist. When you come up against that attitude, it shuts off debate and slams the door. Nothing can get around that. Israel has been a nation for about a half century, and the Jews have discovered that all you can do is cling to your own humanity, try not to be provoked, and when you have to fight, you fight to win."

"Sir, I've said some pretty harsh things to you this morning, things you ordinarily wouldn't hear. You give the impression you don't listen, you don't hear, you just ignore inconvenient facts and try to teleprompter them away with nice words. I'm sure that without the nukes Ayers and Janine would still be in power doing your work. But your words to me this morning are a revelation. I have to say, Sir, that you've convinced me finally something has gotten through the shell. It's a damned shame it cost all those lives to do it, but there's nothing to be done about that now. This is the second time we've been attacked here at home on a large scale. *Is their message getting through?*"

"That aside, Sir, your Office carries within it the love and the profound respect of the American people. America chose you as our leader, and in this time of massacre and war every American will look to you for guidance. But more important, we look to you for a symbol. We know what to do now. We need you to lead. We need a focus for the coming struggle because it will take everything we've got to win it. We can't afford to be stupid about this or in denial any longer. This isn't a game. We have to see these people as genocidal enemies, and we have to strike them and hurt them until they leave us alone. You need to know that this is my attitude, Sir, and I won't work under any other."

The President of the United States was silent for a long time. Then he said, "Gordon, come to DHS. Handle the aftermath as you see fit: I'll endorse anything you do. Your CIA director will be whomever you choose, but I insist it NOT be a political appointment. The new Director must be from the ranks. I will install a new National Security Advisor with your private concurrence so it will be someone you can work with. I envision your office operating as does our Joint Chiefs of Staff on the military side. Your sole directive will be to prevent a recurrence of this horror and in carrying out that mission I expect you to find the perpetrators and assist in bringing them to justice. They are enemy combatants and will be tried in our military courts under military laws of war. You will coordinate continually with the Joint Chiefs so that you have all their resources and they yours. We will drive these murdering animals from our shores for good!"

"I have already taken steps to undo Mr. Ayers' damage. I have ordered the FBI to stand down at the blast sites in their role as preventers of individual will. Director Feeny suggests forming civilian units at each site to assist in home defense while our police services are being put back together. I concurred, but I can't be sure these attacks will be the end of it. So I asked him expand the idea and organize them nationally under the name *Home Guard* after the units formed in Britain in 1940 against a possible Nazi invasion. The FBI will assist in arming local citizen groups if they do not already possess private weapons, and will liaise and generally oversee their activities in protecting their own homes and neighborhoods until their local police can take over."

"With Feeny's agents overseeing the Home Guardsmen, no one will ever again interfere with a private American citizen shielding his own home and family. I will not permit another New Orleans, where private citizens were harassed and abused for trying to protect themselves. The FBI will see that this does not reoccur. I have called Congress into Joint Session next week wherein I shall offer my resignation. I hope it will not be accepted; my vice-president is too weak to run the country and the Speaker of The House next in line is an asshole. I will set forth these things I have told you and others that I hope will keep us safe."

"Mr. President, what you're describing is like a fresh breeze, but it will cost a lot of money."

"Yes, Gordon, it will. I will ask Congress to divert the rest of the Bailout funds, as well as the trillions for our centralized universal health care, to the Defense Budget to be earmarked for anti-terrorist defense. And offense! I may not be much of a commander, Gordon, but I'm a very good politician. The bill will pass unanimously."

One would think that a nuclear attack on the continental United States -- something that even the old Soviet Union had not dared -- would finally convince everybody to stand up and fight. Well, one would have to think again. In the days after the Cleansing Suns, the limousine liberals from Hollywood and New York, once having recovered from their terror at Being Next, fell over themselves condemning the US military for provoking the attack. They seemed unable to connect the fact, intuitively obvious to the flyover people they despised, that the reason we hadn't been attacked for a decade might just have something to do with all those people with the guns and planes around. Well, there's no law in this great land of ours against being rich, handsome and stupid.

Black minority advocate groups and lawmakers whose continuance in office depended on finding new whites to bash, were just having a pretty hard time playing the race card. Their influence was already in steep decline with the movement of blacks to a second-sized minority below Hispanics, and with their constituencies eroding as blacks discovered they could make it on their own, turned away from the cult of victimization, and were replaced in these victim groups by an increasing number of hard-core drug criminals and users whose vision of Black Emergence extended no further than the next corner sale. And since for decades many American blacks had been making successes of their lives on their own abilities, these pols were finding it harder and harder to shoehorn their constituents into a victim status that no longer seemed to describe reality, Nevertheless, as during the aftermath of the New Orleans flooding, they dutifully condemned the American White Power Structure for the attack.

As after 9/11, the American Islamic Community once again outdid itself in its outpouring of sympathetic gales of silence.

And what about the President of the United States? The president who had risen to office condemning the American military, laughing at the idea that America was somehow special in the world? Who had promised to win over the "terrorists" by changing their name to *Vehemently Intense Extremists* or *Dispossessed Rampageous Separatists,* standing down our military and instead calling the police? Whose friends "God-damned" America from their pulpits, quoted Chairman Mao Zedong to innocent graduating seniors, and tried to blow up government buildings? Whose close advisors called themselves "avowed Communists and termed American capitalism a "relic of the past?" What about the President who was elected on his promise to just walk away from Afghanistan and Iraq and who vowed to look to the United Nations to keep America safe?

Day Six of the Cleansing Suns

اليوم السادس من تطهير صنز

On Day Six of the Cleansing Suns, the same President of the United States who had brought into his government people who had done all those things and said all those things stood before both Houses of Congress in joint session. He reported the status of each of the three attack sites. The news was grim.

The nuclear device detonated on Cemetery Ridge had made in the center of Gettysburg Military Park a quarter-mile crater ten feet deep lined with radioactive debris. Everything within a two or three mile radius had been destroyed including most of the town to the north. The bomb had been scheduled to go off just at the start of the business day, so deaths numbered in the tens of thousands, outright injuries at least a hundred thousand and still climbing as new returns came in, and unimaginable long term sickness. The short-half-life isotopes created by the fission reaction were already decaying away, but there were enough heavy elements to make things very hot for a very long time. Rescue teams, unequipped for a nuclear disaster, couldn't get near the site because of the radiation, so anyone left alive was on their own. The President ran portions of a film, so far unreleased to the public, made by a National Geographic film crew who had happened to be on location in tiny Carroll Valley a few miles southwest of the blast site. The cinematographer had just set up an interview shot when his lens was filled with the bomb's mushroom cloud. With the presence of mind and personal courage that would earn each of them a Pulitzer, the crew packed up and raced up US 116 toward the site. As they came near what had been the town, they stopped in horror at the sight of the remnants of survivors. There was nothing they could do for any of them, so, setting up their cameras at what they hoped would be a safe distance from the blast area, they began filming the exodus, a stream of burned and mutilated almost-corpses that the commentator, through his tears, could only describe as "pitiable."

The news from Florida was much worse. The nuclear device detonated close to the center of the Disneyworld theme park near Orlando obliterated almost a square mile of the grounds. All of the approximately 8,000 employees and 32,000 guests present near Ground Zero were incinerated by a fireball running to several thousand degrees Centigrade. The shock wave and firestorm that rolled outward from the blast center consumed people and structures for several miles. About half of the ten square miles developed by the park owners, or 10% of the total park area, was rendered uninhabitable by the blast. The plume of radioactive dust and debris catapulted upwards floated for miles in the prevailing southeasterly winds at 20,000 feet, moving slowly northwest toward the Georgia border, Atlanta, and the Richmond-Boston Corridor.

As in Pennsylvania, none of the police or rescue services were equipped for a disaster of this magnitude. No one had contamination suits, so to approach the blast site meant certain death. Rescuers could only stand by and watch those victims who had somehow remained alive, wither and expire. The few who managed to find transport and drive clear were rushed to burn centers and hospitals.. Later they would be swamped, but in the early stages of response, there was very little crowding in these facilities because there were very few survivors who could reach them.

With shaking hands and tears in his eyes, The President of the United States apologized for leading America down the wrong road. He took full responsibility for the attacks and the deaths of his countrymen and offered his resignation on the spot on a voice vote of the Body Assembled. Even before he finished speaking he was shouted down, the shouting beginning from across the aisle among the party of opposition and spreading throughout the room, lawmakers standing and applauding and bellowing "No! No!" The Minority Leader of the House shouldered his way through the milling, clapping congressmen to offer the President his hand stretched up from the Floor to the podium. From somewhere down below began to be heard the words to the "The Star Spangled Banner" and the old familiar words, seldom heard these days since his party had been in power, swelled out over the din. The shouting died out as more and more took up the old familiar phrases; jostling ceased as they pointed themselves toward the flag behind the Speaker's Chair. Most had hand over heart but here and there a man or woman braced themselves at as rigid a military attention as old muscles could produce, with as straight a salute to their temple as might still be managed after so many years away from duty yet really no time at all if you think about it.

Waving away his teleprompter, the President then spoke from a sheet of lined paper he had torn earlier that morning from his twelve-year-old daughter's composition book. He reported to Congress In Common Assembly his instructions to the Department of Homeland Security to find the perpetrators, his intention to punish them and their national haven even to the last extremity. He outlined his intended funding shifts, his determination to end the regime of the government responsible for what he termed a "cowardly massacre of innocents." He was applauded strenuously from both sides of The Aisle as each line item came out. But when he announced his directive to the FBI to establish, arm and protect average Americans in *Home Guard* defense units so that citizens could keep themselves safe meanwhile, the room went to its feet again and would not be quieted. It was observed that the British Ambassador, ordinarily a rock of phlegmatic imperturbability, who had taken a seat in the gallery to hear the President speak and whose father had died at Dunkirk, upon hearing the name to be given to these citizen safety groups lowered his head into his hands and wept. When some semblance of order was finally restored, The President finished by stating that he sought no additional powers in this national emergency beyond those already granted his Office, and that there would be no resort to single rule on his watch even if America again came under direct attack. As he was ushered out up the middle aisle of the House, he narrowly escaped serious bruising from the press of men and women anxious to pat his shoulder to comfort him and show their love and support.

The President's appearance before Congress had lasted just under two hours and was televised by all major networks. During that time he spoke for approximately twenty-one minutes. The deluge of electronic mail offering support completely overwhelmed White House mailboxes and crashed its servers for three days. A crowd estimated at between two and three million people assembled as close as they could get to the White House and on departing left behind not a single article of trash throughout the National Mall. They stayed for the better part of two days, those leaving being replaced by others, including a group of veterans who set up camp in front of the West Wing and spent their time praying for their government and for the success of American arms. Respectful and orderly, some of them were camped in tents and some had none but simply spread their blankets and sleeping bags on the ground. They were finally supplied with makeshift shelters built by off-duty White House guards.

One night at a very late hour the President himself walked into their small encampment and sat with them awhile to talk things over. He came at night with minimum security so there would be no news coverage, and for months afterward no one even knew he had been there. The old soldiers thanked the President for coming to see them out of his busy days. They tried to convey to him their sorrow that they had no more to offer their country now that she was in peril, that they sort of stood for the larger number of Americans who couldn't be with him but whose respect and hopes went forward with him every day. They urged him to do what he had to do and not worry about being wrong, for to act honestly and courageously in America's defense could never be very wrong. They told him they had been ready to give all for their country and said they spoke for all Americans in uniform and all Americans safe in their homes in assuring him they were behind him in this mortal struggle.

The President told the soldiers that they were the hope of America, that America was the hope of the world, and asked them to continue praying for him at his labors. He said they showed the world that all Americans from every age still stood tall against America's enemies and were glad to give what they had in the common defense. He said they could best serve their country now by remaining here close to him for as long as they could manage to do it, so that he, as well as all other Americans, might notice their vigil and take, from their devotion, increased devotion to the cause.

One old man, not especially well dressed nor particularly well groomed, whose carefully cleaned yellow motorcycle shared space alongside him in his shabby tent, remarked that though he was a veteran, he had never gotten overseas during Viet Nam, just served in the ranks and did little or nothing. Now that his country was at war, he found he was too old to fight and too slow to run away. Said he'd gladly serve again but had no more skills to offer his country and coming here to sit with his government was the best he could do. He said almost every day he prayed a question:

> "Why, Lord, did you take all those good men and leave a man like me behind?"

He told the President he felt a little easier after telling him the way of these things, because he wanted his country to understand he'd serve again if he could. Just didn't want to get in the way. The President asked him if he'd gotten an answer to his question. The old man replied, no, and he supposed he never would. But he figured it was ok to ask it. In fact, he went on, he thought it was all right for any American to ask that question whether they had served or not. And as gently as he knew how to say it – for he knew the President had never served his country and now faced the most terrible of responsibilities – the old man allowed as how it might even be ok for a President to ask it.

As the President of the United States made his way back to the White House between the tarpaper shacks and colorful tents and on out through the roped-up cordon made by the Secret Service, he quietly informed his security detachment that in addition to guarding him, their duties would henceforth include the safeguarding of this group of soldiers for as long as they cared to stay here. They were to be fed from White House kitchens, their food to be paid out of the President's own pocket. His Detail Chief acknowledged she had already checked them out individually and that no harm would come to them, assuring the President, so that he would have no worries on that account, that she would see to it personally. Several of his Secret Service guards, a hard-bitten lot not especially given to emotional display, some of whom during the president's conversation with the motorcyclist had discovered that they had apparently gotten something in their eye, asked to be permitted to contribute to these funds as well. The President considered the matter, then told them he thought it would be all right.

Day Thirty of the Cleansing Suns

اليوم الثالثون من التطهير صنز

Upon direct orders of the President of the United States, the American Ambassador to the United Nations stood before the United Nations General Assembly. She was brand new at the job, appointed by the President from the ranks of conservative national news commentators after the previous incumbent had refused to make the statements desired by the President and had been summarily dismissed. It was widely held throughout the country that an appointment of a woman with absolutely no diplomatic experience was intended among other things to send a clear message to the American diplomatic corps that a new day had dawned for them. Upon being recognized by the Secretary General, Ambassador Shields offered for consideration to the representatives of the nations of the world therein assembled the following Resolution:

> *The United Nations in General Session hereby resolves:*
>
> …*that nuclear attack anywhere in the world will bring upon the first strike nation prompt and utter destruction of its ability to wage war;*
>
> …*that attack against a member of the General Assembly using a nuclear or sub-nuclear device will automatically invoke Article V of the United Nations Charter, being considered to be an attack against all members simultaneously, and will be met with a joint and immediate defensive military response.*
>
> …*that any nuclear attack launched by any sub-national group anywhere in the world will be considered to be a declaration of war from the nation within whose boundaries the attack was physically launched or who can be shown to have supported it.*

The Resolution was referred to the proper committee for deliberation, placed on its agenda and promptly shelved.

Day Forty-two of the Cleansing Suns

اثنان وأربعون يوماً من التطهير صنز

Ambassador Shields again stood before the General Assembly, this time without any suggestions or resolutions, just a statement:

> *"Being apparently unable to enlist the several Members of the United Nations in the common defense against nuclear terrorism, The United States of America hereby notifies the nations of the world and all interested parties:*
>
> *...that supplying or trafficking in nuclear arms, components, material, or processes from a nuclear power to any other nation or group will be considered an act of war against the United States of America.*
>
> *...that attack upon the State of Israel with nuclear weapons will be considered to be an attack upon the United States."*
>
> *...that attack upon the United States from any subnational group will be considered a declaration of war by the nation from within whose boundaries the attack was launched or who can be shown to have supported it.*

As the President expected, his notification to the world was greeted with sulphurous invective by the members of his own party. "Warmonger," "Chauvinist," "Racist," "Class Traitor," and "World Bully" were a few of the kinder labels. But much of this sort of rhetoric died away after publication by the Government Printing Office of a collage of the Three Craters with a caption borrowed from the motto of the State of Israel: 'Never Again!"

Day Fifty-five of the Cleansing Suns

اليوم خمسة وخمسون من فينيكس التطهير

A group calling itself *Tea Parties Dot Fedup* began a grass-roots movement to expose network news programs and other media that pushed a hidden agenda and refused to report balanced news. Only those news programs that claimed to be balanced and fair were candidates for their investigation. News outlets that publicly declared up front to be either liberal or conservative were exempted from analysis, since the intention was to discover agencies whose agendas were being concealed. In order to keep their investigations to manageable size, they decided to limit their investigations to a few issues that were reported frequently. They chose Gun Ownership and Control, National Politics, Campaign Rhetoric, Pundit Interviews, and a catchall category for print media called Above The Fold in which staffers analyzed lead stories in major dailies.

Tea Parties Dot Fedup analyzed reportage for what they called Inherent Bias. If merely reporting the story contained an inherent bias, they looked for a balancing commentary revealing the opposite view and to see whether both points of view were presented uniformly. To do this they passed the wording of the story through the Hopton matrix and graded the result.

The Hopton Index of Propaganda Phrasing and Positioning, which came to be known universally although somewhat inaccurately as The HOPPP Index, had been developed several years previously by an obscure Purdue University scholar as a learning tool in his course on Nazi Minister of Propaganda Dr. Joseph Goebbels. He tried to answer for his students the question that was fundamental to his entire course: what separated propaganda from straight news and how could you identify the difference? Professor Hopton counted certain words and the positioning of facts in a story and derived from his tabulations a simple opinion: the story was either Straight News or Propaganda. He counted words such as "admitted" instead of "stated," noted the presence of the assertion that this or that fact is "troubling," and named the last paragraph in a news story the Golden Throne, asserting that this was where propaganda, if any, would be lodged.

Since Purdue was no more interested in a frank analysis of political correctness than any other seat of higher learning, his book almost cost him his tenure and propelled him unceremoniously into early retirement. In it, one of Professor Hopton's examples was a CBS story, supposedly straight news, about gun control. It seemed at first glance to be balanced between statements from the Violence Policy Center in favor of gun control, and the National Rifle Association against it. But the Hopton Index revealed that according to the reporter, the VPC "stated" while the NRA "admitted, " VPC "asserted" while NRA "claimed; VPC "challenged" while NRA "revealed. Moreover, the question of gun ownership itself was deemed by the writer "troubling," whatever that meant, and in the last paragraph, the writer used "but" and "although" to restate VPC's anti-gun position and imply that it was also the writer's own, thereby causing the reader to infer it was also the view of the media outlet itself. Since the story had been aired, not as opinion but as "balanced" journalism, the implication was clear that not only was gun ownership wrong, but *discussion* of it was also wrong.

These common journalistic tricks were used by agenda merchants everywhere, so they fell easy prey to Dr. Hopton's analytical knife. *Tea Parties Dot Fedup* fed news stories into the HOPPP matrix and graded them either Balanced News or Garbage Propaganda. Then each news program's total in each category was published on *Tea Parties'* web site with an invitation to readers to make their own comments on the news program in question. Interviews conducted by news anchors and pundits were subjected to similar scrutiny, though with the added analysis whether questions were designed to elicit information or merely parrot the anchor's own bias. Names were named with video clips as backup. Scores were posted and web site visitors were invited to vote whether a leftist-lunatic or right-wing-extremist bias existed. Results for each network were published periodically and a running category total maintained.

At the same time, the group collected and published lists of sponsors whose ads appeared during the news broadcast being analyzed, with the suggestion that visitors contact sponsors to express their views on the kind of news the sponsor was "selling." For outlets deemed by web site visitor to be Leftist Lunatic or Right Wing Extremist, the web site suggested that viewers boycott these sponsors or write to them suggesting they get out of the propaganda business and leave politics with the citizenry to whom it belonged. For convenience, each listing included names of chief executives, their addresses, and home phone numbers. Viewers were also urged to write to the manufacturer or service company such as a realty firm, and at the same time contact a local retailer, several of which were also helpfully listed for each product. Rollout of *Tea Parties Dot Fedup's* first Censure Day came on Day Seventy-Two of the Cleansing Suns. MSNBC's Network News stories had fallen overwhelmingly into the Garbage Propaganda category and received a resounding Leftist Lunatic vote from site visitors. The site published its findings, viewers' votes, and the program's sponsor list with executive names, addresses, phone numbers, and selected retailers that carried the sponsors' products.

Nothing happened for about eight weeks, then all hell broke loose. Without warning on Day One Hundred Thirty-One of the Cleansing Suns the MSNBC news anchor was fired along with eight of his staff reporters. Journalists from the other networks came sidling forward uneasily to investigate this extraordinary event and discovered that, of the program's six sponsors, four had seen sales drop an average of twenty-three per cent over a week's period, with one New York City car dealer reporting a sale-per-floor-traffic ratio down a whopping forty-eight per cent. When asked by a reporter how he knew *Tea Parties Dot Fedup* was the cause, the dealership owner, himself a Vietnam era veteran, replied through clenched teeth it was because people were calling him at home and telling him about the cars they *would have bought* from him had he been a "real American." Some of them, the owner added, had sent to his house copies of sales contracts for the same car but from a different dealer with the accompanying admonition to peddle his cars and not his politics.

All the sponsors on the list had been contacted directly by a new consumer watchdog group, *Teeth In Your Leg,* styling themselves the "action arm" of *Tea Parties Dot Fedup,* although no actual connection seemed to exist. *Teeth In Your Leg's* web site refined *Tea Parties'* scale down to two categories and designated each sponsor either *"Self-Reliant,"* or *"Mommy and Daddy." "Teethers",* as they came to be called, contacted the *Mommy and Daddy* sponsors demanding to know why they were supporting political propaganda where they had no business being and began actively campaigning in the marketplace against the sponsors' products. After being subjected to a few weeks of this treatment and seeing sales plummet, each MSNBC's sponsors had informed the network that they would pull sponsorship of its news program unless a balance in reporting was immediately evidenced. The result was an instant and almost complete news blackout as CBS, CNBC, ABC, and the other major TV news programs scrambled to avoid being next to receive *Tea Parties'* analyses and the *Teethers'* attentions. *Fox News,* whose journalism had always maintained its fair and balanced stance but from a conservative viewpoint and was thus outside *Tea Parties'* purview, took up the slack as best it could, but its reporters couldn't be everywhere, so many events simply went unreported.

In their desperate search for a quick way back to profitability, liberal-biased network news programs seized upon Professor Hopton's formerly discredited research. Newly retired from Purdue, the Professor found himself in urgent demand. The networks set him up in an impartial, round-robin-funded commission to vet their stories. Conservative news shows, whose product had not been addressed by *Tea Parties'* staff since they freely admitted their conservative point of view, laughed richly and loudly, and in the spirit of helpfulness suggested the networks could save Dr. Hopton's sizeable salary as well as the huge expense of checking each news story against the Index, by simply firing their entire staffs, hiring "real" reporters directly out of journalism schools, and starting over.

Day Sixty-nine of the Cleansing Suns

يوم تسعة وستون من فينيكس التطهير

A huge rally was convened in San Francisco to protest America's change in policies toward what was described by promoters as "poor, indigenous folk from overseas whose only crime was to be held down by the US." It was led by a major film producer and showcased leading stars from film and the music industry. On the first day of the rally it was met by an even larger crowd of very calm, very silent people who, after surrounding the stage and participants, suggested mildly to the protesters that they might consider whether it would be a good idea to immediately disband and go home. The speaker, a major film star of action type movies, berated the crowd accusing them of trying to stifle free speech. There was a brief halt in the ceremonies during which the film producer who organized the rally was informed that the statements made that day would be taken down verbatim and posted on *Tea Parties Dot Fedup* for the edification of the movie-going – movie *buying* – public. *Teeth In Your Leg,* the producer was advised, would begin posting movie trailers with the political comments of their stars set underneath. The rally quietly dispersed.

Day One Hundred Eighteen of the Cleansing Suns

يوم واحد ومئات من ثمانية عشر لفينيكس التطهير

"Mr. Secretary, Director Baskin is on your inside line."

"Thank you, Jan, would you put it on speaker for me?"

"Mr. Secretary, CIA Director Baskin here. I'm calling to verify that the two Marines you sent over for the eyes-only dispatch pouch are sitting in my office. Thanks for sending them right away. You need to see these latest intercepts and I don't want to send them electronically. I don't want this stuff floating around the internet."

"It's all in the briefing documents, but a couple of things you need to hear about right away. First of all, we think there's a fourth bomb, maybe more. All my people are on it overseas and Feeny's got his assets running it down on this end. We think it's not just dirty like the Lynchburg one, but fully nuclear like Disney World and Gettysburg – Erector Set job, assembled near the site, no casing, just subcomponents, suicide trigger, lying around like swimming pool components in somebody's warehouse. Undetectable. We're working with Ari in Tel Aviv but so far nothing. We've focused on Syria as you asked, but I'm beginning to wonder about that."

"The President's certain the Syrians were involved in the first three blasts," Cubbage replied. "They leaked the plot to him right beforehand and he's convinced they did it pre-emptively to slide suspicion."

"Well," Lorraine was pensive, "That could be…but we're getting some more out of those prisoners now that they're being properly questioned without a lot of *Miranda* bullshit. A couple of them have mentioned a 'Benefactor' – their term – military guy or one masquerading as a soldier. Outsider, maybe not even Middle Eastern. Hard time coming up with a description. Might be the guy who supplied the nukes although that would be a real long shot and more bonus than we deserve. Then there's the Pakistani connection. We did some polite enquiries about that guy Sheridan told us about when she came back to us. But you can't just accuse a senior Pakistani general officer of rape and genocide without a little more proof than what they would call a crazy woman's nightmare. If Sheridan could have told us more about him…well, we're staying on that one but it looks like a real long shot to me—" Lorraine broke off.

"Do you think they're after the government?" Cubbage asked

"Doesn't seem like it. My opinion? They just want to hit us with nukes For their purposes it doesn't really matter where they do it as long as the world sees us being hit with nuclear weapons. Do you know something I don't?"

"Cubbage sighed, "Wish I did. I agree though. Now that they've got hold of nukes they're going to launch more if they can. From their standpoint it's the most bang for the buck, and they know they have to use them before we dry up their supply of material. But they're getting what they want from these bombs. You're already seeing Europe caving in to them and they haven't even been threatened, much less hit. Denmark suspended their Muslim immigration exclusion policy, Germany 's inviting Muslims into its government as a separate party, France reversed its prohibition of the *bhurka*. All this without any demand from anybody, just the fear of what *might* happen to them. What can your life be worth if you get on your knees to save it? But getting back to your question, no, I don't think they're coming after the US government. Hell, our government is what gave them this opportunity in the first place! But even if that's true, we can't trust it. I'm tasked with keeping the Presidential Line of Succession safe and I'm having a hell of a time doing it."

Cubbage referred to the officials succeeding to the Presidency in case the incumbent were killed. Living in Washington and already frightened not only of being a target but also of being the Successor, the Vice-President was fairly easy to guard. However, safeguarding the Speaker of the House of Representatives, next in line after the VP, had suddenly become another matter entirely. Ordinarily safe at her offices in Washington, on Day Fifty-nine of the Cleansing Suns she had found it necessary to return to California to fight a vicious recall election in which, after a number of campaign ads were aired suspiciously similar to the Speaker's own original rhetoric, it was discovered that the name her opponents had put forward in nomination to contest her seat in Congress belonged to a chimpanzee, current resident of the Los Angeles Zoo, who had been taught to speak a few phrases and was being supplied campaign literature consisting of the Speaker's old speeches suitably reworked.

When the California Board of Elections reported this to the State Legislature in session, Democratic lawmakers walked out and Republican lawmakers collapsed in laughter so prolonged that one representative had to be carried out into the lobby and given oxygen. A lengthy floor fight ensued in which opponents of the nomination asserted that the former Speaker would have a hard enough time conducting her campaign without having to debate publicly an opponent who ate bananas with the skin on, was liable to urinate at any moment, and never mind about the inappropriate self touching. The chimp's nominating committee fought for his place on the ballot arguing that in view of the recent terrorist nuclear attacks, the Speaker's former prolonged and continuous attacks on the CIA could be shown statistically to fall well within the IQ range of her opponent. Finally, after weeks of wrangling during which the public was treated to the rare spectacle of American Civil Liberties Union attorneys and representatives of People for Ethical Treatment of Animals working together in common cause, the chimp's petition for candidacy was finally accepted provided the chimp could meet the permanent residency requirement in the Speaker's home district. His attorneys immediately assured the Board that they had a tree already picked out in McLaren Park.

"Well," Lorraine said, "The Speaker did her humble best to get a couple hundred thousand Americans smeared and obviously didn't care as long as her lunatic left agenda got pushed ahead, so she gets what she deserves either way. I would advise her to marry the chimp; then no matter what happens she can't lose the Seat."

Cubbage was laughing hard into the phone so Lorraine switched subjects before he choked, "So how are those Home Guard people getting along?"

"Pretty well actually," Cubbage replied regaining control of his voice, "Bunch of yelling from the anti-gun people for a while until the FBI let it out that in areas patrolled by Home Guard units, looting and home invasion had all but vanished. Or it might have been what happened to the CEO of the Violence Policy Center – you know, the old Brady Handgun Control people? Lives in one of the townships the Home Guard was patrolling. Couple of nights ago four guys broke in and did recreational activities on him for a while. Were just going for his wife and kids when a Home Guard unit coming off duty heard some gunshots from the guys playing around. Went in, killed three of the four, released the wife and kids unharmed, and got the guy to an ER for an HIV check."

Lorraine was aghast, "Holy shit! What happened to him? Is he ok?"

"Yep, couple of treatable STDs but so far no herpes, no HIV, so apparently he lucked out his ass…literally. Made two phone calls from his hospital bed: first one was to NRA for a Life Membership, second was to Fox News for an interview. Fox sent a reporter right over but she had trouble getting through the media crowd. They apparently thought he was going to slam the Home Guardsmen for not keeping him safe and were all set up for a juicy 'right wing extremist' bash; but he insisted the *only* reporter he'd talk to was the gal from Fox. Told her he was resigning from the VPC and buying a Glock. And that was pretty much the end of the anti-gun shit. I'm working to lock the *Home Guard* into our DATAR network. I think they'll be a real asset."

The Defense Appreciation and Threat Axis Response group, DATAR, had been convened by Cubbage shortly after taking the DHS post. It gathered the heads of the American Homeland Security forces – CIA, FBI, BATF, NSA, and so on, and put them with the Joint Chiefs of Staff in a monthly situation analysis conference for threat assessment and response. This was the place to which all terrorist-related information, once vetted by the submitting agency, gravitated. The information rejected for DATAR oversight was then funneled to a second group who asked the question: "Why is this data *not relevant* to Homeland defense?" It was discovered that a great deal of information, thus approached, yielded important intelligence in its own right, and was put back into the DATAR data stream.

It was then analyzed by professionals and acted upon by the military – no politics, no hand-wringing, no agendas; every issue was judged on its potential effect on the defense of the Homeland, and actions were taken without political oversight except for budget. Any American, or any foreigner for that matter, wishing to add to this information stream had a simple conduit right to the top. No data were dismissed based on lower-level analyses until rigorously proven false. *Everything* was examined. Recommendations for action went directly and immediately to the President. So far the track record was good. In its three months of full operation, DATAR had foiled four airline bombings, a plot to bomb the Ohio State campus, and, through Interpol, eight separate attacks in Western Europe, two within hours of their intended execution, including an attempted assassination of the Chancellor of Germany.

"Glad to hear he's ok." Lorraine replied, "Another thing you should know about right away: we think we know how the Disney bomb got planted. All the witnesses went up in the blast, and the ones who might have survived were buried alive when the maintenance tunnels under the park collapsed. So until now we've never had any direct evidence how it got under there in the first place. Disney security is pretty tight because of all the cash around. Now we're fairly sure it was in the armored truck that comes once a day to pick up cash receipts.. The truck has to drive down under the park through the tunnels, and it's big enough and heavy enough to carry a device. This would be a natural way to get one inside right under the Castle where the actual bomb went off."

Cubbage was intrigued, "How did they do it? Steal a truck? Substitute theirs at the last minute?"

"No," Lorraine went on, "Armored trucks are so unusual and so specialized that to steal one or buy one out of the blue would immediately cause talk. Substitution might work but it couldn't be done quietly on the street and would generate an instant police response because one thing the cops have a hot button for are armored bank carriers."

"We're still not sure of all the details but we have a couple of really good leads. A guy came to us the other day who had worked for the armored car service that picks up the Disney cash. Said he had been recruited from that company a year or so ago by another firm trying to expand their business. They offered him about twice what he was making and said it was because they needed his experience. Seemed legit to him. Had actual customer accounts, made drops, pickups, just like normal. All the usual phone book and internet ads, sales people, and so on. But after the bomb went off he got to thinking about it and he thinks the company might have been a stage prop just to get drivers who knew the layout of the tunnels and where the truck had to go inside the park. He said if the attack hadn't happened he wouldn't have thought anything about it, but afterwards it seemed strange that they wanted to know exact routes and timetables for the Disney pickup when they didn't even have the contract yet. They told him they needed to cost things out to the absolute minimum to get under the current bid. He didn't think much about it at the time."

"The exact location of the cash pickup point under the park is a Disney company secret. It's somewhere inside those miles of maintenance tunnels, but a lot of them aren't big enough for the truck, so the driver really has to know exactly where he's going. A truck in the wrong place would cause immediate response from the Disney security people. Most of them are ex law enforcement and they don't fool around. From the epicenter and damage assessment analysis, we conclude that the bomb was detonated almost directly under the Disney Castle. We gave the Disney corporate people the approximate size of the device and they said that to get the device to that place on their grounds, nothing would work except one of the bank trucks. Otherwise, their security would have jumped on it right away. They monitor that area closely because that's where the cash ends up, so their best people are down there on that detail…or were."

"The details of the operation are interesting enough, but that's not what I want you to be thinking about. This kind of company with this kind of local history isn't something you throw together at the last minute. *This has been in the works for years!* We ran a check on the company that hired the driver. It's bogus all right, but it has the best credentials I've ever seen for a sham operation. Looks fine on the surface until you start looking down into their finances. We discovered that they consistently lost huge amounts of money by underbidding legitimate firms in order to build up credible customer base. Their funds were replaced from time to time by 'investments' from people in the area in amounts of less than $10,000 each, which meant the money could pass through banks without triggering the IRS's ten-grand surveillance floor. Treasury is still tracing the cash flow but it appears now that most of these 'investors' were American citizens connected with local mosques."

"Ok, I'll brief the President right away," Cubbage responded. "He's got State working on finding out which countries supported this, and he'll want to know the time line. So what else is up out your way, Director Sugar Lips?"

"Oddest thing, sir...those Marine couriers in my outer office... In addition to taking custody of the pouch, they have very politely informed me that their orders include taking *me* into custody and delivering me to an unspecified location at your orders. Naturally I eagerly await any little thoughts the Director of Homeland Security might be willing to share on that subject."

"Yep," Cubbage replied, "I told 'em as long as they're there after the pouch, duct tape you, roll you up in a rug and bring you on over here. Haven't seen my wife in eight days and I have needs."

Lorraine was thoughtful. "Well, the rug might be fun but I've never been arrested before. Will I be expected to surrender my sidearm?"

"Would you?" Cubbage asked.

"Probably not."

"Hmmm...let me speak to the soldier in charge of the detail."

Baskin switched on the speaker, "Marine, would you please identify yourself to the DHS Secretary?"

"Yes Sir, Mr. Secretary, Gunnery Sergeant Axelrod here."

"Gunny, what's your assessment of your chances of taking Director Baskin into temporary custody, shackling her, rolling her up in a rug, and delivering her to my office?"

Lorraine Baskin Cubbage lounged in her chair, lifted her hands behind head, smiled a huge smile and batted her eyelashes at him. Gunnery Sergeant Axelrod made a quick tactical appreciation, "Sir...Mr. Secretary...ah...well...mmmm...I'm not sure I'd really want to try that, Sir."

"But Sergeant," Cubbage exclaimed, "I sent *two* of you!"

The sergeant glanced at his companion who was looking at the floor and shifting one foot to the other. "Um...if you don't mind, Sir, I'm also speaking for Corporal Gyimesi."

Cubbage sighed audibly into the speaker. "Very well, Gunny, change in orders. First, please tender my compliments and felicitations to the Director and request with my deepest respect that she accompany you to our house."

"Second," Cubbage's voice softened, "Please pass along the following message to the Director *verbatim*: 'Colonel Darlin', I love you with good man's fervent passion and I count the minutes until I may once again hold you in my arms."

Lorraine's smile grew even broader and she nodded vigorously, "I'm on my way, darling; ten minutes. By the way"...she looked the marines up and down. Both he and his companion stood over six feet and bulged their battledress in all the right places, "Your messengers look particularly scrawny and underfed. Do you think we could find a couple of spare plates?"

"An excellent idea, Madame Director, I will assume the invitation has already been delivered."

"Thanks, Ma'am; we'd love to come. But...ah, sir...," began the sergeant.

Cubbage laughed, "Never mind that second part of my order, Gunny. Just ask the Director to come home."

"Ah, no sir, that wasn't what I meant…um…could I speak to you privately for a moment, Sir?"

"Of course."

Lorraine switched off the speaker and handed the marine her handset. He turned toward the window and spoke in a low voice, "Sir, if you don't mind my asking you a personal favor…well, uh, what we said about not wanting to take on the Director even with the two of us… ah…well, Sir…could you make sure that doesn't get around?"

Secretary of Homeland Security Gordon Cubbage relaxed backwards into his chair and slid his hands behind his head locking his fingers comfortably together. He lifted his gaze toward the ceiling, and smiled to himself a smile only one other person in the world had ever seen, "I know exactly how you feel, son, exactly what you mean." Then he tipped forward and resumed his official voice, "Don't worry, soldier, we're all on the same side now. Your secret will be safe with me."

Made in the USA
Lexington, KY
06 June 2013